# PANDEMIC

**Also by James Barrington**

**OVERKILL**

# PANDEMIC

## JAMES BARRINGTON

MACMILLAN

First published 2005 by Macmillan
an imprint of Pan Macmillan Ltd
Pan Macmillan, 20 New Wharf Road, London N1 9RR
Basingstoke and Oxford
Associated companies throughout the world
www.panmacmillan.com

ISBN 1 4050 4582 5 (Hardback)
ISBN 1 4050 4583 3 (Trade Paperback)

1 3 5 7 9 8 6 4 2

A CIP catalogue record for this book is available from
the British Library.

Typeset by IntypeLibra, London
Printed and bound in Great Britain by
Mackays of Chatham plc, Chatham, Kent

Writing this book required extensive research in areas with which I was unfamiliar, including post-mortem examinations, biological warfare and open-water diving. Much of the information was obtained from the Internet and my own resources, but I would particularly like to thank Tony McGovern – a friend, former paratrooper and very experienced professional diver – for casting his expert eyes over the underwater sequences.

I must also thank my friend and agent, Luigi Bonomi, for his unfailing enthusiasm and encouragement, and Peter Lavery at Macmillan for his talented editing, which undoubtedly substantially improved this book. I'm also grateful that Macmillan was prepared to accept without demur a manuscript that, although a work of fiction, is nevertheless highly controversial.

And, of course, Sally.

James Barrington
Principality of Andorra, 2005

## Author's Note

One of the difficulties in writing about a country like Crete, where the language is Greek and uses a completely different alphabet to the rest of the world, is the spelling of place names. In the *Times Concise Atlas of the World*, for example, you will find that the town I have called 'Chóra Sfakia' is spelt 'Khóra Sfakíon', but in the *Collins Road Atlas of Europe*, it's just called 'Sfakia'. I elected to take the spellings I have used in this book from the Automobile Association's *Spiral Guide to Crete*. This is a most useful pocket-sized guide to the island, full of helpful information and with the most detailed maps of any publication I was able to find.

# Glossary

**800 NAS**   800 Naval Air Squadron: Sea Harrier squadron
**814 NAS**   814 Naval Air Squadron: Merlin helicopter squadron

**Aden cannon**   30mm cannon, which can be carried by a Sea Harrier
**AGR**   Anti-gas respirator
**AIM-9L or AIM-9M**   Sidewinder air-to-air missile
**AMRAAM**   AIM-120 Advanced Medium-Range Air-to-Air Missile
**APC**   Air Picture Compiler
**APU**   Auxiliary Power Unit: used to start the main engine on a Sea Harrier
**ASaC**   Airborne Surveillance and Area Control Sea King Mark 7 helicopter
**ASI**   Airspeed indicator
**ASW**   Anti-submarine warfare
**AWO**   Air Warfare Officer. More correctly Anti-War Warfare Officer, responsible for the defence of a ship against airborne threats

**Beretta**   Italian company which manufactures weapons, including the Model 92 semi-automatic pistol
**BIOS**   Basic input-output system: low-level software that runs when a computer starts
**Blue Vixen**   Ferranti coherent pulse-Doppler radar fitted to Royal Navy Sea Harriers
**BLV**   Bovine Lymphotrophic or Leukaemia Virus: a slow-acting virus affecting cattle
**Bogey**   Royal Navy slang for a potentially hostile airborne radar contact
**BSL4**   Bio-safety level four: a maximum-safety biological research laboratory

# GLOSSARY

**CAP**  Combat Air Patrol: defensive air patrol mounted by pairs of Sea Harriers to protect the aircraft carrier and other vessels from air attack

**CDC**  Centers for Disease Control and Prevention, Atlanta, Georgia

**CIA**  Central Intelligence Agency: the Americans' foreign espionage organization

**Cockers-pee**  Royal Navy slang for a cocktail party

**Collective**  The control lever in a helicopter which alters the angle of attack of the rotor blades and causes the aircraft to climb or descend

**CPO**  Chief Petty Officer: senior non-commissioned officer in the Royal Navy. Also known as 'Chief'

**CVS**  The official designation of a Through-Deck Cruiser, like HMS *Invincible*

**DCPP**  *Direzione Centrale Polizia di Prevenzione*: the division of the Italian police force that carries out arrests on behalf of the SISDE

**DECOM**  Type of table (and software program) that allows a diver to calculate decompression stops for specific times underwater

**DP51**  Daewoo 9mm semi-automatic pistol

**Dragunov**  *Snayperskaya Vintovka Dragunova* sniper rifle in 7.62mm Soviet calibre, normally equipped with either the PSO-1 telescopic sight or the NSPU-3 night sight

**DSCS-3**  Defense Satellite Communications System 3. Hardened, jam-proof satellites in geostationary orbit that are designed to provide uninterrupted high-priority secure communications

**E2B**  Simple magnetic compass fitted in Sea Harrier aircraft

**ECG**  Electrocardiogram. Essentially an electronic recording of the heart to allow doctors to assess its condition

**ECM**  Electronic Counter-Measures: devices used to jam or otherwise disrupt radio and radar systems

**EEG**  Electroencephalogram. Essentially an electric recording of the heart to allow doctors to assess its condition

**EMCON**  Emission control policy: statement of intent governing the use of radios and radar

**Enigma T301**  Type of mobile phone allowing totally secure conversation

# GLOSSARY

**EPI1**  Essentially a movement order for CDC (q.v.) personnel. It specifies what the team members are hoping to achieve, where they are going, who they are to contact on arrival, and so on

**ERC**  En-route Chart. Aviation chart showing airfields, airways, upper air routes and other information

**ERS**  En-Route Supplement. Document listing airfield, beacon and other aviation information for a specified geographic area

**FA2**  Fighter Attack 2 variant of the Sea Harrier, also known as the FRS2

**FAA**  Federal Aviation Administration: the American Government organization responsible for all aspects of aviation and air traffic control in the United States

**FADEC**  Full Authority Digital Engine Control: a computerized control system used on the Agusta 109 helicopter

**FDO**  Flight Deck Officer: physically controls all movements on the Flight Deck of an aircraft carrier

**Fibbies**  Slang term for the FBI

**Filovirus**  A lethal thread-like virus found in Africa: there are several different types, the most deadly being Ebola Zaïre

**Flight Level**  Height of an aircraft in thousands of feet based upon the standard pressure setting (q.v.) of 1013.25 hPa (hectopascals) or 29.92 inches (for some American aircraft)

**Flyco**  Flying Control position: located on the port side of the bridge of an aircraft carrier, Flyco controls all launches from, and recoveries to, the ship

**FOE**  Foreign Operations Executive. The fictitious organization that employs Paul Richter. Although FOE does not literally exist, the concept of the SIS employing ex-military personnel to carry out deniable operations is well established. These recruits are known collectively as 'The Increment'

**Fort Detrick**  Location of USAMRIID, the US Army Medical Research Institute of Infectious Diseases, which possesses one of the only two BSL4 laboratories in America

**FRS1**  Early model of the Sea Harrier

**Gazelle**  Two-seat basic trainer helicopter used by the Royal Navy

# GLOSSARY

**Glock**   Austrian-manufactured 9mm semi-automatic pistol

**GSM**   Global Sysem for Mobile Telecommunications. The technical name for the system that operates the ubiquitous mobile phone

**Guard**   Military Emergency frequency of 243.0 megahertz: the equivalent civil VHF frequency is 121.5 megahertz

**Guardian**   Radar warning receiver fitted to Sea Harrier aircraft

**HDS**   Helicopter Delivery Service

**HEPA**   High Efficiency Particle Arrestor: a very efficient filter

**Hi-Power**   Browning 9mm semi-automatic pistol: the standard British Forces side-arm

**Homer**   A radar console manned by a specialist Air Traffic Control officer on an aircraft carrier

**KH-11 or KH-12**   Type of surveillance satellite normally known as a 'Keyhole'

**L4HA**   Level Four Hot Agent: classification of the most lethal known virus types

**Little F**   Lieutenant Commander (Flying)

**Mayday**   Highest state of emergency in an aircraft or ship

**MDC**   Miniature Detonating Cord: thin line of explosive bonded into an aircraft canopy, which shatters it a split-second before the ejection seat is fired

**Merlin**   Agusta Westland Merlin HM Mk 1 ASW helicopter

**MI5**   Military Intelligence 5 – the Security Service – responsible for counter-espionage in the United Kingdom. Also known as 'Five'

**Model 92**   Beretta 9mm semi-automatic pistol

**Mossad**   The Institute for Intelligence and Special Tasks. The Israeli intelligence service, headquartered in Tel Aviv, is one of the most competent and feared services in the world, achieving remarkable results from a total staff of only about 1,200

**NAS**   Naval Air Station (US) or Naval Air Squadron (UK)

**NAVHARS**   Sea Harrier's inertial navigation system

**NBCD**   Nuclear, Biological and Chemical Defence

# GLOSSARY

**N-PIC**  National Photographic Interpretation Center: part of the Science and Technology Directorate of the CIA and based at Building 213 in the Washington Navy Yard

**OOW**  Officer of the Watch

**Pan**  Lower of the two possible states of emergency in an aircraft or ship

**Perp**  Perpetrator

**PGP**  Pretty Good Privacy: a type of data-encryption computer program

**Pigeons**  Magnetic heading to steer and distance to run to reach a ship. Passed to a pilot on recovery to the ship in the format: 'Pigeons two seven five at forty-two'

**Porton Down**  British biological and chemical weapon research facility

**POTUS**  President of the United States

**PWO**  Principal Warfare Officer

**QNH**  Airfield pressure setting calculated so that an aircraft's altimeter will show the airfield's elevation when on the runway

**RC-135**  A highly specialized and very expensive electronic surveillance aircraft based on the Boeing 707 platform

**RDF**  Radio Direction Finder

**RDX**  Cyclotrimethylenetrinitramine. Also known as hexogen or cyclonite, it's a white crystalline substance that is one of the most powerful and stable of the military-application explosives

**RFA**  Royal Fleet Auxiliary: merchant ships that operate under special rules and act as supply vessels to Royal Navy ships

**Ripple Three**  ASW tactic using three helicopters in a screen to protect a group of surface ships: each aircraft is relieved on task by another, so providing a constant ASW protection against the perceived threat

**RPS**  Regional Pressure Setting: the lowest forecast pressure setting for an area that is used by low-level aircraft in transit through that area

# GLOSSARY

**SAMOS**   Satellite and Missile Observation System. Generic term for a series of early American satellites designed to spy on the Soviet Union

**SDS**   Satellite Data System. American satellites used to relay images and data from reconnaissance and geostationary communications satellites, and to detect nuclear detonations. The current version is the SDS-2

**SEM**   Scanning Electron Microscope

**Shareholders**   Naval Air Squadron meeting, normally held every morning, covering administration, flying programme, etc

**SIG P226**   Swiss-manufactured 9mm semi-automatic pistol

**SIS**   Secret Intelligence Service: often but inaccurately known as MI6, and responsible for espionage outside the Unite Kingdom. Also referred to as 'Six'

**SISDE**   *Servizio per le Informazione e la Sicurezza Democratica*: the Italian Secret Service

**SITREP**   Situation report

**Sobs**   Senior Observer of a Royal Navy squadron

**SOP**   Standard operating procedure

**SPC**   Surface Picture Compiler. Royal Navy non-commissioned officer or rating responsible for tracking all surface radar contacts around the mother ship

**Spectre**   Italian-manufactured 9mm sub-machine-gun, unique in that it is double-action, and unusual in having a magazine capacity of fifty rounds

**Splot**   Senior Pilot of a Royal Navy squadron

**SPS**   Standard Pressure Setting of 1013.25 hPa (hectopascals) or 29.29 inches (for some American aircraft). Set on the altimeter sub-scale, it is used above about five thousand feet to ensure all aircraft altimeters share a common setting to allow accurate vertical separation

**SVR**   *Sluzhba Vneshney Razvyedki Rossi*: the successor to the First Chief Directorate of the KGB, responsible for espionage and intelligence operations outside Russia

**SWAT**   Special Weapons and Tactics. Generic term applied to police and other law-enforcement agency paramilitary units

# GLOSSARY

**Two and a half**  Royal Navy slang term for a Lieutenant Commander

**UHF**  Ultra high frequency

**Unsub**  Unknown subject – the unidentified perpetrator of a crime
(US slang)

**USAMRIID**  United States Army Medical Research Institute of
Infectious Diseases. Part of the US Army Medical Research and
Materiel Command and the principal research laboratory of the
American Biological Defense Research Program

**Uzi**  Israeli-manufactured 9mm sub-machine-gun

**Vauxhall Cross**  The headquarters of the Secret Intelligence Service
fronting the Thames in London: the building's bizarre design has
spawned a number of uncomplimentary nicknames

**VHF**  Very high frequency

**Walnut**  Slang term for the CIA's main database

**WASP**  White Anglo-Saxon Protestant. Slang term applied mainly to
young, white, affluent and powerful middle-class Americans in the
1970s and 1980s

**Wings**  Commander (Air): the head of the Air Department on an
aircraft carrier

# Prologue

'So what the fuck did you do?' Jonas snapped, loosening his seat belt and looking across the dimly lit cabin at the tall thin man in the leather seat opposite. The Lear had reached top of climb at thirty-five thousand feet out of Cairo, and was heading west into the gathering dusk.

This atypical expletive – Jonas was the senior man and almost always calm and controlled – shocked Wilson. 'I just did what the three of you refused to do,' he said, looking back at the hostile expressions of the other men. 'I had to – my conscience wouldn't let me ignore it. You know *exactly* what we were doing back there.'

'No,' Jonas said heavily, 'we don't *know* anything. You're just guessing, and you could be guessing wrong.'

Wilson laughed shortly. 'You've seen the file,' he said, 'and you've seen the research. How can you ignore it?'

'Quite easily,' Jonas replied, and turned to glance out of the window at the navigation lights of their escorting F-4E Phantom jet, a dimly seen shape a quarter of a mile out to starboard and slightly behind the civilian aircraft. Then he turned back to face Wilson. 'Look, why didn't you just do what you've been paid – and very well paid – to do?'

Wilson shook his head, rimless spectacles glinting in the cabin lights. 'I couldn't.'

'So you reported it?' Jonas asked, and Wilson nodded. 'Who to?'

For the first time, Wilson looked uncomfortable. 'I knew there was no point in going through the usual channels. That would just make sure whatever I said got buried in a file somewhere.'

Jonas and the other two men stared at him. 'I'll ask you again,' Jonas said, his tone now low and threatening. 'Who did you tell?'

'The President,' Wilson blurted out. 'I wrote to the President, and copied it to the Director of Central Intelligence.'

For a moment, Jonas just stared across the cabin at his subordinate. His voice, when he spoke, was quiet and laden with infinite sadness. 'You fool,' he said. 'You stupid, meddling, ignorant fool. You've probably killed us all.'

'Lima Charlie, this is Tango Three.' The Phantom pilot sounded calm and controlled on the discrete frequency the two aircraft were sharing. 'I have unidentified traffic on radar, sixty miles to port, two contacts, high speed and heading towards. Suggest a precautionary starboard turn onto three zero zero while we check it out.'

'Roger, Tango Three,' the Learjet captain replied, as he disengaged the autopilot and eased the control column to the right.

'I wonder who they are?' the co-pilot asked.

'I don't know, but we're not that far from Libya, so it might be Gaddafi starting to flex his muscles. Probably nothing to worry about.'

The Learjet steadied on its new heading, a track that would take it over to the west of Crete and towards the Ionian Sea.

'Lima Charlie, Tango Three.' There was now a clear note of urgency in the Phantom pilot's voice. 'We're being illuminated by fire-control radar. Recommend you head north. Dash speed. We're—' The transmission broke in a sudden burst of static.

'Oh, shit,' the Learjet captain muttered, pushing the throttles fully forward and moving the control column further to the right.

Wilson had leaned forward, reaching for the case at his feet, then fell back in his seat as the Learjet banked rapidly to the right, the engine noise suddenly increasing.

'What the hell's going on?' Jonas demanded.

Above the cockpit door, the 'Fasten Seat Belts' sign suddenly illuminated, and the cabin speaker crackled into life.

'Buckle up, back there. We've got company, and this may get rough.'

'Tango Three, this is Lima Charlie. Respond.' Silence. 'Tango Three, Lima Charlie.'

'Leave it,' the captain said. 'He's got his hands full, if he's still flying. Kill the lights.' The co-pilot obediently extinguished the Learjet's navigation and anti-collision lights. 'A waste of time if these bastards have got radar-guided weapons.'

'Who the hell are they?' the co-pilot asked again. 'We're not at war with anybody, as far as I know.'

'Who cares? Let's just get the hell away from here. Make a broadcast on twelve fifteen. Give our position and tell anybody who's listening that we're under attack by two unidentified fighter aircraft.'

The co-pilot switched to the civil aircraft emergency VHF frequency – 121.5 megahertz – and started speaking into his microphone. Almost immediately he stopped.

'What is it?' the pilot asked.

'It's just been jammed. There's a tuning tone or something being broadcast. I can't break through it.'

'Try a different frequency. Try Guard, then Athens, or Cairo or Malta.'

The co-pilot tried four, then six frequencies, UHF and VHF, but the result was the same each time. He shook his head. 'They're all blocked,' he said. 'One of those fighters must have an ECM pod fitted.'

The captain's face was noticeably white in the dim cockpit lighting. 'That's real bad news,' he said. 'That means they don't want us to tell anybody what's happening up here.'

'Can we out-run them?' the co-pilot asked.

The Learjet 23 was a very rapid aircraft, with a top speed of almost five hundred miles an hour and a service ceiling of over forty thousand feet. Its performance made it as fast, or faster, than many civilian airliners, but not as quick as most fighter interceptors.

'No idea. We're at maximum velocity now. There's nothing else we can—'

His voice was interrupted by a muffled crump from the port side of the aircraft. Warning lights flared red across the instrument panel, needles on gauges span wildly, and the aircraft lurched to the left.

'We're hit!' the captain shouted. 'Missile in the port engine. Hit the extinguishers.'

The co-pilot pressed the buttons as the captain wrestled with the control column. With the port engine destroyed, the aircraft immediately became asymmetric as the thrust of the remaining turbojet tried to turn the aircraft to the left. The extinguishers fired their foam into the wreckage of the engine, quenching the flames. Hydraulic fluid and aviation fuel bubbled out of ruptured pipes, to be instantly carried away by the slipstream.

'We're losing height! Cabin's depressurizing!'

The altimeter needles unwound in a blur as the Learjet tumbled out of the sky.

The missile that had impacted with the port engine had also blown a two-foot hole at the back of the cabin on the left-hand side. Oxygen masks dropped down in front of the startled passengers from the overhead baggage lockers.

Three of them immediately pulled the masks over their faces. When Wilson didn't follow their example, Jonas turned to shout out to him – but his voice died in his throat. A foot-long shard of aluminium was sticking out of the back of the man's seat, while another six inches protruded from Wilson's throat, thick red blood pouring over it.

In the cockpit, the two pilots pulled oxygen masks over their faces as they struggled to regain some semblance of control.

'Mayday, Mayday, Mayday,' the co-pilot shouted automatically into his microphone, before again hearing the tone in his earphones and realizing nobody would be able to hear his transmission.

At fifteen thousand feet, the captain managed to get the aircraft straight, and more or less level. 'Closest land?' he demanded.

The co-pilot already had the navigation chart unfolded. Using his out-spread fingers as a crude measuring tool, he calculated distances. 'Crete,' he said. 'Come right. Steer zero two zero. Distance about fifty miles to the southern coast, around eighty to the airport at Irakleío.'

'If we can keep this thing in the air that long,' the captain muttered, as he cautiously eased the control column to the right, depressed the right rudder pedal and reduced power slightly on the starboard engine. The flight controls felt soggy and vague, and the gentle turn cost him another three hundred feet of altitude. 'And if whoever's flying those fighters lets us, more to the point.'

The co-pilot's eyes scanned the instruments in front of him. Red and orange warning lights studded the panel, and yellow and red captions had erupted everywhere.

'The fire's out,' he said. 'That's the good news. The bad news is we're losing fuel. We'll be tanks dry in about thirty minutes. The bigger problem is that hydraulic fluid's pumping out of the hole where the port engine used to be. Flight controls are heavy and mushy, and that'll only get worse, and we'll probably have to do a wheels-up flapless landing.'

'If we get that far, I'll be happy to. Tell our passengers what's happened,' the captain said.

As the co-pilot selected cabin broadcast, a stream of tracer shells screamed past the left side of the cockpit, and both men felt the impact as they crashed into the port wing. Panels ripped and buckled, the aileron and flaps were torn away, and then the last eight feet of the wing lifted upwards and backwards before ripping off and tumbling away behind the aircraft.

And then there was nothing anyone could do. The Learjet lost virtually all lift from the mangled wing, turned inexorably to port and began to spin rapidly down towards the sea nearly three miles below. The two men in the cockpit fought it all the way, and managed to straighten the aircraft for a few brief seconds at just under a thousand feet. But they both knew they were going nowhere but down.

'Brace for impact!'

As the glittering surface of the Mediterranean rushed towards them, both men saw a dark shape out to starboard, descending with them.

The captain shook his head in disbelief. 'That's—' he started to say, and then the Lear impacted the water at a little over one hundred and eighty miles an hour.

At that speed, hitting water is pretty much the same as hitting concrete. The remains of the left wing and the nose of the aircraft struck almost simultaneously, the impact killing the men in the cockpit instantly. The aircraft fell onto its back, filled rapidly with water, and sank. Bits and pieces of debris floated up to the surface to mark its grave – but no survivors or bodies appeared.

The fighter aircraft that had followed the Learjet in its final plunge circled the impact site for five minutes, the two-man crew scanning the surface carefully, the pilot's finger hovering over the firing button of the cannon. Finally satisfied, he made his weapons safe, pushed the throttles forward and climbed rapidly away to the west.

# Chapter 1

**Present day – Monday**
**Southern Adriatic Sea**

Paul Richter eased the control column of the Sea Harrier FA2 gently to the left, then pushed it further, turning the bank into a slow barrel roll. He levelled the aircraft for less than a second, then turned sharply to port and accelerated to catch up with the other Harrier, which was already opening to the south-east. He glanced down briefly at the surface of the Adriatic glinting far below, and waited for the Senior Pilot's inevitable rebuke.

'Tiger Two, Leader. Stop buggering about and stay in formation.'

'Sorry, Splot,' Richter said. 'Just checking I could still do it.'

The two Sea Harriers steadied on a heading of one two zero and continued their climb to thirty-one thousand feet, holding four hundred and twenty knots or about eight miles a minute. They were in battle pair formation, Richter holding position about half a mile to the right and behind Tiger One. It was his fifth Combat Air Patrol sortie since his temporary attachment to 800 Squadron, embarked on board HMS *Invincible*, for continuation training.

Richard Simpson, the head of the Foreign Operations Executive and Richter's unloved superior, had bitched about it long and hard. However, Richter was still technically on the Emergency List and in the Royal Naval Reserve, and had argued that he was required to keep up his flying skills. If there had been a good – or even a faintly convincing – reason why he shouldn't have gone, Simpson would certainly have used it. But everything was quiet in London, and Richter had just been sitting in his office moving paper from one tray to another and getting increasingly irritated, so Simpson had reluctantly, and somewhat suddenly, consented.

The previous evening a signal classified Secret, and marked for

7

Richter's eyes only, had been handed to him as he'd emerged from the dining room, and had explained exactly why Simpson had changed his mind.

'Tigers, Alpha Sierra. Snap one eight zero. Two bogeys bearing one nine zero at sixty, heading north. Low.' The voice of the observer in the Airborne Surveillance and Area Control Sea King Mark 7 was slightly distorted by his throat microphone, but perfectly understandable. The ASaC helicopter was positioned at about five thousand feet in a holding pattern some thirty miles ahead of the *Invincible* group.

'Roger, Alpha Sierra. One eight zero.'

Richter followed Tiger One round in a tight starboard turn, rolled out heading south and began to descend, pushing the throttle forward as he adjusted the aircraft's heading.

'Tigers established on south. In the drop passing twenty-eight for fifteen.'

'Roger, Tigers. Bogeys one eight five at forty-two. Low. Below five.'

Fifty miles to the north-west of Richter's Sea Harrier, the *Invincible* group was heading south-east at a steady twelve knots through the Adriatic Sea, about seventy miles off the Italian Puglian coast, and approaching the end of a two-day ship-controlled exercise after an exhausting port visit to Trieste. Accompanying the *Invincible* were two Royal Fleet Auxiliary supply ships, one of them a tanker to cater for the carrier's insatiable thirst for aviation fuel, and two frigates.

HMS *Invincible*, like her sister ships *Illustrious* and *Ark Royal*, is officially known as a Through-Deck Cruiser – a 'CVS'. This somewhat bizarre appellation was forced on the Royal Navy by the political climate in the days when these vessels were constructed, after the word 'carrier' became unacceptable for a variety of reasons.

When the previous *Ark Royal* – the last 'proper' carrier belonging to the Royal Navy – had sailed into the scrapyard, the government of the day had decided, without apparently consulting anybody who might actually know what they were talking about, that in the future the Royal Navy's Fleet Air Arm would only require helicopters. Protection against an enemy unsporting enough to use aircraft to attack a ship would become the sole responsibility of the Royal Air Force.

In theory, and back in the English Channel, this might have worked, but any credible blue-water navy has to carry organic fighter aircraft, and within a short time their lordships at the Admiralty had realized that the *Invincible*-class ships were almost ideally suited to the carriage of Harriers. The result was the Sea Harrier FRS1, which first flew in 1978. Following successful trials, Sea Harrier squadrons were formed and became the principal offensive weapon of the CVS.

The first practical test of the aircraft came in 1982, when Argentine forces invaded the Falkland Islands. A couple of dozen Sea Harriers flying from two small carriers – the *Invincible* and the ageing *Hermes* – were pitched against an air force that was vastly superior both technologically and numerically. The Argentinians fielded supersonic Super Etendards, Daggers and Mirage IIIs, and the small and agile Skyhawk light bombers. Theoretically, the Harriers didn't stand a chance: they should have been overwhelmed by sheer weight of numbers. But they weren't. In a short and bitter campaign, the Sea Harriers shot down twenty Argentine jet aircraft, and several other types, for no air combat losses whatsoever. The reliability and survivability of the type – not to mention its capability – were proved at a stroke.

In the Falklands, the Navy had used the AIM-9L Sidewinder air-to-air missile, but the current variant is the AIM-9M. The newer weapon offers one vitally important advantage – it can lock on to a target from any direction, not just from behind like the 9L, allowing head-on engagements. However, as every fighter pilot knows, the best possible place to engage an enemy is from behind, where you can see him but he can't see you, so air combat tactics have changed little with the introduction of this new weapon.

In its original form, the FRS1 Sea Harrier had usually carried four Sidewinder missiles on under-wing pylons, and a pair of Aden cannon beneath the fuselage. The FA2, the 'Fighter Attack' variant, which entered service in the mid 1990s, added the highly capable AIM-120 Advanced Medium-Range Air-to-Air Missile, which, when matched with the excellent Ferranti Blue Vixen coherent pulse-Doppler radar, offered multiple target acquisition, long engage range and a fire-and-forget capability.

The only problem with the AMRAAM is that it's larger and heavier than the 'winder, and to enable the aircraft to carry more than two of them, the Aden cannon pods were removed, allowing a maximum armament of four AMRAAMs. But the Sidewinder is still an option, and a mix of two AMRAAMs and four 'winders is considered by many Harrier pilots to be the optimum air-combat load.

For exercises, the Royal Navy had decided that AMRAAMs made things just too easy, so most aircraft employed on CAP sorties still used Sidewinders only. The weapon has a maximum engage range of only five miles, and to obtain a kill against another Sea Harrier, with identical performance and armament, is a true test of flying skill and combat ability.

'Bogeys one seven five at thirty. Still low. Vector one nine zero.'

'One nine zero, Tiger One.'

The two fighters were heading directly towards the two inbound aircraft – another pair of 800 Squadron Sea Harriers playing at being bad guys – with a combined closing speed of well over one thousand miles an hour. The Sea King observer, known somewhat unflatteringly as a 'bagman' after the shape of the inflatable fabric dome covering the Sea King's modified Searchwater radar that dangled from the side of the aircraft like a large grey pustule, was vectoring the CAP aircraft to a location above and behind the two targets.

'Tigers, fence out.'

Richter clicked his transmit button once to acknowledge, and immediately began preparing his aircraft for combat. On a pylon beneath the starboard wing of his Sea Harrier was slung a dummy Sidewinder missile pod. Externally almost indistinguishable from a genuine 'winder, the pod contains an infra-red seeker head identical to that in the live missile, but lacks the rocket motor and explosive warhead.

Richter enabled coolant flow through the infra-red head, which would allow it to detect the heat signature of the target aircraft. He switched on the Guardian radar warning receiver, which would tell him if the attacking aircraft had obtained a missile lock on him, then pre-set the Blue Vixen radar to Air Combat mode. The agreed EMCON – emission control – tactics for the sortie required both Tigers to remain radar silent until almost within missile acquisition range of their targets.

The two last preparations were probably the most important. When engaged in high-energy manoeuvring, the airflow through the huge inlets of the Rolls-Royce Pegasus engine can get badly disrupted, and in some cases the compressor may stall or surge and effectively stop. The Harrier glides like the proverbial brick – pretty much straight down – so

Richter selected the 'combat switch' to engage the short-duration high-power setting.

Finally, he checked his anti-g suit. In hard turns pilots' bodies are subjected to very high stresses, and if their anti-g suits don't function properly they can black out, with predictably unfortunate – and sometimes fatal – results.

'Bogeys one seven five at fifteen. Low. Standby hard port turn.'

'Roger.'

'Tigers, turn now, now, now. Roll-out heading zero one zero.'

Richter grunted with the increasing g-force as he hauled the Sea Harrier around in a tight left-hand diving turn. He felt the bladder in the waist section of his 'speed jeans' – the anti-g trousers – inflate rapidly as the g-force increased. It felt like a slow but powerful kick in the stomach, but prevented the blood in his head and torso from plummeting down to his feet and causing a blackout or g-loc.

'Tigers steady on zero one zero, passing twelve for five in the drop.'

'Roger, Tigers. Bogeys zero one five at eight.'

'Tigers, radiate.'

Richter reached down, switched on the Blue Vixen and scanned the display in front of him. 'Tiger Two. Judy, Judy,' he called immediately, the code word signifying that he had acquired the two targets on radar.

'Roger that. Leader's taking west, Tiger Two take east.'

Richter's target – the easterly of the two contacts – was still over six miles in front of him, just outside the Sidewinder's kill envelope. The missile's infra-red seeker head is slaved to the radar antenna: in other words, wherever the radar looks, that's where the missile looks. Already he could hear the faint growl in his headset that told him the 'winder had detected the target Harrier, but he was still too far out of range to engage it.

Richter watched the contacts on radar. As he expected, as soon as the pilots of the 'attacking' Sea Harriers detected the Blue Vixen radar transmissions on their Guardian sets, they split, breaking left and right and climbing. In air combat, height and speed are vital: an aircraft caught at low level is denied freedom of movement and is often an easy target.

'Bogeys splitting. Independent pursuit.'

Richter pulled the Harrier hard round to starboard in a 5g turn. His opponent was passing his level in a steep climb – the Sea Harrier FA2 climbs at fifty thousand feet a minute – and turning rapidly, just under six miles in front of him. The advantage Richter had was that he was still behind his assigned target, which was where he intended to stay until he could engage it with the Sidewinder.

But the other Harrier pilot was having none of it. Realizing that a CAP aircraft was on his tail, he jinked to the left and started a tight diving turn that could bring him up behind and below Richter's aircraft.

Richter saw the manoeuvre, stopped his turn, reversed direction and hauled the Harrier into an even tighter turn to port, following his target, then rolled inverted and powered downwards towards the sea eight thousand feet below. At four thousand feet he forced the Harrier back into a climb. Despite the anti-g suit, Richter felt the blackness of g-loc creeping up on him as he pulled over 6g. The g-force diminished rapidly as the Harrier climbed. Adrenalin pumping, Richter scanned the Blue Vixen scope.

Intellectually, he knew that it was all a game, a kind of maritime *Top Gun*, that the other pilot was from 800 Squadron and that they'd enjoyed a drink together in the Wardroom the previous evening, but in the cockpit it felt different. It felt real, and he reacted exactly as if the other aircraft had been a Russian MiG or a Libyan Sukhoi. The 'enemy' Harrier had rolled out heading east, four miles in front of Richter and three thousand feet above.

'Got you, you bastard,' Richter muttered as he closed with the bogey. The growl in his earphones increased markedly. He checked the head-up display, looking at the voltmeter to confirm the Sidewinder really had locked on to the other Sea Harrier's exhaust and not the other obvious heat source – the sun – and waited for the diamond symbol to appear in the display.

The target aircraft started a tight right-hand turn, but by then it didn't matter. A final check that the bogey was within the missile's minimum and maximum engage ranges, and release. 'Tiger Two, Fox Two,' Richter called. A Sidewinder kill.

'Tiger Two, good kill. Tigers, terminate, terminate,' the Sea King bagman called. 'Pigeons for Mother three five zero at sixty-two. Listen out for Snakes this frequency.'

'Alpha Sierra, roger. Break, break. Tiger Two, Leader. Roll out north at thirty.'

Richter clicked his transmit button to acknowledge, then steadied the Harrier on north, continued the climb and levelled at thirty thousand feet. He scanned his radar, checking for both Tiger One and the other two Harriers. As soon as he identified the Senior Pilot's aircraft, he took up station in battle formation again.

'Tiger Two, Snake One.'

'Tiger Two.'

'Beginner's luck, I'd call it, Spook.'

Richter grinned behind his oxygen mask. 'You know my motto, Randy,' he replied. 'Any time, anywhere.'

'Yeah, right.'

Richter glanced out to starboard, where Snake One had just appeared at his level. The other pilot waggled his Harrier's wings in salute, then moved slightly ahead. Beyond Snake One, Richter could see Snake Two taking up station.

Richter checked the fuel state and his aircraft position on the NAVHARS inertial navigation system. The time was just about right, and he was in pretty much the right place. He made a final visual check that he was in clear air, pulled back on the control column – the classic 'convert excess speed to height' manoeuvre when presented with any kind of an emergency – and simultaneously throttled back so that the other three Harriers shot ahead of him. Then he took a deep breath and transmitted.

'Pan, pan, pan. This is Tiger Two with a rough-running engine. Request diversion to the nearest shore station.'

## Between Gavdopoúla and Gávdos, Eastern Mediterranean

Spiros Aristides had spent his entire working life as a professional diver, primarily in the Aegean, and in retirement he still enjoyed – albeit outside the law – what had once been his livelihood. Scuba diving in Crete is technically illegal, unless the diver holds a permit from the Department of Antiquities, but Spiros had never been particularly concerned about the legality or otherwise of what he was doing. He always carried his diving gear in a couple of sacks, just in case there were any prying eyes trying to monitor his activities, but in the eight years he'd been living on Crete he'd never so much as caught a glimpse of a police-man in the village where he resided, let alone a man from the ministry.

Most weekdays he left his small house in Kandíra on the south-west coast, packed his equipment into his eighteen-foot workboat and headed off into the Mediterranean. Not much to look at, with faded blue and red paintwork and a bunch of old car tyres acting as fenders, the *Nicos* was nevertheless a well-equipped diving tender, fitted with a Gardner diesel engine, radar set, echo-sounder and even a Global Positioning System unit.

Spiros had been given the last piece of equipment by one of his many nephews as a birthday present, which was the only reason it was still attached to the bulkhead in the tiny wheelhouse. He had never used it, and he never would. He knew the waters around Crete the way a gardener knows his lawn, and almost never even glanced at a chart. To have utilized the small digital display of the GPS would have been, for Spiros, an admission of defeat.

Although Crete is one of the most visited holiday islands in the Mediterranean, attracting more than two million tourists every year, it has never been particularly popular with devotees of recreational div-ing. Quite apart from the prospect of a fine of up to one hundred and fifty thousand pounds if caught diving without a permit, the island of Crete is the top of a submerged mountain and, although there are excel-lent bathing beaches, around most of its coast the seabed slopes rapidly away, plunging precipitously to depths of hundreds of feet.

If Crete isn't a popular diving destination, the islands of Gavdopoúla and Gávdos are even less so. The only above-surface projections of another seamount lying some twenty miles to the south of Crete, the islands are tiny – Gávdos is the biggest at about five miles long by three wide – and, as with Crete itself, the seabed slopes rapidly to depths in excess of a thousand feet. Gávdos has a population of around fifty, while Gavdopoúla is unoccupied apart from a bunch of goats.

But between Gavdopoúla and Gávdos lies a saddle, a section of seabed that almost joins the two islands and lies at an average depth of only one hundred feet below the surface of the Mediterranean. And it was there that Aristides had found the wreckage.

When he first spotted the case, he didn't realize what it was. Caught in the powerful beam of the underwater torch, the object swayed slightly, almost imperceptibly, from side to side. A bulky, squared shape festooned with brown and green marine growth, it rocked very gently with the slight current. But it caught his attention because of where it was, rather than what it was.

Visibility underwater in the Mediterranean is usually good, but at a depth of eighty-five feet the light is grey and weak, and Spiros Aristides could see clearly only what his torch beam illuminated. And what it illuminated puzzled him. He lowered the beam and again played it around what was left of the aircraft's cabin.

Aristides knew little about aircraft but even he could recognize an executive jet when he saw one. Or what once had been an executive jet.

After he'd discovered the seat the previous afternoon, he'd guessed that there was more to find, but it had taken him all of three dives to locate the remains of the cabin. The section of wing, torn away from the fuselage, had been easy, one end embedded in the sand, the other pointing up towards the surface in mute entreaty. He'd found bits of unidentifiable twisted metal, and a long and heavy chunk of corroded steel and aluminium that he'd guessed was an engine, but it wasn't until he looked among the rocks fifty metres to the south of where the wing lay that he'd found the cabin. And even then he'd nearly missed it.

Covered in marine growth, it had looked pretty much like another rock, until Aristides's trained eyes had spotted the three more or less regular shapes of what had once been windows along one side of it.

Aristides had checked his chronometer before doing anything else, and realized any exploration of the wreckage would have to wait. He'd looped a rope through two adjacent holes in the fuselage and secured it with a loose knot, then tied the other end to one of his lifting bags. He'd partially filled the bag, using expelled air from his aqualung, enough to give it sufficient buoyancy to hang in the water some twenty feet above the wreck. That had acted as a marker on this, his next dive.

The front of the fuselage had been ripped off, leaving a wide opening through which Aristides now peered. Bubbles from his exhaled breath foamed and swirled above his head, forming an irregular silvery mass in the centre of the cabin roof. There had once been six seats in the passenger compartment, but only five were still secured to its buckled floor. The sixth lay about two hundred metres away, tipped on its side on the seabed some ninety feet below the surface. That same seat, and its grisly occupant, was what Aristides had found first.

Three shrunken, skeletal shapes peered impassively back at him from the seats they had now occupied for over thirty years. He rested the beam of his torch on them, one at a time. Their clothing had largely vanished, as had their flesh and the fabric of the seats they rested in. The two bodies closest to him had slumped down, but a third, towards the rear of the cabin, still sat unnaturally upright.

Aristides crossed himself, then eased forward gently into the cabin, careful to avoid touching either of the first two bodies, until he could see the third one clearly. Then the reason for the corpse's unnatural stance immediately became clear. A shard of metal, probably aluminium and apparently ripped from the fuselage of the aircraft itself, had speared through the back of the seat and was still lodged between two vertebrae of the corpse's neck.

Hanging suspended centrally amid what was left of the cabin, Aristides swung round in a complete circle, his eyes following the torch beam as he searched for anything of value or interest. He stopped the beam between two of the seat frames and focused it on a dark bulky shape squatting among the marine growth and debris covering the buckled floor of the cabin.

Aristides moved carefully towards this object, transferred the torch to his left hand and then extended his right arm. He gave the thing an experimental prod, and it moved slightly across the floor. Then he pulled it towards him and studied it more closely. Made of what appeared to be rotting leather, it looked like the kind of bag usually carried by doctors.

Putting the torch down carefully on the floor, and wedging it so that it illuminated the bag, Aristides pulled the heavy diving knife from its sheath strapped to his right calf. Holding the bag firmly with his left hand, he stabbed the knife into the side of it and then ripped it open. He tipped the bag onto its side and looked down in puzzlement as a cascade of corroded medical instruments tumbled out.

Aristides mentally shrugged and transferred his attention to the object that caught his attention immediately he had peered into the cabin. Unlike the leather bag, this was bouncing gently and improbably against the ceiling of the aircraft cabin, rather than lying on the floor.

That meant that it was either naturally buoyant or, more likely, water-proof and airtight.

Picking up his torch again, Aristides reached for the object of his interest. Only then did he notice what appeared to be a small silvery tail dangling from it. As he peered more closely, he realized that this tail was actually a handcuff and immediately he recognized the bulky briefcase. The handcuff, which had presumably once been fastened around the wrist of one of the corpses below it, suggested that the case contained something valuable. Light, certainly, but valuable.

Professionally conscious of the passage of time, Aristides checked his chronometer and backed out of the aircraft's cabin, now holding the briefcase in his left hand. He wanted to try to identify the aircraft itself, if he could, before having to surface.

Aristides secured the case to the line holding the lifting air bag, then swam back to the remains of the fuselage. He noticed what appeared to be part of a registration number visible near the rear end of the cabin, on the starboard side, and rubbed his gloved hand over it until he could make out the first letter. He couldn't interpret any of the following digits until he'd scraped off some of the marine growth with his diving knife. That revealed three numbers which, together with the initial letter 'N' – Spiros instantly interpreted this as the Greek capital letter *nu* – he wrote on his waterproof pad. It looked to him as if there was another number, perhaps even two numbers, but it or they were indecipherable without shifting more growth.

Aristides wondered if the registration would be repeated on the other side of the cabin, and swam around to check. But when he spotted the jagged hole in the fuselage, he forgot all about checking numbers.

## Southern Adriatic Sea

There was a brief silence on the frequency, then the squadron Senior Pilot, flying Tiger One, responded.

'Tiger Two from Leader. Can you make it back to Mother?'

'Negative,' Richter snapped. 'I need a long concrete runway to put this down on, not a steel postage stamp.'

'Roger. Go to Guard and check in with Homer. Suggest you steer two four zero initially. I'll accompany you. Snakes, Tiger Leader turning port and following Two. See you back on board.'

Richter was already in the turn onto south-west, as he switched frequency and selected the emergency code 7700 on his Secondary Surveillance Radar transponder. This setting generates an unmistakable, and absolutely unmissable, symbol on air traffic control radar displays.

'Homer, this is Pan aircraft Tiger Two on Guard.'

On all warships, the Operations Room is a darkly colourful, and invariably noisy, environment. The illumination is derived from the reddish glow of radar screens, from small reading lights mounted on the consoles, from the myriad multi-coloured tell-tales and illuminated controls. The noise is caused by the constant chatter on Group Lines, intercoms and radio frequencies as specialist officers and ratings do their work.

The Operations Room on Five Deck is in every sense the nerve centre of the *Invincible*. Around the perimeter, information is gathered from the ship's own sensors – principally radar and sonar – and from sensors mounted on other vessels and aircraft that transmit to the ship using secure data-links. Here the Air Picture Compilers track and identify all airborne radar contacts, while Surface and Sub-surface Compilers perform identical functions for their specific areas of responsibility.

The collated data provide the Warfare Officers, working at consoles in the centre of the room, with a complete picture of the air, surface and underwater environment around the warship, and enable them to act or react as the situation warrants. Surprisingly to the uninitiated, during any kind of action or alert the Captain will be found sitting on a swivel chair virtually in the centre of the Operations Room, and he will direct all aspects of the ship's activities from there. No longer does he fight battles from the bridge, as was the norm during the Second World War. Today, instead, a seaman officer will take the bridge watch, to visually ensure the safety of the ship and to check that helm and engine revolution orders don't run the vessel aground or into a collision.

Inside the Operations Room, close to the port-side door and beneath the printed title 'Homer', is a radar console manned by a specialist Air Traffic Control officer whose principal responsibility is the safe recovery of the ship's organic air assets. The Military Emergency (Guard) frequency – 243.0 megahertz – is monitored whenever the ship is at sea, but is generally patched through an Ops Room speaker rather than listened to by Homer, who normally has more than enough traffic on his primary aircraft recovery frequency.

As soon as he heard the Pan call – 'Pan' being the lower of the two states of aircraft emergency, the more serious one being 'Mayday' – Lieutenant John Moore leaned back in his seat and looked up at the Radio Direction Finder display mounted above his console, simultaneously selected Guard on the frequency selector panel, and pressed the transmit key.

'Pan aircraft Tiger Two, this is Homer. You're loud and clear. State the nature of your emergency.'

'Tiger Two has a rough-running engine and is requesting diversion ashore. Present heading is two four zero at Flight Level three five zero, squawking emergency. Tiger One is in company to relay as required.'

'Roger, all copied, and you're identified by your emergency squawk. You're forty-two miles off the coast, and estimate you'll be feet dry in about six minutes. Standby for airfield information.'

The moment the call had been heard on Guard, Homer's radar console had become the focus of most of the activity in the Operations Room. His assistant had pulled out the relevant en route chart and the en route supplement covering Italy and was scanning the ERC, looking for the closest airfield that could take the Sea Harrier.

Moore's next priority was to shed his other traffic so that he could concentrate on the emergency aircraft. In fact, he had nothing else on frequency at that moment, but he was expecting Snake One and Two to check in imminently. To pre-empt them, he called the Air Warfare Officer on Group Line Six.

'AWO, Homer. Snakes should be on recovery soon, and I don't want them on my frequency until we've sorted out Tiger Two. Can you raise the ASaC Sea King and get Snakes to call Director for recovery?'

'Already doing it.'

'Thanks.'

Then Moore looked at the chart his assistant was holding, glanced across at the airfield details listed in the ERS, nodded and transmitted again.

'Tiger Two, Homer. Suggested diversion airfield is Brindisi-Casale.

Runway is eight thousand six hundred feet in length, airfield location approximately one nine zero range fifty from your present position.'

'Roger,' Richter said. 'Turning port onto one nine zero and starting a cruise descent.'

'Initial Contact Frequency for Brindisi-Casale Approach Control is three seven six decimal eight, but suggest you call them first on Guard.'

'Roger.'

Commander (Air), who'd been up in Flyco when Richter made the Pan call, had immediately left his position and arrived at that moment in the Operations Room.

'Where is he?' he demanded.

Moore glanced round then pointed over to the south-western side of his radar screen. 'Here, sir. He's about to call Brindisi.'

As Moore spoke, Richter's voice echoed round the Ops Room from the Guard speaker. 'Brindisi, Brindisi, this is Pan aircraft Tiger Two.'

In the Operations Room, a long silence followed, because the ship was out of radio range of the airfield, but Richter and Splot in Tiger One heard the reply clearly, and the Senior Pilot then relayed the airfield's response to the *Invincible*.

'Pan aircraft Tiger Two, this is Brindisi Approach. What is your emergency, and what is your position, level, aircraft type and number of persons on board?' The Italian's English was perfectly clear and understandable – English being the international language of aviation and air traffic control – but with a quite unmistakable accent.

'Brindisi, Tiger Two is a British Royal Navy single-crew Harrier aircraft with a rough-running engine. Position approximately forty miles north of you, in descent passing Flight Level two zero zero.'

'Roger, Tiger Two. What are your intentions?'

'Request navigation assistance and a straight-in approach to a priority landing.'

'Roger. You are identified by your position report and secondary radar return. Steer one eight five and continue descent to Flight Level one zero zero. Standby to copy the weather and airfield missed approach procedure.'

'Tiger Two is ready to copy.'

Tiger One was still at thirty-five thousand feet, holding clear of Italian airspace and loitering to relay information to the ship.

'Homer, this is Tiger One relaying for Tiger Two on Guard. Two is in descent out of twenty thousand down to ten, and receiving nav assistance from Brindisi Approach.'

Richter saw the airfield from twelve thousand feet and fifteen miles, and throttled back even further.

'Brindisi, Tiger Two is now visual with the field.'

'Roger, Tiger Two. Report approaching five thousand feet on the airfield QNH with Tower on two five seven decimal eight. We have no traffic in the circuit or local area.'

As Richter pulled his Sea Harrier round in a gentle turn to starboard, he glanced down and in front of his aircraft at the airfield below him. The Italians were obviously taking no chances: he could see an ambulance waiting near the control tower, and at the holding point for the main runway two emergency vehicles – known in the UK as 'Crash' and 'Rescue' – were already in position, blue and red lights flashing. 'Crash' was a primary unit – a first-line heavy fire engine designed to dowse aviation-fuel fires using a foam compound known as A Triple F (Aqueous Film-Forming Foam) – flanked by 'Rescue', a small four-wheel-drive go-anywhere vehicle.

Inside seven miles and nicely settled on the runway's extended centreline, but well above the normal glide path to provide the margin of safety a prudent pilot would want with an engine that might fail at any moment, Richter hauled the Harrier's speed back to below two hundred knots. Once his speed was within the aircraft's parameters, he dropped the landing gear, checking the enunciator as four green lights illuminated, indicating that both the main wheel assemblies and the wheels at the ends of the wings were down and locked.

'Tiger Two, Brindisi Tower, confirm landing checks are complete.'

'Checks complete, four greens,' Richter replied.

'Roger, Tiger Two. Land runway three two. Wind is green one five at ten gusting fifteen.'

Richter played with the throttle all the way down, but he didn't attempt to adjust the nozzle angle: he had over a mile and a half of asphalt and concrete in front of him, and was quite happy to use all of it if he had to.

He flew over the touchdown end of the runway, coming in very high and very fast – the kind of profile one of his flying instructors had dubbed an 'elephant's arse approach' because it was high and it stank – then flared the Harrier and dropped it onto the rubber-streaked runway about four hundred yards beyond the piano keys. The moment the tyres touched the concrete, Richter throttled back completely, and the aircraft's speed began falling away.

'Thank you, Tower,' Richter transmitted. 'Request taxi instructions.'

'Take the next exit right and follow the taxiway to the first hangar.'

As Richter made the turn he saw the fire-and-rescue vehicles following behind him, the ambulance in trail. He waved an acknowledgement from the cockpit and received an answering flash from the primary unit's headlights in return.

Fifty-eight miles away and thirty-five thousand feet above the surface of the Mediterranean, the Senior Pilot in Tiger One, who had followed Richter's frequency changes down to touchdown, heard the transmission and pulled his aircraft around in a starboard turn onto east.

'Tiger Two from Tiger One on Brindisi Tower frequency. Copy that you're down safely. See you around, Spook.'

'Roger that, Splot.'

The Senior Pilot checked his fuel state, selected Destination One – the *Invincible*'s programmed position – in his NAVHARS, and settled his Harrier into a high-level cruise. Then he switched back to Homer frequency.

'Homer, Tiger One. Tiger Two is down safely at Brindisi, my estimate at minute two six. Tiger One is now on recovery and requesting pigeons.'

'Tiger One, Homer. Good news, sir. Pigeons zero seven five at fifty-three.'

At Brindisi-Casale, Richter switched off his Harrier's electrical systems and then shut down the engine. The ground crew didn't have a proper set of steps designed for the Harrier, so they improvised with a small fork-lift truck, against the raised prongs of which they rested an aluminium ladder.

When Richter reached the ground he shook hands solemnly with each of the ground crew, then followed their hand signals and sign language towards the squadron building adjacent to the hangar. He walked into the white-painted, single-storey building and followed another Italian's directions to what he assumed was the squadron briefing-room.

The first, and in fact only, person Richter saw when he pushed open the door was Richard Simpson.

# Chapter 2

What may be termed the militarization of space began in 1960 when the US Air Force successfully recovered exposed film from Discovery 13, the first photo-reconnaissance satellite, and when in a parallel but unrelated operation the US Navy orbited a Transit bird.

These two successes were quickly followed by a series of SAMOS (Satellite and Missile Observation System) reconnaissance satellites. The launches of these early and very basic vehicles were followed by satellites of increasing complexity, and near-space orbits are now filled with a plethora of highly sophisticated, complex and very specialized pieces of equipment. These include Defence Support Program infra-red early-warning satellites, Magnum electronic intercept birds, SDS information-relay satellites, and DSCS-3 jam-proof high-frequency communication platforms.

Project 467 began in the 1960s and culminated in the first long-lived surveillance satellite that included data transmission facilities. This was Big Bird, the first of which was launched in 1971. Compared to the early surveillance satellites, it was huge: forty-nine feet long, weighing nearly thirty thousand pounds, launched by a specially modified Titan 3D rocket, and with a design life of months.

Its on-board equipment included a general area survey scanner developed and manufactured by Eastman Kodak, and a Perkin-Elmer high-resolution camera designed for detailed analysis of specific areas of interest. Pictures taken by the area scanner went through on-board processing, and were then scanned and the data transmitted down to earth using a twenty-foot-diameter antenna located at the end of the satellite. To provide hard copy for the analysts, up to six recoverable film capsules were carried, which could be ejected at intervals and recovered by air-snatch using a converted C-130 Hercules transport aircraft.

Five years after the first Big Bird launch, an entirely new surveillance satellite was lifted into orbit. This was the KH-11, or Keyhole, vehicle. Only two-thirds the size of the Big Bird, at just over twenty thousand pounds, but with an operational life of about two years, the KH-11 was initially employed as a back-up to its larger cousin, following an identical orbital path and employing its higher-resolution cameras to take detailed pictures of areas identified by Big Bird as being of special interest. Unlike Big Bird, the KH-11 didn't scan processed photographs: digital images were produced immediately and the data transmitted to earth in near real-time. The Keyhole could also provide television pictures from its normal orbital elevation of one hundred and twenty miles. In the late 1980s the more efficient KH-12 bird supplemented the KH-11.

Depending on the location of the satellite, digital images are beamed either directly, or via one of a number of dedicated communications satellites in geo-stationary orbit, to the Mission Ground Site at Fort Belvoir just outside Washington, DC. The pictures are then forwarded to Building 213 in the Washington Navy Yard, home of N-PIC – the National Photographic Interpretation Center – part of the Science and Technology Directorate of the Central Intelligence Agency.

Resolution, with particular respect to surveillance satellites, is defined as the minimum distance separating two point light sources so that it can clearly be determined whether those points are dots or a line. The first reconnaissance satellites had an optimum resolution of just over eight feet from their normal maximum elevation of one hundred and twenty-four miles. Big Bird was a huge improvement, and provided resolution of slightly under twenty-four inches from an orbital height of one hundred miles, and the KH-12 brought this figure down to a whisker under six inches from a maximum orbital elevation of two hundred and fifty miles, close to the theoretical limiting resolution of just under four inches.

What all this means in practical terms is that if a man is sitting outdoors reading a newspaper anywhere on the surface of the earth for more than about an hour, an analyst sitting at a purpose-built computer console in Washington will be able to identify which newspaper he's reading, while he's still reading it.

Surveillance satellites follow standard and pre-determined polar orbits. They can be manoeuvred to some extent to provide additional pictures of particular areas of interest, but this costs fuel and reduces the life of the bird, so most agencies simply study the 'take' obtained when the satellite passes over a particular location during its normal operations.

Frequently, the bird's sensors are deactivated when it crosses large stretches of water, simply because there's generally nothing much to see, but there are exceptions. One such exception, originating from the Intelligence Directorate of the CIA at Langley, Virginia, was somewhat unusual, for three reasons.

First, it was old now, having been initiated in the winter of 1972. Most satellite imagery requests have immediate and obvious relevance to whatever troubles are currently being fomented in the world. Second, the area specified was simply a ten-mile square of the eastern Mediterranean, of no obvious strategic or any other importance. Third, it asked for the simplest possible report – the identity and type of any vessel remaining in the same location within that square for more than three hours, or any vessel which returned to the area twice or more in any thirty-day period. No follow-up, no further action.

Since 1972, N-PIC had forwarded some two hundred and eighty reports to the Intelligence Directorate, had received an acknowledgement each time, and had heard nothing further. The report that morning was almost identical to every other one they had sent, with one exception – they hadn't been able to identify the *Nicos*, simply because the vessel had no identification marks visible from above, but they had been able to state exactly what the boat was, because they could see the purpose-built racks for the aqualungs.

This time, they got the usual acknowledgement from Langley, but also an instruction for additional material on the next and all subsequent passes by the bird, and a request for the hard-copy pictures to be forwarded immediately.

# PANDEMIC

## Aeroporto di Brindisi, Papola-Casale, Puglia, Italy

'So just what the hell is all this about, Simpson?' Richter said, putting down his flying helmet and life vest, and sitting opposite his superior. 'I don't appreciate being told to pull stunts like this. Scrambling safety services raises pulse rates and costs money, not to mention the fact that the ship's now going to have to send a team of maintainers all the way out here by helicopter to spend a couple of days examining a perfectly serviceable Sea Harrier.'

Simpson waved one small pink hand dismissively. 'Your comments are noted, but this seemed the easiest way to get you into Italy without anyone knowing you've been here.'

'And that's important, is it?'

'Yes,' Simpson said flatly, 'or it could be.' He gestured towards a small brown suitcase standing upright against the wall. 'You might be here for a day or two, so I brought you a change of clothes. You can hardly,' he added, with a glance at the flying overalls and anti-g trousers Richter was wearing, 'wander around wearing *that* outfit.'

'I *thought* you had a sudden change of heart about my doing a bit of continuation training,' Richter said. 'And I suppose it also explains why I had to fly down at such short notice to join the ship at Gib. So what am I supposed to be doing in Italy? Are we working for the Mafia now?'

'Not that I'm aware of, Richter,' Simpson replied. 'We have a little business to take care of here in Italy. I suppose it is faintly possible that the Mafia might be a beneficiary, but our real client is the SISDE – the Italian Secret Service.'

'And what exactly does the *Servizio per le Informazione e la Sicurezza Democratica* want with us?' Richter asked, in perfect Italian construction yet badly mangling the pronunciation. Simpson even looked impressed. 'I do know my business, Simpson,' Richter added.

'I've no doubt you do. We – or to be more accurate *you* – have been sort of lent to them for a while.'

'There's a quid pro quo lurking here somewhere, I presume?'

'You presume correctly, but it's none of your business. You just do your bit and then you can fly your pretty little grey fighter back to the ship, and finish off your pleasure cruise in the Med.'

'And my "bit" is what, exactly?'

Simpson looked at him steadily for a few moments before he replied. 'We think Andrew Lomas has resurfaced, and we need you to finger him for us,' he said.

## Between Gavdopoúla and Gávdos, Eastern Mediterranean

In a sudden flurry of bubbles and foam, Spiros Aristides's head broke the slightly choppy surface of the Mediterranean less than a metre from the stern of the *Nicos*. Immediately the Greek stretched out his hand and grabbed the diving ladder. He reached down, pulled off his fins and tossed them on board, and followed them with his mask. Then he climbed up the ladder and into the boat, shrugged off his scuba set and placed it carefully in a rack on the starboard side. The racks were covered with a tarpaulin whenever the boat was in harbour, but at sea Aristides didn't bother.

There was a practised haste in his movements. Decompression stops had kept him below the surface for the better part of fifty minutes, and Aristides was eager to get himself and his prize back to his house in Kandíra as soon as possible.

He pulled off the neoprene hood and unzipped and removed his wet-suit jacket – it was cold at the depths he had dived to, but very warm now he was back at the surface – and next his gloves, then rummaged in a locker until he found another pair of gloves of an entirely different type. These were tough workman's gloves made of stiff canvas, and with leather strengthening patches sewn onto the palms.

Pulling on the gloves, Aristides stepped over to the port side of the *Nicos* and reached down. Securely attached to two cleats was a one-centimetre-diameter orange nylon rope, which descended vertically into the azure waters of the Mediterranean. Taking a firm grip, Aristides began hauling the rope inboard, hand over hand. The first scuba set appeared in seconds, and he paused only to detach it and place it carefully beside him before continuing to pull on the rope.

Within five minutes, Aristides had three scuba sets sitting on the bottom of the boat – he'd used them all during his decompression stops on the way up to the surface – and some eighty metres of orange rope coiled about him. But still he hauled on the rope. Finally he saw a glint of something metallic in the water below him, and pulled more gently, stopping when the object hung suspended just below the surface of the sea, and he then expertly secured the rope around the cleats. He walked back to the wheelhouse where he had an unobstructed view, and surveyed the sea around him carefully, in a complete circle, before walking back to resume hauling on the rope after he felt quite certain nobody could observe him.

Twenty seconds later, Aristides was crouching in the bottom of the *Nicos* to untie the rope from around the metal briefcase he'd pulled from the wrecked aircraft.

Five minutes after that, all the scuba sets were secured in their racks under the concealing tarpaulin, the orange rope was coiled and stowed in a seaman-like fashion, the lead weight he'd used to anchor the rope was back in its locker, and the briefcase was hidden below a set of foul-weather gear on the floor of the wheelhouse. The *Nicos* was under way, making directly for Kandíra at about two knots faster than her usual cruising speed. Spiros Aristides was a methodical man, but today he was a methodical man in a hurry.

A little under three hours later, he unlatched the door of his small white-washed house, opened it and walked through the tiny hall into the main room. Light from the afternoon sun streamed through the closed slatted-wood shutters, creating Morse-code patterns across the rough tiled floor, as dust-motes danced in the air. Aristides switched on the overhead light and lowered his large canvas sack to the floor.

Then he walked back into the hall, opened the door and looked up and down the dusty street. Nobody in sight, and nothing moving apart from an elderly marmalade cat cleaning itself in the shade of the fig tree on the other side of the narrow lane. No sound but the ever-present cicadas zithering their drowsy salute to the late-afternoon sun, that was now shading into evening. It was a good time to return home for a man who didn't particularly want to meet any of his neighbours. Aristides nodded his satisfaction, pulled the door closed, locked it and walked back to where he'd placed the sack.

To one side of the room was a small sturdy oak table and two upright chairs, the table still bearing the remains of Aristides's simple breakfast – a bowl containing a few black olives, a small piece of feta cheese on a plate, and a cup half-full of the thick black coffee he favoured. He flapped his hand ineffectively at the flies crawling sluggishly over the remnants, then removed the debris to the kitchen. After that he gave the top of the table a cursory wipe with a damp cloth. Before doing anything else, Aristides walked across the room and seized the standard lamp that stood next to one of the easy chairs positioned either side of the small fireplace. He dragged it across to the table, stretching it to the very end of its lead and switched it on.

Bending down, he loosened the draw-string closing the neck of the sack, then carried his prize to the table and put it down carefully. He'd scraped off most of the marine growth before he'd started the Gardner diesel of the *Nicos* and hauled up the anchor. His neighbours were quite used to the smell of decaying seaweed emanating from his property, but he would still rather avoid them asking awkward questions.

The case was bulky, in size about mid-way between a briefcase and a small suitcase. It was made of metal – steel or perhaps aluminium – and had originally been covered with leather or plastic since in places there were still small patches of coarse, dark material adhering to it. Aristides pulled a clasp knife from his pocket and snapped it open, then ran the point of it lightly along the side of the case for a couple of centimetres. The knife-point barely scratched the metal, so he knew it was steel.

When he'd hauled it out of the sea and into the *Nicos*, Aristides had been surprised at how light in weight his discovery seemed. He'd realized, because of the way he'd found it floating, that it was airtight, but he had still been hoping for something of substance inside it.

He sat down at the oak table and studied the outside of the case for a few moments. There were no distinctive markings of any sort that he could see, not even a manufacturer's name or number. The case had one large central catch and a lock on either side of it, both quite simple affairs and each with an over-centre latch holding the lid closed. Aristides guessed that the primary security of the case and its contents had been the man carrying it, whose wrist had originally been secured to the handcuff still dangling from a steel chain welded to the case – a man whose bones now lay lost and unremembered ninety feet below the surface of the Mediterranean.

Underneath the old stone sink in his kitchen, Aristides kept a metal toolbox containing an assortment of screwdrivers, pliers, files and a hammer, useful items for tackling the odd household problem. He got up to collect the toolbox and placed it beside the mysterious case on the table. He selected a small screwdriver and measured the size of its point against the keyhole in one of the locks. A little *too* small. He picked one slightly larger, stuck the point into the keyhole and gave the handle a sharp rap with the hammer. The point drove about half a centimetre into the lock. Aristides seized the handle firmly and twisted the screwdriver – gently at first, then with increasing force. With a snap, the lock gave, the screwdriver turned, and Aristides freed the latch.

He pulled the tool out of the ruined lock and repeated the treatment on the second one. The catch, between them, had no lock, so he simply unclipped it and eased the lid open slightly. There was a sudden hiss of escaping air. Aristides leaned back, then opened the lid all the way and peered cautiously inside.

### Aeroporto di Brindisi, Papola-Casale, Puglia, Italy

Richter just stared at Simpson, ice-blue eyes unblinking as his mind span back through the years to the last, in fact the only, time he'd seen Andrew Lomas. And whenever he thought of Lomas, Richter remembered Raya Kosov.

Richter had been the totally expendable bait in a complex trap laid by Richard Simpson to ensnare a high-level traitor somewhere within British Intelligence. Sent to Austria on what purported to be a courier assignment, Richter had unwittingly been set up as the tethered goat to attract the tiger. Not knowing where the traitor was employed, Simpson had disseminated his story throughout all arms of the intelligence community. He had portrayed Richter as a disaffected Russian cipher clerk, a renegade from the SVR, a man running from his former masters and carrying documentary evidence that would expose the traitor. His confrontation with Gerald Stanway, the treacherous SIS officer, had nearly cost Richter his life, but when the shooting stopped it had been Stanway who lay dead.

Then, in a bizarre example of reality imitating art, a genuine cipher clerk – in fact the deputy manager of the SVR computer network – had run from Russia to seek sanctuary in the West. Raya Kosov had had her own agenda and her own reasons for running, and she had applied her own conditions. One of these was that she would not meet with any serving or even retired member of British Intelligence. Richter was not only on the spot, he was the only man Simpson could find who met all the criteria that Raya had specified, and Simpson was desperate to access the information she possessed before the CIA, or even worse the SVR, found her.

It was only after Richter had met Raya, and the two were making their way through France to Britain, that he had learnt the reason for her refusal to be handled by a 'proper' intelligence officer. She knew the identity of a traitor so highly placed in the British Secret Intelligence Service that she wasn't prepared to trust anybody in that organization or in any of the other arms of the intelligence community. And the man she could identify wasn't Gerald Stanway.

With both SVR hit-squads and SIS assassination teams looking for them, Richter and Raya had literally run for their lives and, perhaps inevitably, had become 'involved' with each other. Finally they had made it to London, where an analysis of the data Raya had obtained pointed at one man – Sir Malcolm Holbeche, the head of the SIS – and Richter and Simpson had confronted him together.

And then, as the operation wound down, Holbeche's own Russian case officer, Alexei Lomosolov – a deep-cover illegal using the cover name Andrew Lomas – had counter-attacked. With Holbeche dead, and the operation over as far as Richter was concerned, he had let his guard slip and had been followed back to the hotel where he had hidden Raya.

Ten minutes after he got in, there had been a knock at the door. Without thinking, Richter had opened it and looked straight into Andrew Lomas's dark, almost black, eyes for less than a second before the taser dart had stabbed into his stomach. When he had come round, he found himself lying on the bed – and Raya's horribly mutilated body was lying beside him. The only good news was that Simpson had already taken custody of the disks and data that Raya had smuggled out of Moscow.

'Where is he?' Richter growled, finally.

'Here in Italy – somewhere near Taranto, to be exact,' Simpson replied. 'At least, that's what the Italians think. They've got a couple of photographs of somebody who matches Lomas's description, and also a copy of the photofit you did back in London. But you need to confirm his identification, because you're the only person in the service who's known to have met him in the flesh, so to speak. And Richter,' Simpson warned, 'we – that's myself as well as the Italians – want Lomas in one piece, not diced, sliced or blown away.'

## Kandíra, south-west Crete

Spiros Aristides slumped back in his chair, disappointment evident in every line of his face. He didn't know exactly what he'd been expecting, but what he'd actually found definitely wasn't it. The case was lying on the floor, where he'd tossed it in irritation, and its contents were now spread across the table in front of him. The biggest and heaviest item was a thick file enclosed in a bright red cover. Aristides had opened it and looked at some of the papers it contained, but they'd been meaningless to him. He'd simply recognized that the writing was in English, a language he didn't speak, though he could read the odd word.

The only other things in the case were four small heavily sealed steel vacuum flasks, each bearing a white label with the legend 'CAIP' on it, and below that a number. Their tops were held in place with red wax and wire, and the flasks had been fitted snugly into shaped and padded recesses inside the case. There were also spaces for a further eight flasks of the same size, but none of these had been occupied.

The flasks were light and, as far as Aristides could tell, empty, but that made no kind of sense. Why would anyone seal up empty flasks and lock them securely in a briefcase then chained to a courier and carried on board an expensive private jet? There simply had to be something significant inside them.

For the third time, he picked one up and shook it, close to his ear, but could still detect no sound of anything moving inside. Perhaps, he surmised, they might contain small amounts of some very pure drug: heroin or maybe cocaine. The only way to find out was to open one.

Aristides studied the top of one flask. He couldn't see the stopper at all, because the whole top end of the container was covered in a thick red covering of some sort, as if the mouth had been dipped into a bowl of molten wax to seal it. Confining the wax was a wire net, whose thin strands cut deep into the surface and were twisted together round the neck of the flask to secure it. Whoever had sealed these flasks had definitely not intended that one might come open by accident. Aristides nodded to himself. Perhaps it *was* drugs. Perhaps he might be able to make a profit out of his efforts after all.

In his toolbox Aristides had a pair of sharp wire-cutters, and it was the work of only a few seconds to snip off the twisted knots of wire at the neck of the flask. Pulling the wire strands out of the wax took longer, but after ten minutes he had removed them all, and was examining the unconfined wax itself.

The simplest way to get the stuff off, Aristides thought, was to melt it again, so he walked through to his kitchen and reached down beside the cooker to turn on the gas supply from the large blue cylinder attached to it. Then he rotated the discoloured knob on the front of the cooker and struck a match to light the gas. He'd actually walked back to his dining table and picked up the sealed vacuum flask before his natural caution re-asserted itself.

Suppose the heat from the gas destroyed the contents before the wax melted? Or, worse, what if he was wrong about what it contained – maybe an explosive, not drugs – and the flask blew up in his hands?

No, the safest option was his knife. Aristides went back and switched off the gas cylinder, then returned to the table. He opened his old clasp knife again and eased its point gently into the red wax covering the neck of the container, then rotated the flask in his left hand while the right held the blade of the knife firmly, at an angle, against the flask itself. The knife was sharp and cut easily through the wax, the blade spiralling closer and closer to the top of the flask as he turned it. Then he stopped, put down the knife and seized the loose end of the wax, pulling it off like the skin of a peeled apple. The wax covering the actual mouth of the flask was much thicker than that on its sides, so he had to insert the point of the knife blade under it to lever it off.

Aristides looked carefully at the stopper – now revealed – and raised his eyebrows. It had been locked in place, with a small keyhole right in its centre, and the Greek could tell immediately that this was intended for some kind of security key. His trick with a screwdriver wouldn't work again.

He sat thoughtfully at the rough oak table, hefting the small steel flask in his hand, considering his options. The precautions that had been taken with these containers were like nothing he had ever seen before, and in his long career as a diver he'd been involved in the recovery and opening of numerous safes and strongboxes found on wrecked ships. Some had been little more than padlocked containers, yielding to a simple wrench from a pry-bar or a blow from a hammer, while others had required oxy-acetylene cutters or even a thermic lance to cut around the lock or slice an access hole in the back or side of a safe. But none that he could recall had ever involved such serious multi-layered protection for such a small object.

Aristides could think of only two possible reasons why such elaborate precautions had been taken: the contents had to be either extremely valuable or very dangerous. The question was, which?

### Central Intelligence Agency Headquarters, Langley, Virginia

The top-floor office was spacious, light and airy, and had a clear and unobstructed view of the Virginia woodlands surrounding the Head-quarters complex, but the big man wearing the charcoal-grey suit and sitting in a leather swivel chair had no eyes for the natural beauty of the locality. His attention was fixed on six eight-by-ten black-and-white photographs spread out on the desk in front of him.

The desk itself was big and impressive, an oak-framed antique with a walnut veneer. It was his personal property, having been in his family for at least eighty years. Apart from the photographs and three steel-mesh document trays, the only other objects on the desk were two tele-phones and a solid silver writing set. A tidy and organized desk, he had always believed, denoted a tidy and organized mind.

Beside the desk stood a purpose-built console, which housed a computer terminal with direct access to the CIA's extensive databases, to the Internet, and to a host of other data sources including all the major news feeds.

He had arranged five of the photographs in a curving horizontal line across his desk, and in chronological order. The sixth picture he had placed off to one side. That one had been taken on the transit by the KH-12 bird three days earlier, and just showed an open boat, but no sign of an occupant.

It was that picture that had originally both alerted and alarmed the Director, particularly when he had checked the precise geographical location specified by the satellite, and printed at the head of each photograph. The next few passes had revealed nothing in that area, and he had for a brief period hoped and almost believed that the first picture had been an isolated occurrence of no long-term significance.

Then another pass had generated the remaining five pictures, taken at thirty-second intervals as the Keyhole satellite had over-flown the target area. These were superficially very similar. Close to the centre of each frame was the unmistakable shape of the same open boat – N-PIC had measured its length at just over eighteen feet – with a small wheelhouse at its stern.

The CIA officer wasn't Photographic Interpretation trained, so each picture had been annotated by the N-PIC analysts at his request. Most of the labels were self-evident – wheelhouse, ropes, cleats, radar reflector, tyres acting as fenders, and so on – but he was going to have to accept their word that the vague oblong shapes visible along both sides of the boat towards the stern were aqualung racks, one with a set still in place.

In the first two pictures, the single occupant of the boat was leaning over the side, reaching down for something, or hauling something in. Until he'd studied the third picture, the CIA officer had wondered briefly if perhaps this was all a false alarm, and that what he was looking at was nothing more than a fisherman hauling up a lobster pot. Then he'd checked a Mediterranean chart and realized that the water there was far too deep for any lobster fisherman to foolishly try to catch anything.

And, anyway, in the third photograph the shape of an aqualung tank was clearly visible beside the man in the boat, even without the N-PIC label, so the analysts had been right about the type of boat, although they hadn't been able to identify it by a name or a number.

The fourth picture showed three aqualung tanks resting beside the anonymous figure in the diving boat, but it was one N-PIC label in the fifth and final photograph that had caused the CIA officer most concern.

The major difference between this picture and the preceding four was that the figure was no longer bending over the side of the boat. Instead, the KH-12 camera had caught him just entering – or perhaps standing beside – the wheelhouse. For at least the sixth time, the CIA officer leaned forward over the last photograph and stared intently at one tiny section of it through his desk magnifying glass.

Clearly visible on the side of the boat, where the man had been bending over earlier, was a very slight protuberance. Next to that was an inked line joining it to the N-PIC label, that simply stated 'ROPE IN WATER AND CLEATED TO GUNWALE'.

And that meant, or it could mean, that there was something at the submerged end of the rope.

### Aeroporto di Brindisi, Papola-Casale, Puglia, Italy

'Where did you spot him?' Richter asked. It was late evening and he and Simpson were sitting in a military briefing-room at the Brindisi-Casale air base. Brindisi is a small airport, just outside the town of that name, handling a couple of dozen civilian flights a day to and from Rome, Milan and Venice. It is home to 9 Brigata Aerea of 15 Stormo, which flies Sikorsky HH-3F Search and Rescue helicopters, and also to the United Nations Logistic Base, which supports humanitarian aid and peacekeeping operations.

Rather than go to Rome or to any other location where the Italian Secret Service maintained a presence, they had decided it was both safer and easier to brief Richter within the confines of the airfield. He was, after all, the only member of any Western Intelligence service who could positively identify Lomas/Lomosolov. Even Simpson had wanted reassurance on that point.

'You can do it, Richter?' he had asked.

Richter thought back to that hotel in West London, and to the image of Lomas's smiling face staring at him from the doorway of the room. It was an image that he knew, without a shadow of a doubt, would be with him for the rest of his days, no matter what happened now in Italy.

'No problem,' he had confirmed. 'I'll know him.'

'Lomas – or the man we believe is Lomas – was spotted eight days ago by a covert operative, one of our watchers, at Rome's Fiumicino airport,' explained Giancarlo Perini, a senior operational agent of the

SISDE who had flown into Brindisi-Casale an hour earlier by helicopter, specifically to brief Richter.

'He arrived at the international terminal, Terminal Three. Because he was spotted before he reached passport control, the immigration people were able to record his details. He was travelling on a German passport, in the name of Günther, and had just arrived on a flight from Geneva. The purpose of his visit, he claimed, was tourism. We checked with Swiss – the airline he was flying with – and learned he has a return ticket to Geneva, due to fly out of Rome in three days. That was when we contacted your Secret Intelligence Service, Mr Simpson.'

Richter glanced over at Simpson and did some swift mental calculations. The timing for this was almost exactly right. As soon as Simpson had been informed by SIS about the possible sighting of Andrew Lomas – who was on the alert list of every Western Intelligence service – he had suddenly, miraculously, changed his mind about Richter's long-standing request for two weeks' continuation training on board the *Invincible*.

'So where is he now?' Richter asked, putting the thoughts from his mind.

'Not too far from here,' Perini replied, 'and he's led us on quite a dance so far. He took a taxi from Fiumicino to the Stazioni Termini – Rome's main railway station – and there bought a ticket to Naples. One of our men got close enough to him to hear him speaking to the ticket clerk.'

'Why didn't he just fly direct to Naples, then?' Simpson asked.

'He couldn't,' Perini replied. 'There are no direct flights from Geneva to Naples. They all route through an airport in some other country first, usually Paris or Munich, and our guess is that Lomas didn't want to risk being spotted either in France or in Germany.'

'So he's now in Naples?'

'No. Let me explain,' Perini shook his head, looking slightly embarrassed. 'We got one of our men on to the train that Lomas caught, and briefed watchers to wait for him at Naples. That train makes three stops before it gets there: Latina, Formia and Aversa. Lomas got off at Aversa – the station serving Caserta, a few miles north of Naples. Our man followed him out, and then used his mobile phone to let us know what had happened, but we had nobody waiting at Aversa and the station's at least a half-hour drive from Naples. That was our mistake.

'Lomas got into a taxi and our man followed in another, but it was late afternoon and the traffic was very heavy. When he got boxed in, the taxi carrying Lomas slipped away.'

'We tend to use motorcycles,' Simpson remarked shortly.

'So do we,' Perini replied with a frown, 'and we had two waiting at the station in Naples, but unfortunately nothing at Aversa. There had been no indication that Lomas realized he was being followed, and we assumed incorrectly that he would proceed to Naples. It was just an unfortunate oversight.'

'He probably *didn't* know he was being followed,' Richter said sympathetically, 'but for men like Lomas taking precautions becomes a way of life. He'd probably never buy a ticket to any railway station he was actually intending to use – always for somewhere further down the line, and then get off earlier. So how did you find him again?' Perini stared at him. 'You obviously did find him,' Richter went on, 'otherwise I wouldn't be sitting here trying to develop a taste for *pasta al forno* and with a Sea Harrier parked outside that the Royal Navy would quite like to get back safely.'

Perini nodded. 'Yes, we did find him again. Our man had the registration number of the taxi Lomas hired, and we interviewed its driver. He took his fare to one of the smaller hotels in the centre of Caserta, but when we checked with the hotel reception, nobody resembling Lomas was registered there.'

'I'm not surprised,' Simpson snorted. 'As Richter's already said, Lomas is an accomplished professional. He was a deep-cover illegal in Britain for years, and for at least the last ten of them he was running the head of the Secret Intelligence Service as a source for the SVR. We had no inkling this man even existed until we got to interrogate Malcolm Holbeche. What he certainly isn't going to do is take a taxi to any hotel that he's actually staying at. So where did you pick him up?'

'We had a bit of luck then,' Perini admitted. 'We circulated all the hotels in Caserta, searching for a guest who looked like Lomas or who was using the name Günther. As we had expected, that produced no results, and neither did canvassing taxi drivers and car-hire firms. But, like you, we have watch teams permanently in place around all the foreign embassy buildings in Italy, and three days ago—'

'Don't tell me Lomas actually went to an East European Embassy?' Simpson interrupted.

Perini shook his head. 'No, and we didn't expect him to either. But we did wonder if he was in Italy to receive instructions, or perhaps to deliver a report, so we blanketed the whole area. We positioned pursuit crews – on motorcycles, Mr Simpson – outside all buildings known to be used by East European officials and businesses in the Caserta, Naples and Salerno areas. Each operative was briefed to follow any known or suspected intelligence officer, to stay out of sight, and to report any contact with anyone who looked anything like Lomas.

'For the first few days we used up a lot of petrol and covered a lot of kilometres, and discovered absolutely nothing that we didn't already know. And then, as I said, three days ago we got lucky. One of our watchers followed a mid-level consular official, believed to be an SVR agent, to a restaurant on the eastern outskirts of Salerno. He went inside and bought a drink at the bar, and appeared to be waiting for someone. Our operative followed him into the restaurant, bought herself a drink and—'

'A woman?' Simpson asked, recalling the motley collection of hairy-arsed men employed in the same role by MI5 and to a lesser extent by SIS.

Perini nodded. 'We have always used women in preference to men. They tend to be more observant, and they can get into most places a lot easier, and with far fewer questions asked, than any man. They are also rarely perceived as a threat. Anyway, our operative sat and sipped her drink and waited. About fifteen minutes later a man entered the restaurant and walked straight over to the bar. He greeted the consular official like an old friend, then they had a drink together and a light lunch.'

'But it wasn't Lomas,' Richter said.

Perini looked surprised. 'You're quite right. It wasn't Lomas. How did you know?'

'I didn't,' Richter said, 'but from what we know of the man, he always tries to use cut-outs. My guess is that the man the official was meeting was just a go-between sent by Lomas to receive a verbal briefing, or whatever, on his behalf.'

The Italian nodded again. 'We don't know what information was exchanged but, when the two men parted, our operative decided to follow the unknown male. It was a good decision – he climbed into a car and drove off, heading east. All the motorcycles our people use are fitted with long-range tanks, which is just as well because he kept on going for over two hundred kilometres. He finally led her to an isolated villa just outside a town called Matera. That's on the main road between Taranto and Salerno, and about one hundred and twenty kilometres – around seventy-five miles – west of Brindisi. As the man went inside, she stationed herself in a position from which she could cover the front of the villa. She stayed there, tucked behind some bushes on the hillside, for the rest of the day.

'She had called in a progress report as soon as she reached the restaurant, and another when she got to the villa, but neither her description of the man she'd followed nor the address of the villa meant anything to us, so we did nothing from this end. All our watchers use the latest surveillance equipment, including binoculars fitted with integrated digital cameras. Because she was using one of these devices, as dusk fell she was able to take two photographs through an uncurtained window of the villa.'

Perini opened a manila envelope and slid a number of large black-and-white photographs onto the table in front off him. He separated them into piles, then passed two pictures each to Richter and Simpson.

'These are enlarged copies of the two photographs she was able to get.'

Richter looked down at them and saw, for the first time, a picture of the face that still haunted his dreams.

# Chapter 3

**Monday**
**Kandíra, south-west Crete**

Brilliant white stars studded the sky over Crete, but Spiros Aristides saw none of them as he trudged from his simple home down the narrow unlit streets towards the centre of the village. He was both preoccupied and irritated, and badly needed a drink – or, better, several drinks.

He had hoped – in fact, he'd felt certain – that the steel case contained valuables, but unless something remarkable popped out when he finally opened those flasks, as far as he could see he'd just been wasting his time. He would have done better to have just left that damned case where he'd found it.

The murmur of conversation stopped briefly as Aristides pushed open the pale green door of the *kafeníon*, the café-bar, and stepped inside. Kandíra was well off the tourist track and had been spared the dubious 'improvements' visited on most coastal towns in the Mediterranean. There were no illuminated signs above the door or flickering in the small and dirty windows, no signs of any sort, in fact, to announce that the place was a bar. No juke-box, no gaming machines, no bar meals or shaded terrace where a passing tourist could pass a pleasant half-hour sipping red wine and writing postcards.

It was just a small, scruffy room with half a dozen tables and twenty or so assorted chairs, most in need of some repair. Down one side ran a battered oak bar behind which Jakob – that wasn't his real name, but the previous incumbent had been called Jakob and old habits died hard in Crete – stood wearing a once-white apron and dispensing drinks with the kind of ill grace that frequently made his clientele wonder why he hadn't opted for a different profession, like tax collector or maybe New York yellow cab driver.

As far as Aristides could tell, the bar hadn't changed in any significant way since he had first arrived in Kandíra a little over eight years earlier, and nor had its occupants. Every evening the old men of the village trickled in, in their ones and twos, took their usual seats at the discoloured tables and, without a word being exchanged, were served their usual tipples by Jakob. Then they talked or just sat in silence. Sometimes a pack of cards would be produced and the usual bar noises would be punctuated by the slap of pasteboard on a table and the cries of exultation or recrimination as some game progressed.

After Aristides pushed the door closed behind him, the murmur of conversation began again. Two or three of the customers smiled or lifted a hand to acknowledge the Greek, gestures to which Aristides responded with a nod, but most of the old men ignored him. He was, after all, a relative newcomer who wasn't even Cretan, and he was still considered by many of them to be a suspicious foreigner.

Aristides walked across to the bar and looked at Jakob, who looked straight back at him. The Greek had been drinking in the bar three or four nights every week for the past eight years, but Jakob still pointedly regarded him as a stranger.

'Whisky,' Aristides snapped. Greek he might be, but he didn't have a Greek's palate for retsina or ouzo.

Jakob slapped a small glass on the bar and poured a measure of golden liquid into it from a bottle labelled 'Glenfiddich', but which Aristides was quite certain the man kept topped up with the cheapest whisky he could find on his weekly trips to the supermarkets in Chaniá. He had never, since he first walked into this bar, seen the bottle anything other than half-full, and he had never seen Jakob open a new bottle of Scotch of any brand. There were two other permanently half-full bottles of whisky on the shelves behind the bar, one of them labelled 'Johnnie Walker' and the other 'Famous Grouse', and the contents of all three tasted absolutely identical. Only their prices were different.

Aristides drained the Scotch in two gulps, gestured for Jakob to refill his glass, then dropped some coins on the bar, picked up his drink, walked across the room and sat down at an unoccupied table in the corner.

He'd been sitting there for something over half an hour and three Scotches, when the bar's door opened yet again. Like everyone else, Aristides looked up at the new arrival and, for the first time since he'd walked in, he smiled. The man at the door smiled back and walked over to join him at the corner table.

'I tried your house, but it was in darkness, so I guessed you'd be here.'

'Sit down, Nico, sit down. A beer? Something stronger?'

Nico Aristides, one of Spiros's numerous extended family, pulled up a chair and sat down. He gestured to Jakob, and the swarthy unsmiling Cretan plopped a beer bottle and a chipped and dirty glass down on the table in front of him. Nico took one look at the glass and decided to drink straight from the bottle.

'You were out again today?' Nico said, more of a statement than a question. 'Anything?'

Nico had never enjoyed diving but he had numerous clients on Crete, and scattered around the Eastern Mediterranean, who were always keen to purchase any interesting objects that his uncle recovered from the bottom of the sea. And, whenever possible, Spiros obliged, hauling up ancient artefacts that the archaeologists, given the choice, would far rather were left in situ. Nico, in effect, acted as his uncle's fence.

Spiros shook his head, deciding in that instant to say nothing, yet, about the flasks in the steel case.

'Nothing, really. A wrecked plane, but nothing of value inside.'

'A plane?' Nico's eyebrows rose in surprise. He was used to his uncle finding amphorae, statuary, pots and occasionally ancient jewellery, but he'd never expected him to find a recent wreck, far less so an aircraft. 'Where?'

Aristides gestured vaguely to the south, but didn't specify a location.

'What sort of aircraft? Fighter? Bomber? From the war?'

Spiros grinned at him, revealing a selection of yellowish teeth amid an almost equal number of gaps, then shook his head.

'No, a modern one. Some kind of a small jet – a private jet, that kind of thing. But it had certainly been in the wars,' he added enigmatically.

Nico looked at him, then glanced around the tiny bar. Almost every seat was now occupied, and as he looked at the table a couple of feet to his left, he met the level stares of two Cretans who had obviously over-heard Spiros's last remark. Under Nico's gaze, the two men looked away and seemed to resume their conversation.

'I don't follow,' Nico said, leaning closer, and gesturing to Aristides to do the same. 'What do you mean?'

'I mean,' Aristides rasped in his gravelly voice, 'that there were three bodies inside it, and another one lying on the bottom, all of them still strapped in their seats.' Nico's eyes widened and he shivered involuntarily. 'And I'll tell you something else,' Aristides added, more loudly now, settling down to tell his story and oblivious of the interest still being shown by the occupants of the adjacent table. 'That plane didn't crash. Somebody shot it down.'

### Aeroporto di Brindisi, Papola-Casale, Puglia, Italy

'Is *that* Lomas?' Perini asked.

Richter took his time, studying both photographs with exaggerated care. They weren't bad either, bearing in mind the circumstances in which they had been taken. Each showed two men standing inside a house, illuminated by the light of a small chandelier and framed by a tall window, apparently talking to each other. Because the pictures had been shot from a distance, and through the window glass, the images naturally weren't as clear as if taken in the open air.

In both of them, the man on the right-hand side was in profile. In the first shot, the other man was also in profile, but in the second photograph he appeared full-face, apparently staring straight into the lens of the camera. Richter had no doubt, absolutely no doubt at all, that this was Lomas, but he shook his head.

'I don't know,' he said. 'It's very like him, but I really need to see him in the flesh. Photographs can be deceiving.'

Perini looked disappointed. 'We had hoped you could provide us with a positive identification just from these pictures,' he said.

Richter shook his head again. 'I'm sorry, but I can't be completely certain. It could be Lomas, but to be absolutely sure I'll have to see him face-to-face.'

Simpson eyed Richter with deep suspicion. 'Remember what I said, Richter,' he snapped, 'not sliced or diced.' Richter put down the photographs and looked back at him without expression.

'I'm sorry?' Perini said, with a puzzled frown, as he looked from one man to the other.

'Nothing,' Simpson replied, still staring at his subordinate. 'Can you arrange for Richter to see this man?'

Perini was silent for a few moments, then replied slowly. 'We were going to arrest him tomorrow afternoon,' he said, some doubt in his voice. 'I suppose Mr Richter could accompany our team, purely as an observer, of course.'

'Of course,' Richter echoed. 'But what are you going to arrest him for?'

Perini smiled slightly. 'We hadn't decided,' he said. 'If you had positively identified him, it would have been for murder, acting on behalf of the British Government. As you haven't, we'll probably start with charging him for using a false passport or maybe illegal entry into Italy, and see what happens after that.'

## Kandíra, south-west Crete

Spiros Aristides staggered slightly as he walked through the bar doorway and out into the cool of the night. It was nearly midnight, and he knew he'd drunk far more of the cheap Scotch than he should have. He would no doubt suffer for it tomorrow, but tonight he would certainly sleep soundly.

Nico put a steadying hand out to the older man, but Spiros shrugged it off. Side by side they each retraced their separate steps back from the bar through the narrow streets until they reached the Greek's tiny house, where Spiros fumbled for a moment with the door handle.

'You'll take a last glass with me?' he inquired. Nico nodded and followed him inside.

'That was all I found,' Spiros gestured towards the still-open steel case lying on the dusty floor. Nico walked across and picked it up. He opened and closed it several times, and looked closely at the shaped and padded recesses designed to hold the flasks.

'This is a very expensive item,' he murmured. 'This case was custom-made for some very special purpose, I think.'

'Can you sell it?' Spiros demanded somewhat hoarsely as he walked into the kitchen, returning with an open bottle of beer. He put the beer down on the table, sank into a chair and filled a glass with Scotch.

'No,' Nico replied firmly, sitting down and picking up the beer, 'or not easily, anyway. It's too specialized in purpose, and in any case it's been in the water for too long.'

He studied the objects on the table with interest, picked up first the red-covered file, flicked through it, then put it down. Unlike his uncle, Nico spoke a little English – it was always useful in dealing with the annual influx of tourists – but he'd never learned to read more than a few words of the language.

'Those were in the case as well,' Spiros said, nodding at the objects on the table.

'Twelve of them?' Nico asked, pointing at the case.

'No,' Spiros said, 'just the four. All the other spaces were empty. And look at this,' he added, picking up the flask from which he'd stripped the wax and passing it to Nico.

His nephew hefted the flask in one hand, exclaimed at how light it was, and peered closely at the lock securing the top.

Spiros looked at him appraisingly. 'Something valuable inside, maybe?'

'Maybe, maybe,' Nico replied. 'This was sealed just like the others?'

'Yes. I cut the wire away and stripped off the wax.'

'It's very light, but there must be *something* inside, otherwise it makes no sense to seal it.' He looked over at his uncle. 'I don't think we can pick this lock,' he said, 'but we could still open the flask. Do you have a hacksaw handy?'


### Central Intelligence Agency Headquarters, Langley, Virginia

'Elias? It's the Director. I need to pick your brains for a minute. You've done plenty of recreational diving, right? Why would a diver attach aqualungs to a rope dropped underneath a boat?' On the top floor at Langley, the CIA officer leaned back in his chair and gazed out of the window as he waited for David Elias, a junior officer in his own section, to reply.

'That's easy, Director. If you dive using compressed air cylinders –

what you would normally call an aqualung – below a particular depth for longer than a certain time, you have to decompress yourself before you surface, otherwise you could suffer from the bends.'

'That's a bit vague. "Particular depth" and "certain time"? What depth, and what time?'

Three floors below, David Elias unconsciously mimicked his superior officer, leaning back in his seat and staring out of the window. 'I can't tell you precisely, sir,' he said. 'It's variable, depending on a lot of different factors. Should I come up? I can explain it better in person.'

'Yes, do that.'

Elias entered four minutes later, holding a dark blue book in his hand. John Nicholson waved him to a chair and watched as his subordinate opened the book.

'I've some idea about the bends, but what's the actuality of them?'

'It's all to do with pressure, sir. The deeper you dive, the greater the pressure on the human body from the water surrounding you. The pressure increases by about one atmosphere for every thirty feet of depth. When there's significant pressure, say when you dive below about sixty feet, the nitrogen in the compressed air mixture you're breathing isn't expelled completely from your lungs, but starts going into solution in your bloodstream.'

'Is that dangerous?'

'Not as long as your body is under pressure, no. The problem comes when you re-surface. If you come up too fast without decompressing, the nitrogen comes out of solution as bubbles in the blood, usually at your joints. That will cause excruciating pain and often forces the sufferer into physical contortions, hence the name. To prevent that, a diver must pause at certain depths on the way back up to the surface and wait for the nitrogen to emerge from the bloodstream gradually.

'The simplest way to cope is to lower a line with a heavy weight on the end from the diving tender, and attach separate sets of aqualungs to the line at the correct decompression depths. Then all the diver has to do is ascend until he reaches the lowest set, wait there for the appropriate time, then ascend to the next one. You have to use these additional compressed air cylinders,' he accurately anticipated his superior's next question, 'because after a very long or deep dive the diver would use up all the remaining air in his aqualung long before he could safely surface.'

Elias gestured to the book he'd opened on the desk in front of him.

'These tables show the recommended decompression depths and times for particular diving depths and durations, sir. Unfortunately, as I said on the phone, the equations are highly variable, and to complicate things there are a whole bunch of different tables to consider. The US Navy's tables, as a matter of interest, acquired themselves some notoriety for getting divers out of the water quickest but also into the decompression chamber fastest.'

Nicholson looked at him blankly, and Elias explained.

'It's a kind of joke, sir. If a diver surfaces too quickly, which anybody using the US Navy tables would almost certainly do, getting them straight into a decompression chamber is the only way to stop them suffering from the bends. The chamber is basically a pressurized cylinder carried on the deck of the bigger diving tenders, which allows divers to get re-pressurized in controlled conditions. No aqualungs involved, so no hanging around twenty feet below the surface for half an hour.

'To give you an example, sir, the US Navy tables list a total decompression time of only twenty-one minutes for a dive of half an hour down to a depth of one hundred and thirty feet. The Buhlmann tables give twenty-eight minutes as a minimum, and the DECOM tables, which are derived from the Buhlmann figures, recommend thirty-eight minutes, which is nearly twice as long as the US Navy suggest. Me, I'd go for the DECOM figures every time.'

'So,' the Director asked, 'taking a hypothetical case, what would be your best guess at a dive depth that required three aqualung cylinders for the decompression pauses?'

'It's impossible to be sure,' Elias replied, 'but if I had to guess I'd say you were looking at either a very deep dive – down to maybe one hundred and fifty feet – or an unusually long dive at some intermediate depth.'

When the door had closed behind Elias, Nicholson opened the wide central drawer in his desk, pulled out the photographs and spread them out in front of him again. He was once more examining the fifth picture through his magnifying glass when the telephone rang.

'This is the Duty Interpreter at N-PIC, sir, with a follow-up call. On the Keyhole's next pass, the diving tender was no longer in the area. We're doing a wide area survey to see if we can pick it up in port somewhere, but that might be difficult. That area of the Med is full of boats just like the one in question, and it'll be a real needle-in-a-haystack job to find it.'

'Did you have any other assets in range between the Keyhole's passes?'

'No, sir, sorry. It's a low-interest area.'

'OK, do the best you can. On my authority, identifying and finding that boat is now a Class Two priority task. Use all available assets, but do not deviate any of the birds from their normal routes.'

'Understood.'

The Director replaced the telephone and bent again over the photographs. The fifth picture had been taken at a somewhat oblique angle, as the satellite was moving away from the target, which paradoxically made it slightly clearer than all but one of the preceding shots, because the sun was no longer reflected off the surface of the sea directly towards the camera. Of course, the surface of the Mediterranean was still dappled with light reflected from wavelets, but the area on the port side of the diving tender was comparatively dark.

But there in the water, close to the protuberance identified as a cleated-down rope by N-PIC, was a small bright blob. Even using the magnifying glass, Nicholson was unable to determine what it was. To his naked eye it looked like either an unusually square-shaped wavelet or something metallic hanging suspended just below the surface. Through the magnifying glass it looked exactly the same, only bigger.

He thought back over what Elias had just told him. This could be merely the weight the diver had used to anchor the rope to which he had attached his compressed air cylinders. But, in that case, why hadn't he recovered the rope and its weight immediately? Why would he stop hauling in the rope with the weight so close to the surface, cleat it down and go to the wheelhouse? Perhaps he'd received a call on his radio, if he possessed one. Or maybe he'd gone to make a radio call. An urgent call?

No, that didn't make sense. Only one possible sequence of events made sense, and that was the one that for thirty years he had endured nightmares about.

'Oh, fuck,' he muttered grimly. He shook his head and reached out a hand to the black telephone.

## Kandíra, south-west Crete

Spiros didn't own a vice, so he clamped the flask as firmly as he could against the edge of the wooden table with his hands and a towel, while Nico began to use the hacksaw on its neck. The blade was blunt, with teeth missing, which didn't help, and the steel was tougher than it looked. And Spiros's hands shook a little after so much whisky.

But finally the blade began to bite, and after five minutes Nico had cut about a quarter of an inch into the neck of the flask. He stopped for another swig of beer, and then they turned the flask over to rest on its base before he continued cutting, just in case any contents escaped through the incision before he finished. Holding the flask upright against the pressure of the hacksaw was much more difficult, and it took another twenty minutes before the last unsevered fraction of steel finally parted and the top of the flask tumbled to the floor.

Nico put the hacksaw down on his chair and opened up the metal case resting on the table. Then he positioned the flask over the lid, carefully tipped it on its side and gently tapped its base. A thin trickle of grey-brown dust emerged, then with a rush a small piece of what looked like dried mud shot out of the flask, and landed on the centre of the case's lid.

'What is it?' Spiros asked.

'I have no idea,' Nico replied, prodding at the strange lump with a screwdriver. As the blade touched it, the solid piece crumbled into the same grey-brown dust.

'Drugs?' Spiros inquired hopefully, pinching some of the powder between forefinger and thumb and smelling it.

'I don't know. It could be heroin, perhaps. I've heard that some of the very pure varieties are brown in colour.'

Nico was almost right. About ninety per cent of the heroin that finds its way to Western Europe, and particularly to Britain, is extracted from the opium poppies – *Papaver Somniferum* – of Anatolia in Turkey. Known as Turkish Brown, among other pseudonyms, this heroin looks something like Demerara sugar, and it's usually either smoked or the fumes inhaled as the heroin is burnt in a spoon or piece of tinfoil held over a candle.

In contrast, the American addict's heroin of choice is Thai White, culled from the poppy fields of Thailand's Golden Triangle. Pure white, and suitable for snorting or injecting, this is gram for gram the most expensive heroin, and hence by definition the most expensive illegal drug, in the world, worth about three times as much as Columbian Pure, which is the very best quality cocaine.

Nico leaned forward to smell the powder and found it was almost odourless – perhaps just a slight hint of mushrooms. He dampened the end of one finger and applied it gently to the edge of the little heap of powder, then touched it to his tongue. He grimaced and spat. 'This is not heroin,' he complained. 'Whatever it is, it's disgusting.'

'That's it, then,' Spiros muttered. 'This can go to the dump.' He tossed the two pieces of the opened flask into the steel case and snapped it shut, securing the lid with the over-centre catch. 'Five days I've wasted on that aircraft wreck, and nothing at all to show for it.'

Nico shrugged and looked over at his uncle. 'If you really don't want it, I'll take the case and see if I can get something for it.'

'Take it, take it,' Spiros grumbled. 'And take the rest of this rubbish as well.' He opened the case once again, dropped the three remaining flasks into their empty recesses, added the red file, and slammed the lid shut.


Ten minutes later, Nico left Aristides's house and began the short walk to his own apartment – actually three rooms, accessed by an outside staircase, on the upper floor of a two-storey house owned by a friend – which lay on the northern edge of the village. As he walked through the silent streets, deserted but for a handful of near-feral cats noisily disputing their territorial rights, Nico became more conscious of the weight of the object he grasped with his right hand.

From what Spiros had told him, it seemed that the case had remained underwater for a long time, several years at least. It was therefore probably unlikely that anyone would take an interest in it now. And it was just a steel case after all, though specially constructed for carrying those strange flasks. The flasks themselves were something else. He still had no idea what the brown powder was, but it just had to be valuable to somebody somewhere, otherwise the comprehensive sealing and locking of the stoppers on the flasks made absolutely no sense. And if it was valuable, there was always the chance that someone might come looking for it.

Nico stopped at the end of the street and considered for a few moments. It might be best to handle the steel case and its contents the same way he treated most of the other prizes that Spiros had wrested from the Mediterranean over the years. Taking it back to his home might be asking for trouble. On the other hand, it was late and he was tired. He could hide it somewhere else in the morning.

Yes, he nodded, and turned right. Three minutes later he opened the door to his apartment and stepped inside, placed the steel case in the bottom of the free-standing wardrobe in his bedroom, and walked straight through into the bathroom.

Spiros Aristides put down the toolbox just inside the kitchen door, walked back into his sitting room and looked sourly at the three fingers still remaining in the bottom of his bottle of Scotch. What the hell, he thought. He'd be in no fit state to dive tomorrow, but he hadn't planned to go anywhere. He settled down at the table and poured himself another glass. He'd finish the bottle and then call it a night.

Twenty minutes later, as he drained the last remnant of Scotch from his glass, and lay down fully clothed on his unmade bed, Spiros Aristides sneezed. Forty-five minutes after that, sitting on the edge of his own bed in the upstairs apartment on the northern edge of Kandíra, Nico Aristides sneezed as well.

# Chapter 4

Christina Polessos was seventy-eight years of age, and had lived in Kandíra most of her life. Burnt brown by the sun, she invariably wore black – almost the Cretan national colour – in memory of her husband, dead some forty years. And that, coupled with her stooped posture, noticeably hooked nose, large dark eyes and thin and somewhat mean mouth, gave her a quizzical, crow-like appearance. Everyone knew her, but few really liked her. She knew everyone, and returned the favour by liking almost no one.

She especially didn't approve of Spiros Aristides. He was a mainland Greek for openers, and had never married, which were two strikes against him right away. He drank far too much, as she made sure everyone knew, and she was quite convinced that he was involved in something illegal every time he went out in his boat. In this, of course, she was perfectly correct, although her oft-repeated tales of gun-running and drug-smuggling bore no relation to the truth.

And his house! In contrast to most of the white-washed houses in the narrow street, it looked a disgrace. The paint on the shutters was faded and peeling, the tiny garden overgrown and weed-strewn, and even the roof tiles looked scruffy and ill cared-for. She deliberately averted her eyes every time she passed it, muttering imprecations under her breath.

But even if on principle she didn't look, she could certainly still listen as she trudged down the street, hoping maybe to hear some spoken titbit from within its walls that she could embellish and re-tell later to her few cronies in the square.

And that morning she was rewarded: not by a snatch of incriminating conversation but by a long, pain-racked moan seeming to emanate from one of the upstairs rooms. This was so unexpected that she

54

stopped dead in her tracks and looked up, listening intently. The sound was shortly repeated, then followed by a sobbing, bubbling noise that might almost have been an attempt at speech.

She shook her head grimly, lowered her eyes and walked on. She was almost a hundred yards further down the street, and had nearly reached the square, when she stopped again, turned and looked round. Her brain had been niggling away at what she'd just heard, and some part of it had decoded the final sounds. It could, she suddenly realized, have been the single Greek word – *'voíthya'* – 'help me'.

She looked back up the street. Nobody else had passed the elderly mainlander's house since she'd walked by, and possibly nobody would – few of the villagers living beyond his property – at least not until later in the day. Had that been a cry for help or just the moaning of a man after far too much to drink the previous evening? No, there had been a peculiar choking sound about that utterance. Whatever was wrong with the old man, it was more than just simple drunkenness.

And this was, she realized, a golden opportunity to establish for herself that the inside of Aristides's property was just as disgusting as the outside. But to find out what was wrong with him, she would have to actually go into the Greek's house, and she couldn't do that alone, as a widowed woman. That would be highly improper and would set tongues wagging, something she couldn't tolerate.

She pursed her thin lips, walked on into the tiny square, and looked around her. Maria and Luisa were usually to be found there at this time of the morning, chatting outside one of the small handful of shops before heading home to prepare lunch. Luisa, she saw, wasn't anywhere in sight, but then Maria Coulouris appeared around the corner, shopping basket in hand, and almost bumped into her.

'Good. Come with me.' Christina grabbed the younger woman by the arm.

'Where to?'

'That old Greek's house. I think he may be dying,' Christina said with some relish.

'What?'

Christina explained to her the sounds she had heard minutes earlier.

'He's probably just drunk again,' Maria hazarded.

Christina shook her head. 'He may well be, but the sounds I heard were strange. I'm sure there's something else wrong with him, something much more serious.'

They walked back up the street together, Maria still protesting ineffectually. Outside the tiny house they paused and listened, but no sounds floated down now from the upstairs windows.

'We'll shout out,' Christina announced, and yelled 'Aristides!' in a surprisingly loud voice.

There was no response, no sound at all.

'Perhaps he's gone out.'

'No. I walked past here no more than five minutes ago. He was in one of the upstairs rooms then. We'll just have to go inside and look.'

'Must we, Christina? I have so many things to do.'

The older woman ignored her half-hearted protest and seized the handle of the street door. Like just about every property in Kandíra, it was unlocked. Some of the other doors in the village didn't even possess locks. She pushed the door open and both women peered inside. The narrow hall was empty, the house silent as the grave. Maria suddenly sneezed and Christina frowned at her.

'Sorry. It's the dust.'

'Aristides!' Christina called again, with the same lack of response.

'I don't like this at all.'

'We have to go upstairs,' Christina said firmly, and the two women began slowly and quietly to ascend the wooden staircase.

At the top, Maria halted suddenly. 'What's that smell?' she muttered.

Christina sniffed suspiciously, then shook her head. 'I can smell it too, but I don't know what it is.'

There were only two doors leading off the tiny landing. One stood open and they could see clearly that it was a spare bedroom, with a wooden-slatted steel-frame bed pushed against the far wall, a small chest of drawers opposite it. No mattress or bedding was visible. The other door was closed, and the two women approached it.

Christina knocked firmly twice on the wooden panel, again calling out the old Greek's name, but still without apparent result. She looked questioningly at Maria, who nodded, then she turned the worn brass handle and pushed against the door.

They both stepped into the doorway and stared. Then Maria began to scream.

# PANDEMIC

## Aeroporto di Brindisi, Papola-Casale, Puglia, Italy

Richter and Simpson had spent the night in a hotel in Brindisi as the guest of the SISDE, but early the following morning Simpson had been whisked off in a chauffeur-driven car to attend some kind of briefing or liaison meeting – he had seemed somewhat evasive when questioned – leaving Richter to cool his heels.

Actually, that had suited him quite well. He'd first grabbed a light breakfast in the hotel dining room, then used his credit card to obtain some cash and gone shopping. There were two items he had particularly wanted to buy, and he came upon both of them in the fourth shop he tried.

The 800 Squadron maintainers arrived from the *Invincible* by Merlin late that same morning. They had first been briefed by the Squadron Engineering Officer, and then Commander (Air) had taken the Chief Petty Officer in charge aside for a few minutes, and explained exactly what he wanted the team to do here at Brindisi.

Richter was meanwhile back at the airfield, standing outside the squadron building and wondering what to do about lunch, and also why he hadn't bought something to read in the airport shop, when he heard the distinctive clatter of the Merlin's rotors. The helicopter approached Brindisi from the south-east at five hundred feet, dropped down to fifty feet once inside the airfield boundary, then air-taxied over to the dispersal area where Richter's Sea Harrier was parked. Once the big helicopter had settled on the ground, its engines shut down and the rotors stopped, Richter walked over and waited while the squadron maintainers climbed out.

The CPO spotted Richter immediately – it wasn't difficult, as he was the only person anywhere on the dispersal who wasn't wearing either an Italian air force uniform or maintainer's overalls – and walked over to join him. 'Wings had a word with me before we left the ship, sir,' the Chief said, 'so I know what we're supposed to be doing.'

Richter grinned in a conspiratorial fashion. He knew exactly what Wings had told the CPO, because he had spent half an hour with the Commander explaining precisely what was going to happen, before he left the ship. 'Thanks, Chief. Can you just make sure she's fully fuelled and ready to fly before you leave? I may need to get out of here fairly quickly.'

'Consider it done, sir. Do you want us to pre-flight her as well?'

'Yes, please, that's a good idea. Turn the aircraft round so that she's facing the taxiway. When you're working on her, don't forget that the Aden cannon are loaded. I know it's not SOP, but could you remove all the external locks and pull and stow all the pins except for the ejection seat and the MDC. Oh, and can you leave a ladder attached, so I don't need to bother the ground staff?'

'No problem.' The CPO winked.

### Kandíra, south-west Crete

The police arrived first because, from the telephone description furnished by a tremulous Christina, supplemented by hysterical squeals from her friend Maria, it was clear that Spiros Aristides had been murdered – hacked to death.

The first two police cars arrived from Chaniá an hour and a half after Christina's excited phone call, and the officers immediately set up a cordon around the victim's house. The senior officer pulled on latex gloves, then opened the street door, entered the building and climbed the staircase to the upper floor. There he took one look inside the bedroom and quickly closed the door. It would definitely be better, he decided immediately, to wait for the arrival of the forensic team and scene-of-crime officers he'd requested from the main police station in Irakleío.

Ninety minutes later a white van arrived. Three men wearing white overalls and carrying plastic cases full of gloves, pads, bags, tweezers, cameras and all the other paraphernalia of criminal investigation, climbed out of it. The forensic scientist in charge – who also happened to be a medical doctor – introduced himself to the senior policeman.

'Dr Gravas,' he said, 'Theodore Gravas. And you are?'

'Inspector Lavat. The house is cordoned off, and nobody's been inside except those two women' – he gestured across the street where a grim-faced Christina stood with one arm protectively around the shoulders of her tearful friend – 'and me. I wore gloves, of course, and touched nothing inside the house apart from the bedroom door handle. I didn't even enter the bedroom, nor, I understand, did the women.'

'*They* found the body?'

'Yes. According to the older one, she heard a moaning sound from the bedroom window.'

'Hacked to death, I believe?' Gravas said.

Lavat nodded. 'I didn't approach the body closely, but that's certainly what it looks like.'

'Right.' Gravas turned to brief the other two members of his team. 'I'll go up myself first to confirm that death has occurred and to perform an initial examination. Then we'll follow the standard procedure, starting with the bedrooms and working down through the house.'

Gravas pulled on plastic overshoes, thin latex gloves, and a paper mask to cover his mouth and nose. He picked up his small scene-of-crime bag, and stepped over to the door, turned the handle and eased it open. He climbed the stairs slowly, peered inside the spare bedroom, then switched his attention to the closed bedroom door across the landing. He slowly and carefully opened it wide, then propped it open with a chair from the landing. Only then did he turn his attention to the corpse lying on the bed.

His first impression was that the attack must have been almost incredibly brutal. The old man's entire face was a mask of blood, only the very top of the forehead and his hair seeming untouched by the viscous red liquid. Below, his chest was a carpet of red, and the bedding beneath him soaked through. It looked almost as if the body had been completely drained of blood, there was so much of it evident around him.

Gravas sniffed, trying to identify conflicting odours. Blood, definitely and unarguably. Urine, faeces – and something else? Something faint, unfamiliar and unpleasant.

He walked across the room to the bed, eyes flicking from side to side as he looked for any clues, any sign of a weapon or anything out of place. Any incongruity, in fact.

He stopped beside the bed and looked down. One glance at the body told him this was a complete waste of effort, but he stretched out his hand and felt for a pulse in the side of the man's bloodied neck. Nothing, of course. Then he bent forward and gently touched the flesh of the face with his gloved fingertips. He looked more carefully, then used both hands to search for the wounds that he was sure were there.

Two minutes later he turned his attention to the torso, and five minutes after that he stepped back from the bed. Behind the mask, his expression was puzzled. Nothing that he'd seen and felt on this body made any sense.

Spiros Aristides was undeniably dead, and from the initial approximate body temperature measurement – obtained simply by placing a long thermometer in the dead man's armpit for two minutes – he had probably expired about three to four hours earlier. But at that precise moment Gravas had not the slightest idea what had killed him.

He was reasonably certain that death had not been caused by any kind of sharp-edged weapon, nor as far as he could see, probing the skin underneath the sodden clothing, by a bullet. He had found no lesions of any kind on the face or head. The torso was another matter, because there could be wounds he had failed to detect still hidden beneath the carpet of blood. For a definitive answer he would have to wait until he got the corpse back to the mortuary.

What he did know was that whatever had killed the Greek had caused virtually all his blood supply to haemorrhage from every orifice. The bloody facial mask was the result not of some frenzied attack by a machete-wielding homicidal maniac, but of blood pouring from eyes, nose, ears and mouth.

And that was something Gravas had never seen before, and hoped never to see again.


## Central Intelligence Agency Headquarters, Langley, Virginia

David Elias had just decided to lock up his desk and office safe, and head off for an early-morning coffee and a crap, not necessarily in that order, when his internal phone rang.

'Elias? I've got a few questions for you. Come up.'

The coffee would have to wait, Elias decided. By now the crap couldn't, but he'd have to be quick. 'On my way, Director.'

When he reached the top floor, John Nicholson's door was already open, but Elias knocked anyway and waited for a response before entering and standing beside the leather armchair that faced the big oak desk. The Director, he thought, looked somewhat irritated, and Elias wondered which of his own recent reports was responsible, and exactly how severe a dressing-down he was about to receive.

Elias was essentially an analyst, and had only worked in the Intelligence Directorate for a little over a year, although altogether he'd been employed by the Central Intelligence Agency for almost ten years. He had been drafted into Intelligence from Administration, where he'd worked as a bean-counter, after a senior officer had noticed that he spoke fluent Malay and workable Japanese. He now specialized in the Pacific Rim, and enjoyed what he did.

'Sit down, Elias,' Nicholson said, looking up from the open file lying on the desk in front of him. 'This has nothing to do with your work here,' he began. Elias relaxed noticeably, but still felt puzzled. 'Tell me about your diving skills.'

'What? Sorry, Director?' Elias's puzzlement increased.

'Your diving. Have you had formal training or is it just a hobby for you?'

'Both, really, sir. I got given my first scuba outfit when I was a teen-ager, and it just sort of took off from there. I joined the local sub-aqua club, got all the qualifications I could, and I've been diving ever since. I'm a qualified blue water instructor, and I've spent about, oh, fifteen hundred hours underwater, I guess.'

'You done any deep diving, then?'

Elias nodded. 'I was involved in a couple of projects down in Florida, where we worked at depths in excess of a hundred feet. I've used exotic gases a few times, done a bit of saturation work.' Nicholson now looked puzzled, so Elias enlightened him. 'You can't dive safely to great depths by just using compressed air,' he said. 'You remember I explained to you earlier about the bends, and about decompressing before you surface?'

The Director nodded.

'There are other problems as well, like nitrogen narcosis, and believe it or not even oxygen can become toxic in certain conditions. So for very long and deep dives the nitrogen is removed from the air you breathe and replaced with an inert exotic gas, usually helium. That won't go into solution in your blood, so it doesn't cause the same problems that nitrogen does.'

'Any other problems with that sort of stuff, though?'

Elias grinned. 'Only one. While you're breathing it, you sound like Mickey Mouse, because the helium affects the vocal chords. Professional divers use voice-alteration devices on their major underwater projects, so that they can be clearly understood.'

'You mentioned saturation work. What's that?'

'It's a technique which makes for more efficient use of divers. Instead of surfacing at the end of a deep dive, with all the decompression time that requires, saturation divers live for days at a time in a diving bell, or some other kind of underwater habitat, which is anchored to the seabed or in mid-water at the depth at which they're working.

'That means they can go out, work for a couple of hours, go back into the habitat, have a drink or a meal, get suited up again and go back out for another dive. They only need to decompress once, therefore, at the very end of their time underwater and before they finally surface.' Elias smiled at a memory. 'It's not too much fun, actually. Everything you eat or drink down there seems to taste of either salt water or rubber – or both.'

'OK,' the Director said grimly, 'I'm satisfied you're competent.' He wrote something on a slip of paper and passed it across the desk. Elias looked at it and read the words with increasing confusion. 'Be there this morning,' Nicholson said, 'at ten fifteen. And take your passport.'

### Kandíra, south-west Crete

Gravas was still standing irresolute in Spiros Aristides's simple bedroom, staring down at the body. He looked around the room, then back at the corpse, and realized he had to decide soon. Normally, once he had certified that the victim was dead, photographs would be taken and drawings made of the position of the corpse, the hands would be bagged to preserve any trace evidence, and the body would then be placed in a fibreglass coffin and transported to the forensic suite back at Irakleío for the post-mortem examination.

But something about the man's death simply wasn't making sense, and Gravas felt certain that he should look more closely here, in the place where the death had occurred, before moving the body. So he decided to break the rules.

There was a glass tumbler beside the bed and Gravas picked it up and sniffed it. He detected the faint odour of Scotch, and guessed that Aristides had been drunk, or at least intoxicated, when he climbed the stairs to his bedroom the previous evening. The old man hadn't even undressed, just lain down on the bed wearing his outdoor clothes.

Gravas made a decision. He took a pair of eight-inch scissors from his bag and cut a more or less straight line down the front of the blood-sodden checked shirt, and peeled it away from the torso. He undid the old black leather belt on the jeans, then with some difficulty cut the denim down the top of each leg, and again peeled the material away from the body. Finally, the underpants got the same treatment.

Now Aristides lay naked on his back, exposed to the early-afternoon sunlight streaming in through the window, and Gravas bent to examine the corpse minutely. He began, as he had been taught to do, at the top of the head, and worked his way steadily, and without haste, down along the entire body.

Just below the left breast his sensitive fingertips detected a small lesion, and he carefully cleaned away the crusted blood to examine it more closely. It could, if it proved to be a knife thrust to the heart, explain the huge out-pouring of blood that had soaked the old man's shirt and the bed sheet underneath the body. But after a few seconds Gravas realized that it wasn't. The lesion was clearly an old scar, a skin tear from some sharp object years earlier, which had healed badly with a ragged edge.

Gravas continued his examination, but found nothing else. Then he took hold of the right side of the body and gently turned it to allow him to examine the back. He followed exactly the same procedure, and found precisely nothing. No wounds, no lesions, no signs at all of external damage.

He returned the body to its original position and gazed down at it. As far as he could tell, the blood on the chest appeared to have come from the Greek's mouth, spewed out like crimson vomit. And the blood encrusting the sheet on which the body lay had a most unusual source

– it had been ejected from Aristides's anus. And still Gravas didn't know what had killed him.

His forensic team was elsewhere in the house, combing it room by room, but so far he had let nobody else into the bedroom. Something was niggling at the back of his mind. Something he'd read or heard somewhere, something that was relevant, that might explain what had killed this elderly man.

He shook his head slowly. It would come to him in time. It always did, sooner or later. The autopsy might clarify things, he hoped. Meanwhile, there was nothing more he could do with the body. It was time to move it and then let his team begin their examination of the bedroom.

He skirted the bed and reached up for the handle of the latch window, intending to call down to Inspector Lavat, when he suddenly stopped, freezing into immobility. The realization had come sooner rather than later, and suddenly he knew, or thought he knew, exactly how Aristides had died.

Gravas walked away from the window, giving the body on the bed as wide a berth as possible and stepped out onto the landing. He turned and pulled the door closed behind him and called out to his forensic team.

'This is Gravas. Listen, both of you, and stop whatever you are doing immediately. Put your equipment down and just leave it where it is. Ensure that your masks and gloves are securely in place, then stand up and walk out of the house, touching nothing else. Do not even touch each other, and wait for me in the street outside.'

Two very puzzled men emerged rapidly from the spare bedroom and walked in single file down the narrow stairs. Gravas first checked that all the upstairs windows and doors were closed, then followed them down. On the ground floor he checked too that all the windows were secured, then he himself walked out of the house, pulling the door firmly shut behind him.

'Dr Gravas?' Lavat called to him as he watched this procession emerge.

'Inspector,' Gravas said, his voice slightly muffled by his mask, 'don't come near me or my team. Ensure that nobody else approaches the house. Set up a cordon around the whole village. Nobody must be allowed in or out until we have this situation under control.'

'Situation? What situation? This is a murder, clearly a *brutal* murder, but to cordon the whole village? Is that really necessary?'

Gravas almost smiled. 'I wish it were that easy,' he replied, 'but I'm afraid this particular killer can slip through any cordon you are able to erect.'

Lavat looked startled. 'You mean you know who killed Aristides?'

Gravas nodded. 'It's not a who, Inspector, it's a what. If I'm right, what killed the Greek was a thing called Ebola.'

# Chapter 5

Tyler Q. Hardin – the 'Q' wasn't short for anything; his middle name really was 'Q', which Hardin presumed had been his father's idea of a joke – had actually got one foot in the shower stall when his pager went off. He snapped off the shower, which he'd just spent nearly five minutes getting to precisely the right temperature, picked up the pager and looked at the display. It showed a single acronym: 'L4HA'.

'Oh, shit,' he muttered, forgot all about his shower and climbed back into the clothes he'd just taken off. He ran out of the house, slamming the door behind him, got into his two-year-old Grand Cherokee Jeep, started the V8 engine, pulled the shift lever into 'drive' and raced off down the street.

Traffic was heavy at the intersection, so Hardin reached down and flicked a couple of switches on the dashboard. Two red lights fitted behind the radiator grille began alternately flashing, and a two-tone siren started its discordant wailing. Traffic parted, Hardin hauled the steering wheel around to the right and floored the gas pedal.

Eighteen minutes later he walked into the CDC and three minutes after that he opened the door to Walter Cross's office. Cross was Hardin's immediate superior and head of the Special Pathogens Branch, but the two men had worked together for so long that they were firm friends.

They had to some extent been thrown together by their qualifications. Although the Centers for Disease Control is a major organization, employing around seven thousand people and with an annual budget in excess of two billion dollars, there are exactly eight employees who are qualified to work in the Bio-Safety Level 4 laboratory. One was

Walter Cross, the Head of Special Pathogens – a highly specialized department within the Division of Viral and Rickettsial Diseases – and another was Tyler Hardin.

The CDC BSL4 laboratory is one of two maximum-safety biological research laboratories in America, and one of only six in the entire world. Entry is by ID card and a personal identification code punched into a keypad by a scientist wearing a totally sealed biological spacesuit, who even then has to enter through a negative-pressure airlock, to ensure that air can only bleed into the laboratory and never out of it, and a powerful decontamination shower.

Only inside one of these secure laboratories is it safe to examine any of the handful of microscopic and utterly lethal species-killer viruses.

Viruses are usually named after the places where they were discovered, and the first of what became known as the species-killers emerged in 1967 in Marburg in Northern Germany. The Marburg virus arrived at the Behring Works factory inside an infected African green monkey, the kidney cells of these animals being used by Behring to produce vaccines. Somehow, the Marburg virus jumped from the monkey into the immediate human population working at the factory. By the time the outbreak was over, thirty-one people had been infected and seven were dead. Marburg proved it had about a twenty-five per cent lethality.

Marburg is a type of organism known as a filovirus, one of a small and highly lethal family of haemorrhagic fever viruses, which closely resemble one another but which bear little resemblance to other known viruses. Under the impartial gaze of an electron microscope, the reason for the appellation filovirus (from the Latin *filo*, meaning 'thread' or 'threadlike') becomes immediately obvious, the shape of the virus being just that.

Marburg was the first, but unfortunately it wasn't the last.

The Ebola River is a tributary of the Congo or Zaïre River and, just under ten years after Marburg began its rampage in Germany, a new and even more deadly filovirus emerged from the rainforest. Named Ebola Zaïre after the river and the country, it appeared almost simultaneously in over fifty native villages scattered near the headwaters of the Ebola River, and killed nine out of every ten people who became infected.

Ebola Zaïre was and is the most lethal fast-acting virus the world has ever seen, killing its victims in a matter of days, spreading easily and swiftly through any close-knit population through body-fluid exchange. A drop of infected blood on a cut finger is quite enough to start the infection.

It is popularly believed that Ebola attacks every organ in the body apart from skeletal muscle and bone, multiplying at a terrifying rate and converting body tissues into active virus particles. It is reported to liquefy the internal organs, resulting in uncontrollable bleeding from every orifice.

In fact, it does nothing of the sort. Almost all these 'facts' – repeated in countless books, magazines, television programmes and films – are either simply fiction or misconceptions promulgated by writers who haven't bothered to do their research. True, Ebola does multiply at a terrifying rate, and uncontrollable bleeding from every orifice does frequently occur during the terminal stages of the disease.

But Ebola actually attacks only the circulatory system, and merely two components of that. It targets the platelets responsible for blood clotting, and the endothelial cells that line the inside of veins and arteries and essentially keep the blood contained inside. It launches, in effect, a two-pronged attack: the circulatory system begins to leak as the endothelial cells fail to function, and the blood that then leaks out doesn't clot.

The effects are usually first apparent in those organs where the membranes are the thinnest and most vulnerable: typically the lungs, eyes, mouth and nose. Tissues and organs become soggy as they fill with blood; the lungs stop functioning properly; blood enters the digestive system; the throat becomes bloody and infected, making swallowing impossible; blood leaks from the eyes and other orifices; in the latter stages brain functions become erratic and then cease almost entirely, as the skull fills with blood.

Again contrary to popular belief, a notable peculiarity of Ebola and the other viral haemorrhagic fevers is that the organs themselves are not destroyed. Despite the huge amounts of blood present in them, the actual tissues of the organs remain perfectly healthy – in effect, they have ceased to function because they have drowned in blood. And if a patient does manage to survive an attack by Ebola, he or she will normally suffer no lasting ill-effects: once the virus has been eliminated from the body, the organs will begin working normally once again.

In short, an attack by Ebola is essentially functional – the virus attacking the whole body through the circulatory system – rather than biochemical, in that there is no destruction of cells or organs. The attack is always very fast but the recovery, if the patient is lucky enough to survive, is also both fast and complete.

But one other popular 'fact' *is* true: in the latter stages of the infection, one drop – a single millilitre – of a victim's blood can contain as many as one hundred million virus particles.

The Ebola virus is an extremely simple yet very mysterious organism. Like the other filoviruses, it is a microscopic thread visible only at magnifications in excess of one hundred thousand, and is characteristically very twisted and convoluted at one end – a feature that some virologists call the 'shepherd's crook' or the 'eyebolt'.

Structurally, it consists of a single strand of ribonucleic acid, containing the virus's genetic code, encased in a sheath of structural proteins of seven different types. Three of these proteins are partially understood, but virtually nothing is known about the other four. The structure and function of these four proteins is a mystery, but the combination in Ebola is lethal – the virus appears specifically adapted to attack the circulatory system, and the human immune system seems completely incapable of fighting back.

It is also, using the tense terminology of the virologists, a *badly adapted* parasite. A well adapted parasite lives in some kind of harmony with its host: the relationship becomes almost symbiotic, and both host and parasite will survive. Ebola can kill its human host within days, and will itself die unless it can migrate rapidly to another human being.

This fact suggests that Ebola has another host somewhere, some animal or bird living in the tropical rainforest in Zaïre which carries the virus but is essentially unaffected by it, yet nobody has any idea what that host might be. It also implies that either Ebola has mutated naturally, or it has been manufactured, to become capable of attacking the human immune system.

In its effects, if not in its appearance, it does resemble some other viruses. It appears to be distantly related to those which cause mumps, measles and rabies, for example, and also pneumonia and influenza. But these are all benign compared to Ebola and, unlike them, there is no known cure or even treatment for attack by a filovirus.

Marburg, Ebola Zaïre and its slightly less lethal cousin Ebola Sudan, which has only about a fifty per cent lethality, are all classed as Level Four Hot Agents – L4HA – hence Hardin's speed of reaction once he had read the message on his pager.

'What have you got?' Hardin demanded immediately, as he shouldered open the door.

'It sounds quite like Ebola,' Walter Cross explained, 'but if the agent is a filovirus, it's a hell of a long way from home.'

'Where is it, then?'

'Crete,' Cross replied shortly.

'That's Crete as in Crete in the Mediterranean?' Hardin's surprise was obvious in his voice.

'Yup. We – or to be accurate you – are going to have to go in to confirm it, but the message from the reporting doctor makes it sound pretty much like a filovirus infection of some sort. Maybe even some kind of totally new strain.'

Hardin sat down, slid a sheet of notepaper across the desk and began scribbling on it. 'Ebola in Crete is really scary,' he continued. 'An infection in a major holiday area like that could scatter the virus over most of Europe. What about jurisdiction? Do we have an EPI One?'

The Centers for Disease Control is a federal agency. That means before the CDC can send anyone to investigate something within America, the state in which the outbreak occurs or its local health authority has to formally request assistance from the CDC. Outside the United States, exactly the same rules apply: the CDC has to be officially invited to assist by the government or its health ministry.

The form known as EPI 1 is basically a movement order for a CDC officer or team. It confirms that assistance has been requested from the agency, provides a brief summary of the investigation which the CDC intends to undertake, and what it hopes to achieve, lists the names of the CDC personnel who will be involved, and specifies which authorities in the destination government's health department are to be contacted on arrival.

'It's being typed right now,' Cross replied. 'We've been formally requested to assist by the Cretan health ministry, but the contact list is real short. It's just one man – Dr Theodore Gravas – and he's actually now on the scene at this village called Kandíra.'

'What else have you done so far?' Hardin asked.

'I've faxed the Cretan health guys the standard list of instructions and warnings. I've got people making airline bookings right now, and others recalling the staff you'll need with you. And I paged you, of course. Good response time, by the way.'

'Thanks,' Hardin grunted, abstractedly.

## Kandíra, south-west Crete

It had taken Inspector Lavat some three hours to set up the cordon, and would have taken a lot longer if the village hadn't sat almost on the edge of the cliff. Therefore the seaward side fortunately required no action, but summoning the men he needed from Chaniá and Irakleío had taken time, and even then they were too thinly spread for his liking around the hastily created perimeter.

Gravas had been adamant: nobody was entering or leaving Kandíra until he said so. And that would not occur until he knew for sure exactly what had killed Aristides. The big problem was that he couldn't perform the diagnosis himself. He and his men would need expert help and specialist equipment, not least biological space suits, just to go anywhere near Aristides's body again.

When he had telephoned the Cretan Ministry of Health, requesting they contact the Centers for Disease Control and Prevention for urgent assistance, the officials there hadn't argued for long. Most health professionals would know about Ebola, and the consequences of any kind of a filovirus outbreak erupting in a highly populated tourist destination like Crete simply didn't bear thinking about. And even that might be the least of their worries. If tourists, returning home to America, Britain and Europe, began incubating any filovirus with a lethality similar to Ebola, they could soon spread an uncontrollable plague that would make the Black Death seem like an attack of head colds.

With the Ministry of Health informed, and the wheels set in motion, Gravas had turned his attention back to his more immediate problem – Kandíra and the people who called the small isolated community home.

There were now several problems he had to address. First, he had to ensure that anyone who had already stepped inside Aristides's house was fully quarantined. He realized this could be overkill, because Ebola and Marburg are normally spread by body-fluid exchange from an infected victim. But there was a third, little-known, Ebola variant called Ebola Reston, which was lethal to monkeys but for some reason appeared not to affect human beings, and was believed to be transmitted by airborne particles. So it was better not to take any chances.

He also needed, urgently, to find out where exactly the Greek had been, and who he had been with, over the last few days – especially the previous day. Those who had last seen him could provide valuable clues to his physical appearance, which might give Gravas some pointers indicating how fast the disease had progressed. And of course there was the real possibility that some of the people who had been in Aristides's company were now also incubating the virus, in which case there would be more deaths, possibly a lot more, over the next few days.

His final problem was the biggest: he had to find out exactly how and where Aristides had become infected by the virus that had killed him. And, as he looked up and down the dusty street, baking in the afternoon sunshine, Gravas had no idea how he was going to determine that.

### Irakleío, Crete

The faxed message from the Centers for Disease Control to the Cretan Ministry of Health was in English and ran to some eight pages of single-spaced typing, but what it said could be condensed into a simple five-word instruction: 'Touch nothing. Wait for us.'

It also contained a request for two large chest freezers, and if necessary a generator to power them, to be shipped to the site of the outbreak if such facilities weren't already available there. The duty officer at the Ministry made two telephone calls, got no sense out of either party, shrugged, and then made another two calls. The first went to a domestic appliance supplier in Irakleío, the second to an industrial equipment company.

Within thirty minutes of the telephone call received from Dr Gravas, an urgent meeting had been convened to decide on necessary action before the CDC team arrived. It was short and fairly acrimonious. The Minister of Tourism, concerned primarily with the island's image as a holiday resort, had opposed almost everything pending confirmation of exactly what had happened in Kandíra, but had been over-ruled every step of the way.

Fifteen minutes after stepping out of the conference room, the Minister of Health issued a series of instructions that only reinforced the isolation of Kandíra. An hour after that, he finally issued a short statement to a handful of waiting pressmen, but refused to answer any of their questions.


### Aeroporto di Brindisi, Papola-Casale, Puglia, Italy

Looking pink and well fed, Simpson returned to the squadron building just after four in the afternoon, and noted the two empty sandwich wrappers and a paper cup – evidence of Richter's rather less than gourmet lunch – with a certain amount of dissatisfaction.

'Why don't you ever eat properly?' he demanded.

'Unlike you,' Richter retorted, 'I don't have an unlimited expense account. And food is just food: protein, carbohydrate, starch and fat. As long as you get enough of it inside you, it doesn't much matter what the source of it is.'

'God, you're a Philistine, and a scruffy one at that.' Simpson glared at Richter's faded jeans and T-shirt.

'These are the clothes you brought out for me,' Richter observed.

'Yes, but you're the one wearing them, and they were pretty much all we could find usable in your flat.'

'I prefer jeans, and T-shirts are comfortable.' Richter was tiring of the subject. 'I take it you had a good lunch? Largely liquid, perhaps?'

'None of your business,' Simpson replied sharply.

The door opened behind him, and Giancarlo Perini entered the briefing-room. He carried a large plastic bag which he placed on the table only after Richter had removed the debris he had left there.

'What's this?' Simpson asked.

'A Kevlar jacket,' Perini replied. 'We have no idea if Lomas – if it is him – will be armed, though we're assuming he will be. I want everyone who gets close to him to be protected – including Mr Richter here.' Richter himself thought this was an excellent idea. 'You, Mr Simpson, will presumably not be at the scene yourself?'

Simpson shook his head firmly. He was an organizer, not an operative. 'When do we leave?' he asked.

'In half an hour or so,' Perini replied, and gestured out of the window at the sleekly pointed shape of the Agusta 109 helicopter squatting outside on the tarmac. 'We'll fly to a location a mile or so from the villa, and meet the DCPP officers there.'

The SISDE, like Britain's Security Service, has no law enforcement powers, and relies on a division of the police force – the *Direzione Centrale Polizia di Prevenzione* – to carry out arrests on its behalf. In the United Kingdom, the Metropolitan Police Special Branch fulfils the same function for MI5.

'How many men are you using?' Richter asked.

'Ten including the drivers,' Perini said. 'They'll all be armed with automatic weapons and side-arms, and wearing body armour.'

That was pretty much what Richter had expected, so he didn't foresee too much trouble.

Simpson nodded approval. 'That should be enough for getting just one man.'

'More than enough,' Richter said, though he was agreeing with what Simpson had said, rather than what he meant.

Fifteen minutes later Richter pulled on the Kevlar vest and secured it around his torso. The vest was, in fact, a bonus that Richter hadn't anticipated. He'd expected that the DCPP officers themselves would enter the property to arrest Lomas, then call him in later to carry out the identification, but it now looked as if he would actually be on the scene when they first entered the villa, which might make things a lot easier for him.

Richter and Simpson headed out of the building towards the Agusta 109, following Perini. The pilot was strapped in and running through his pre-take-off checks. A ground marshaller and fireman stood in front of the helicopter waiting for engine start. Richter increased his stride to fall into step beside Perini. 'Could I ask a favour?' he said.

'Of course, Mr Richter, what is it?'

'It seems a long time since I've flown in a helicopter. Could I ride in the front seat?'

Perini had no objection to this seating arrangement. 'That's fine by me.'

'Thanks.'

The right-hand-side rear sliding door on the Agusta was already open for them, so Simpson and Perini climbed aboard and strapped themselves in. Richter opened the much smaller door of the cockpit and manoeuvred himself into the right-hand seat. The Kevlar vest, being heavy and bulky, made his movements slightly awkward. He strapped in too, then put on the headset.

It was already plugged into the intercom system, but before Richter introduced himself to the pilot he could hear Perini gabbling away in what Simpson would probably describe as 'high-speed foreign'. When he finally stopped, Richter addressed the pilot. 'Hi, I'm Richter,' he said. 'Do you speak English?'

In many ways it was a silly question, for English is the international language of aviation, and all commercial pilots can be guaranteed to speak at least some English.

'Of course.' The pilot extended a hand across the cockpit. 'Vento. Mario Vento. Signor Perini tells me that you are a qualified Sea Harrier pilot.'

'That's right,' Richter replied, 'but this is all new to me.' He settled back in his seat as Vento made a twirling motion with his right forefinger to the maintainer – the signal for engine start. He looked with interest around the cockpit as the Italian started the two Pratt & Whitney 206C engines in sequence.

The Agusta was very different to any helicopters Richter had previously flown in. Quite apart from the long 'bonnet' sloping sexily away from the cockpit windshield, the A109 Power model has full LCD instrumentation, meaning that the dials found in a conventional helicopter cockpit are replaced by a pair of computer screens. This reduces the cockpit workload considerably, as the screens only display what the flight control system computer deems to be relevant.

When computerized cockpits were first introduced, there was both resistance and suspicion on the part of the pilots. In fact, shortly after its introduction into service, one of the most common remarks made by pilots on the flight deck of the Boeing 757 aircraft, one of the first to possess a semi-computerized cockpit, was: 'What's it doing now?'

Time and technology have marched on, and nowadays on most commercial airliners and a large proportion of military aircraft the cockpits almost entirely lack the traditional engine and navigation instruments. And there are some, particularly the new generation of American air-superiority fighters, which are inherently aerodynamically unstable, and literally impossible to fly if the computers fail.

'This is fitted with the FADEC system,' Vento explained, as the noise from the engines increased to a dull whistling roar. The Full Authority Digital Engine Control system applies a level of digital control to the twin engines, and has been responsible for both reducing the fuel consumption and increasing the helicopter's range and payload.

'That,' Vento added, releasing the rotor brake and watching as the main blades began turning slowly, 'and the better aerodynamics, have given us a range of over nine hundred kilometres, a top speed of one hundred and fifty knots, and a service ceiling of six thousand metres. It's a truly delightful aircraft to fly.'

Vento then called Brindisi Tower and obtained taxi and take-off clearance. The ground marshaller watched as the helicopter lifted into the air and turned to the west, accelerating as it crossed over the main runway. The Italian retracted the undercarriage as they cleared the airfield and climbed up to two thousand feet for their transit to Matera.

It was late afternoon, but the sun was still high in the sky as the Agusta flew swiftly across the fairly flat terrain lying to the north of Taranto. Vento pointed out the villages, towns and roads as they passed near them; San Michele Salentino; Villa Castelli; Montemesola; the sprawl of Taranto itself looming to the south; Crispiano beneath the *autostrada* that runs from Bari down to Massafra skirting Taranto; then Palagiano and Laterza.

A couple of minutes after they'd flown past Laterza, Vento descended the Agusta to one thousand feet. 'That's Matera,' he said. 'Right one o'clock at about five kilometres.' Richter peered forward, as did Simpson and Perini. 'We'll be landing a couple of miles outside the town. There's a convenient field right alongside the road, and that's where the cars will be waiting.'

Vento dropped the undercarriage as he descended the helicopter further and, as he brought the Agusta in to land, Richter could see four dark-coloured vehicles parked nose-to-tail in a lay-by immediately adjacent to a small and level field. Three minutes later they were on the ground, and walking towards the gateway by the road.

### Kandíra, south-west Crete

Gravas and his assistants had carefully stripped off their white overalls and overshoes, and had placed them beside a wall right across the street from Aristides's house. Gravas also issued orders that nobody was to approach the clothing, except to add to the pile.

Everything any one of them had been wearing was possibly or probably contaminated, so should really have been placed in a sealed bag for destruction in a furnace. But they possessed no bag big enough to hold everything, and Gravas had decided that simply getting out of the clothes was probably the best they could do in the circumstances. Originally they had anticipated investigating a murder scene, which had dictated the equipment carried in their vehicle. Some lethal and invisible virus was a very different situation.

The last items to be removed were their gloves and masks, though Gravas ordered them to don fresh ones immediately. He also told Inspector Lavat to remove his uniform jacket, his trousers and shoes, and provided him instead with a white overall and a pair of rubber boots from the back of the van. The two Greek women, as Gravas had silently predicted, were more difficult to sway.

'This is for your own safety,' Gravas insisted, for at least the third time, while Christina Polessos stood in front of him, hands on hips and rock-like in her defiance. 'We believe that house has been contaminated with some kind of deadly virus, a germ that killed him and might kill both of you too.'

Christina snorted. 'Call yourself a doctor? We saw Aristides and he was covered in blood. Somebody killed him, with a knife or a club or a gun. It wasn't some germ – germs just give you a cold.'

Maria Coulouris, still tearful, added her contribution. 'And we are respectable women. We cannot disrobe here in public, out in the street.'

'Not even if it kills you?' asked Gravas, in exasperation.

This blunt remark stunned both women into a momentary silence.

'But we didn't touch him,' Christina insisted. 'We never even went near him.'

Gravas shook his head. 'That doesn't matter,' he said. 'The virus I mentioned could be anywhere in that house: on the floor, the walls, the door handles, or just floating in the air. And now it could be somewhere on your clothes, so if you breathe it in, you could end up like Aristides.'

The two village women looked at each other, then back at Gravas. 'And if we do take off our clothes?' Christina was the natural spokes-woman of the two.

Gravas shrugged. 'I can give no guarantees, but the risk would be much less.'

Again the women exchanged glances. 'Very well,' Christina said, 'but you must erect a proper screen, and provide us with something decent to wear.'

Gravas rapidly gave instructions for his assistants to rig up a tempo-rary screen using waterproof tarpaulins from the back of the van, behind which the women could decently undress. The older one, Christina Polessos, could just about fit into a set of his one-size white overalls, but the younger, Maria Coulouris, had an ample girth and spectacular breasts, so would have to be content with a large blanket.

Gravas walked back over to Lavat, who stood waiting.

'What now?' the inspector asked.

'*Now* it's over to you,' Gravas replied. 'It's time for your detective work. We have to find out exactly what this Aristides did yesterday. We have to identify and locate everybody he met or talked to. It might be worth starting with those two women, once they've sorted themselves out.'


### Outskirts of Matera, Puglia, Italy

Perini asked Richter and Simpson to wait by the gate while he went for-ward to check that the senior DCPP officer and his men were ready. Then he returned and motioned them to get into the last of the four Alfa Romeo saloons parked in the lay-by.

'Everything is prepared,' he said, sitting in the passenger seat and turning round to look at them. Behind him they could see the para-military police officers, looking to Richter something like a group of Special Air Service troopers, climbing into the other three cars.

As the last car door slammed shut, the leading vehicle indicated briefly then pulled swiftly out of the lay-by and onto the road, the others following promptly. It was only a short drive because the helicopter had landed no more than a couple of miles from the villa itself. The lead car indicated again – something Richter had previously believed Italian drivers never did – and pulled off the road onto some waste ground, the driver turning his vehicle to face towards the road.

The other drivers followed suit, but this time when the men emerged from the cars they were obviously taking care to be quiet, so Richter realized they must be fairly close to the villa where Lomas was believed to be hiding. The officers checked their weapons – they were carrying Spectre 9mm sub-machine-guns and Beretta Model 92 pistols in holsters – each man inserting a magazine, working the action to chamber a round, and then setting the safety catch. The Italian-made Spectre is the only double-action sub-machine-gun in the world, and is also unusual in having a magazine containing four columns of cartridges, thus allowing fifty rounds to be carried in a magazine that is vertically smaller than the thirty-round units fitted to most similar weapons.

Once they had all reported themselves ready, Perini, who had donned a Kevlar vest and was also now carrying a Spectre in his left hand, crossed over to where Richter and Simpson leaned against the bonnet of one of the Alfas. 'We're ready to go,' he announced.

'Are you sure he's still in there?' Simpson asked.

'Yes,' Perini replied, 'we've had at least one watcher covering that villa ever since our operative took her photographs. We'll now be leaving one man here to watch the cars, Mr Simpson, and I suggest you stay well to the back until the target area has been secured. Mr Richter: the same applies to you, but please be ready to come forward as soon as we have captured the suspect.' As both men nodded their understanding, Perini walked back to the DCPP officers.

Four minutes later the armed men were crouching in a small copse of trees that looked down over a gentle incline towards a shabby white-painted villa about one hundred yards away, nestling in an overgrown and obviously untended garden.

## Kandíra, south-west Crete

'He would have been out in his boat all day,' Christina Polessos stated definitively, 'and drinking in the *kafeníon* all evening.'

'Boat? What kind of boat?' Lavat asked, opening his notebook.

'He was a smuggler, or worse,' Christina continued, 'but he claimed he was a diver. He has a boat moored somewhere out there in the bay.'

'What do you mean "or worse"?' Lavat demanded.

Christina suddenly seemed to realize that she was talking to a policeman rather than one of her gossiping cronies from the village, and began to clam up. 'That's not for me to say,' was all she murmured.

'Right, we'll find his boat later. Which bar did Aristides normally use?'

Maria Coulouris laughed suddenly, the unexpected sound incongruous in the silent street. 'You obviously don't know Kandíra, Inspector. There is only one bar – Jakob's.'

When Lavat and his sergeant reached the *kafeníon*, Jakob was just opening up.

'I'm Inspector Lavat,' the officer announced, keenly aware that he didn't look much like a policeman in his white overalls. He showed his identity card to the scowling Cretan, who stood peering out from behind his street door. 'We need to talk to you about last night.'

Jakob looked closely at Lavat's identification, slowly comparing the man with the photograph, before he answered. 'What about last night? Nothing happened here.'

'We know that. We just want to ask about one of your customers.'

For a moment Lavat thought Jakob was going to slam the bar door in his face, but instead he shrugged and opened it wide. 'Very well, come in. But I have customers to serve, so you must be quick.'

Lavat glanced up and down the street, then into the echoing emptiness of the bar, redolent with the stale odours of coarse tobacco, cheap beer and hard liquor. 'Yes, obviously,' he said, the sarcasm lost on Jakob, who had moved behind the counter and was now ostentatiously wiping it with a dirty grey cloth.

'Which customer?' Jakob demanded curtly, pointedly not offering either man a drink.

'Spiros Aristides,' Lavat replied. 'He was drinking in here last night?'

'Don't know him,' Jakob muttered.

'Look,' Lavat said, tiring of the Cretan's sullen and stubborn attitude, 'this is a murder investigation, and you have two choices. You can talk to us here, which means your bar will stay open and you won't lose any valuable custom.' Lavat glanced round at the conspicuously empty tables as he said this. 'Or you can get in the back of a police car and we'll drive you over to our headquarters in Irakleío, and we'll talk to you there. Of course, we have a lot of potential witnesses to interview meanwhile, so we can't guarantee how long all that might take. Could be a day, maybe two or three. Maybe even more. Now, let's try one more time. Was Spiros Aristides drinking in here last night?'

Jakob stared at Lavat for a long moment, then reached below the counter and brought out three beers. He snapped off the caps, pushed one bottle towards each of the policemen, picked up the third and took a long swallow. 'You mean the Greek?' he demanded.

'Yes,' Lavat said, picking up the beer, 'we mean the Greek. Was he in here last night?'

'Yes,' Jakob nodded. He pointed at the far corner of the room. 'He sat over there.'

'Did anyone speak to him? Did he meet anybody here?'

'Some of my customers know him,' Jakob conceded reluctantly, 'but I don't think anybody else talked to him until the other Greek arrived.'

'Other Greek?' Lavat asked. 'What other Greek?'

# Chapter 6

**Tuesday**
**Outskirts of Matera, Puglia, Italy**

Richter watched with professional interest as the DCPP officers moved out of the copse and headed down the slope to his left, carefully keeping out of sight of the villa. The house was located a short distance from the road and accessed by a rough gravel track, the property itself bordered by low stone walls and shrubs.

Richter waited until the Italians were almost at the villa, then stood up to follow them.

'Where are you going?' Simpson demanded.

'Down to the villa,' Richter replied. 'I'd like to be in at the kill, so to speak.'

Simpson glared at him. 'Make sure that's just a figure of speech, Richter,' he said. 'We want Andrew Lomas in one piece. I know you have issues with him, but—'

'I don't have *issues* with Lomas, as you put it,' Richter interrupted. 'He and his minders tied Raya Kosov down in a chair and sliced bits off her until she died of pain and shock and blood loss, and then they dumped what was left of her body on the bed next to me, so the first thing I'd see when I came round was her mutilated face. I don't think the word *issues* actually covers something like that, do you?'

Simpson waggled a warning finger. 'You just let the law handle Lomas, Richter. I don't want to see any kind of vigilante action from you when those Eyeties pull him out of that house.'

'Oh, come on, Simpson, there are ten heavily armed men down there, and all I've got is a Kevlar vest. What are you expecting me to do, choke him with it?'

'Just remember what I've said, Richter.'

'Yeah, yeah,' Richter muttered. 'I'll take care of it.'

# PANDEMIC

It was five minutes after Richter had slipped from sight behind the stone wall that Simpson finally realized his employee hadn't actually confirmed that he wouldn't try to kill Andrew Lomas. 'Oh, shit,' he murmured, then got to his feet and began picking his way through the trees, following the path Richter had taken down to the road.

## Atlanta, Georgia

Just over three hours after his pager had summoned him from the shower, Tyler Q. Hardin was buckling his seat-belt for the flight north from Atlanta to New York's John F. Kennedy Airport. In his pocket was an onward ticket to London Heathrow first and from there a direct flight to Crete. About four hours behind him would come the other three members of his team, now hastily assembling protective clothing and equipment.

CDC personnel are given automatic priority on all US carriers when responding to a request for assistance, and two disappointed passengers had been bumped from the flight to provide Hardin with a seat. In fact, only one had been bumped for the seat, and the second to ensure sufficient space in the hold of the Boeing 757 for the two large reinforced cases, sealed with tempered-steel padlocks and carrying Customs-exempt labels, which contained everything Hardin hoped he would need for carrying out his initial investigation.

What little clothing he had brought with him was crushed into a leather carry-on bag sitting in the locker above his head, and beneath the seat in front of him was stashed his Toshiba Satellite laptop. As soon as the seat-belt sign was switched off, he was going to haul out the computer and call up everything in the database about Ebola and other members of the filovirus family and start preparing a series of protocols for whatever he might find on Crete when he finally got there.

## Outskirts of Matera, Puglia, Italy

The villa looked quiet and peaceful as Perini and his men approached it. To satisfy legal requirements, the DCPP had in their possession a warrant to search the property, and Perini had received permission to gain access by whatever means he, the man on the spot, felt necessary. Knowing Lomas's reputation, the Italian had decided that the best means of entry was to kick down the front door and go in with, metaphorically speaking, all guns blazing.

About twenty yards from the boundary of the property Richter stopped and watched. Perini had briefed the DCPP officers to effect their planned assault in two groups, which made obvious sense as the villa would undoubtedly have both a front and a back door. The groups were clearly all linked by radio, because Richter could hear nothing apart from the furtive movement of the men across the ground. Perini stood off to one side of the drive curving up to the front door, a broad sweep of old gravel flecked with grass and weeds. He was watching as his men deployed.

Five black-clad figures soon grouped by the front entrance and Richter watched one of them reach out, turn the handle and press his hand firmly against the door. When it didn't open, a second DCPP man began pushing at its right-hand edge, starting at the top and working downwards. Richter could see the ram leaning against the wall near by, and knew that they were trying to locate the locks or bolts so that they could target the ram against them.

On a silent command, three of the five stood back, Spectre sub-machine-guns at the ready, while the other two picked up the ram. Richter saw Perini's lips move as he issued an order – and suddenly it started.

With a shout that echoed around the quiet valley, the two DCPP men smashed the heavy steel ram into the villa's entrance door just above the lock, and Richter could clearly hear a splintering of wood. When the door didn't budge, they propelled the ram forward again, slightly below the lock this time. Abruptly it gave and the door crashed open. The men immediately dropped the ram, swung their Spectres to the ready, and burst inside.

Standard special forces assault tactics call for the use of noise and violence so as to shock, intimidate and hopefully persuade suspects to disarm. These DCPP types certainly knew how to make a noise. Richter heard two stun grenades detonate, then shouts and bellows from the interior of the building as the men systematically cleared one room after another. And suddenly two single shots sounded, followed by a three-round burst of sub-machine-gun fire, then finally silence.

Perini approached the door of the villa, and Richter followed a few feet behind. When the Italian heard him, he turned round and gestured. 'They've found three people inside,' he said. 'One is the man we believe to be Lomas himself, one we presume is the man Lomas sent to meet the consular official in Salerno, and the other was probably just a body-guard.'

'The shots?' Richter asked.

'The one that we think was a bodyguard fired his pistol. He missed, and now he's dead. The other two men weren't armed. They're bringing them out now.'

Just as Perini finished speaking, two DCPP officers approached, half-carrying, half-dragging a dazed-looking man. Richter stepped forward and pulled his head up by the hair. 'That's not Lomas,' he said.

Perini nodded. 'He matches the description our watcher gave for the go-between.' He then issued instructions for the prisoner to be taken away and processed.

Another three men emerged, two black-clad DCPP officers flanking a slightly built middle-aged man. Richter stepped forward, but this time he had no need to lift the suspect's head: the man was walking normally upright, except with his hands tied behind his back, and secured at the wrist with plastic cable ties. Richter took one look and turned to Perini.

'That's Lomas,' he said. 'No question.'


### Arlington, Virginia

David Elias looked down at the piece of paper in his hand and then up again at the building in front of him, checking the address carefully. It was five past ten, so he was ten minutes early for the meeting the Director had instructed him to attend.

He walked up the steps of the house and pressed the bell push set in a polished brass plate beside the door. Immediately, lights flared on above his head and he was suddenly conscious of the empty stare of two security cameras mounted behind protective grilles set on either side of the entrance.

A minute later a hidden speaker crackled. 'Yes? Please press the button again and state your name.'

Elias pressed it and spoke towards the brass plate. 'My name's David Elias. I think I'm expected.'

The speaker clicked off, then the door opened and a squat, heavy-set man peered out at him, shoulder holster clearly visible beneath the open jacket of his dark blue suit.

'Your ID, please, Mr Elias?'

Elias dug in his jacket pocket, pulled out his CIA card and handed it over. The man scrutinized it carefully, handed it back and then opened the door wide. 'OK. Come in.' The hallway was spacious and high-ceilinged, an elegant entrance to an obviously expensive property. 'Follow me.'

Elias walked down the hall, following the man in the dark suit. The man stopped beside a mahogany door at the far end, knocked twice, and opened it without waiting for a response. He gestured inside. Elias entered and heard the door close behind him.

Probably originally a formal drawing room, it was large and square, with comfortable sofas and easy chairs. In the far corner a youthful dark-haired man sat behind a small oak desk in a leather wing chair, looking slightly ill at ease. Elias had never seen him before, and neither did he recognize the two other men sitting in front of him. He walked across the room and paused beside a third chair as the man behind the desk stood up.

'Welcome, Mr Elias,' he said, and gestured to the other two men, who both now stood. 'To your immediate right is Roger Krywald, and on his right is Richard Stein. This is David Elias.'

Elias shook hands with both men, then sat down and waited expectantly.

'My name is McCready,' the dark-haired man continued, accurately anticipating Elias's unspoken question, 'and I'm your briefing officer for this operation.' He scanned the faces of the three men sitting in front of him, then opened a red folder on the desk. 'As at least two of you know,' he said, 'we normally conduct operational briefings at Langley, in one of the secure briefing-rooms there. But the circumstances in which we now find ourselves are not normal, which is why we're meeting here in this safe house.'

Elias tentatively raised a hand. 'Sir,' he began, 'I'm not really sure I should be here. I'm an analyst. I'm not part of the operational staff.'

Out of the corner of his eye Elias saw a sneer cross Krywald's face. The antipathy between the operational staff – the coal-face warriors of the Agency – and the analysts, who sat at desks or in front of computer screens evaluating the take from technical intelligence mechanisms, was well known.

Each denigrated the work of the other, and each was to a certain extent justified. Technical intelligence was vital – you simply had to know what weaponry the opposition possessed, but without the humint – human intelligence – gleaned from operatives under cover and on the ground, you would have no idea at whom those weapons were likely to be aimed.

McCready looked at Elias and smiled slightly. 'That's right, David. Unlike Roger and Dick here, you're not. But in one way you're the most vital member of this team, because of your other skills.'

'My diving?' Elias hazarded, after a moment.

'Exactly, your diving. In the initial stages of this operation, Roger and Dick will be supporting and assisting you, because without you there could be no operation.' McCready paused and again eyed each of the three men in turn.

'Before we start, some housekeeping. David, as he's already mentioned, is not a member of the operational staff, and is essentially a passenger on this mission, along just to carry out one specific task, and therefore we've decided that for him to use an alias is an unnecessary complication. He can use his genuine passport and he'll be issued with a credit card in his real name.

'You two' – he gestured towards Krywald and Stein – 'will travel under assumed surnames, but retaining your real first names, and we'll have appropriate documentation issued to you. You'll each have three aliases, but this should be a simple enough operation so I doubt that you'll be needing more than one. Is that clear?'

McCready got three nods in exchange. 'Right,' he continued, 'the situation the Agency has found itself in is somewhat unusual, for a number of reasons. First, you need to know some history. This operation essentially began,' he settled himself more comfortably in his chair, 'over thirty years ago, on the other side of the world.'

## Outskirts of Matera, Puglia, Italy

That afternoon Richter had made two purchases in a shop in Brindisi: one was a whetstone, and the other was a flick-knife with a five-inch blade. When he'd arrived back at the airfield, he'd spent a couple of hours honing the blade of the knife until it was quite literally razor-sharp. He wanted there to be no mistake because he knew he'd get no second chance.

As Perini leaned forward to study Lomas, Richter took a step closer to the captive and eased his right hand out of his pocket. Behind him, he was dimly aware of Simpson approaching the villa, puffing from the unaccustomed exercise.

Lomas looked at Richter, a faint light of recognition in his eyes, and Richter knew that the Russian was desperately trying to place him.

'Hullo again, Andrew,' Richter said. 'Or should that be Alexei? Remember me?' And as his mouth formed the last syllable, Richter moved. Moved too fast for Perini or Simpson or the DCPP officers or anyone else to stop him. His right thumb had been resting on the button of the flick-knife while he'd been talking. He depressed it and the lethally sharp blade snapped out and locked into place. In a single fluid movement Richter rotated the knife so that the cutting edge of the blade faced up – the way a professional would hold it – and whipped his right hand forward and upwards.

The entire length of the blade sliced effortlessly through Lomas's shirt and entered his stomach just above the navel, and before he could do anything but open his mouth and take a huge gulp of air prepara-tory to a scream, Richter's left hand was encircling his right and he was lifting the knife, lifting it with all his considerable strength, powering it up through Lomas's body, almost pulling the Russian off the ground, the knife point seeking out the vital organs located above his diaphragm.

'Let me remind you then, you bastard,' Richter hissed, his face close to Lomas's right ear. 'Raya Kosov, West London. You and your hoods sliced her to pieces. This is payback.'

And then Lomas finally screamed, his howl of pain echoing off the sides of the valley and the villa walls. Perini began yelling and then grabbed Richter from behind, trying to pull him away, but it was like trying to shift a rock. Simpson, Richter realized, was somewhere over to his left and shouting for him to stop. The two DCPP officers were standing stock-still, stunned into immobility by the sudden and completely unexpected attack, while still detaining Lomas by the arms.

And still Richter pulled the knife upwards, the blade slicing through skin, fat, blood vessels and intestines. Blood poured out of the gaping wound, down over Richter's hands and forearms, soaking the front of the Kevlar jacket and his jeans, and splattered on to the gravel. Perini moved back, then forward again, and then Richter had no option but to stop, and pull out the knife, because the Italian had placed the muzzle of his Beretta Model 92 coldly against his temple.

Simpson grabbed Richter's left arm and swung him back and away from Lomas who, finally released by the two DCPP men, tumbled forward to the ground, collapsing clumsily into the dark spreading pool that was his own life blood. 'You treacherous fucking bastard, Richter,' Simpson spat. 'You disobeyed my direct order. I told you we wanted Lomas alive.'

'Tough,' Richter snapped back, 'I wanted him dead. If you'd had your way he'd have been stuck in a comfortable safe house and gently debriefed over a year or so, then handed back to the Russians or whoever he works for now with a note of apology. You probably wouldn't even have got anything useful out of him. This bastard killed Raya Kosov, who I was protecting, and I believe in an eye for an eye.'

Behind the two men a scene of noisy chaos unfolded. Somebody had found a towel in the house, and the two DCPP men were clamping it down over Lomas's stomach, trying, without a great deal of success, to staunch the flow of blood. Perini had lost interest in Richter as soon as he'd pulled out the knife, and was barking orders into his headset radio. Simpson turned round to see what was happening, to see if Lomas was still alive and if they could salvage anything from this disaster. When he turned back again, Richter had simply vanished.

## Kandíra, south-west Crete

Inspector Lavat pulled the paper mask tighter around his mouth, and checked his rubber gloves and overshoes. Dr Gravas looked him up and down critically, and nodded. They were ready, although they both anticipated this would be a very short visit.

Jakob had been considerably less than helpful, but they had finally deduced that the 'other Greek' who had visited the bar was probably Nico Aristides, the only other member of Spiros's family known to reside in Kandíra. Finding out where he lived had taken a further two hours, due to the in-built reluctance of all Cretans to divulge any information whatsoever to any police officer, or indeed any other authority figure.

While it would not be true to say that the Cretans hate the police, they certainly dislike and distrust them, and the police, for their part, are cautious and suspicious, not least because of all the Western European nations, the Cretans are by far the best armed. Almost every family possesses at least one gun, and usually these are serious weapons ranging from combat shotguns up to sub-machine-guns, while virtually everyone seems to own a pistol. And the single characteristic of almost all these weapons is that they are completely unlicensed.

When they knocked at Nico's door there had been no reply, only an echoing silence that both men found ominous, though it could simply mean that Nico was out fishing or drinking or something. Unusually for Kandíra, his door was locked. In fact, Nico had acquired that habit long ago, when he'd first started 'helping out' his uncle with some of the objects he hauled up illicitly from the seabed.

Now, with Lavat's authority, they were going to break into the apartment. The policeman lifted a crowbar and placed the end of it firmly between the door itself and the jamb, directly above the lock. He heaved but for a few seconds nothing happened, then with a sudden crack the lock gave way and the door swung open.

Lavat peered inside, listening intently. 'Nico Aristides, this is the police,' he called out, more in hope than anticipation. He was rewarded only by silence, glanced back at Gravas with a shrug and stepped carefully into the small apartment, keeping well to the centre of the hallway and away from the walls.

He pushed open the second door he encountered with the tip of his crowbar. It proved to be the bedroom, and one glance was all he needed to realize that Nico Aristides would never go out drinking or fishing or anything else, ever again.

## Outskirts of Matera, Puglia, Italy

The moment Simpson turned away, Richter had seized his opportunity. He'd taken off down the gravel drive, the crunch of his footsteps lost in the shouting that emanated from the men surrounding the villa. He turned left outside the gateway and ran back up the hill towards the waiting cars. He had to get there as quickly as possible, before Simpson or Perini did something to stop him.

The Kevlar vest had been a potentially useful protection during the assault on the villa, but now it was just a liability. Richter undid the straps as he ran, then lifted the jacket over his head and tossed it to one side.

Heart pounding, breath coming in short gasps, Richter ran off the roadway and onto the waste ground. The driver Perini had left to watch over the cars was still standing beside one of them, his head cocked to one side as he listened to some message relayed through his earpiece.

As Richter came into view, the man's eyes widened on seeing the massive bloodstains down the front of his jeans. The driver first slid his hand up towards his lapel microphone, then thought better of that and reached into the left side of his jacket. Richter had barely two seconds to act, no more. He accelerated his pace as much as he could, reaching the Italian just as the man pulled the Beretta clear of his shoulder holster.

This was no time for finesse, and Richter just kept up his momentum, slamming his right shoulder into the Italian's chest and knocking the breath from his body. The two men tumbled backwards, crashing into the side of the Alfa Romeo.

The driver was still holding the pistol in his right hand, and Richter knew he must disarm him before he could train the Model 92 and pull the trigger. The Italian chopped Richter in the kidneys with his left hand, but because he was backed up against the car there was little room to swing, and it was thus a weak blow Richter could ignore.

He turned his body to the left, placing his back towards the man's chest, and reached up and out with both hands, grabbing his arm just above the wrist. Then Richter continued his turn to the left, bent forward at the hips and pulled downwards. The Italian flew over Richter, hitting the ground hard, to fall flat on his back and losing his grip on the pistol.

Richter scooped up the Beretta and hurled it as far as he could, right over a low hedge and into the scrubby field beyond, then turned his attention back to the driver. He was trying to get up, had made it onto his hands and knees. Richter had no quarrel with the man, but he hadn't got time to mess about.

He stepped across, kicked the Italian hard in the stomach, the impact virtually lifting him off the ground. He began retching, but he was young and strong, and Richter knew he'd recover in seconds, so he closed in again and hit him with a rabbit-punch, hard on the side of the neck. The driver collapsed in an unconscious heap.

Pausing for a second to catch his breath, Richter then removed the keys from the ignition switches of three of the Alfas, locked each one carefully and then lobbed the keys in the same general direction that he'd earlier thrown the Beretta. He climbed into the fourth Alfa and started it up, powering it off the waste ground and up the hill, heading away from the villa.

Richter was off and running, if not for his life then at least for his freedom.

### Kandíra, south-west Crete

Nico Aristides was very clearly dead, apparently killed by the same unknown pathogen as his uncle. The policeman and doctor stood side by side in the doorway of his bedroom and looked across the small room at the still and silent body lying collapsed beside the bed.

Unlike Spiros, who'd become fairly intoxicated, Nico had had little to drink the previous evening, and perhaps as a result his death had not been easy. There was blood everywhere, trailing across the floor, smeared on the walls and doors, a mute testament to the younger man's desperate and ultimately futile attempts to find relief from the killer that was destroying him from within.

'The same?' Inspector Lavat asked, his voice slightly muffled by the mask he clutched carefully to his face.

'The same,' Gravas agreed. 'We don't go near him. Seal the door of the apartment, then close all the windows in the rest of this house. Best to put a policeman in the street outside. Nobody should come in here until the American specialists arrive.'

### Outskirts of Matera, Puglia, Italy

'Where is he?' shouted Perini, his face, contorted with rage, only inches from Simpson's.

The Englishman took a handkerchief out of his pocket to wipe a trace of spittle off his cheek and then shrugged his shoulders. 'I don't know, but it's easy enough to guess. He'll no doubt try and take one of your cars, then either head for the border or make for some airport, so that he can get out of Italy as soon as possible.'

Perini stepped back and shouted orders to his men. Simpson watched as two of the DCPP officers left their current posts and began running up the hill towards the spot where they'd parked the cars. Then he glared at Simpson. 'The French border?' he demanded.

'Maybe. Richter knows France well.'

Perini shook his head. 'He'll never make it. It's about twelve hundred kilometres up the length of Italy to get to France. I'll put police check-points on the north-bound carriageway of every road in the country, and have a watch on all the airports and ferry terminals within the hour. And, Simpson,' added Perini, menace in every syllable, 'he's *your* man and that makes his actions your responsibility. Don't think for a moment that it's finished here.'

Simpson said nothing, just stared at Perini. The Italian dropped his eyes first, then glanced over his shoulder. Lomas was still alive but in excruciating pain, and weakening steadily from massive blood loss. The towels pressed against his stomach were sodden with blood but helped contain the bleeding. What everyone knew was that the wound was too big and too deep for any such crude effort to stem the flow. Unless

Lomas received medical attention within a matter of minutes he was going to die.

Seconds after the attack, Perini had called for an air ambulance. The helicopter was on its way from Bari, but there was no way it could get there for at least fifteen minutes. As far as Perini could see, Andrew Lomas was going to bleed to death here in the garden of the villa, and there was nothing any of them could do about it. And if he did die, then Perini wanted to see Paul Richter standing in front of an Italian judge on a charge of wilful murder.

Simpson walked away a short distance and sat down on a wooden garden seat that was missing two slats. From the moment Richter had run, his priorities had changed. He had been absolutely furious when Richter attacked Lomas, although he could understand the reason for it, and would have done anything to stop him.

But Simpson was a realist. Nothing he could say or do would alter the fact that Lomas lay dying fifteen feet away, and now the most important thing was to ensure that Richter didn't fall into the hands of either the Italian police or the SISDE. He was simply too valuable to lose, and the last thing Simpson wanted was to see him banged up for years in some Italian prison.

And, despite his comments to Perini, Simpson thought he knew precisely where Richter was heading, and exactly what he was going to do when he got there, because he knew one other important thing about Richter that the Italian didn't.

Richter was by now nearly two miles down the road, holding the Alfa at a steady hundred and thirty kilometres an hour. But he was heading south, not north.

He had always possessed a highly developed sense of direction, so he knew precisely where he was and where he was going. He was retracing the route that the four cars had taken earlier that day, and the field where the helicopter had landed was now less than one minute away. And what Simpson knew, but nobody else involved in the incident was aware of, was that Richter was a qualified helicopter pilot.

He'd joined the Royal Navy as a pilot, training first on fixed-wing aircraft, as was usual, and then cutting his teeth on the Gazelle trainer.

He'd had two squadron tours, first flying a Wessex 5 and then a Sea King, before transferring to Sea Harriers. Like riding a bike, piloting a helicopter is a skill that, once mastered, tends to endure.

Richter saw the lay-by just around the bend and hit the brakes hard, hauling his speed down and looking ahead for any oncoming traffic. There wasn't any in evidence, so he waited until he was almost at the lay-by, then span the wheel hard left, pulled on the handbrake and executed a perfect bootlegger turn, sliding the Alfa across the road and into the lay-by, the vehicle facing back the way he had come.

'I enjoyed that,' he muttered to himself, pushing open the car door and running into the field, but it wasn't obvious whether he was referring to what he'd inflicted on Lomas or to the manoeuvre just performed in the Alfa. Or maybe to both.

Richter had noticed that Vento had been a passenger in one of the cars, so was presumably still somewhere near the villa. He ran across to the helicopter and seized the door handle, praying that Vento hadn't locked it before he'd left.

Aircraft aren't like cars: any teenager with a modicum of intelligence can learn how to hot-wire a car within a few minutes, and can then get the vehicle moving as long as he's got some basic knowledge of how it works. Aircraft, both fixed and rotary wing, are different. Typically, to get to one-circuit solo standard – in other words, to be able to taxi, take-off, fly around the airfield and land – in a single-engine, fixed-wing aircraft will take most people about fifteen hours of instruction. To become a competent amateur pilot will take fifty hours at the very least. The upshot of this is that aircraft are very rarely stolen, so pilots don't usually bother locking them.

As he had hoped and expected, the door handle turned easily. Richter climbed nimbly into the left-hand seat – the pilot's. He'd earlier asked Perini if he could travel in the front seat for only one reason: he'd wanted to watch exactly how Vento started the aircraft. As soon as he sat down, Richter ran through precisely the same sequence of actions.

Within two minutes of opening the pilot's door, he had both engines running and the rotors starting to turn, and just thirty seconds after that he was ready for lift-off. Muttering a silent prayer to whatever gods looked after the welfare of pilots not qualified on type, Richter eased back on the control column and smoothly lifted the collective lever, increasing both the power of the engines and the angle of attack of the main rotor blades. The Agusta lifted somewhat jerkily into the air.

It wasn't one of Richter's better take-offs, but he was off the ground and that was all that mattered. He pulled up the collective further, pushed down gently on the left rudder pedal, and moved the control column slightly further back and over to the left. The helicopter banked sharply to port and began increasing speed. As Richter straightened up and the Agusta soared over a clump of poplars at the edge of the field, he knew for sure that he was going to make it.

Perini had just enjoyed an unexpected piece of good fortune. The air ambulance was still at least ten minutes away when a black BMW saloon slowed down at the end of the drive leading to the villa, where some of Perini's men were still standing, weapons held loosely in their hands. The driver peered curiously over at the activity outside the house, then braked to a stop and climbed out, clutching a black leather bag. He ran up to where Perini was standing, took one look at Lomas and pushed the DCPP officers aside.

He pulled off the sodden towel and looked in horror at the gaping wound running from Lomas's navel almost up to his breastbone. '*Per l'amore del Dio*,' he muttered, then opened his bag and pulled out a dozen or so self-locking forceps, which he used to clamp all the larger of the severed blood vessels. The doctor then used gauze and adhesive strapping, and quickly contrived a makeshift pad to cover the gaping wound and hold Lomas's intestines in place.

Only then did he turn and look up at Perini. 'This man requires emergency surgery,' he said. He may have been a doctor, but that clearly didn't exempt him from stating the blindingly obvious.

'I know,' Perini said. 'The air ambulance should be here any minute now.' And, as he said that, they all heard the distinctive throbbing of rotor blades and a bulky white helicopter with red crosses marked on the side swung into view. After the pilot had carried out a single sweep of the area, it landed in the road just beyond the doctor's car, and in seconds its two crewmen were running up the drive, carrying a stretcher.

Lomas had slipped into unconsciousness. Speed was the only thing that could now save his life, and without ceremony the crewmen lifted his body onto the stretcher. The doctor checked his pulse then listened to his heartbeat with a stethoscope. One of the crewmen ripped open an intravenous drip set, tore the sleeve off Lomas's shirt, found a vein and slid the needle expertly into it. He pushed the other end of the tube into a plastic bottle of saline solution and opened the sliding tap on the tube all the way.

'His heartbeat is erratic and his pulse is weak,' the doctor said to Perini, raising his voice against the roar of the helicopter's engines and the clatter of the rotor blades. 'We have to put fluid into his bloodstream to replace what he has lost. And now we must get him into an emergency room. I'll go along with him.'

The two crewmen picked up the stretcher and swiftly carried Lomas down the drive. The doctor trotted beside them, holding the bag of saline solution high and squeezing it gently to ensure a steady flow into the body. Less than three minutes after the helicopter had landed, it was airborne again, heading north-east for the main hospital at Bari, the doctor already using the radio to advise the emergency staff of the nature of the injury and what needed to be done as soon as they touched down.

'Will he live?' Simpson asked, stepping forward to stand beside Perini.

The Italian shook his head, staring into the sky at the departing helicopter. 'I don't know. The doctor wouldn't say, because he doesn't know either. If they can get him into surgery immediately, perhaps he'll survive.' Perini swung round to look at Simpson. 'Now we have other matters to attend to. Your man Richter.'

One of the two DCPP officers Perini had sent off now re-appeared in front of the villa, ran across to the Italian and spoke rapidly. Perini nodded but didn't look surprised at whatever the man was saying: he issued further orders and three more DCPP men took off up the road at a trot.

Perini walked back to Simpson. 'Richter's taken one of the Alfas and he's locked the other three. I've got my men searching for the keys in case he just threw them away, and I've ordered an automobile locksmith to get out here immediately. Your man has also badly beaten the driver we left in charge of the cars, and that's another strike against him.

Despite what you said, Simpson, he won't try for the northern Italian border. It's too far, he doesn't speak the language, and he'd be too easy to intercept. He'll be trying to get out of the country some other way.' Perini stopped short. 'Of course, how stupid of me. He already has a way out – his Sea Harrier. We have to stop him reaching Brindisi.'

He called for a map of Puglia, identified the half-dozen or so roads that led from Matera to Brindisi, and immediately issued orders through his DCPP men to have them all blocked with checkpoints. As a further precaution, he also ordered a checkpoint on the E55 coastal *autostrada* running down from Bari to Brindisi, and some others on the roads further south, between Brindisi and Lecce.

Finally, he called Vento over and ordered him to get airborne in the Agusta as soon as possible, to try to identify Richter's car from the air.

'How will I do that?' Vento asked.

'Use your initiative. Break a window on one of the Alfas and hot-wire it. Or stop a passing motorist and commandeer his car. Or take the doctor's BMW – I don't care. Just get back to the helicopter, get it airborne, and then find Richter.'

As Vento and the DCPP driver hurried away, Perini stared down at the map and nodded with satisfaction. 'He's boxed in,' he said. 'There's no way he's going to get to the airfield. We've got him.'

# Chapter 7

**Tuesday**
**Aeroporto di Brindisi, Papola-Casale, Puglia, Italy**

In fact, Richter was almost at Brindisi. Vento had been right about the speed of the Agusta. Richter had wound it up to an indicated one hundred and fifty knots and climbed to two thousand feet. He could have stayed low, but he thought that would probably attract more attention than a transit at a normal height. It also meant he didn't have to worry about power lines, pylons, higher ground or any other obstacles, and he was also too low to conflict with most fixed-wing aircraft.

When he'd lifted off from the field he knew he had about seventy miles to cover before he reached Brindisi, but that was less than a half-hour flight in the helicopter. At the moment when Perini was ordering checkpoints to be positioned, the Agusta was less than five minutes from the airfield boundary, and Richter was already in descent.

Like any competent pilot, Vento had put a note of Brindisi's frequencies on the instrument panel, and as Richter pulled the Agusta round in a tight right-hand turn over Punta Penne, due north of the town, he selected VHF frequency one one eight decimal one, picked a callsign and called Brindisi Tower.

'Brindisi, this is helicopter Lima Whisky at three hundred feet over Punta Penne.'

'Lima Whisky, Brindisi, roger. State your intentions.'

'Lima Whisky would like to refuel, sir. We're running a little low.'

'Roger, Lima Whisky. Cleared for a visual approach to land by the two northerly hangars and await a fuel bowser. Wind is light and variable. The active runway is three two. Hold well clear of the active; we have inbound heavy civilian traffic long finals.'

'Thank you, Brindisi. All copied.'

That had been Richter's biggest gamble. By flying low to the north of the airfield and making his approach from Punta Penne, he had been hoping that the Tower controller would instruct him to land somewhere to the north-east of the active runway, which meant he could put the Agusta down not far from where the Sea Harrier was parked.

Two minutes later Richter lowered the undercarriage and landed the helicopter about fifty yards from his Harrier. He shut down the Agusta, pulling on the rotor brake a little sooner than he would have liked, but he was in a hurry, then climbed out and trotted over to the squadron building he and Simpson had been using.

### HMS *Invincible*, Ionian Sea

Just over an hour earlier, the *Invincible* had increased speed by about two knots and altered course slightly. The rate at which rumours travelled throughout the ship never ceased to amaze newcomers, and they were, perhaps surprisingly, usually reasonably accurate. Almost as soon as the engine revolutions increased, the word spreading on the lower deck was that the planned visit to Athens had been cancelled, or at least postponed, and the ship was now proceeding to Crete. Or maybe Malta? The Wardroom didn't get to hear about Malta, but the word 'Crete' was certainly being bandied about.

'So what the hell's going on in Crete that involves us?' The inquiry from the lieutenant filling a cup at the coffee urn was plaintive and somewhat querulous. 'My wife's flying out to Athens tomorrow. What's she supposed to do all by herself in Greece while we're poncing about the Med?'

'That's life in a blue suit, mate. You may not like the fucking Navy, but the Navy likes fucking you. Anyway, you'll find out what we're supposed to be doing in about ten minutes. The Old Man's going to brief us all on the CCTV system. What your wife'll find to do in Athens for the next week or so with all those randy Greek men is something else.'

The Wardroom filled rapidly. With no flying operations planned and the ship winding down in preparation for a planned port visit, most of the officers had time on their hands, and when the big TV screen in the corner of the room flickered into life and a familiar face, flanked by epaulettes bearing four gold stripes, appeared on the screen, it was quite literally standing room only.

'Good afternoon, this is the Captain. As you are all no doubt aware, our planned visit to Athens and Piraeus has been delayed for operational reasons, and we are at present proceeding on a south-easterly heading towards Crete. The current situation is still somewhat confused, but we have been advised that a state of medical emergency exists on part of the island. At least one person has died, and there are fears of a major epidemic. The Cretan authorities have requested international assistance in containing this situation.

'I should emphasize that at this stage we have no further information concerning the nature of the epidemic, or the disease or illness involved, and I think it unlikely that we will become too involved in the detailed management of the crisis. I anticipate that our involvement is likely to be purely supportive. We will probably act primarily in an off-shore replenishment role, and assist the Cretan authorities in the movement of personnel and supplies around the island.

'I am sorry that our scheduled visit to Athens has been disrupted, and I am keenly aware that many members of the ship's company have arranged for their wives or girlfriends – in some cases perhaps both – to travel out to Greece over the next few days. Those of you who wish to do so may avail yourselves of the communications facilities to make brief telephone calls to Britain to cancel or modify these arrangements. Please contact the Operations Office to arrange a schedule for such calls.

'That is all I have for the moment but, in view of the changed circumstances, Commander (Air) will now address the Air Group.'

The television screen blanked for a few seconds, then a swarthy, darkly bearded face appeared. 'Good afternoon, this is Commander (Air). As the Captain has just outlined, it is likely that we will have to begin flying operations, possibly intense flying operations, at fairly short notice. The nature of the emergency on Crete suggests that it is unlikely that the Sea Harriers will be required, but rotary wing operations are almost certain to be carried out. There will be an initial briefing in the Number Two Briefing-Room at twenty-one hundred today. All rotary wing squadron personnel are to attend. That is all.'

Commander (Air)'s face was replaced on the TV screen by a sudden grey snowstorm and a buzzing sound, and someone switched off the big set with the remote.

'Isn't that typical?' an anonymous voice piped up. 'The bloody stovies get to sleep through this lot as well.'

Sporadic laughter greeted this remark. It was true that the Sea Harrier pilots – the 'jet jockeys' or 'stovies' – flew fewer hours than the helicopter crews, but this was primarily because of their very different roles. Nevertheless, it was popularly rumoured that the most common medical complaint suffered by 800 Squadron pilots was bedsores.

### Outskirts of Matera, Puglia, Italy

'It's gone,' Vento shouted out, as he ran back up the villa's drive towards Perini. They'd found one set of keys in the field adjoining the wasteland, and Vento had immediately set off with the driver to where he'd left the Agusta.

'What?'

'The helicopter,' Vento said, 'it's gone. And the other Alfa Romeo was parked in the lay-by. Richter must have taken the Agusta.'

For a moment Perini said nothing, then he span round to face Simpson. 'You *knew*,' he said. 'You knew he could fly a helicopter.' Simpson nodded. 'Why didn't you tell me?'

'You never asked,' Simpson replied, with a wintry smile. 'And let's get something quite clear, shall we? I will do nothing at all to assist you in capturing Richter. He's one of my most valuable assets, and I will not tolerate seeing him incarcerated pointlessly in Italy, or anywhere else for that matter.

'I don't condone what he did here, but I do understand why he did it. Lomas killed a woman Richter had become personally involved with. He killed her slowly and with incredible precision so as to cause her the maximum possible pain, and when he'd finished he dumped her body next to Richter himself while he was unconscious. What Richter did was actually rather less than Lomas deserved. If it had been my decision, Lomas would have taken days to die.'

'I have no interest whatsoever in Richter's reasons,' Perini snapped, then turned away and told one of the DCPP officers to contact Brindisi airport immediately and place the Sea Harrier under armed guard. Then he faced Simpson again. 'The fact is that he made a murderous attack upon a bound and unarmed prisoner in full view of four witnesses. If Lomas dies, I expect Richter to be charged with murder. If he survives, I expect him to be charged with causing grievous bodily harm.'

'Expect away,' Simpson replied coldly. 'As I've said, I'll do nothing to help you. And you should also know that any attempts to extradite Richter from Britain will not succeed. I will see to that. If you persist with this vendetta, I promise you I will produce witnesses of unimpeachable probity who'll be prepared to swear that at the moment this attack took place Richter was actually in London.'

'Or Paris or Berlin or Madrid, I suppose,' Perini said bitterly.

'Or anywhere else I choose. Exactly,' Simpson nodded. 'I can see you're finally getting the hang of it.'

### Aeroporto di Brindisi, Papola-Casale, Puglia, Italy

Inside the squadron building, Richter dropped the flick-knife into a large plastic bag, then stripped off his T-shirt, jeans and trainers and stuffed them into it as well. Then he climbed into his flying overalls, pulled on his speed jeans and flying boots, slipped on the life-saving jacket, grabbed his helmet as well as the plastic bag and ran out of the building.

A fuel bowser had just arrived beside the Agusta and the driver was looking around in a puzzled fashion, presumably wondering where its pilot had got to. Richter strode briskly across to the Harrier, his eyes roaming over the control surfaces, but the Chief had been as good as his word, and all the locks had been removed. Richter climbed nimbly up the red ladder secured to the side of the aircraft, sat down, strapped himself in and pulled on his flying helmet. He shoved the plastic bag awkwardly over to one side of the cockpit.

He rushed through the pre-flight checks – again, the Chief Petty Officer had done those that he could – and as soon as he had completed them he reached out and levered the ladder away from the side of the cockpit. As it fell with a clatter on to the concrete hardstanding, the fuel bowser driver turned round to stare curiously at the Harrier.

Richter closed the canopy and removed the last two pins that primed the ejection seat. There are five pins altogether, but the Chief had already removed and stowed the other three. Out of the corner of his eye he saw a truck and a car approaching the hardstanding along the taxiway, headlights blazing and travelling at speed, but he ignored them.

He flicked the start switch and pressed the button next to it. The Auxiliary Power Unit started to whistle, and then Richter heard the sound he'd been waiting for: the mechanical whine as the APU started the Pegasus engine turning. This whine grew louder as the turbine span ever faster and then the jet settled into a steady, comforting roar.

Richter checked all the engine instruments, then glanced up the taxiway. The truck and car were almost at the edge of the hardstanding, but he really didn't think they were going to pose a problem – for one very simple reason.

During practice air combat, live missiles are never carried, and the Sidewinder fitted below the starboard wing of Richter's Harrier was a dummy apart from its seeker head, but the pair of Mark 4 Aden cannon – essentially a multi-barrelled Gatling gun similar to those fitted to American tank-busting helicopters and A10 aircraft – located in pods under the belly of the aircraft were very real, and he had persuaded Commander (Air) to authorize the loading of two ammunition packs of one hundred rounds for each gun.

Normally the FA2 Sea Harrier carries only missiles in various combinations. Richter had seen no point in asking Wings to let him carry live Sidewinders or AMRAAMs, but because he had no idea what Simpson was planning for him in Italy, some kind of self-defence capability had seemed prudent. The obvious solution was the Aden cannon, and the squadron maintainers had spent some hours fitting this pair of weapons.

The truck swept onto the hardstanding and screeched to a halt almost in front of the Harrier. Armed airmen poured out of the back and pointed their assault rifles at the aircraft. Richter did nothing, because he was waiting for the car to stop. When it did, blocking the access to the taxiway, two more armed soldiers climbed out.

Then Richter acted. He increased the power setting on the Pegasus slightly and pressed down on the right rudder pedal: the Harrier swung gently to the right until the nose of the aircraft was pointing directly at the back of the parked truck. He selected the Aden cannon, sighted carefully, making sure that none of the soldiers was in the firing line, and depressed the trigger, releasing it after about a second. There was a sound like tearing calico and the back of the truck simply ceased to exist as some fifty 30mm shells smashed into it from a distance of less than twenty yards. The impact swung what was left of the vehicle around in a half-circle, and Richter found himself looking into the terrified face of the driver, who was still in the cab.

The results were immediate and exactly what Richter had expected. The soldiers scattered and, as they disappeared into whatever cover they could find, he wound on the power and the Harrier began to move again, turning directly towards the car on the taxiway. The driver suddenly decided he'd be more likely to survive if he moved his vehicle, so floored the accelerator, swinging the wheel so that the car shot onto the hardstanding, well clear of the Harrier's path and leaving the taxiway clear.

The Italians' second line of defence was even then being assembled: three heavy fire vehicles were being parked nose to tail across the full width of the runway. But Richter didn't need the runway. He turned the Harrier onto the taxiway, slammed the engine to full power, and the Harrier began to roll. He hit one hundred knots in four seconds, and less than two seconds after that, with one hundred and fifty knots showing on the ASI, he rotated the nozzles to fifty degrees and the Harrier leapt into the sky.

## American Airlines 747, direct Baltimore-London Heathrow, western Atlantic

David Elias picked at the meal on the drop-down table in front of him with preoccupied disinterest. Although it seemed a hell of a long time since breakfast, he wasn't particularly hungry, and even the best of airline food only ever seemed barely edible to him.

But it wasn't the food that was concerning him. Ever since the man calling himself McCready had begun that briefing in the safe house in Arlington, Elias had been wondering what the hell he was doing getting involved in this thing. Not, he reasoned, that he had been given much of a choice. His superior officer had told him to attend. Any dissent would reflect badly on Elias professionally. And, in any case, his role had seemed simple enough.

All operational matters, McCready had told them, were the sole responsibility of Krywald and Stein, with Krywald as the senior officer. Elias was simply along for the ride, and to carry out a solo dive – possibly a deep solo dive – once they reached their destination.

That, too, had been a surprise. All Elias knew about Crete was that it was a popular holiday destination in the eastern Mediterranean. As far as he was aware, the Company had no assets on, or interest in, the island, and McCready had been carefully non-specific about the purpose of the dive. Krywald, he had said, would brief Elias when the time came. For the moment, Elias didn't need to know more.

He may not have needed to know, but Elias was certainly curious. He was also aware that the bulk of the briefing in Arlington had been completed well before his own arrival – he had been told almost nothing about the true purpose of the operation. All he did know was that some thirty years earlier an aircraft had crashed somewhere near Crete, and there were indications it had been found recently by a local diver. He presumed that the wreck was the focus of the dive he was going to have to undertake, but that was about all.

He was also puzzled by the haste involved. Less than two hours after the briefing had concluded, the three of them were sitting in the 747 out of Baltimore on a direct flight to London Heathrow – the first available aircraft across the Atlantic – and with onward connections to Crete. He'd presumed he would be given time to go back to his apartment to collect some clothes before departure, but that hadn't been allowed. A carry-on bag filled with clothes, pyjamas and washing kit had been provided, together with five hundred euros in cash and a new credit card issued under his real name.

If the sole purpose of the operation was to look for a thirty-year-old crashed aircraft, it all seemed unnaturally hasty. There had to be more – a lot more – to this business.

# PANDEMIC

## Sea Harrier 'Tiger Two' and HMS *Invincible*, Ionian Sea

As soon as the Harrier had cleared the airfield boundary, Richter pulled back on the control column and continued his climb to thirty-five thousand feet. He also, as a precaution, switched on his Guardian radar warning receiver, but he doubted if the Italians were likely to send anything up after him.

Richter didn't know exactly where the *Invincible* was, but he knew the ship had to be somewhere between the heel of Italy and the Peloponnisos at the southern tip of Greece, so he set an initial course of one six zero magnetic. As he reached top of climb, and passed abeam Lecce, he selected Homer's discrete frequency and called the ship.

'Homer, this is Tiger Two.' For a few seconds there was no reply, and Richter repeated the call. 'Homer, Homer, this is Tiger Two.'

With no planned flying, the Operations Room was almost deserted. Lieutenant John Moore, one of the two Air Traffic Control officers on board, was sitting in his usual seat, but with his feet up on the swivel chair next to him and reading a book. His headset was draped over the top of the console, and the Homer and Guard frequencies were being relayed through a speaker. The delay in replying was caused simply by the time it took Moore to put down his book and don his headset.

'Tiger Two, this is Homer. Good afternoon, Spook.'

'Good to hear your voice, John. OK, Tiger Two is at Flight Level three five zero, heading one six zero magnetic and approximately twenty-five miles south east of Lecce in Italy. Request ship's position and pigeons. Note that my NAVHARS is non-functional and I'm using only the E2B magnetic compass.'

'Roger, Tiger Two,' Moore replied, looking up at the RDF display, which shows the direction from which a radio transmission has come. 'Steer one five five magnetic for Mother. Understand your NAVHARS is unserviceable?'

'Negative,' Richter responded. 'It's working, but I had to leave Italy in a bit of a hurry and I didn't have time to set it up.'

The Sea Harrier's inertial navigation system – the NAVHARS – requires the pilot to input both an accurate geographical start position and the aircraft's heading to enable it to function correctly. Without accurate start data, it's virtually useless. Richter hadn't had time to do anything with the system when he left Brindisi – he'd had other things on his mind.

'Roger,' Moore replied. 'Ship's position is forty miles due west of Cape Matapan, which gives you, ah, wait one –' Moore fumbled with an en-route chart and roughly measured distances using his chinagraph pencil '– about a three-hundred-nautical-mile transit from Lecce. Say your endurance.'

'I was tanks full at Brindisi,' Richter replied, 'so well over one hour. I should reach you in about thirty minutes.'

'Roger that.' Moore released the transmit key and pressed the intercom button to Flyco.

On the port side of the bridge, with a clear and unobstructed view of the whole of the Flight Deck, is Flyco, the Flying Control Position. Manned by Lieutenant Commander (Flying), the second-in-command of the Air Department, or his deputy, the Air Staff Officer, Flyco controls all take-offs and landings, and all flying operations within the visual circuit of the ship.

Roger Black, Lieutenant Commander (Flying), known as 'Little F', was sitting in his usual seat, a month-old magazine in front of him, dividing his attention between that and the Flight Deck below him, where a single Merlin helicopter was lashed down on two spot, carrying out an engine run. As the intercom buzzed he pressed a key. 'Flyco.'

'Flyco, Homer. I've just had a call from Tiger Two. He's on recovery now, estimating about a half-hour transit from Brindisi.'

'Excellent. I'll get the deck cleared.' Black selected the deck broadcast and leaned close to the microphone. 'Flight Deck, Flyco. We have one Harrier on recovery. Estimate for landing is thirty minutes. Ensure two spot is clear by then.'

On the steel deck below, the Flight Deck Officer raised an arm in acknowledgement.


### Arlington, Virginia

Once the three-man team was on its way to Crete to try to recover whatever the meddling diver had found, and with firm instructions to bury whatever evidence there was of the thirty-year-old plane wreck, John Nicholson had completed the first phase of the recovery operation.

McCready – who knew nothing more than the brief outline provided by Nicholson – had given Krywald the most specific instructions: the plane was to be totally destroyed and the diver silenced one way or another. The only thing Nicholson expected the team to recover from the wreck was the steel case and its contents, and that was to be returned to Langley as quickly as possible.

But his work was far from finished. The men he had dispatched were en route but, without the proper equipment and support on Crete, their mission was doomed to failure from the start. Nicholson ordered a pot of coffee from the kitchen, pulled out a dark blue file from his briefcase, opened it and began making notes. Then he reached for the phone – the number of which was not listed in any directory, anywhere, and that was checked at least once every two days to ensure there were no taps on it – and began making calls.

Just over an hour later he drank the last of the coffee and leaned back. Through a series of cut-outs, Agency sleepers and even some legitimate channels, he had arranged everything he thought the team would need: the hire of a boat, the provision of a quantity of plastic explosive and under-water detonators, a complete set of diving equipment including extra compressed-air tanks, a hire car, hotel accommodation, press credentials – ostensibly the three men were travel reporters – and personal weapons.

His final task was handling Krywald and Stein once they had completed their part of the mission: McCready had already issued instructions to Krywald about Elias.

Nicholson was fighting a rearguard action, protecting the Company, but also his career and everything he had worked for over the last forty or so years. All other considerations, in his opinion, were secondary, and all the assets he employed were ultimately expendable. He had made plans to ensure the permanent silence of the only three surviving former CIA officers who had been deeply involved in Operation CAIP thirty years earlier, and McCready's usefulness was already over.

What he couldn't and wouldn't permit was any hint of his activities leaking out. That meant no loose talk, and that in turn meant that all three of the men even then approaching Crete at around five hundred miles an hour were expendable too.

And even before he'd started arranging the overt and covert support they would need on Crete, he'd made one other, very short, phone call.

## Sea Harrier 'Tiger Two' and HMS *Invincible*, Ionian Sea

Twenty minutes after Richter's initial call, and with his radar selected to a one hundred mile radius, John Moore noticed a contact that could be the returning Sea Harrier, close to the edge of the screen and heading directly towards the ship.

'Tiger Two, Homer. Transmit for bearing,' Moore requested.

'Homer, this is Tiger Two, transmitting for bearing.'

With no flying operations under way, the Ops Room had retained skeleton manning only, but the Air Picture Compiler (APC) on watch had already allocated the label 'I2' – Interceptor Two – to this return, based on secondary surveillance radar interrogation, and the RDF bearing confirmed that identification.

Moore depressed the transmit switch again. 'Tiger Two is identified. Pigeons one six zero at ninety miles. Flying course will probably be due west, and we have no circuit traffic at present.'

At six hundred and thirty knots, it doesn't take long to cover ninety miles. When the return on his radar set reached twenty-five miles, John Moore made a slight adjustment to Richter's heading and instructed him to descend to two thousand feet, and advise when visual with the ship.

Moore leaned forward and selected an intercom line. 'Flyco, Homer.'

'Flyco.'

'Tiger Two is on recovery just inside twenty-five miles.'

'Thank you, Homer.'

Close liaison between Flyco and the Officer of the Watch on the bridge is essential, for both Sea Harriers and helicopters require very specific wind speed and direction for take-off and landing, and the ship has to manoeuvre quickly and accurately to achieve this.

As soon as he'd deselected the intercom to Homer, Roger Black bent forward over his flying course calculator, an analogue device designed to predict the course and speed the ship would need to achieve in order to generate the correct wind over the deck. He checked his calculations twice, then called through to the bridge. 'Bridge, Flyco. I've got one Sea Harrier to recover in around five minutes. Request flying course of two seven five, speed eighteen.'

'Flyco, Bridge. We're well ahead of you. Turning to starboard.'

Black grinned. Already he could feel the faint vibration that told him the ship was increasing speed, and the bearing on the compass repeater was moving steadily clockwise. Malcolm Mortensen, the young lieutenant Officer of the Watch, was highly efficient and well attuned to the requirements of the Air Department. Black enjoyed working with him.

'Flight Deck, Flyco. Stand by to recover one Sea Harrier, number two spot.' Roger Black's voice boomed out over the tannoy system, and two seconds later he received an acknowledgement from the FDO. Black glanced down at the deck to ensure it was clear and ready, nodded to Commander (Air) who'd just appeared beside him, and began looking out to the east for the returning aircraft.

In the Operations Room the RDF tube sprang to life again.

'Homer, Tiger Two is visual and level at two thousand.'

'Roger, Tiger Two,' John Moore replied. 'When ready, descend to six hundred feet and contact Flyco.'

'Roger, Homer.'

In the descending Sea Harrier, Richter changed his UHF box to Flyco frequency. *Invincible* was now clearly visible, nine miles ahead and slightly to port, the ship's wake a slowly straightening white curve against the aquamarine of the sea.

'Flyco, this is Tiger Two. Visual with Mother, request flying course.'

'Tiger Two, Flyco, roger. Steady on flying course of two seven five, speed eighteen. Wind straight down the deck at twenty-three knots, gusting twenty-eight.'

In Tiger Two, Richter held two thousand feet and aimed straight for the ship, flying directly overhead. As soon as he'd passed, he throttled back slightly and began his descent, simultaneously pulling his Harrier into a hard port turn. He levelled at six hundred feet above the surface of the sea and continued the turn until he was flying parallel with the ship's course and just off to the port side of the *Invincible*'s track.

Six hundred feet, four hundred knots, past the bow. Then throttle back to idle, airbrake out and bank left, hard, into a 4g turn. The speed bled down to three hundred knots, and he heard and felt the growl as the Pegasus hit idle. Then briefly downwind, looking left to check the Flight Deck before pulling the Harrier round into its final approach.

Richter wound on the power again and pulled back on the silver-coloured lever that controlled the nozzle angle, preparing the Harrier for transition to vertical flight. Astern and to port of the ship, steady on west and down to one hundred and fifty feet, he watched his airspeed carefully.

The most critical period during a carrier landing is when the Harrier's weight is transferred from the lift generated by the wings to the delicate balancing act required to support the aircraft solely on the twenty-one thousand six hundred pounds' thrust of the Rolls-Royce Pegasus engine. And the most dangerous phase of this procedure comes when decelerating from about one hundred and twenty knots down to around forty. The pilot must progressively increase engine power as lift from the wings is reduced, but ensure that the nose points into wind and that the angle of attack is within limits. Get this wrong and it bites: the aircraft will flip onto its back and hit the sea in a little under one second. Neither the pilot nor the aircraft will survive.

Richter checked the Flight Deck. As his Harrier approached the stern of the *Invincible*, slightly to port of the ship and still travelling at over one hundred knots, he pushed the nozzles into the braking stop position – fully forward – and then began using the speed trim on top of the throttle to control his approach. This allowed him to adjust the nozzle angle within ten degrees of the vertical position, and enabled him to position the aircraft with remarkable accuracy.

Richter made his final landing checks, lowering the undercarriage and checking the engine temperature to ensure that he had sufficient thrust margin to transition the Harrier into a full hover. He was already 'wet-committed' – to stop the Pegasus overheating, a powerful pump forces water into the engine during a vertical landing. Once started, the pump cannot be switched off, and it runs for only ninety seconds, so Richter had to be on deck in under a minute and a half.

Toggling the speed trim backwards, Richter slowed the Harrier until he'd exactly matched the ship's forward speed. He looked over at the

Flight Deck, watching for the signals from the FDO, eased the control column over to the right, then almost immediately moved it left to stop the Harrier drifting too far.

Richter established his aircraft in the hover, checked the deck markers to ensure he was positioned correctly over two spot, then reduced thrust to start the Harrier in descent. Immediately the aircraft began losing height, Richter increased thrust again. This was essential to avoid the Pegasus engine pop-surging as it ingested its own hot exhaust gases, that were bounced back from the steel deck below.

The Harrier landed, as usual, fairly hard, bouncing a few inches upwards before settling back on the Flight Deck. Richter hauled the power back to zero, rotated the nozzles to the fully aft position, and wound a little power on again to move the aircraft away towards the parking area. This would avoid the heat from the deck melting or exploding the tyres on the Harrier.

The yellow-jacketed ground marshaller directed Richter forward and to starboard into a parking space, and then gave a balled fist gesture to indicate brakes on. Richter waited, engine running, until the ground crew had finished chaining his aircraft to the deck, then methodically switched off all the Harrier's electrical systems and shut down the engine.

A detachable red ladder had already been secured to the side of the Harrier when Richter slid the canopy open, replaced the ejection seat and MDC – Miniature Detonating Cord – pins, and climbed out.

# Chapter 8

In his cabin Richter peeled off his flying overalls and underwear, wrapped a towel around his waist and headed straight for the Two Deck showers. He ran the water hot and long, washing the blood off his hands and forearms. Fortunately most of it had dried before he'd pulled on his flying overalls at the airfield, and what stains there were on the material he'd easily brushed off.

Back in his cabin he dressed in 5J rig – black trousers, white shirt and black pullover – then looked at the plastic bag containing the clothes he'd worn at Matera. Richter was acutely aware that he had attempted to kill Lomas – and he hoped he had succeeded – in full view of a number of hostile witnesses. He had also, without question, left hairs, fibres and who knew what other trace evidence behind at the villa, in the Alfa Romeo and the Agusta helicopter that he had 'borrowed', and in the squadron briefing-room at Brindisi, not to mention the blood-stained Kevlar jacket he'd discarded. And there was absolutely nothing he could do about either the witnesses or this evidence.

But he could at least get rid of the clothes and the knife. What he needed was some kind of a weight that would take that specific evidence straight to the bottom of the Ionian Sea. There was nothing in his cabin that would help, so he locked the door and walked down to Five Deck, opened the bulkhead door and entered the hangar.

As always, it was a scene of coordinated chaos as maintainers worked on the Sea Kings, Merlins and Harriers. The helicopters were both parked and serviced at the aft end of the cavernous structure, where there was a little more width available, and the Harriers at the opposite end. With a full complement of aircraft on this ship, the hangar was always noisy and crowded, so Richter took care not to trip over or walk into anything as he made his way forward.

The squadron Chief Petty Officer who'd headed the team that had flown to Brindisi spotted Richter and immediately walked over to him.

'You made it back, sir,' he said.

'Thanks to your efforts, Chief, I did,' Richter replied, shaking the CPO's slightly grubby hand. 'If you hadn't pre-flighted her it would have been rather a close call. As it was, I had to get quite persuasive to leave that airfield.'

'That would be thirty-millimetre persuasion, as supplied by a pair of Aden cannon?' the Chief asked.

'Got it in one,' Richter said. 'Thank you again. Now, a small favour. I need something reasonably heavy that can also be discarded.'

'Discarded as in dropped over the side?'

'Pretty much, yes.'

Four minutes later Richter was walking back through the hangar, heading aft, clutching a collection of nuts and bolts with stripped threads, and two small pieces of steel plate.

Back in his cabin he laid out his bloody T-shirt on the floor, put the flick-knife and the metal bits and pieces in the middle of it, and rolled it up. Then he wrapped the jeans around the T-shirt and put the whole bundle into the carrier bag. He put his discarded trainers right on top and then tied the neck of the bag securely. Richter made his way down the stairs to the Quarter Deck, walked over to the starboard side guard rail, and dropped the bag straight down. As it hit the water, it floated for a couple of seconds as the air was expelled from it, then sank swiftly beneath the waves.

### Kandíra, south-west Crete

It was late afternoon before the first reporters began to arrive at the cordon surrounding the village, but by early evening it seemed to Inspector Lavat that almost every newspaper in Greece had at least one man standing at the police barrier either asking questions or taking pictures. There were even a couple of stringers for the international press hovering at the edge of the group.

What was unusual was that none of them showed any inclination actually to cross the cordon and enter the village itself. But they did talk persistently to the police officers manning the barriers, and they shouted questions at anybody they saw moving inside the cordon. This story, Lavat knew, was going to be known world-wide within just a few hours.

About an hour after the first of these pressmen had arrived outside the cordon, an elderly Suzuki jeep rattled down the road towards the village and stopped well short of the barriers. The two elderly Cretan men in the car looked about them in some astonishment and confusion for a few moments, then got out of the vehicle and made their way over to one of the police officers manning the barricade.

'What's going on?'

'We have a medical emergency here,' the policeman recited the formula that Gravas had instructed them to memorize. 'No one is allowed to enter or leave Kandíra until further notice.'

'But we live there,' the second man spluttered. 'I want to get home.'

'I'm afraid you can't. One man is already dead, and the doctors fear an epidemic.'

'Dead? Who? Who's dead?'

The policeman shook his head. 'I can't tell you that,' he said.

A reporter for one of the Irakleío papers who had overheard the exchange came trotting over. 'It was a Greek,' he interrupted, 'by the name of Spiros Aristides. One of the forensic people told me.'

'Aristides? But he was fine last night – we saw him in Jakob's. What happened to him?'

Immediately the Cretan said these words, the reporter sensed a story. What he had here was not an eyewitness to the actual death of Spiros Aristides, but almost certainly someone who had seen the Greek just hours before he died. Even if this man had only seen the casualty in the street, he could still use what the Cretan said to embellish the story he was already mentally composing.

He took the man quietly by the arm and led him and his companion across to his own car. He opened the rear door, took out two cans of beer and offered one to each of the old men, then took another for himself.

'A bad business,' he said, 'very bad. Did you know Spiros well?' The use of the dead man's first name was quite deliberate. It implied a familiarity and acquaintance where none existed, and was a device this reporter used frequently. As he had hoped, the elderly man took a swallow of lukewarm beer, then began to talk.

'No, I didn't know him well,' he said. 'We exchanged only a few words if we met in the street, you know, or in Jakob's.'

'Jakob's?'

'The *kafenion* in the middle of the village.'

'And last night?' the reporter prompted.

'Just like any other night, really.' The Cretan indicated his companion and took another mouthful of beer. 'We were there, in Jakob's, just talking and drinking, when Aristides came in. He looked tired and a bit irritated. He had a drink at the bar, then came over and sat down by himself at the table next to us.'

'Did he say anything to you?'

The Cretan shook his head. 'No, he just sat drinking whisky for a while, until Nico arrived.'

'Who's Nico?'

'Nico Aristides. He's a nephew or cousin. I think they do business together.'

The reporter made a mental note to talk to this Nico Aristides as soon as possible. 'And then?'

'They sat together and talked, you know.'

'What about?'

The Cretan glanced at his companion, as if for reassurance, before replying. 'I don't know if we should tell you,' he said. 'You see, Spiros wasn't talking to us. We just happened to be sitting at the next table. But we did overhear them talking about some aircraft.'

The reporter didn't even blink. 'Oh, yes,' he said, lying with the aplomb and confidence that come only after years of newspaper work, 'I heard something about that, too. What did they say?'

The reporter's apparent prior knowledge reassured the naturally suspicious old man. 'Well, you know that Spiros was a diver?' The reporter nodded encouragement and the Cretan continued. 'He was a diver, but he hadn't got a permit – you know, from the Department of Antiquities – so he never said to anyone where he'd gone diving. We couldn't help hearing him say how he'd found some kind of a small aircraft, but he didn't say where it was. It had been there a long time, though, so it wasn't a recent crash.' The reporter nodded again, and the man continued. 'The water was quite deep so he'd had to make several dives to search it.'

'Did he say what he'd found there?'

The Cretan shook his head. 'No, but he thought the aircraft had been shot down. It hadn't just crashed, you see.'

'Did he say anything else you can remember?'

'No, nothing, really. The only other thing was the piece of paper.'

'What paper?'

'Spiros passed Nico a piece of paper with numbers on it. He said it was the registration of the crashed aircraft. Just a short while after that they both left Jakob's, and Nico dropped the paper when he stood up to go. After they'd left, I picked it up.'

'Do you still have it?' the reporter asked eagerly.

The Cretan nodded, fished around in his jacket pocket, pulled out a torn and crumpled slip and handed it over.

'Can I keep this?' the reporter asked, looking at the single letter and three numbers written on it in thick pencil.

The Cretan nodded. 'It's no use to me,' he muttered.

The reporter extracted another four cans of beer and handed them over. 'Thank you,' he said. 'You've been very helpful. Could I take your names for my newspaper?'

'No, no,' the Cretan said firmly. 'I don't want my name in the paper.'

No matter, the reporter thought to himself. He already had enough to scoop his rivals, and the story about a wrecked aircraft could become central to the mystery of Aristides's sudden death. Maybe whatever had killed the Greek had been found on that aircraft. The possibilities were endless.

And he could quote the elderly Cretan as being a 'close friend' of Spiros Aristides. After all, the Greek himself wasn't around to dispute it.

## HMS *Invincible*, Ionian Sea

'Looking forward to getting back to your Secret Squirrel outfit, Spook?' In the dining room located across the corridor from the Wardroom on

Five Deck, Roger Black grinned at Paul Richter over the remains of his dinner.

With the exception of the Captain and Commander (Air), nobody else on the ship actually knew what Richter did or how he was normally employed, but a rumour had quickly spread that he worked for one of the deniable outfits – MI5 or SIS – and the nickname 'Spook' had been attributed to him almost as soon as he had arrived on board.

Richter looked back at him, speared a final carrot, then put down his knife and fork and shook his head. 'You mean, am I looking forward to traffic fumes and miserable weather, and the pointless paper-shuffling that passes for my normal employment in London? Meanwhile you and the rest of the WAFUs can get comprehensively laid in every brothel in Athens and Piraeus, once we've finished whatever it is we're supposed to be doing on Crete.'

'WAFU' is a less than complimentary term used by non-naval aviators to describe aircrew officers: it stands for 'Wanked-out And Fucking Useless'.

Richter paused and looked up and down the long table at the grinning faces of most of 800 Squadron. 'No, not really,' he said. 'The only thing that keeps me going is the thought that at least some of you will get the clap or worse, and have a hell of a time explaining it to your wives when you get back to Yeovilton.'

Black shook his head. 'I'll have you know we're all officers and gentlemen.'

'And that means what, exactly?'

'That we never pay for it. The Captain's Secretary has assured me that there'll be tons of available crumpet at the cockers-pee in Athens – if we ever get there, that is – and all we'll have to do is decide what shape and colour we want and take it from there.'

'Dream on, Blackie,' Richter replied to the gathering at large. 'He said the same thing about the cocktail party in Trieste, remember, and the youngest woman there was fifty-five if she was a day, and had a face like a Doberman – all nose, teeth and attitude.'

'Well, you should know best. Somebody told me you left with her.'

'That,' Richter said, 'is a lie. I retired to bed alone, with an improving book, and well before midnight.'

'And we believe that, of course.' Black smiled. 'Anyway, all kidding aside, when are you off?'

'The day after we dock at Piraeus, probably. I'll hop a flight from Athens to London and be back at work the next day, I suppose.'

'No long weekend, then?'

'Well, maybe.' Richter grinned. 'I'm in no hurry, no hurry at all. And I'll probably need a day or two to recover from the rigours of about four hours in a 737, enduring that new British Airways crap-class seating.'

'Well, now that you've flown your last sortie with us, and managed to return our Harrier more or less in one piece,' Lieutenant Commander David Richards, the 800 Squadron Commanding Officer, spoke up, 'I would just like to say that it's been good having you here as a temporary squadron member.'

'Thanks,' Richter said, sincerely. 'I've really enjoyed being back in the saddle, even for just a few days. Maybe I'll be able to do it again some time.'

'Hang on,' Richards said, frowning. 'We didn't enjoy having you here as much as that.'

## Arlington, Virginia

Mike Murphy was known to his few friends as 'The Double M'. His given name was actually George, but ever since high school he'd been called Mike because, apart from anything else, he didn't really look like a George. And the reason he had few friends, he told anyone who asked, was because of his job.

He'd joined the Central Intelligence Agency straight out of college and immediately gravitated into the Directorate of Operations, more commonly known throughout the Company as Clandestine Services, and he'd spent the next fifteen years working pretty much everywhere except mainland America. Then he'd abruptly retired, ostensibly on the grounds of ill health. In fact, he'd received what amounted to a better offer.

Mike Murphy's personal specialization was cleaning things up – he sometimes even referred to himself as 'The Cleaner' – and the offer he'd received was to continue working for the Agency but as a freelance operator under contract, at a substantially increased salary and with a complete absence of the bullshit invariably associated with any organization funded by any government. The downside was that, as a contract employee, the CIA could legitimately disavow him if the manure impacted the air-conditioner. If Murphy made a cock-up, he had to face the consequences without the protecting hand of the US Government to help him. Even so, it hadn't been a difficult decision.

The call from John Nicholson had reached him as he was heading out to do some grocery shopping, one of the more boring tasks faced by any bachelor, and he'd happily postponed that one when he heard what Nicholson had to say. Ninety minutes later he was walking down the hallway of the Arlington safe house, instructions memorized.

He was going to return to his apartment in Falls Church to pack what he needed before getting a cab to Baltimore to catch a transatlantic flight. Nicholson had calculated that Murphy would arrive in Crete about twelve hours after Krywald, Stein and Elias, which was just about right.

But before he went home, he had an extra job to do for Nicholson, immediately.

## Number Two Briefing-Room, HMS *Invincible*, Sea of Crete

The Operations Officer stood waiting for them at the front of the room, a clipboard of notes in his hand. Before him, in tiered seating that ascended towards the rear, sat most of 814 Naval Air Squadron. Some looked interested, some looked bored, but most just looked irritated. Their run ashore in Athens had been keenly anticipated.

'Commander (Air),' the Operations Officer announced as the heavily built, bearded officer walked into the briefing-room and down the steps to the front row. Everyone not already standing stood up, then relaxed back into their seats as the Commander himself sat down.

'Carry on, please.'

'Thank you, sir. Gentlemen, this will be an outline briefing only, as we have yet to receive detailed tasking instructions, and we have no confirmed start time for any flying operations. For this reason I have dispensed for the moment with the meteorological briefing and other detailed information on the area. You will be briefed on terrain, high ground, safety altitudes, inbound and outbound routes, operational frequencies and so on, before your individual sorties.

'This briefing will cover five topics: ship's position, other forces present in the area, operational background, anticipated tasking and forecast operation timing.' He picked up a pointer and turned to the bulkhead behind him, where a large map of the island of Crete was displayed.

'*First*: ship's position. *Invincible* is currently here,' he said, pointing to a location about ten miles to the north east of Andikíthira, 'and we're making our way to here,' he pointed again, 'just north of Réthymno, which is more or less the mid-point of the island. The ship will be holding clear of the civilian ferry routes into and out of Irakleío and Chaniá, but we will only be about thirty miles from the Nikos Kazantzakis International Airport here at Irakleío and around the same distance from the island's second airport on the Akrotíri Peninsula. We will remain in the same general area until further notice.

'*Second*: other forces. As some of you will be aware, the airport at Akrotíri has three different functions. First, it's the civilian airport serving Chaniá and the western end of the island of Crete. Second, it's the home of the Hellenic Air Force's 115th Combat Wing, which operates two squadrons of A-7H Corsairs. It's also home to the US Naval Support Facility of Soúda Bay, with quite a large presence – over one thousand people altogether. The primary function of the base is to provide support to US and allied ships and aircraft operating in the eastern Mediterranean.

'We're not concerned about the surface vessels they may have, because we are unlikely to become involved with them, but you should be aware of the range of air assets they can deploy. Currently, the Americans have based their Fleet Air Reconnaissance Squadron Two Detachment at Soúda, flying two EP-3E Aries II aircraft. Their Patrol and Reconnaissance Squadron Five, operating P-3C Orions, and Detachment One of the 95th Reconnaissance Squadron, flying RC-135s, are also based there. Additionally, there's an Air Mobility Command weekly trooping flight from the Naval Air Station at Norfolk, Virginia, to Soúda Bay and back again for personnel and light stores. What you will have noticed immediately is that neither the Greeks nor the

Americans operate a dedicated helicopter squadron out of Soúda, which is where we come in.

'*Third*: operational background. We now have some further information about the medical emergency on the island. Apparently the disease broke out in a small village called Kandíra, which is here on the southwest coast of Crete.' He pointed to a location on the coast about halfway between the small town of Soúgia and the equally small settlement of Agía Rouméli, and south of the peak of Psiláfi, then turned back to face his audience.

'The latest information we have is that one person is confirmed as having died, and we now have unsubstantiated reports of a second death. What worries the Cretans is that the man whose death began this emergency was reported as being alive and apparently healthy late on Monday evening, yet dead by the following morning.

'The cause of his death is still unknown, but the Cretan Health Ministry believes, based upon the initial report from the doctor who examined the victim, that he could have been attacked by a very fast-acting virus, possibly a filovirus like Ebola. For those of you who don't know, Ebola is a very rare virus previously only encountered in the Congo. It is highly contagious and normally fatal.

'The only good news is that this outbreak has occurred in one of the smallest villages on Crete, which is perhaps why the death toll up until now is so low. Kandíra has a population of under five hundred: if this had happened in Irakleío, Chaniá or Réthymno, and if the causative agent is indeed some kind of virus, there could already be dozens dead and hundreds infected.

'The consequences of an Ebola-type epidemic anywhere are horrific to contemplate, so the Cretan authorities are well aware that swift and decisive action is necessary to contain the situation. They have therefore requested the assistance of the Centers for Disease Control at Atlanta in Georgia, and have already established a police cordon around the village of Kandíra. Nobody is to be allowed into or out of the village until the CDC personnel arrive to assess the situation.

'We have been informed that the Cretan authorities have begun transporting tents, bedding, clothing, latrines and washing facilities, cooking equipment and provisions to Kandíra. These are obviously for the benefit of the police and other personnel assisting in this operation.

'Some police officers are already inside the barricade because they had been originally tasked with investigating the first death, so were actually there in the village itself when the doctor realized that they were facing a possible epidemic. Because they are possibly contaminated by the pathogen, they will have to remain within the cordoned-off area for the foreseeable future.'

The Operations Officer – Ops One in the parlance of the Royal Navy – turned back to the map and pointed again at Kandíra.

'*Fourth*: anticipated tasking. The biggest problem the Cretans have in this emergency is access,' he said, tracing a route on the map.

'The only road to Kandíra runs through Soúgia, and I understand that this road here is almost literally a cart track, heavily rutted and barely wide enough for a large van to pass. From Soúgia the road winds north up a fairly narrow valley to the west of Lefká Óri before dropping down to Néa Roúmata. From there, vehicles have to continue north-east through Chiliaró and Alikanos before they reach the main east-west coast road at Chaniá. There are other routes out of Soúgia, but that is probably the fastest and most direct, which is why moving personnel and equipment into and out of Kandíra is inevitably going to be slow and difficult. Quite apart from the mountainous terrain, most of those roads are narrow and twisting, and in many places in a poor state of repair.

'That is the principal reason why we have been called in. Driving to Kandíra from the closest large town, which is Chaniá, could take two hours or more, but a helicopter can cover the same distance in a few minutes. The Cretans will continue to use road vehicles to transport the heavier items to Kandíra, so we will probably be asked to move only personnel or small pieces of equipment required urgently.'

The door into the briefing-room stood open, not least because the room was actually too small to accommodate all the squadron personnel, and several were listening intently from the outside corridor. Ops One heard a slight commotion and looked up to see Ops Three pushing his way down through the crush. He finally reached the lowest tier and handed Ops One a flimsy.

'Sorry to interrupt, sir, but we've just received this tasking signal.'

'Thanks.' Ops One scanned the page rapidly, nodded and looked up at the clock on the bulkhead. 'Right, this more or less confirms what I've been saying. Our first task is to collect a civilian specialist from the CDC. He will be arriving at Irakleío Airport early tomorrow morning and will need to be flown immediately to Kandíra. There will be a dedicated briefing for the crew involved at zero six-thirty tomorrow.

'That really covers topic *five* as well – collection of this CDC official will mark the start of our involvement in this matter.

'Finally, to facilitate HDS operations, I will be sending one of the Ops staff ashore to Kandíra to liaise with the CDC people there on the ground. He will have a radio, and will relay requests for transport as and when required. He will also be able to talk to arriving and departing helicopters, and crews should establish two-way communications with him as soon as their aircraft have left the visual circuit and once cleared by Soúda Bay Tower. Helicopters will have callsigns allocated by Mother, but we will probably use the aircraft side-numbers to keep things simple.

'The Ops staff on the ground will use the callsign "Fob Watch", derived from "FOB" –"Forward Operating Base".' Ops One looked round as if expecting applause, and was rewarded with a handful of polite smiles. He paused and looked down at Commander (Air). 'Have you anything to add, sir?'

The Commander stood up and turned to face the assembled aircrew.

'Thank you, Ops One, only two things. First, I need hardly remind you all that this is not an exercise. This is a real operation involving real people quite probably facing mortal danger. I want no mistakes from anyone, and I expect you to operate with all the skill and professionalism you've shown in the past.

'Second, as you're aware from what Ops One has already said, this epidemic apparently involves some kind of fast-acting virus or other pathogen, so any direct contact with it could prove fatal. But I should emphasize that there is no suggestion that any of *Invincible*'s aircraft will be required to do anything other than ferry personnel and equipment to or from a landing site well outside the cordoned-off area around this village.

'As things stand, therefore, neither I nor the Senior Medical Officer see any necessity for aircrew to wear AGRs or NBCD suits, but obviously we will review the situation as this operation progresses.'

That was a small relief. AGRs – anti-gas respirators – are somewhat cumbersome whole-face gas masks designed to prevent the wearer from inhaling chemical or biological agents. Uncomfortable enough to wear in a ground environment, they are very awkward in an aircraft, making the hearing of radio messages and transmitting responses – both vital to all aircrew – very difficult and prone to misinterpretation. NBCD suits, whose initials stand for Nuclear, Biological and Chemical Defence, are one-piece suits covering the whole body apart from the face, where the AGR would be worn, and the hands, which would be gloved.

'However,' Commander (Air) continued, 'any aircrew who start feeling unwell after a flight to Kandíra are to report to the Sick Bay immediately. That is all.'

'Thank you, sir. Briefing complete.'

Paul Richter, who'd been leaning against the door jamb for the entire session, nodded briefly to himself and walked away. Rotary wing flying only, and basically HDS – Helicopter Delivery Service – operations at that, so just a glorified taxi service. He decided to visit the ship's library and find another couple of books to read, because it now looked like being a long week, with almost exactly nothing for him to do.

It would be a long week – Richter was right about that – but in fact he would have plenty to do.

### George Washington Memorial Parkway, Virginia

The briefing Dave McCready had given in the safe house in Arlington had been his first. As an inexperienced agent, he'd been flattered when John Nicholson had summoned him to his office and told him what he wanted done, and he'd taken care to follow his superior's instructions to the letter.

McCready had only been with the Agency for a couple of years and had spent most of that time working in the Intelligence Directorate, but outside Langley at one of the numerous satellite establishments the Company maintained in Virginia. He wasn't to know that Nicholson had picked him primarily because he was quite certain that he had never met Elias, Stein or Krywald. All he'd needed was a buffer, some-body who could deliver the necessary briefing to the recovery team, but who would be unknown to all the members of that team, and McCready had seemed ideal.

Once the three agents had left the safe house, Nicholson had said nothing about his performance, but simply told McCready to go out and get himself some lunch and to return to the house for a debrief at three-thirty in the afternoon. That, McCready had guessed, meant that he had been inadequate in some way. The Director was not known as a man who lavished praise on anyone – his direct subordinates were more usually the recipients of caustic tongue-lashings, if canteen gossip was to be believed – and he'd been somewhat apprehensive when he'd walked back into the building.

But to his surprise and relief Nicholson had declared himself more than satisfied: in fact, his comments to McCready had bordered on the fulsome. As he headed north-west back towards Langley along the George Washington Memorial Parkway out of Arlington, the Potomac glinting in the sun over to his right, McCready wondered idly if Nicholson might be grooming him for some kind of advancement, or maybe a different job within the Agency.

If he hadn't been quite so preoccupied, McCready might have registered the old and battered tan Chevrolet following him, three cars behind his two-year-old Ford compact. If he'd been a more experienced agent, he might also have noticed that the same car had been parked about seventy yards down the street from the safe house, and that the driver had eased it out of the parking space seconds after McCready had accelerated away.

As it was, he didn't register anything until he was a couple of miles short of the off-ramp for State Route 123. And when he did finally notice the Chevrolet, it was too late for him to do much about it.

McCready was in one of the centre lanes, passing a line of trucks, when the tan car accelerated and moved into a position directly behind his Ford. As McCready reached the cab of the leading truck, the Chevrolet driver accelerated hard, swinging his car to the left, apparently trying to overtake the Ford and making a pretty bad job of it.

'What the hell?' McCready muttered to himself, as the image of the Chevrolet filled his door mirror. Instinctively, he steered a little to the right, giving the other driver more room, but supremely conscious of the forty-ton eighteen-wheeler travelling at sixty miles an hour eight feet to his right.

It didn't help. The bigger car moved over with him, the driver apparently having difficulty controlling the vehicle and, as the two cars cleared the front of the truck, they touched, the Chevrolet's bumper hitting the left rear of the Ford and forcing McCready further over to the right.

As his Ford lurched forwards and sideways under the impact, McCready suddenly realized that the man in the Chevy might be something more than just another incompetent road-user. He touched his brake pedal, thought better of it and pressed the accelerator instead. If he could just get ahead of the Chevrolet and clear of the Mack truck he might just make it.

The blare of the truck's horn momentarily deafened him, but McCready was concentrating only on the tan Chevy. Time seemed almost to stop, and the Ford's pick-up seemed slower than normal, the speedometer needle moving with treacle sloth around the dial. The bigger car dropped back slightly, then accelerated again, its big old V8 engine giving it a degree of mid-range acceleration denied the Ford. The Chevrolet smashed into the left rear of the compact car, pushing it sideways and directly into the path of the truck.

Now McCready braked hard, ramming his foot onto the pedal, and wrenched the steering wheel to the left, but the bigger car had the weight and the speed, and the Ford swung right, directly across the inside lane, right-hand wheels lifting. Tyres howled in protest, blue smoke swirling as rubber was torn off them.

The truck's horn blared again, then McCready heard the hiss of the air brakes as the trucker hit the pedal. As his car lurched directly in front of the eighteen-wheeler, McCready looked with horrified fascination through the passenger side window, and saw nothing but a huge vertical radiator bearing the word 'Mack'.

Half a second later the truck hit the Ford, its massive steel bumper smashing into the right rear of the car. Immediately, the Ford swung hard to the right, broadside-on to the front of the truck.

In the car, McCready's body lurched to the right, then left, crashing into the driver's door, his seat belt tensioning automatically and the airbags deploying. In a normal crash, that might have been enough to save him, but this was far from normal.

The airbag forced McCready back into his seat, tearing his hands from the steering wheel and turning him into a helpless passenger as the Ford lurched under the colossal impact of the forty-ton weight of the Mack truck. For maybe half a second McCready thought that the Ford would stay upright as the truck's speed fell away, but then he felt the unmistakable lurch as the car was lifted onto its left-side wheels and it slammed over, rolling onto its roof.

The last image that registered in McCready's brain was the grooved tread of an immense tyre, inches from his door, just before the left-hand front wheel of the Mack lifted up and over the Ford's chassis and crushed the vehicle beyond recognition. The momentum of the massive truck bounced the left rear wheels of the cab over the wreck, finishing the job the front wheel had started, and when the Mack finally stopped the Ford was just a mess of twisted steel and leaking fluids.

Murphy pulled the Chevrolet onto the shoulder a hundred yards or so beyond the wreck and stopped the car. He took a pair of compact binoculars from his pocket, turned round in the seat and looked carefully back up the Parkway. Cars and trucks had stopped at all angles, hazard lights flashing, their drivers staring in horror at what was left of the Ford, which lay, like some obscene roadkill, half-under the trailer of the Mack. Already people were milling around, talking on mobiles, pointing at the car. One guy was even taking pictures.

He couldn't see clearly, but Murphy was as certain as he could be that McCready was dead. The left wheels of the Mack's cab seemed to have gone right over the passenger section of the Ford and the whole of the bodywork looked as if it had been flattened. Even if he hadn't been killed outright, McCready would probably be dead long before the fire service and paramedics could cut him out.

Murphy tossed the binoculars onto the passenger seat, pulled the shift into 'drive' and eased the Chevrolet down the road. As he accelerated away, he switched on the radio, found an easy-listening station and tapped his fingers on the steering wheel rim in time to the music as he drove. Faintly in the distance he heard the wail of a police siren and automatically checked his speed, then smiled slightly. His 'extra' job for Nicholson had gone without a hitch, as he'd expected.

McCready's death would be classed as just another unfortunate traffic accident on a busy stretch of road. It didn't really matter if anyone had noticed the manoeuvres he'd performed in the Chevy. The police would likely assume the driver had been drunk or on drugs, and would probably disbelieve any witness who claimed that the driver's actions – actions which Murphy had been specially trained to execute – were deliberate.

He'd stolen the car in Tysons Corner late that morning, and he was going to dump the vehicle once he got clear of the Parkway. Even if somebody had been able to note down the plate number, and the police tracked it, there would be nothing in the car to provide a link to Murphy. He'd worn thin rubber gloves when he'd jacked the Chevy, and he'd leave them in the car when he walked away from it. In the glove box was a small incendiary charge, slim enough to slide into the fuel tank, fitted with a time switch. Once that blew, any forensic evidence he'd left would burn up along with the car.

Murphy pulled off the Parkway onto State Route 123, heading for McLean. He'd dump the Chevy there and catch a cab back to Falls Church. He'd already set the timer on the incendiary charge for ninety minutes, so all he had to do was flip the switch and slide it into the gas tank as he left the car. He glanced at his watch: if he didn't meet any problems, he'd be halfway to the airport at Baltimore before it blew.

## Irakleío, Crete

It had taken the editor less than twenty minutes to be persuaded to put the story of the mysterious epidemic at Kandíra on the front page of the following day's paper.

The reporter had taken the few crumbs he had extracted from the policemen guarding the barricades and from the two village men he had interviewed, and he had concocted a story that sounded dramatic in almost every way. It was dramatic in what it said, which was actually very little, and in what it implied, which encompassed almost every possible permutation of the 'Unknown Pathogen Kills Villager' angle. And most of all in the heading, which screamed the story across the top of the front page: *Biological warfare in the Mediterranean. Diver killed by deadly germ found on seabed.*


## Arlington, Virginia

Nicholson was just about to leave the safe house when his mobile phone rang.

'Yes?'

Murphy didn't bother introducing himself, because he had no idea who might be listening in to either his or Nicholson's mobile. The fact that both numbers were unlisted provided some security, but these days you never knew. It was better to be circumspect. 'That matter we discussed,' he said. 'It's been taken care of.'

'Good,' Nicholson replied, and ended the call.

He put the mobile down on the desk, reached inside his jacket pocket and extracted a slim black diary. All the entries in it were entirely innocent and innocuous, apart from those on a single page at the back. That contained seven lines of what appeared to be code.

In fact, the lines looked very much like the product of a single or double transposition cipher, created by nothing more complicated than two memorized key-words and a knowledge of how to encode and decode a message. One of the characteristics of a message enciphered in this way is that all the groups are the same length, usually four, five or six letters. The lines in Nicholson's diary were all five-letter groups:

```
MVCJV     HWMZU
HFWGT     JSWLY
RTCGU     CHSKG
BQTFR     NSKGP
ERIDG     GFRDY
SQEXZ     LSJVR
KEYTK     QXPFG
```

The lines *were* a form of code, but Nicholson hadn't used any kind of transposition cipher, or indeed any enciphering method at all, though he'd deliberately arranged the letters to look as if he had. He was fairly certain that his diary, which he kept with him at all times, was safe enough, but he hadn't wanted a clear written record linking him to any of the people involved in the current operation. But as a methodical man, he had wanted to record their names for his own benefit, hence the code.

If any security organization did get possession of the book, he imagined that they would spend tens of hours trying to make some kind of sense of what he'd written, because his 'code' was logically uncrackable by conventional cryptanalysis for one very simple reason: he had picked all the letters entirely at random, with the exception of the first and third letters of the groups in the left-hand column. With that knowledge, the decode was childishly simple; the 'code' was simply a list of seven names – McCready, Hawkins, Richards, Butcher, Elias, Stein and Krywald.

Nicholson opened the diary at the note page and laid it flat on the desk in front of him. He took a black Mont Blanc fountain pen from his pocket and a ruler from the desk drawer and drew a single line through the first two letter groups. McCready was dead, and so the entry was no longer required.

'One down, six to go,' Nicholson muttered, with a slight smile of satisfaction. He closed the diary, then opened it again and added a further, eighth, group:

$$M Q R D F \qquad H D G T N$$

He would, he promised himself, deal with Murphy personally once the steel case had been retrieved and delivered to Langley. Nicholson nodded, slipped the diary back in his pocket and left the room.

### HMS *Invincible*, Sea of Crete

Paul Richter leaned against the aft guardrail on the Quarter Deck in the darkness of late evening and looked back at the wake stretching out behind the ship as *Invincible* ploughed through the Sea of Crete.

Astern and a mile or so to port he could see the lights of the Royal Fleet Auxiliary tanker, and behind that one of the frigates, both ships keeping station on the carrier. And a long way out to starboard, Richter could just make out a line of brightness, which marked the location of, he guessed, the town of Chaniá on the north coast of Crete.

Beyond the wake, above that faint trail of phosphorescence that stretched arrow-straight into the darkness, the sky was alive with stars. Without the constant glare of the lights of London to dim their glory, they appeared brighter and more numerous to Richter, beyond counting or comprehension. He craned his neck to look up at them, turning left and right as he picked out the constellations and individual stars. Orion, with Sirius blazing down to the apparent south-west. The Great Bear. Leo. Dracos. Some he knew, most he didn't, but all were glorious to behold.

He looked down again at the endless wake and thought back to the conversation over dinner, the light-hearted bantering that overlaid the total professionalism of the Air Group. Was he looking forward to getting back to London, back to the covert life that he'd been coerced into living? No – no way. But even as that thought crossed his mind, he realized again that his time here on the *Invincible* had been what amounted to a holiday, a brief return to a former life, and he also remembered why he'd left the Navy in the first place.

A cruise like this was the cream. Flying a state of the art jet fighter in wonderful weather, playing war games, relaxing in the Wardroom – just the cream. He thought back to the twenty or so years he'd spent as a squadron pilot, first on Wessex and Sea King helicopters and then flying Sea Harriers, some of it on 800 Naval Air Squadron under an older, less congenial management, and he remembered the other times, the other duties, that were less pleasant. The secondary duties, the divisional work, implementing change for the sake of change, and those pointless little jobs that senior officers always seemed to think were essential and urgent, but which were usually little more than a comprehensive waste of time and effort.

And then there was Richter's big problem, of course. When he'd first been appointed to 800 Naval Air Squadron the CO had disliked him on sight. Richter could have handled that – nobody said you had to like the people you worked with – but he had never been able to tolerate fools, and the 800 Commanding Officer had definitely been a fool, one of a small number of naval officers somehow promoted by the system into a position well above their abilities.

Richter's mistake had been to point out to him, in unequivocally clear language, that he was an illiterate idiot. The mistake was not what Richter had actually said – that was neither more nor less than the undeniable truth – but that he had said it with a large and attentive audience of senior officers present. An audience that neither forgot nor forgave his blatant insubordination, and which had ensured Richter's naval career was stymied from that moment on.

Richter shrugged at the memory. It was water – even a flood – under the bridge now, he thought, clutching at a convenient cliché. Look on the bright side. He was still in employment, which a lot of ex-service fixed-wing aviators weren't, there being very few openings for former Harrier pilots in the world of civil aviation, and he was getting paid reasonably well, too.

And, despite the fact that he didn't like his superior, Richard Simpson, and had frequent disagreements with him, he did actually enjoy what he did. The fact that he occasionally got shot at when he wasn't submerging amid terminal boredom in a sea of paperwork and files, did lend a certain frisson of excitement to his work. In fact, Richter realized that, despite his earlier denial, he was actually looking forward to getting back to his small and rather grubby office in Hammersmith. And, even, back to his piles of files.

He shivered slightly as a cool breeze lanced off the sea and across the Quarter Deck. Red Sea Rig – open-necked shirt with his lieutenant commander rank badges on the epaulettes, black trousers and a borrowed squadron cummerbund – was comfortable enough, but once the temperature dropped the wearer certainly knew about it.

Richter glanced out into the darkness again, casting an eye over the stars and the steadily unrolling wake, then looked down at the luminous dial of his watch. Just time for one final coffee in the Wardroom, and then bed.

'Good night,' he called out to the anonymous figure standing at the aft port side of the Quarter Deck.

'Good night, sir,' the Lifebuoy Sentry murmured, and watched as Richter walked forward to the starboard-side door, leading through to the Wardroom on Five Deck. As soon as the door had closed behind him, the Sentry reached into his trouser pocket, extracted a packet of cigarettes and lit one. He was gasping for it – he'd thought that WAFU two and a half would never bloody well leave the Quarter Deck.

# Chapter 9

**Wednesday**
**Outside Kandíra, south-west Crete**

They spotted the helicopter long before they heard it. A dark grey speck against the blue sky over the two and a half thousand metre peak of Lefká Óri, it grew rapidly in size as it descended the southern slope of the great mountain. Within seconds, it seemed, it was right above them, rotors clattering, jet engines roaring. The pilot swung the Merlin around in a tight left-hand turn, to point the aircraft's nose into wind, then settled the big helicopter on the ground.

Dust rose all around it, then began to settle again as the pilot dropped the collective and throttled back the engines. The door on the right-hand side of the aircraft slid open and the aircrewman kicked down a set of folding steps. A slim middle-aged man descended them uncertainly. He was carrying two small bags, and looked around before walking over to the group of watching men. Behind him, two aircrewmen began manoeuvring the first of two large cases out of the rear compartment of the aircraft.

Three minutes later the dust rose again, as the Merlin lifted into the air and wheeled around to the north-east on a direct track over Lefká Óri back to the *Invincible*.

**Kandíra, south-west Crete**

The accommodation wasn't ideal by any means, but it was better than nothing.

Three large tents had been erected within the cordon late the previous afternoon. One held a bottled-gas-powered cooking range and sufficient provisions for about a week, though everyone hoped they'd be out of there long before that. The second had a dozen camp beds and the third a couple of chemical toilets, four sinks and two showers. Hot water was supplied by an on-demand gas heater fed by three one-thousand-litre plastic water tanks.

Well away from these three tents was a single, much smaller, one. It held only the two large chest freezers that had been requested in the CDC response to the Cretan Ministry of Health. These were powered by a Honda petrol generator sitting outside the tent in a sand-bagged enclosure, the noise of which provided a constant throbbing background hum.

Inspector Lavat, after consulting the doctor, had insisted that everyone who had been in recent contact with Spiros Aristides or his house should take a shower as soon as the system was working. All their clothes were then placed in the same cordoned-off pile in the street, which already held Dr Gravas's and his assistants' white coveralls, as well as Lavat's discarded uniform. Only when the last person had emerged from the shower tent, wearing fresh clothing brought in from outside the village, did Gravas begin to relax.

They heard the helicopter arrive, like everyone else in Kandíra, so Lavat and Gravas were waiting as the sandy-haired civilian walked up and stopped by the cordon. Behind him, four police officers struggled under the weight of the cases.

'I'm Tyler Hardin, from the Centers for Disease Control. Does anybody here speak English?'

'Welcome, Mr Hardin.' Lavat extended a hand and gestured for the police officer to let the American through. 'I'm Inspector Lavat of the Crete police force and this is Dr Gravas. We both speak English. Are you by yourself?'

'Pleased to meet you,' Hardin said, shaking hands with both. 'Yes, I'm just the advance guard. The rest of my team will be arriving soon with more equipment. Dr Gravas, you're the person who alerted us, I think?'

'That's correct. I've been hoping ever since that I didn't over-react, but I've never seen anyone die like this man Aristides. And,' Gravas added, 'there has been a second death, superficially identical.'

'Another one?' Hardin asked. 'What do you mean "superficially identical"?'

'I mean it looks as if this second man, called Nico Aristides – he was a nephew of the first victim and had been drinking with him in the local bar the previous evening – was killed by the same pathogen. But all we did was to enter his apartment and view his body from a distance. I made no examination of the corpse, and we have also had the apartment sealed ever since, just like the other property.'

Hardin nodded in satisfaction, and the three began walking towards the tents erected at the periphery of the village.

'OK, I see you've got a cordon in place but what restrictions have you imposed?'

'Everyone who was already here in the village when I examined the first body has been kept inside the cordon, including the police officers and my assistants. Except for yourself, nobody has been allowed into or out of the village since.

'All those who had any recent physical contact with either of the properties where the bodies were found have been identified and we've tried to decontaminate them with showers and changes of clothing. And, as I said, the properties themselves have been sealed.'

'Good. That's very good,' Hardin said. 'With the limited facilities you've got available here I can't think how you could have done better.'

Gravas smiled and led the way into the first tent. 'We can offer you some coffee? Or perhaps you'd like something to eat?'

'Coffee, please,' Hardin replied, 'but no food, thank you. I seem to have eaten my way non-stop across the Atlantic.'

Lavat asked the woman serving behind the counter – one of several villagers offering to help the investigation – for three cups of coffee, then the men sat down together at a table.

'Right,' Hardin said. 'We received your initial report at the CDC, but I'd appreciate it if you could just run the sequence of events by me again, in case there's anything I missed or you overlooked. Your English, by the way, is excellent.'

'Thank you,' Gravas said. 'I had the benefit of two years at Oxford. Now, what happened here was simple enough. Yesterday morning a village woman heard a moan of pain coming from Spiros Aristides's house. She gathered up a friend, and a few minutes later they entered the house and made their way upstairs. Looking into the bedroom, they saw Aristides lying fully clothed on his bed but completely covered in blood. Assuming he had been hacked to death, they ran out of the house and called the police.'

Lavat took up the story.

'I was then summoned from Chaniá and arrived here about an hour and a half after the alarm was raised. I set up a cordon around the house, then went inside myself. I looked into the bedroom and saw exactly what the women had reported. I touched nothing in the room, just closed the door and waited for the forensic specialists to arrive.'

'A question,' Hardin interrupted. 'You said that one of the women heard a moan of pain, but when they entered the house the man was already dead. What was the interval in between?'

Gravas looked at Lavat.

'No more than ten minutes,' he said. 'She headed from Aristides's house to the square, found the other woman almost immediately, and they went straight back.'

'What, exactly, did she hear? Was it just moaning, or did she hear any words?'

Lavat consulted his notebook. 'She said it was a moan, but she's here, close by, so I can go and ask her again, if you think it's important.'

Hardin nodded. 'It could be vital, Inspector,' he said.

As Lavat walked out of the tent, Gravas looked questioningly at the American. 'Why is what the dying Greek said important?'

'What he actually said is of no importance at all. All I really want to know is whether he was still capable of speech. That could be a vital indicator.'

Gravas was still looking puzzled when Lavat walked back into the tent. 'She's not absolutely certain,' he began. 'She thinks he called out "Help me" in Greek, but Aristides's voice was very distorted, so she might just have interpreted some sounds as speech. She can't be certain he actually said anything, but she definitely heard him making noises – he was in distress.'

Hardin nodded. 'OK, so the victim was able to emit sounds, speech or otherwise, up until about ten minutes before he finally died. That's interesting. What happened next?'

'I arrived some time after the police,' Gravas intervened, 'because I was over in Irakleío when I was alerted. The Inspector here explained what had happened. I usually enter the scene of a crime first by myself

to make an initial survey and to confirm that the victim is actually dead
– being a medical doctor as well as a forensic scientist – before bringing
in any of my team members. In this case, I entered the bedroom and saw
the body exactly as Inspector Lavat has described. From my initial
inspection I was certain that he had been butchered, probably with a
knife or an axe. His corpse appeared almost drained of blood. Once
I confirmed that he was dead, I called in my team to begin checking the
rest of the house.

'I remained in the bedroom to carry out a physical examination of the
corpse, and that was when I discovered no evidence whatsoever of any
kind of physical injury. I had expected at the very least to find one or
more puncture wounds in the chest to account for the amount of blood
on the body itself, but there was nothing.

'Normally, we would then remove the corpse to our mortuary without further examination, but this absence of wounds troubled me, so I
broke the rules. I cut off the man's clothing and carried out a detailed
examination of his body. I found no fresh wounds of any kind, but
I did find indications of severe internal trauma. He appeared to have
haemorrhaged blood through every orifice, something I have never
encountered before.

'I was about to finally order his body taken out of the house when
I suddenly recalled an article I had read years ago about the disease
Ebola. I remembered it describing how the bodies of victims almost
liquefied, with blood erupting everywhere, and that seemed to me to be
the only explanation that made sense. I ordered my team out of the
house, closed the bedroom door and, to use your American expression,
called in the cavalry.'

Hardin smiled briefly and looked down at the notes he had been
making. 'As I said before, Dr Gravas, you seem to have done everything
exactly as it should be done. I hear what you say about Ebola, and from
your description of the dead man here there are certainly some disturbing similarities. But actually I don't think it's Ebola we're dealing with,
mainly because of the timescale involved.'

'What do you mean?'

'Two reasons. First, Ebola takes a lot longer than that to kill its victims. Typically the time between the onset of the infection and the death
of the victim is a minimum of four or five days, sometimes a week or

even more. You told me that this guy Spiros Aristides was drinking in the bar here in Kandíra on Monday evening, but on Tuesday morning he was dead. That's one reason.

'The second reason is what the woman heard. Ten minutes or so before his death, the victim moaned or perhaps cried out. In fact, and contrary to anything you may have read, Ebola actually attacks only the circulatory system, causing uncontrollable bleeding within the body and affecting every organ. That includes the brain as the skull fills with blood. Victims may suffer what appear to be epileptic seizures, strokes or convulsions, but they invariably go into a deep coma in the last stages of the infection, as brain functions cease. If Aristides had been suffering an attack by Ebola, he couldn't possibly have cried out.

'Instead, I think what we're dealing with here,' Hardin looked from Lavat to Gravas, 'is a brand-new hot agent that could make Ebola look like a mild case of influenza.'

## HMS *Invincible*, Sea of Crete

Paul Richter's cabin was on the starboard side of Two Deck, almost directly below the Harrier tie-down spot, a fact that quickly became obvious to him at a little after eight ten that morning when the 800 Squadron maintainers began slam checks on a Harrier that had just had an engine change. With about half an inch of steel plate and pretty much no sound insulation between him and a Rolls-Royce Pegasus running at full power, Richter woke up fast and stayed awake.

He shaved and showered and decided not to bother with breakfast. He grabbed a cup of coffee in the Wardroom, then walked up to the Harrier briefing-room on Two Deck to be in time for Shareholders. He didn't actually need to attend, as he was in reality little more than a passenger, and there were no more fixed-wing flying operations planned until after the ship left Piraeus, but Richter made the effort anyway.

Just after nine he wandered up to the bridge and sat down in Commander (Air)'s swivel chair in Flyco, staring out at the Mediterranean.

*Invincible* was maintaining station about five miles north of

Réthymno, so the north coast of Crete was clearly visible to the south of the ship, extending from left to right as far as the eye could see. The Merlin that had been used earlier to ferry the CDC specialist to Kandíra from Irakleío was lashed down on three spot, rotors folded, and the Flight Deck was more or less deserted, apart from a handful of goofers peering through cameras and binoculars at the distant shoreline.

He had been sitting there ten minutes when somebody spoke from behind him. 'A penny for them, Spook.'

Richter recognized Roger Black's voice immediately. 'Hi, Blackie. Just taking a last look around. Don't know when – or even if – I'll ever be aboard this war canoe again.'

'Oh. I thought you might be bored here: no flying, nobody shooting at you.'

'Nope.' Richter grinned. 'Boredom's a state of mind, not a state of place. I never get bored, even when nobody's shooting at me.' He took a last glance round the horizon, then got up from the seat. 'Come on,' he said. 'I'll buy you a coffee.'


## Kandíra, south-west Crete

The three men sat in silence for a few minutes, seemingly stunned by the possible implications of what had happened in the quiet village.

'OK,' Hardin said, rousing himself. 'The diagnosis can come later. Before I get suited up to take a look at this man, I've got a few more questions. First, you said that both Spiros and Nico Aristides were drinking in a bar last night. Have you traced anybody else that was there? Anyone who saw them, I mean.'

Lavat nodded. 'Yes, we interviewed the owner, who's also the bartender. He saw the two men together, but said they were acting normally – no signs of illness or anything else. We spent most of yesterday afternoon locating the other customers from the bar that night, and all those we managed to trace seem fine. No health problems, and none recalled anything unusual about Spiros or Nico.'

'Apart from finding the aircraft, that is,' Gravas murmured.

'Aircraft? What aircraft?' Hardin demanded.

'It's probably unrelated,' Lavat said, 'but two drinkers overheard

Spiros telling Nico about a crashed aircraft he had found somewhere off the coast. He's a diver – he was a diver, I mean. To be exact, he was an unlicensed diver. Unfortunately, those two locals turned up outside the cordon and talked to one of our local reporters, with the result that the papers have been splashing a lot of nonsense about some poisonous germ from the seabed all over their front pages.'

Hardin grunted. 'Another question. Did Spiros and Nico arrive at the bar together or separately?'

'They met there,' Lavat said firmly. 'Apparently Spiros arrived first, in a bad mood, and sat drinking whisky for quite some time before Nico walked in. The barkeeper's impression – but he's definitely not the best of witnesses – was that Spiros didn't expect to see his nephew, and was pleased when he showed up.'

'Ah,' Hardin said, 'that could be important.'

'I don't follow you,' Gravas murmured.

'I'm trying to work through the timescales involved,' Hardin replied. 'We have to assume that we're dealing with an unknown pathogen that possesses some of the gross characteristics of Ebola, but which is real fast acting. We know that these two men were drinking together in a bar on Monday night, and we also know that less than twelve hours later they were both dead.

'It seems reasonable to assume that the victim of any pathogen capable of killing that quickly would show signs of illness fairly soon after becoming infected. Now, if Spiros and Nico had been together when they entered the bar on Monday night, they might already have been incubating the agent. The fact that they arrived separately, and met there by chance, suggests to me that they were both uninfected when they left the bar.

'And that,' he added, 'means that they had to have come into contact with the pathogen somewhere here in Kandíra, so we've got to find the source real quick before somebody else goes down. It also means that this hot agent, whatever the hell it is, works exponentially faster than anything that I've encountered before.'

# JAMES BARRINGTON

## Central Intelligence Agency Headquarters, Langley, Virginia

The Central Intelligence Agency has a section whose multilingual personnel do nothing all day but read the world's newspapers and magazines, searching for any snippet of information that might be of value, or simply of interest, to the Company. Another section does precisely the same thing with books, whether non-fiction or fiction. As a result, the officers employed in these two sections are probably the best-informed men and women on the planet, but you'd never know it because, like all CIA officers without publishing contracts, they never talk about their work.

At 0713 local time, Jerry Mulligan – who despite his Anglicized names had been born on Corfu and spoke fluent Greek and workable Turkish – pulled up a scanned image of the front page of an Athens paper on the twenty-one-inch computer monitor in front of him.

Most major newspapers, and almost all of the international ones, publish extracts of their daily editions on the Internet. Smaller papers don't have either the money or the resources to do the same, which was why since the 1960s a CIA agent or asset in every city in the world has been employed to purchase daily copies of all local papers. Originally the newspapers were analysed there on site and any relevant cuttings sent to Langley by mail, but the growth of the Internet and the availability of email has greatly automated the process, effectively eliminating any kind of local analysis. These days, agents just scan the entire paper into a computer, one page at a time, and then send the scanned images as email attachments to one of several CIA-owned email accounts over in the States.

The Athens paper in question was definitely the product of a smaller publisher. Parochial in content, and lacking the advertising clout of its bigger brothers, it was nevertheless interesting, and Mulligan actually looked forward each time to reading it.

The 'Cretan epidemic' had made its front page, and as Mulligan read the text he immediately realized that this item was of potential interest to the Company for at least two reasons. Any kind of epidemic or outbreak of unexplained illness was relevant to them, because it might indicate some terrorist organization testing a biological weapon, or even foreshadow the start of a full-scale biological attack, while finding the remains of a crashed aircraft might close a still open Company file.

Mulligan flicked the trackball and sent the cursor shooting across the screen to the top left-hand corner of the news item. He depressed the left-hand key with his thumb, and with fingers made sensitive by years of practice, used the trackball to move the cursor down the screen, highlighting the entire text of the story. He pressed 'Ctrl' and 'C', the keyboard shortcut to copy the text, opened up a new file in the word processor and pasted the text into it. Then he quickly read the article again to make sure that the optical character recognition software hadn't made any errors, like reading a capital 'i' instead of the letter 'l' or the number '1', added the source of the story and the publication date, and saved it.

That was the easy bit. Next he ran the automatic translation program to produce a first-draft version of the whole article in English. This would be accurate in that it was an exact translation from the Greek, but difficult to read because of the inevitably stilted nature of the grammar and unusual sentence construction. Mulligan spent another twenty minutes smoothing out the rough edges, then he read the translation through one more time. Satisfied, he saved the final version, together with the original, and loaded them both onto the Agency's central computer system's main database as text files.

The last action he had to take was technically easy, but almost always took him some minutes to complete. All data – including photographs, text files, communications intercepts and even unattributed gossip – that was loaded onto the database had to be allocated both a security classification and a so-called 'importance' code.

Mulligan had no trouble deciding the classification – the source of the story was a newspaper so anything extracted from it had to be considered unclassified – but he mulled over the importance code for a couple of minutes.

The code consisted of a two-digit alphanumeric and was simple enough to interpret. The first letter indicated the region which was the source of the incident. 'A' was mainland America; 'B' was South America; 'C' was Canada; 'D' was what used to be termed the Eastern Bloc and which is now the Confederation of Independent States and the various satellite nations; 'E' the rest of Eastern Europe; 'F' Western

Europe; 'G' the Middle East; 'H' the Far East including China and Japan; 'I' all other countries and locations, such as Antarctica, and 'J' was used for any non-region-specific reports, such as atmospheric or oceanographic events.

The numbers ran from '1' to '6'. '1' was the highest code and implied that the incident had probable direct and urgent relevance to the CIA, to America or to one of America's allies. At the bottom of the scale, '6' meant that the incident possessed interest only, but no particular relevance or urgency.

The letter was simple – obviously it had to be 'F' for Western Europe – and Mulligan eventually decided it merited a class '2' coding for importance and relevance. He added the 'F2' code to the text, closed the file and moved on to the second page of the same Athenian newspaper.

### HMS *Invincible*, Sea of Crete

Paul Richter walked into the Wardroom after lunch, poured himself a cup of coffee from the urn by the door and crossed to a chair in the corner of the large room. He picked up a travel magazine from the table in front of him and began flicking through it.

Richter didn't often take holidays, because he usually didn't have anybody to go anywhere with, and when Simpson allowed him any time off he normally went down to his tiny cottage on the east side of the Lizard Peninsula in Cornwall and spent a few days playing with his motorcycles.

But he had travelled around most of the world, or at least the wet bits of it, courtesy of the Royal Navy's Grey Funnel Line cruising organization, when he had been employed as a regular pilot in 800 Squadron and earlier when he'd flown helicopters, so he liked looking at the pictures. He'd been sitting there for about ten minutes when he heard his name called in a tannoy broadcast: 'Lieutenant Commander Richter is requested to report to the Communications Centre.'

'They're playing your tune, Spook,' John Moore called from the adjacent table, and Richter grinned at him.

'If it's what I think it is, it's not going to be a fun few minutes,' he said. 'I'm already right at the top of my boss's shit list and my guess is he's about to drain all over me again.'

'Something went wrong in Italy, I presume?' Moore asked.

'He seems to think so,' Richter replied, 'but from where I was standing everything worked out pretty much the way I'd planned it.'

In the CommCen on Five Deck, Richter was directed to a secure telephone apparatus in one corner of the room. All around him was the hum of electronic equipment, the clattering of teleprinters and the sound of the Communications staff talking to each other. He picked up the handset and said one word: 'Richter.'

'And about bloody time too. Do you know how long I've been kept hanging on this line?'

Simpson's voice was quite unmistakable, and he sounded extremely irritated, but he was, in Richter's experience, irritated most of the time, so that was probably understandable.

'No, of course I don't,' Richter said. 'I've only just been called down from the Wardroom. Where are you?'

'Not that it's any business of yours, but I'm still in Italy.'

'Brindisi?'

'Rome,' Simpson snapped. 'For reasons that don't make any sense to me, you can't fly direct from Brindisi to anywhere useful, so I'm in the Six office in Rome, waiting for the afternoon Alitalia from Fiumicino to Heathrow.'

'OK,' Richter said, 'what do you want?'

There was a short appalled silence on the line, and Richter could sense – in fact, he could almost feel – Simpson's anger building.

'What the fuck do you mean what do I want? What do you think I want? I want to talk about that fiasco in Italy.'

'Well, there's a surprise.'

'Don't get clever with me, Richter. You tried to kill a helpless and unarmed man who had his hands tied behind his back while he was being held by two other men. To make things worse, you did it in front of witnesses. Then you beat up a police officer, stole a car and a helicopter, and finally you shot your way off the airfield at Brindisi, writing off one of their military trucks on the way. The Italians, in case you hadn't noticed, are supposed to be our fucking allies.'

'I was in a hurry,' Richter said. 'I'm sorry about the cop, but I didn't have time to stand around and argue with him. I could have killed him instead of just giving him a headache. And I didn't steal either the car or the helicopter: I just borrowed them for a while.'

'Don't quibble. Fortunately for you, the policeman will recover. The car and the chopper are incidental, the truck too, but what you did to Lomas isn't. I've been fending off some heavyweight diplomatic pressure to have you arrested the moment your ship reaches port, and then extradited to Italy to face charges. The Italians are extremely annoyed about this, Richter, and so am I.'

'Get used to it, Simpson. What's done is done, and if I was in the same position tomorrow I'd do exactly the same again. Lomas was an animal, a vicious, rabid beast and I think of myself as the pest-control man. He deserved to die.'

'Wrong tense, Richter,' Simpson said, 'and watch your tongue. I've stopped their extradition attempts so far, but I can always change my mind.'

'What do you mean, "wrong tense"?'

'Just what I said. Your little attempt to bisect Lomas didn't succeed. A doctor turned up a few minutes after you'd headed for the hills and he managed to stop most of the bleeding. The air ambulance arrived straight afterwards, so Lomas made it to the hospital at Bari, went into surgery immediately and was still alive this morning. It's going to be a long time before he's walking around again, but it looks like he'll pull through.'

'Oh, shit,' Richter said.

'That, in fact,' Simpson added, 'is probably why the Italians haven't been trying as hard as they might to get hold of you. They'll have plenty of time to debrief Lomas once he's out of danger, and he'll be in no fit state to resist. What they probably won't do, though, is share the take with us, which has certainly pissed me off and is hardly going to make you flavour of the month with Vauxhall Cross and Five when they find out about it.

'It's also worth your while remembering that Lomas has shown himself to be extremely vindictive. If he does recover from what you did to him, he's going to want blood in return. You'll need to watch your back.'

'I've got used to that ever since I started working for you,' Richter said. 'I hope Lomas does come after me – I'd like to finish the job. So what's next?'

'In view of the hostile vibes you're likely to receive if you come back to London right now, you might just as well stay on that ship for at least another week. Let things cool down a bit.'

'Fine with me. I can't fly back from Athens for the next few days, because we're standing off Crete.'

'Why?'

'Some kind of medical emergency. The ship's been positioned here to ferry goods and bodies around the place.'

'OK, stay on board for the next seven days. If their operation runs on for more than a week, get yourself ashore and buy a ticket home from Crete. Economy class, of course.'

'Of course.'

'Oh, and Richter.'

'Yes?'

'I wouldn't take a holiday in Rimini for a few years if I were you.'

# Chapter 10

**Wednesday**
**Réthymno, Crete**

Sometimes it's not the direction of travel, or even the duration of the journey, that causes the greatest discomfort and jet-lag. Sometimes it's just the circumstances, nothing more.

When he had driven his Lincoln to Langley the previous morning, all David Elias had been expecting was another routine day of analysing raw intelligence data from the Pacific Rim area and writing reports and summaries based upon that intelligence.

What had actually happened was that he had been summoned to his first-ever operational briefing, where he had been given what were clearly highly edited instructions about his intended role, and received background information that frankly made little sense. Then he'd been appointed the third member of a covert team comprising two men he'd never met before, and who clearly weren't particularly enamoured with the idea of a mere analyst hitching a ride with them, and finally hustled into a car and rushed to Baltimore to catch a Jumbo to London Heathrow.

There had been a twenty-minute delay in landing the 747 and, despite their best efforts to get to the departure gate in time, they'd missed their connection to Crete. Nearly three hours later, most of it spent sitting around in startlingly uncomfortable seats in the departure lounge, they'd boarded the next available flight to Irakleío. The taxi ride to Réthymno had seemed interminable and, when they finally arrived, the hotel was hardly five star.

So it was, perhaps, not altogether surprising that Elias simply walked into his room, dropped his bag on the floor, took off his jacket, tie and shoes, and then crashed out on the bed. Within three minutes he was sound asleep.

Krywald and Stein were made of sterner stuff, or perhaps they were just more used to such things. They had been booked into adjoining rooms – Elias was occupying a single down the corridor – and as soon as they'd stowed their gear and cleaned up, Krywald switched on his laptop computer, plugged in the connecting lead to his mobile phone, and dialled an unlisted service provider in the United States.

There were three email messages waiting, all signed McCready but which had actually been sent by Nicholson. All three messages were scrambled using the PGP (Pretty Good Privacy) encryption program, but it took Krywald only minutes to decrypt them. The first simply confirmed the details of the overt support Nicholson had arranged – where they should go to collect the hire car, the boat and Elias's diving equipment, and so on – while the second message provided similar information for obtaining the covert support, like the explosives, detonators and personal weapons. The third email was perhaps the most interesting – or rather the most alarming.

Nicholson had sent it soon after he had read the translated newspaper report on the CIA database of the apparent filovirus death at Kandíra. The message was brief and to the point: Krywald and his team were to amend their pre-briefed roles. They were to pose now as either American journalists or CDC personnel investigating the medical emergency on Crete. They were to enter Kandíra as soon as possible, gain access to Spiros Aristides's house and search it thoroughly. Nicholson had a plan for them that, Krywald thought to himself as he scanned the email for the third time, might even work.

The case containing the flasks, Nicholson suggested, was probably still in the dead man's home, overlooked or ignored by the local police. Destruction of the wrecked aircraft was now to become the secondary priority.

'Just as well,' Stein remarked, somewhat sourly, 'as our highly trained diver is sound asleep down the hall and in no fit state to get into a bathtub without help, never mind dive to the bottom of the ocean.'

'Right,' Krywald agreed. 'OK, let's do things in order. You go collect the car. I'll pick up some maps of this goddamned island, then we'll grab a drink and work out how the hell we're going to get inside this Kandíra place.'

## Popes Creek, Virginia

Charles Jerome 'CJ' Hawkins had retired from the Central Intelligence Agency over twelve years earlier, but unlike most of his contemporaries – who had moved their entire families south to Florida, 'God's waiting room', as soon as they'd completed their time with the Company – he had elected to remain in the area where he had lived and worked for so much of his life.

His home was an elegant four-bedroom property on the edge of the small town of Popes Creek, overlooking the Potomac a few miles south of Washington, DC. He and his wife Mary lived there quietly, their three children long grown up and with families of their own, two living in Idaho and one up in Michigan.

For most of his career with the Company, Hawkins had worked in the Operations Directorate, much of it in the Covert Action Staff, responsible for disinformation and propaganda. He had been involved in hundreds of operations during his employment, some successful, many not, but the only one that he ever thought about these days still gave him sleepless nights. Not because of the operation itself – Hawkins had believed totally at the time in what they were doing – but in the possible consequence for both the Central Intelligence Agency, and even America itself, if details of it ever leaked out.

And early this morning, that nightmare from the past had suddenly loomed in front of him. It began, innocuously enough, with a phone call. The voice at the other end was familiar, although it was five years since they had last spoken together.

'We need to meet,' the man said. 'It's been found.'

Hawkins was silent for a few moments, and when he spoke there was a slight tremor in his speech. 'When?'

'A few days ago.'

'Have you told the others?'

'I've told Richards. Butcher is in a coma in a hospital in Baltimore, and the prognosis isn't good.'

'The meeting – when and where?' Hawkins asked.

'Tonight. We have to move quickly. Take a drive out to Lower Cedar Point, just west of Morgantown. Arrive at eight fifteen and park close to the water. I'll find you.'

# PANDEMIC

## Central Intelligence Agency Headquarters, Langley, Virginia

John Westwood had been head of the Foreign Intelligence (Espionage) Staff for a little over three years, after a career spent entirely in the CIA's Operations Directorate, most of it located outside the United States. He hadn't been particularly impressed with the idea of driving a desk after so many years in the field, but he had recognized the inevitability of the promotion and, being head of department, he was still deeply involved in the conduct of operations abroad.

One of the things that he had always done, as a matter of routine ever since his appointment, was to scan the main database for all new entries given an importance classification of '3' or higher, and especially those from geographical regions 'D', 'E' and 'G' – respectively the Confederation of Independent States, Eastern Europe and the Middle East – those being the areas in which most CIA espionage operations were kept running for most of the time. But he also scanned the other regions as well, and the 'F2' code with an attached headline 'Cretan epidemic linked to crashed aircraft' was sufficiently intriguing for him to not simply read the entire translation, but also to print it as hard copy.

The Athens newspaper had picked up the story from the first report filed by the journalist based on Crete, and comprehensive information on the incident was somewhat lacking. However, the two locals sitting in Jakob's bar that night had overheard just enough of what Spiros had said to make the story compelling. And because what he said was so intriguing, they had remembered enough to re-tell it later to a newspaper reporter – suitably embellished, no doubt.

But, even without embellishment, there was actually quite a lot of hard data. The crashed aircraft was definitely small, there had been bodies inside, its registration began with the letter 'N' and contained at least three numbers, and it was lying on the seabed somewhere near Crete.

Westwood read through the report three times, and each reading persuaded him that this was something worth looking into, not least because the 'N' in the wrecked aircraft's number meant that it had been originally registered in the States, and the fact that the diver had found bodies suggested that there might somewhere be a still-open file on that missing aircraft – a file that could now perhaps be closed.

The first thing, he decided, was to try to identify the aircraft, which shouldn't be that difficult if the Greek diver had noted down the right letter and numbers and, perhaps more importantly, had remembered them correctly when he wrote them on the piece of paper he'd handed to his nephew. And, of course, if the reporter who had talked to the two Cretans had transcribed them correctly when he wrote the story. Westwood mentally corrected his 'shouldn't be that difficult' assumption to a definite maybe.

But he tried it anyway. Westwood used his desktop PC to log on to the Federal Aviation Administration database through the Internet and input 'N176' in the search field. That turned up a light aircraft, certainly not an executive jet, and it was still flying around – at least as far as the FAA knew.

Within three minutes Westwood knew he was wasting his time. The initial letter confirmed the aircraft's country of registration, but the missing one or two digits – even assuming that the three the diver had reported were correct, and in the right order – expanded the number of possible aircraft to a huge extent, not least because one or both could be letters or numbers. He would have to try a different approach.

## Outside Kandíra, south-west Crete

Stein was driving the rental car – a white four-door Ford Focus – that he had collected from the agency in Réthymno. Krywald was sitting beside him, studying a tourist map of the island. David Elias sat in the back seat, bleary-eyed and yawning, as the Ford bounced over the rough road – actually little more than a track through the olive groves – out of Soúgia towards Kandíra.

The car crested a slight rise and Kandíra lay before them. Stein pulled the car off the road, and for a couple of minutes Krywald studied the scene before him through a small pair of binoculars. It looked much like any of the other small villages they'd already passed through on their seemingly interminable drive over the mountains from Máleme, where they'd left the main road. A cluster of white-painted houses perched almost at the edge of a cliff overlooking the Mediterranean. To one side a path snaked away towards the cliff itself, presumably leading down to a beach or a small harbour. On the slopes to the north of the village, their bases hidden by the stunted olive trees that covered the hillside, three circular white windmills sat, with their fabric-clad skeletal sails turning slowly in a gentle breeze.

'OK,' Krywald said, turning to Stein. 'They've got a cordon in place around the village, but it's real thin, just a local cop every fifty yards or so. I don't think we'll have any trouble getting in.'

Stein nodded and swivelled in his seat. 'You ready, Elias?'

David Elias smothered another yawn and nodded.

'Right,' Krywald said, and gestured down the hill towards a point next to the cliffs and well away from the open space where three large tents had been erected within the cordon.

'We'll do it over there. There are two cops, one by the cliffs, the other about fifty yards inland. They can see each other, but I don't think they can see any of the other guys forming the cordon, because there's a stone outbuilding right next to them, blocking their view that way. Let's get ready.'

Stein started the engine, turned the car around and drove it a short distance down the track away from Kandíra. Once out of sight of the village, he stopped the vehicle and all three men climbed out.

Stein opened the boot and pulled out two pairs of white coveralls which he and Krywald pulled on over their other clothes. Each had the initials 'CDC' roughly stencilled on the left breast. There was one small case in the boot, black and square, the kind that might well be carried by a doctor or a forensic scientist. It was empty but big enough to accommodate the steel case whose dimensions had been supplied by McCready at their briefing in Virginia. Stein pulled out the case and handed it to Krywald.

'You know what to do?' he asked Elias.

Elias nodded. 'I know what we discussed, but I'm not sure I can carry it off. I know just about enough Greek to order a cup of coffee.'

'That's exactly the point,' Krywald said. 'You'll have to use a phrase-book and that's going to spin everything out. That'll give us time to get into the village. Look, David,' he added, his tone friendly and persuasive, 'I know you're an analyst and this really isn't your scene or anything that you've been trained for, but there's just the three of us here, so you're going to have to pull your weight.'

'OK, OK, let's do it,' Elias grunted, and climbed into the driver's seat. Stein and Krywald got into the back, crouching down below window level. Elias started the engine and the car moved off, over the rise and down the track towards Kandíra.

Directly in front of Elias the road ran straight into the village, but there were barriers across it, manned by policemen, and several of their vehicles parked close by. Following Krywald's directions, Elias turned right, towards the coast, and drove around the village on the track which they assumed led to the beach or harbour. Just short of the cliffs he stopped the car and turned it round, parking it in the shade of an olive tree about thirty metres from the temporary barricade. Then he got out, clutching the tourist map Krywald had bought earlier and also a Greek phrasebook, and walked over towards one of the policemen standing by the village perimeter, watching him.

'Excuse me,' Elias said in halting Greek, his finger tracing each word on the page of the phrasebook as he said it. 'I am looking for the town of Palaiochóra.' He distorted the name as much as he could, which wasn't difficult for him. The policeman looked at him blankly, so Elias repeated his inquiry, making a further conscious effort to mangle the Greek. Then in English he asked if the policeman spoke English, which it soon became apparent he didn't.

At this point, just as Krywald had predicted, the policeman waved to his colleague, who wandered over to help them. Elias was the first other person they'd needed to talk to since their shift had started nearly three hours earlier, and any diversion, no matter how mundane, seemed welcome. Elias placed his back squarely towards the spot where he'd parked the hire car, and opened up the map. As both policemen studied it, it meant their backs were towards the vehicle as well.

Crouching in the car beside the olive tree, Krywald nodded to Stein and quietly opened the rear passenger door on the side of the car opposite the village. He and Stein slipped out and crouched behind their vehicle, pushing the door to, but not audibly closing it. As Krywald glanced across at Elias, both policemen had their backs still towards them. One was pointing up the track leading out of Kandíra, towards the west, indicating the direction in which Soúgia lay, and beyond that Ánydroi and Palaiochóra.

*Perfect.* Krywald estimated they had at least a couple of minutes.

The two men stood up and walked calmly, and without haste, towards the nearest houses. The distance they needed to cover was less than forty yards, so within seconds they were out of sight, heading down a narrow twisting street towards the village centre.

## Hammersmith, London

The Central Intelligence Agency isn't the only organization that reads newspapers gathered from around the world.

The British Secret Intelligence Service, popularly and incorrectly known as MI6, has a section which is given very much the same remit as that for which Jerry Mulligan worked at Langley. The source they were using was different: the SIS man on the spot in Athens had missed the local press but had picked up a broadcast on one of the radio stations. He had then telephoned three of his local contacts – two of whom were newspaper reporters and believed that he was too – and within an hour he had amassed pretty much the same information as Mulligan had gleaned from the newspaper.

Rather than wait for the normal end-of-business encrypted email to Vauxhall Cross, the SIS officer had then written, enciphered and dispatched a one-off high-priority email to SIS London, with a copy to his opposite number on Crete.

In London, after the message was decrypted and its originating station identified, it was automatically diverted into the electronic 'in-box' of the head of the Western Hemisphere Controllerate. He scanned it, and copied it to his number two, with a bald instruction to investigate and report.

Ninety minutes after this email had arrived at Vauxhall Cross, Richard Simpson, who'd arrived at Hammersmith from Heathrow Airport less than ten minutes earlier, was looking at a hard-copy printout of the message, which was annotated with the 'investigate' request from SIS.

Simpson hated computers and refused to have a terminal in his office, which meant that every message for which the Foreign Operations Executive was an action addressee had to be printed out and presented to him. This caused a considerable amount of irritation to –

and a lot of extra work for – the staff at Hammersmith, but as Simpson was the head of the department there wasn't a lot, apart from muttering and complaining to each other in the canteen, that anyone could do about it.

'Typical of bloody Six,' Simpson muttered sourly into his empty office, putting down the printed message. Then he glanced at his desk calendar, nodded, picked up his telephone and pressed three keys for an internal number.

'Simpson,' he said when his call was answered. 'Come up, please.'

The Intelligence Director walked into Simpson's office four minutes later and sat down in front of his desk.

'Have you seen this?' Simpson demanded, passing the printed sheet across.

The ID looked at it and nodded. 'Yes. It could, of course, just be a bad case of Asian 'flu, but I doubt it. I have been wondering whether it might be some kind of biological weapon test. The obvious worry is that al-Qaeda or some other group of terrorists might have developed a biological weapon of mass destruction and they're trying it out on Crete as a sort of test run. If so, it would be somewhat reminiscent of the Aum sect in Japan.'

Simpson looked irritated. He had great respect for the Intelligence Director's breadth of knowledge, but had always found his pedantic delivery and frequently incomplete answers somewhat annoying. He was, however, well aware of the details of the Tokyo attack.

In March 1995 the Aum sect – its full name was Aum Shinrikyo, which translates more or less as 'Aum Supreme Truth', and it was led by Shoko Asahara who was half-blind and certainly more than half-mad – launched a gas attack using sarin on the Tokyo subway on a Monday morning in the middle of the rush hour. Twelve people died and over five and a half thousand had to receive hospital treatment. The low mortality rate was attributed to impurities in the sarin nerve gas manufactured by the cult. Because of the inevitably confined space and lack of fresh air in the subway, the death toll would have been hundreds or even thousands if the sect had developed a pure strain.

'And what exactly has a gas attack in Tokyo got to do with a virus infection on Crete?' Simpson demanded.

'Nothing directly, but it might indicate the same kind of pattern.

What isn't generally known is that before the Tokyo attack the Aum sect carried out a trial run in Australia of the sarin gas it had itself developed. They bought a remote sheep ranch – the Banjawarn Station deep in the outback of Western Australia – specifically to test their concocted strain. It was an expensive test, since the ranch alone cost them four hundred thousand Australian dollars.'

'Casualties?' Simpson asked.

'Twenty-nine sheep, no humans, but that was because the only people in the area were Aum technicians wearing full biological space suits. Despite its impurities, the Australian test proved that the sarin they had manufactured was lethal – which was all Asahara needed to know. The Aum sect is long gone, but what worries me is if al-Qaeda are following a similar path and they've chosen Crete as a testing-ground for some bioweapon they've developed or, worse, bought illicitly.'

'From Russia?'

'From Russia, or Britain or America or Iran or Syria or China or any one of about a dozen other nations. There are hundreds of biological and chemical weapon stockpiles dotted around the world, and making such agents isn't actually that difficult as long as you possess the right facilities. Sarin – its chemical title is isopropyl methylphosphonfluoridate – is basically an insecticide, so its ingredients are readily available. You have to take care in making it, to ensure that there are no leaks, but any reasonably well-equipped chemical laboratory could manufacture it easily.'

'The Tokyo death toll seems low. How dangerous is sarin?'

'Very,' the Intelligence Director replied. 'The lethal dose is about six milligrams – that's about decimal zero zero zero two of an ounce – and it doesn't have to be inhaled. Just getting a drop of it on your skin is enough to kill you. And sarin is benign compared with some of the more modern concoctions.'

'And you think this might be a bioweapon attack using sarin?'

The Intelligence Director shook his head.

'Yes and no. Sarin is a nerve gas. That makes it a chemical agent, not a bioweapon. If sarin had been used and had been properly deployed it would have affected a large number of people – perhaps even the entire population of this village on Crete. It would also have affected them all at about the same time, and in more or less the same way. No, what we're looking at here is almost certainly some kind of a biological agent, but it could also be entirely natural and nothing to do with any terrorist organization.'

'Explain.'

'In my opinion, this incident on Crete is one of two things. The most likely explanation is that it's just an isolated outbreak of some already known but rare disease that the local doctor hasn't recognized for some reason. Despite what the medical profession would like us to believe, no doctor knows everything, and a Cretan general practitioner is going to spend most of his time treating tourists for sunburn and stomach upsets. He isn't likely to be familiar with some of the rarer illnesses, like Lassa Fever, Marburg or Ebola—'

'Hang on,' Simpson interrupted. 'I know a bit about those myself, and they're *highly* infectious, so we wouldn't just be looking at a single case.'

'That's not necessarily true. Even if this Greek diver had contracted Ebola, the disease's incubation period is long enough that he may have been infected with it some time ago. He could subsequently have infected other people, but they may not yet be showing any signs of the disease. Within a week or two, there might be another dozen cases.'

'OK,' Simpson brooded, 'that makes sense. What's the other explanation?'

'The least likely, but most worrying, scenario is that it is some kind of a biological weapon, but one with a low mortality or low infectivity. Only one death has been confirmed, I understand, and unless there are a lot of other very sick people in that village right now that we haven't heard about, it suggests the cause is an inefficient killer.'

Simpson stroked his chin in silence for a few moments.

'Right, the problem as I see it is that there's no way of telling at this stage which explanation is the right one. The potential causes are completely different – a rare but naturally occurring virus or other biological agent, or some kind of manufactured bioweapon – but the result at this stage is the same: one man is dead and there are possibly a number of other people incubating the virus but not showing any signs of distress at the moment.'

'That's a fair summary.'

'Well, Vauxhall Cross have asked us to investigate it, so we'd better do something. What are your recommendations?'

'There's not a lot we can do from here. No doubt the Americans will be taking satellite pictures of the island that we'll be granted access to, and I'm sure Sky News and CNN and the rest of the news organizations will be sending teams out to the Mediterranean if they haven't already done so. Six have got a small presence on the island. Probably our best option is to analyse the data already in the public domain and supplement that with satellite and local intelligence.'

Simpson nodded. 'I agree with that for background and general analysis, but I've a better idea. Richter.'

The Intelligence Director looked interested – puzzled, but interested. 'Sorry?' he asked, glancing over at Simpson.

'Richter. He's been taking a holiday on that floating gin palace in the Med, and when I spoke to him this afternoon he told me the ship was loitering off Crete to help with this medical emergency, so he's right on the spot. After the cock-up he made in Italy he can bloody well start earning his money again. Tell the duty Ops Officer to signal him to find out what's going on. Richter's good at digging. If there's anything we need to know about happening in Crete, he'll find it for us.'

## Kandíra, south-west Crete

'So what now?' Dr Gravas asked. 'I presume you'll want to examine the bodies of the victims?'

Hardin's answer surprised him.

'No, not yet. I'm quite satisfied with your preliminary diagnosis of what killed these two men, at least in broad terms. It was definitely some kind of fast-acting hot agent, perhaps a filovirus, or maybe something totally unknown. Once my people get here we'll be able to do complete autopsies, take tissue samples and so on, but if I go and look at the bodies, pretty much all I'll be able to confirm is that they're dead, and that isn't a lot of help to us right now.

'The normal procedure in an investigation is to take blood samples from anyone who may be infected. Then we separate the serum from the red blood cells using a centrifuge: there's a small battery-powered unit in one of the cases I brought. Then we separate the different sera into aliquots, label them, pack them in dry ice and send them back to Atlanta. Our technicians there will try to confirm the virus, and even its precise strain, by identifying specific antibodies within the sera.

'Our problem here is that the subjects are dead and their blood will by now have degraded, so will probably be useless for that kind of test procedure. This case is very different, and not simply because the only two victims known to have contracted this illness are already dead. Our first priority, I suggest, is to try to find out how and where Spiros and Nico Aristides became infected. If we can localize the source, we might be able to prevent any further casualties.'

'And how do we do that?' Lavat demanded.

Hardin grinned somewhat ruefully. 'I don't have a comprehensive answer to that, Inspector,' he said, 'so all we can do is apply simple logic and start from the last place the two men were seen together alive.'

'The *kafeníon*?'

'Exactly. We start from Jakob's bar and work our way slowly along towards Spiros Aristides's house.'

'And what will we be looking for?' Gravas asked.

'I have no idea. All we can assume is that somewhere along that route they saw something sufficiently interesting or unusual that they stopped and touched it, or tasted it, or otherwise allowed the infection to enter their systems. I'm just hoping that we'll see and recognize the same thing.'

'Suppose they picked up whatever this thing is and took it into Aristides's house with them?'

'Then we'll find it there, I guess,' Hardin replied. 'OK, could you ask a couple of your men to take the bigger of my two cases over to Spiros Aristides's house? I'll need to put on a space suit before I go inside, but I don't think we'll need to take any precautions until we actually get there.'

'Why? Isn't there a risk that this agent is still outside somewhere, and still infectious?'

'Yes, of course, but whatever the source is, I don't think it uses airborne transmission.'

Lavat looked quizzical, but it was Gravas who answered. 'Look at the timescale, Inspector,' he explained. 'Spiros and Nico were drinking in that pigsty Jakob calls a bar until around midnight, but by mid-morning next day Spiros was dead, and probably Nico as well. The two women went into Spiros's house just after he died, and they're still both fit and well and complaining about having to stand around in the street without their clothes on.

'Whatever this thing is, the one thing we do know for certain is that it attacks really quickly. If the two women had breathed in any virus particles – assuming for the moment that it *is* a virus – I would have expected one or both of them by now to be showing some signs of physical distress. I mean bleeding, choking, vomiting or something, to show that the infection had taken a hold.'

Lavat nodded slowly. 'Yes,' he said. 'That makes sense. I think you're probably right.'

'And,' Gravas added, 'I'm pleased to say that the same logic applies to us as well. We've been inside both properties without wearing the right protective equipment – the paper mask would help, but it's certainly not a proper defence against an airborne pathogen – and we're still fine.'

'So now what?' Stein asked, after they rounded a corner that took them well out of sight of the police manning the cordon around the village.

'We find the house where this Greek diver died, get inside it and search it.'

'How?'

'Easy,' Krywald replied. 'We're inside the village now, so everyone will assume that we're supposed to be here. You speak Greek – so we'll stop somebody and ask the way.'

Sitting on the steps of a white-washed cottage they found an elderly Cretan man, wrinkled and burnt umber by the sun, smoking a foul-smelling cigarette, obviously hand-rolled. Stein stopped to explain that he and Krywald were part of the American specialist team, then asked directions to Aristides's house.

The old man wrinkled his eyes against the glare of the sun, and looked up at the two Americans. He took his time removing the cigarette from his mouth, then replied briefly in his native language.

'What did he say?' Krywald demanded.

'He asked "Which one?"' Stein replied.

'What the hell does that mean? The one that's dead, of course.'

Stein switched back to Greek and addressed the old man again. 'We're looking for the house belonging to the Aristides who died because of this illness we're investigating.'

The old Cretan grinned up at him and took another drag on his cigarette. 'Which one?' he asked again.

'Either this guy's an idiot or Spiros isn't the only dead Aristides in this village,' Stein muttered to Krywald, then turned back to the Cretan. 'Do you mean there's more than one man here dead with this disease?' he asked.

The old man nodded. 'Spiros Aristides and Nico Aristides – and both of them are dead.'

'OK,' Stein took a small notebook from his pocket. 'Can you tell me where they lived?'

# Chapter 11

His check of the FAA Registry hadn't helped Westwood much, or even at all, so he turned his attention to the CIA's own database, known to Agency insiders as 'Walnut', which had been the source of his interest in the first place. Walnut is actually several databases, some containing purely unclassified background information, being data in the public domain, and others allotted varying security classifications, some with heavily restricted access.

Using the custom-designed search engine, which accepted almost every kind of permutation within its parameters including Boolean logic, he keyed in a simple enough search – 'Mediterranean+aircraft+crash' – specified the entire database rather than just a particular section of it, sat back and waited.

A little over three seconds later the first page of results appeared on the screen in front of him. There had been a surprising number of air-craft crashes in the Mediterranean, it seemed. Maybe this indicated that there was a 'Maltese Triangle', Westwood thought with a wry smile, mirroring the so-called Bermuda Triangle on the other side of the world, about which so much complete and unsubstantiated rubbish has been written over the years. Or maybe it was just that the airspace over the Mediterranean is particularly busy, and has been ever since man first took to the air.

Westwood realized he was going to have to tighten his search if he didn't want to spend all day reading through aircraft crash reports that were of no interest to him. He read through the Greek newspaper article again and then entered a new search command, looking within the results the system had already generated, and specifying only air-craft that had crashed since 1960.

That still threw up a couple of dozen reports, so he refined the search again, using the registration letters reported for the crashed aircraft: 'N', '1', '7' and '6'. The screen cleared and he was now looking at three reports only, all classified 'Restricted' – the lowest possible rating above 'Unclassified' – and all referring to the same incident: a Learjet that vanished somewhere over the Eastern Mediterranean in 1972. The first file was the reported loss, the second a compilation detailing the various stages of the surface search that had been mounted, and the third noted when the search had been abandoned without result. Westwood printed them all as hard copy and began to read through them.

It wasn't a great leap of logic to connect this report with the wreckage of the aircraft that the Greek diver had reportedly found at the bottom of the Mediterranean, particularly as the registration number of the missing aircraft was N17677, but as he studied the printed pages in front of him Westwood realized that something didn't gel.

The location of the missing Learjet was necessarily imprecise, as the aircraft had been outside radar cover when it went down, and the search teams had simply extrapolated the aircraft's predicted route from its filed flight plan, and then concentrated on the area the aircraft should have reached when the en route controlling authority lost radio contact with it. But the location where the Greek diver had apparently found the wreckage was nowhere near either this predicted course or the original search area. It was a long way to the north, which suggested that the pilot of the Learjet had for some reason waited until his aircraft was outside radar cover, then turned north towards Crete, and that didn't make any sense unless the aircraft was lost – which was most unlikely – or on some kind of covert mission.

Westwood turned back to his computer terminal and on a hunch typed in a new search solely for 'N17677'.

The result surprised him. Realistically, he had been expecting to see only the same three reports that the system had already generated, but the more specific search had now added a fourth file. Its title was 'N17677'.

That didn't make sense. The search parameters he had entered previously – the partial registration number 'N176' – should also have located this file. Westwood bent over the keyboard again and entered 'N*7677', then pressed the 'Enter' key. The '*' symbol is a wildcard that can mean any letter, number or symbol, so that search string should bring up the 'N17677' file reference – but it didn't. Once again, Westwood was gazing at only the original three references.

He tried again, this time inputting 'Learjet N17677', but with the same result: only the same three Restricted reports about the missing aircraft. That had to mean that the 'N17677' file was protected. It could only be located by typing in the exact filename – a primitive, but actually quite effective, means of ensuring that the file could only be accessed by somebody who already knew about it.

Again, Westwood typed in 'N17677' and glanced at the screen. Next to the filename was its classification, 'Ultra' – one of the highest classification levels above 'Top Secret' – and the cryptic note 'Cross-reference: CAIP'. Beside this was a warning: 'Access prohibited. File sealed July 02, 1972'.

'What the hell is CAIP?' Westwood muttered to himself. He tapped the letters into the search field and pressed 'Go'. Almost as he had expected, the result was virtually a mirror image of what he had already seen – 'Cross-reference: N17677. Access prohibited. File sealed July 02, 1972' – and again the security classification 'Ultra'. The only additional information provided were the names of the six senior CIA officers who had been responsible for CAIP, whatever it was, but Westwood had never heard of any of them.

For a couple of minutes he sat silently, staring at his computer monitor. Then he opened Internet Explorer, moved the cursor into the 'address' field, and typed in 'www2.faa.gov', the address of the Federal Aviation Administration's website. He selected 'Information' and 'Pilots and Aircraft Owners', then 'Services' and 'Query the Aircraft database'. He clicked the link at the bottom of the 'Aircraft Inquiry Site' page, waited while the 'FAA Registry Aircraft Registration Inquiry page' loaded and chose 'N-Number'. In the query field he typed '17677' and pressed 'Go'.

Then he leaned back from the screen and shook his head. In front of him were details of the aircraft bearing the North American registration N17677. It was a Learjet 23, exactly the same type of aircraft as the one that had been lost in the Mediterranean in 1972, but according to the FAA database, it hadn't crashed or gone missing – it had been retired from service in 1979.

But an aircraft's registration number, just like that for a car, is issued only once, so either the FAA had made a mistake and the details Westwood was looking at on the screen were incorrect, which seemed extremely unlikely, or the registration of the aircraft referred to in the CIA database was wrong.

Or, Westwood suddenly thought, maybe not. There was a possible way in which they could both be right.


### Kandíra, south-west Crete

As Krywald and Stein walked around the corner, they spotted the policeman immediately. He was leaning against a wall in the shade, opposite a scruffy white house, and smoking with the cigarette cupped in his hand. As the two men appeared he dropped the stub to the ground, trod it out and straightened his uniform jacket.

Stein walked over to him. 'We're from the CDC, the Centers for Disease Control,' he announced in Greek, and displayed one of the ID cards that he and Krywald had faked by using the laptop computer, a portable printer and a mugshot acquired from a passport-photograph booth before they left Réthymno.

One of the major problems with an identity card is that unless the person to whom it is presented knows exactly what the real one looks like, he has no idea whether it's the genuine article. This particular policeman had spent his entire life and career on Crete, and had never even heard of the CDC until Inspector Lavat had told him earlier that the team from Atlanta was expected on the island. The card he studied looked perfectly correct to him, so he just nodded and handed it back.

Stein pulled a notebook from his pocket. 'Is this the house where Mr Spiros Aristides lived?'

'Yes, sir,' the officer replied. 'The door is not locked, and his body is still upstairs in the bedroom.'

'Thank you.' Stein and Krywald then pulled on surgical gloves and paper face masks. 'Make sure nobody else goes inside until we have completed our examination of the premises.'

*

'Do you want to check inside?' Lavat asked. The three men stood in the street outside Jakob's bar, eyeing the faded and peeling paintwork on the door and windows.

Hardin shook his head. 'Not particularly. I don't believe for a moment that the infective agent was encountered in the bar, otherwise we'd be looking at a dozen deaths by now, not just two. So, exactly where is Aristides's house from here?'

Lavat pointed along the dusty street, and the three men turned as one to glance that way.

'Again,' Hardin said, 'I don't know what we're looking for, or even if there's anything here to find. Just be careful, and always look but don't touch. If you see anything, anything at all, that seems in any way unusual or out of place, inform me immediately. But, I repeat, don't touch it, OK?' Lavat and Gravas both nodded. 'Right, masks on. Spread out and let's make a start.'

Each man pulled a disposable paper mask over his nose and mouth, and they set off, walking very slowly down the centre of the street, their eyes roaming the ground, the walls of houses, even the trees and bushes.

'Nothing here,' Krywald muttered. 'We'll try upstairs.'

They'd searched the tiny patio garden, and then the downstairs rooms first as they had been taught, moving swiftly and working efficiently, but it was quickly obvious, once they'd checked the various rooms and pulled open the doors of all the cupboards, that nothing the size of the steel case described to them could possibly be hidden there. Only then did Krywald lead the way up the old wooden staircase.

'Hell of a smell in here,' Krywald remarked as they reached the upper landing.

'According to that cop outside, the Greek's body is still lying dead in here somewhere.'

'OK, we'll just ignore it. I want to be out of here in five minutes.'

They checked the spare bedroom first, but found nothing there, then Krywald walked across the landing and stopped outside the closed door of the only other bedroom.

'Hear that?' he asked, leaning his head close to the door panels.

'What?'

'I dunno – kind of a faint buzzing sound. Like a chopper a long way off, but it seems to be coming from in here.'

'I don't hear it,' Stein said.

Krywald listened for a few more seconds, then shook his head and pushed open the door. The faint buzzing noise was suddenly loud enough for Stein to hear it too.

'Jesus Christ,' Krywald said, stopping dead in the doorway and looking across the room. 'What the hell happened to him?'

Like Krywald, Stein was no stranger to death, sudden or otherwise, but the sight of the blood-soaked bed, and Aristides's bloody corpse, turned him pale. 'Fuck knows,' he said, 'but at least now we know what you were hearing a minute ago.'

Krywald looked where Stein was pointing, and realized that what he had initially taken for dried blood covering Aristides's corpse was actually moving – and buzzing. It was a carpet of what looked like thousands of flies, black, blue and green, their bodies heaving and wriggling in an almost solid mass as they fed greedily upon the dead man's body.

'Jesus Christ,' Krywald said again. 'OK, let's make it quick.'

Two minutes later they were out of the bedroom and back on the tiny landing, having checked every possible nook and corner in the bedroom that could have concealed the steel case. They had found nothing.

'Shit,' Krywald said. 'If he ever had it, he's hidden it somewhere. There's no way it's still in this house. Let's hope our friend Nico took it home with him.'

The two men walked quickly down the stairs and headed out of the house. As they opened the door to the street they both unconsciously took a long, deep breath of the fresher air, but it would be a long time before they would get the smell of that house out of their memories. They nodded briefly to the policeman on guard, then walked back the way they had come.

After having found exactly nothing in the intervening streets that looked as if it shouldn't be there, the other three men also arrived outside Spiros Aristides's house.

'Is this it?' Hardin asked.

Lavat nodded and gestured to the police officer standing near by.

'I've had a guard outside ever since we found the body.'

'OK,' Hardin said, 'as I explained before, there's nothing much I can do until my own people get here, but I will go in now and at least take a look at him. Dr Gravas, could you give me a hand?'

Hardin walked over to the red fibreglass box positioned close to the wall opposite the house. Biohazard symbols – similar to the familiar radiation warning markers but with their own distinctive spiky appearance – adorned the lid and sides. He removed his jacket and hung it on a rusty nail protruding from the wall at a convenient height, then snapped open the catches on the box and flipped up the lid.

It contained all the basic equipment needed to carry out a field investigation: masks, gloves, caps, syringes and needles, microscope slides and covers, glass and plastic sample tubes, sealable plastic bags in a variety of sizes for organ storage, reagents for specimen testing, scalpels, forceps, saws and other dissection instruments, packs of scalpel blades and stainless steel pins for holding apart sections of an organ during a post mortem examination. The box also contained a host of other, non-medical, equipment such as torches, batteries, paper, pens, pencils, erasers, Magic Markers, adhesive tape of various types, two portable recorders with spare cassettes and batteries, and even a bottle of bleach.

On top of all this was, neatly folded, a lightweight orange Racal biological space suit, which Gravas eyed with interest. Hardin noted his keen attention.

'It's made of an airtight fabric called Tyvek,' he explained, pulling the suit out of the box. 'It's not like the ones we use back in Atlanta in the Level Four lab,' he added. 'We call those "blue suits". They're made by a company called Chemturion and are connected to a central compressed air system to provide positive pressure within the suit and also supplies the air we breathe. They're noisy to work in because of the air constantly rushing in, so trying to talk to other people or use a telephone is difficult, verging on the impossible, unless you're prepared to switch off your air supply for a few seconds.

'This suit isn't pressurized because there's just no practical way to do that out in the field. It's just a neutral-pressure whole-body suit, but the hood – it's called a Racal hood – is pressurized to protect the lungs and the eyes, which contain two of the membranes most vulnerable to virus attack.'

As he was speaking, Hardin had unfolded the suit and stepped carefully into it, pulling the orange Tyvek up his legs and then thrusting his arms into the sleeves. He slipped off his shoes and pulled on rubber boots, then spent several minutes taping the legs of the suit over the boots, to make sure there were no gaps and that the joins were completely air-tight.

'Doctor, if you please.' Hardin handed Gravas a small paper sachet.

'Talcum powder?' Gravas hazarded, and Hardin nodded.

Gravas opened the sachet and sprinkled the white powder over Hardin's hands, then handed the American a pair of thin rubber surgical gloves to pull on. Following further directions, Gravas taped the wrists of the biohazard suit over the gloves, ensuring an air-tight join there too. Then Hardin pulled another sachet of powder out of the box and a second pair of surgical gloves and repeated the procedure, but this time Gravas taped the gloves *over* the sleeves of the Racal suit.

'Now the hood and blower,' Hardin said. He secured a thick webbing belt around his waist and clipped on a heavy square battery box, a large purple filter and a blower.

'That's a special filter?' Gravas asked.

Hardin nodded. 'Yes, a HEPA – High Efficiency Particle Arrestor. It's designed to trap biological particles present in the air so that what I breathe in won't kill me. At least, that's what the manufacturer claims.'

Gravas smiled at the weak joke, then helped Hardin settle the Racal hood over his head. The hood comprised a soft and fairly flexible breathing helmet, like a transparent plastic bubble connected to the blower and filter assembly at his waist. Hardin switched on the blower as Gravas checked the pipe connections for leaks. Satisfied, Gravas positioned the double flaps that hung down from the hood over Hardin's chest and shoulders, then zipped up the biohazard suit over these flaps and sealed it at the neck.

'How long does the battery last?' Gravas asked.

Hardin's reply was somewhat muffled by the hood, but clear enough.

'Eight hours, but I'll be out long before then. Now, if you could just apply tape over the main zip and anywhere else that you think it needs it.'

'That's it.' Gravas stepped back, satisfied, a couple of minutes later.

'Thanks,' Hardin said. 'Just walk all round me and check if there are any tears or splits anywhere in this suit, please.'

Three minutes later, Hardin picked up his small bag of instruments and approached the street door of the house that belonged to the late Spiros Aristides.

## Central Intelligence Agency Headquarters, Langley, Virginia

Westwood accessed the FAA database again, and grunted in satisfaction. He hadn't bothered looking before, but this time he checked carefully. The registered owner of the Learjet 23, registration number N17677, was the American Government. The State Department, in fact.

That single fact meant there was a very good chance that the FAA aircraft registry and the CIA's central database were both right, despite their apparently contradictory information.

Westwood guessed that the Learjet had been a Company plane, but a ringer – one of two identical aircraft wearing the same tail numbers, thus allowing a measure of deniability if one were spotted somewhere that it shouldn't be.

What he wasn't sure about was where he went from here, but he knew he was going to carry on digging. Thirty years ago, the Company had probably been involved in some form of covert operation in the Eastern Mediterranean, but that was hardly surprising news. Back in the 1970s the CIA had been involved in covert operations almost everywhere on the surface of the globe. And all he had here was a Learjet that had crashed off-route, somewhere near Crete: it was hardly another Watergate.

Westwood checked the database again, looking for any clues to indicate what the Company might have been up to in 1972, but he found nothing to suggest that anything of any interest to either America or the CIA had been happening around Crete in that year.

But still he sat and worried, about two things in particular. Why had both the CAIP and Learjet files been sealed since July 1972, a full two weeks *before* the search for the missing Learjet had been abandoned? And, even more fundamental, just what the hell was CAIP?

## Kandíra, south-west Crete

Tyler Hardin's gaze took in the flaking white-wash on the walls and the faded light green paint of the door and windows. He wasn't looking for anything in particular, but he was keenly aware that he was entering a potential hot zone, where something too small to be seen except through the magnified gaze of a scanning electron microscope was lurking in wait to kill him. He wouldn't be able to see it, feel it, smell it or taste it, but that didn't alter the fact that it was there, and all that stood between him and this unknown pathogen was a thin layer of Tyvek, a plastic helmet, two pairs of rubber gloves, a battery-driven blower and a HEPA filter.

Inside his suit, Hardin shook his head slightly in self-admonishment, then lifted the latch, pushed open the solid old wooden door and stepped from the sunlight into the sudden cool darkness of the house.

## HMS *Invincible*, Sea of Crete

The communications rating stopped outside the open door to the Wardroom and peered inside hopefully, clutching a buff envelope and a clipboard with a single sheet of paper on it. He'd already tried Richter's cabin on Two Deck and found that empty, and the Wardroom was his second, and last, option before requesting a tannoy broadcast.

'Who is it you want?' Malcolm Mortensen asked, approaching the rating from the starboard passageway.

'Oh, Lieutenant Commander Richter, sir,' the rating replied, turning to the young lieutenant.

Mortensen walked into the Wardroom and peered round. 'Right, he's over in the far corner. Give that to me and I'll take it to him.'

To Mortensen's surprise, the rating shook his head firmly. 'Sorry, sir. I have to hand it to him personally and he has to sign for it.'

Mortensen raised his eyebrows slightly, then nodded. 'OK, wait here.' He walked across the Wardroom to where Richter sat, an inevitable cup of coffee in front of him, leafing through a three-month-old copy of *Country Life*.

'Spook, your presence is required.'

Richter looked up, an expression of mild surprise on his face. 'By whom, pray?'

'There's a lad at the door with a clipboard and a brown envelope. You're to sign one and he'll give you the other. I'll leave it to you to work out which is which.'

'Thanks, Malcolm,' Richter said. He got up and shambled over towards the door. Mortensen watched him cross the Wardroom. Richter really was a scruff, he thought. He was amazed he'd actually got his half-stripe, but Mortensen supposed, correctly, that Richter's undoubted flying ability had counted for more in the eyes of the Promotions Board than whether or not his shirts were properly pressed or his hair combed.

'You've got something for me?' Richter asked the communications rating, at the entrance to the Wardroom.

'Yes, sir. Message classified Secret, precedence Immediate and for your eyes only,' he added, with a hint of a smirk.

'Are you taking the piss?'

'No, sir, it really is. Just sign here.'

Richter scrawled an approximation of his signature in the space indicated by the rating's slightly grubby finger, added the date and time, and handed back the clipboard. He took the envelope and tore it open as the rating walked off along the passageway leading back towards the Communications Centre on Five Deck.

Richter glanced at the red 'SECRET' stamps at the top and bottom of the single sheet of paper. He quickly read the message printed in capital letters – all military communications printers generate their output in capital letters – and then he read it again, carefully.

'Bugger,' he said, and walked off towards the starboard-side staircase, heading for Flyco, because that's where he expected to find Commander (Air).

## Kandíra, south-west Crete

The house was exactly as Lavat and Gravas had described it, so Hardin knew precisely where he was going. But he didn't immediately head for the stairs. First he looked carefully around the tiny hall, checking to see if he could spot anything out of place, anything that looked as if it shouldn't be there. Nothing was evident.

Then Hardin walked through to the kitchen. He looked in the stone sink, above which a handful of flies buzzed in erratic circles. The sink contained a single plate bearing a small piece of cheese, a bowl holding half a dozen black olives and a number of olive pits, and a slightly grubby cup half-full of what looked like strong, almost black, coffee. He carefully pulled open the single drawer, which held assorted bits of mismatched cutlery, and inspected the two cupboards, which contained plates of different sizes and other pieces of crockery, and about half a dozen pans. The cooker yielded nothing, but Hardin spent a couple of minutes looking through the contents of the toolbox he found beside the kitchen door.

Another door, at the rear of the kitchen, led to a tiny bathroom, obviously a later addition to the property, which contained a toilet, a small sink and a narrow shower stall, down the inside of which a constant stream of rusty-brown water trickled from the shower head. It didn't look as if Spiros Aristides had used this shower very often. On the other hand, Hardin reflected with a wry smile, if he went diving in the Mediterranean most days he probably wouldn't need to.

There was a single small cupboard with a mirrored door attached to the wall above the sink. It contained pretty much what one would expect: a bar of soap, a small bottle of shampoo, a twin-blade razor with half a dozen spare blades, and two cans of shaving foam. There was nothing else of interest.

Back in the main room, Hardin switched on the centre light, glanced around and then walked across to the scarred wooden table. There was an empty Scotch bottle more or less in the middle, and next to it an empty beer bottle. This, Hardin deduced, probably meant that Spiros had been drinking Scotch while his nephew had drunk the beer, or perhaps vice versa. Assuming, of course, that Nico had returned here with his uncle after their meeting at Jakob's, which seemed likely.

All that appeared normal. What struck Hardin as he looked more closely at the table was that the other things on it were not quite what one would expect to find on a piece of furniture used for eating meals. There were a couple of screwdrivers, a pair of pliers and a hacksaw with a damaged blade, all of which properly belonged in the toolbox.

Hardin bent down and peered very closely at one corner of the table. Small but perfectly clear: definite scratch marks. Fresh scratch marks, as if some work involving the tools scattered across the table had been done there recently. Hardin stood up and looked around the room, wondering if he was just chasing shadows, if he was inferring something complex from what might have been some simple domestic chore. Maybe the Greek had trouble opening a jar of olives or something, and had simply used these tools to wrench off the top.

He glanced around again, and was heading for the door into the hall when his subconscious stopped him. He'd seen something out of the corner of his eye, something that didn't fit. He turned back and looked down behind the table, at the dusty flag-stoned floor. Something small and red was lying there against the wall, something he hadn't spotted when he'd first looked round the room.

Hardin carefully moved the chair away from the table and eased himself down into a crouch to study what he'd found. At first, he couldn't make out what it was: it looked like a thin red cylinder of some sort.

Ever conscious of the possibility of damage to his protective clothing, and the potential dangers lurking within this house, Hardin stood up again without touching the object. He walked out into the hall, picked up the small instrument bag he had brought with him and pulled out a pair of long-handled forceps. Back in the room, he crouched down again and cautiously prodded the strange object with the end of the instrument.

It moved and rolled and then Hardin realized exactly what it was – a length of thick red wax, cut off the neck of a bottle or something similar, which had curled itself up again, re-forming into its original shape.

'Curious,' he murmured, and picked up the wax by threading the end of the forceps through the centre of the coil. He stood up, placed the wax on the table and examined it, but in the gloom it was difficult to see much detail. Hardin reached out and touched the switch on the standard lamp that stood next to the table, flooding it with light.

Then he realized something else. The standard lamp didn't belong where it was now standing. The electric cable was plugged into a socket nearly ten feet away, close to the fireplace, and was stretched to its limit, though there was another power socket closer to the table, less than three feet from the lamp base. That didn't really make sense. Hardin stepped back and glanced around him.

The room's central ceiling light was comparatively dim – only a sixty-watt bulb, Hardin guessed – so the owner would probably want a stronger light by the two easy chairs beside the fireplace. That was where a man would take his book or newspaper, to sit in one of the more comfortable chairs and toast his feet against the fire in the comparative cool of a winter evening. Hardin walked across and peered down at the floor beside each chair.

Faintly visible there was a circular area that didn't reveal the same amount of dust as the rest of the floor around it in that corner. Hardin estimated its diameter at just over a foot, so he walked back and studied the base of the standard lamp. Also about a foot.

He nodded in satisfaction. He didn't know exactly what Aristides had been up to, but it looked certain that he had been opening something at the table in this room. Something that had been sealed with red wax. He or they had dragged the standard lamp over so that they could see better, while using the tools still scattered across the table.

Hardin bent over to inspect the coiled wax more carefully. It looked as if it had originally encased some kind of small bottle or flask. Still using the forceps he opened it out, checking the inside of the loose cylinder it formed. It was completely smooth, so he looked again at the outside. Clearly visible there was a cross-hatched pattern, as if the wax had been encased in some kind of securing wire.

He stepped back from the table and scanned the floor behind it, then murmured in satisfaction and bent forward to again use his forceps. He dropped the tangle of wires – they formed a kind of loose cage, the ends of the strands bright where somebody had cut them with pliers – on the table next to the coil of wax. Hardin studied both objects for a few moments, considering.

Then he headed back into the kitchen and inspected the contents of the small rubbish bin. Next he peered outside the rear door, then checked again in every cupboard and drawer. No sign of any kind of a flask or bottle, so maybe the nephew Nico had taken it away with him.

But even without the hard evidence of a flask, he knew his diagnosis made sense, and it probably explained why Spiros and Nico were both dead, and why nobody else in Kandíra was apparently affected. Both men had been killed by an unknown pathogen stored in some kind of a small flask, which had been heavily sealed with both wax and wire. They had presumably opened the flask here inside Spiros's house, infecting themselves immediately, and both were dead within a few hours.

Hardin still didn't know what had killed these two men, but he already knew much more than he had when he'd entered the house. He could still be dealing with some rare but naturally occurring pathogen, a lethal virus or such like, which for some reason was stored in a heavily sealed flask, which the two Greeks had unfortunately opened. But the other, more likely, possibility was that this pathogen was a manufactured agent, a bioweapon deliberately created in some unacknowledged and secret Level Four laboratory – an illegal, fast-acting and clearly lethal virus or toxin.

It was warm in the house, and Hardin was sweating inside his biological space suit, but still he shivered at the thought.

# Chapter 12

'So what do you want us to do?' Commander (Air) asked Richter, who was leaning against the bulkhead in Flyco on the port side of the bridge.

'My instructions are somewhat vague,' Richter said, with a slight smile. 'In fact,' he added, 'they often are. What my section wants me to do is go ashore in Crete and find out if this epidemic is natural or if it's been caused by the release of a manufactured agent. My section' – Richter almost never mentioned the name of the organization that employed him – 'is concerned that this may be some kind of a trial run for a terrorist attack.'

'Is that likely?'

Richter shrugged. 'Frankly, sir, I don't know. The obvious worry is that al-Qaeda or some other terrorists have developed a biological or chemical weapon which they're planning to use on a population centre, and that this is just a trial to confirm that the agent actually works. September the eleventh proved how these people have the resources and the determination to attack the West, and the beauty of these agents is that they can be triggered remotely, just by using a timer on a capsule of some sort. They don't even need to recruit a suicide bomber to make them work.'

'I can understand that if this involved an attack on London or New York,' Commander (Air) said, 'but Crete is hardly a hotbed of American or British interests. Why would they attack here?'

'As I said, just as a trial, nothing more. The supposition is that some organization has chosen Crete simply to check if some agent they've cooked up, bought or stolen, is effective. If nobody dies, they go back to the drawing board and tweak it some more. If people die, that proves it works, and they then haul their box of bugs off to Islington or

**180**

Washington or wherever, and open it up there for real. Anyway, all that I have to do for the moment is go ashore and talk to the CDC people, to find out what they think caused this little epidemic.'

'Do you want to fly straight to Kandíra?'

Richter shook his head. 'No, I'll need somewhere to stay and I need to be mobile as well. From what little we know of Kandíra, there's no hotel and the most they're likely to have for hire is a donkey. The airport at Irakleío will do fine. I can hire a car there, find a hotel for tonight and drive over to Kandíra tomorrow morning.'

'Right,' Wings said. 'Rather you than me, but I'll tell Ops One to put you on the next available chopper.'

### Kandíra, south-west Crete

At the northern end of Kandíra, another policeman had been stationed outside the house containing Nico Aristides's small apartment, but again this officer had no idea what a genuine CDC identification card looked like, or even if such a document actually existed. However, unlike his colleague earlier, he didn't just accept them at face value and step aside.

'First, I must check with Inspector Lavat and obtain his permission,' he insisted, and turned back towards the house. Stein noticed an old-fashioned, bulky two-way radio perched on one of the wide window sills and motioned to Krywald, but the other American was already moving.

As the Cretan police officer stretched out his hand towards the window sill, Krywald stepped up directly behind him, lifted his right arm and brought a blackjack crashing down on the back of the man's head. The officer staggered forward and crashed into the wall, but his peaked cap had deflected and reduced the impact of the blow. He cried out with pain, immediately reaching for the pistol at his belt.

It would have been better for him to have just lost consciousness. Then he might have woken up a few hours later with a really bad headache.

Krywald instantly moved forward and span him round until they were face to face. Dropping the blackjack, the American grabbed the policeman's hand to stop him from drawing his weapon. For a few moments they struggled together, Krywald's left hand clutching the police officer's right wrist, as the other man swung a series of clumsy left-handed blows at his head.

Krywald ducked and dodged easily, then seized his opportunity. He brought up the heel of his right hand, hard, against the officer's nose, shattering the fragile nasal bone and maxilla and driving the fragments deep into his brain. The man's head snapped backwards and he tumbled limply to the ground. He wasn't dead, but he was dying quickly. He was also making a lot of noise about it, emitting a high-pitched wail that Stein feared would attract unwelcome attention within seconds. Krywald stopped this by kneeling down and smashing the side of his hand into the officer's throat, crushing the man's voice box and silencing him instantly.

'Shit, another problem,' Stein murmured. 'We really didn't need a local hero.'

'He's not a problem any more,' Krywald said, 'and I guess he's a dead local hero. Here, give me a hand. Oh, and thanks for helping out here.'

'The day you can't take care of a hick cop, Krywald, is the day you should start seriously thinking about another career.'

The policeman's body was still twitching as they carried it across the road. At that exact moment two elderly Cretans walked round the corner and stopped dead, staring.

Krywald and Stein reacted immediately, silently, without hesitation, in the way they'd been trained. They simply dropped the policeman's body and charged towards the two Cretans, who stood rooted to the spot, with their eyes and mouths wide open. In any other context it might have been funny.

Stein thought it would all be over in seconds, but just as he reached them, one old man raised his walking stick and brought it round in a vicious swinging arc. Stein was forced to stop sharply and dodge the gnarled end as it whistled past about an inch in front of his face.

But the old man's valiant swing had unbalanced him. Before he could bring his stick back ready for another blow, Stein stepped in close and slammed his right fist deep into the Cretan's solar plexus. The air was expelled from the old man's lungs in a wheezing gasp and he folded forwards as if hinged at the waist.

As the man collapsed to the ground, Stein knelt down in front of him and reached out almost casually. He took a firm grip on either side of the Cretan's slightly grubby shirt collar, rolled his fists so that his knuckles pressed against the sides of the neck and pushed inwards. The flow of blood through the carotid artery ceased almost immediately.

The Cretan struggled briefly, but he had no chance at all. He lost consciousness within seconds, and was dead in little over a minute.

Stein straightened up, then kicked the corpse onto its back. He next reached down, to grab the old man's right arm and haul him roughly onto his shoulders in a travesty of a fireman's lift. He glanced round to see Krywald already carrying the other Cretan towards a wide ditch running along beside the unmade track that snaked away into the open countryside to the east.

Stein jogged across the track, the old man's body bouncing grotesquely on his shoulders, where it followed Krywald's victim into the ditch. Then, still without exchanging a word, the pair ran back to the policeman sprawled lifeless on the ground, picked him up between them and tossed his body on top of the other two.

Stein looked around and found a sheet of rusty corrugated iron leaning against a fence, and pitched that over the three bodies. It wasn't perfect cover by any means, but as long as nobody stumbled on the corpses for about fifteen minutes, that was going to be fine.

They checked up and down the street but there was nobody in sight. Krywald led the way up the outside staircase and stopped at the single door at the top. He checked the door first, noting the splintered jamb and official seal, placed there on Lavat's instructions, then pushed it open, ripping the fabric seal apart. The two men pulled on their face masks and surgical gloves and stepped inside.

The search didn't take long, because there were only three rooms to check – a double bedroom, a bathroom and a living room with a dining area and what the apartment's developer had apparently hoped was an 'American-style kitchen' at one end.

They found Nico in the bedroom, wearing just a pair of pyjama bottoms and lying beside the unmade double bed. Like his uncle, Nico's body was covered in blood, as was the floor all around, and there were even splashes on the walls and the back of the door. Bloated blue and green flies fed on the blood and the body while others buzzed drunkenly around the room.

'What the hell's been going on here?' Stein demanded. 'Looks like somebody hacked him to death. And there's that same goddamn smell.'

'God knows, because I sure as hell don't,' muttered Krywald, then snapped. 'OK, this is a real small place, so we should be out of here in no time. I'll check the other rooms, you take a good look in here.'

Krywald had barely reached the living room before he heard Stein call out to him from the bedroom.

'Bingo,' Stein said, gazing down at the steel case sitting in the bottom of the free-standing pine wardrobe.

Four minutes after that they walked out of the house, the steel case now tucked inside the square black case that Stein had been carrying. They didn't even glance towards the ditch that they'd turned into a temporary tomb for three innocent Cretans.


Tyler Hardin opened the street door of Spiros Aristides's house and stepped outside. Lavat and Gravas headed over towards him, but kept some four feet away from the American to avoid any possibility of physical contact with him or his space suit.

'That was quick,' Gravas said.

Hardin shook his head. 'I haven't examined the body yet, but I think I know the source of the infection.'

'What was it?'

'I don't know exactly what the agent itself was, but I believe I know what it was inside. I think the two men found a small bottle or flask, which they opened inside there,' Hardin gestured back towards the small, shabby white house, 'and whatever was in that container killed them.'

There was silence for a few moments as the two Greeks digested this, then Gravas spoke. 'So this can't be Ebola or anything natural like that,' he said. 'You're suggesting we're dealing with some kind of *manufactured* agent – a biological weapon?'

Hardin nodded. 'It could be,' he replied. 'Or, possibly, it's some kind of unknown natural virus that had been collected and stored inside the flask for research purposes. Thousands of laboratories store viruses that way, and some of them are lethal, like smallpox, anthrax and so on. You can even buy them on the Internet, if you know where to look.

'What worries me is that I still have no idea what could have killed those two men so quickly. Viruses,' he added, 'are my business, but even I don't know of any virus that can kill as quickly and efficiently as this sucker has. It's more like some sort of chemical agent, but again I don't know of any capable of producing this kind of result within this short a timescale. Whatever this thing is,' he concluded, 'I think it's entirely new, something that's never been seen before, and that really worries me.'

'What about the flask you found?' Lavat asked. 'Can't you identify the agent from the residue left inside it?'

Hardin shook his head. 'I didn't say I'd found the flask. I said I'd found the wax and wire that had clearly been used to seal it, but there's no sign of the container itself. That's what I came out to tell you. I've looked all around the ground floor and if it's there I haven't spotted it. Obviously I'll check upstairs as well, but there's no particular reason why Spiros would hide the flask, so I'm assuming that it isn't here. And that means—'

Inspector Lavat interrupted. 'That means the most likely person to have taken it would be Nico, so it's probably somewhere in his apartment.'

'Exactly,' Hardin said. 'As soon as I've had a good look at Spiros we have to get over there and find it.'


### Irakleío, Crete

Mike Murphy had achieved rather better time than Krywald's team, principally because he had managed to make the connection at Heathrow, so he landed at Irakleío just over eight hours behind them. He was in no hurry, because he couldn't do anything until Nicholson confirmed that Krywald and his team had completed their part of the operation – about which Murphy himself knew nothing – so he took his time.

He collected his single bag from the carousel, queued for about fifteen minutes to collect a pre-booked Peugeot hire car and a map of

Crete, then drove out of the airport. He stopped at what looked like quite a reasonable restaurant and had a meal, then drove west along the north-coast road of Crete to Réthymno and checked into his hotel. He inspected the room Nicholson had booked for him, checked the location of the lift, the main stairs and the fire escape – he had saved his own life at least twice in the past by knowing the back way out of a building – then sent Nicholson, who was still using the 'McCready' alias, an encrypted email announcing his arrival at Réthymno.

And then, because he would have almost exactly nothing to do for a minimum of twelve hours, Murphy stretched out on the rather hard double bed and went to sleep.

## HMS *Invincible*, Sea of Crete

The sun was sinking steadily towards the horizon as afternoon shaded into evening. The western sky was an incredible artist's palette of pastel hues and primary colours – pinks, reds, blues, yellows and greens – splashed in slowly-changing bands above the horizon. The *Invincible* was barely moving through the flat calm sea, easing east at less than three knots, holding position just to the north of Crete.

The slight tang of salt in the air was overlaid by the unmistakable smell of burnt kerosene from the Merlin's three Rolls-Royce Turbomeca gas turbines, and the noise of the aircraft – a mix of the whine of the engines and the clattering of the rotor blades as they turned above the bulky shape – drowned out all other sounds on the Flight Deck.

The Merlin sat, turning and burning, on number three spot, its side access door open and a clutch of Flight Deck personnel clustered around it, carrying out a rotors-running refuel. Each rating wore an appropriate coloured jersey, identifying his specialization to anyone who knew the colour code. The ones that stood out most were the fire-fighters, trolley-mounted A-Triple F extinguishers to hand and clad entirely in what looked like heavy silver coats and trousers, but which were actually made of a fire-resistant asbestos fabric.

Paul Richter watched the helicopter from where he was standing on the port side of the island superstructure, ear defenders on his head and a black leather overnight bag sitting on the deck beside him. He was now wearing civilian clothes and the bag contained enough personal stuff to last him for the couple of days he anticipated it might take to find an answer that would satisfy Simpson.

It was the last flight from the ship that evening, a late addition to the flying programme, and its only outbound passenger was to be Richter. The helicopter was planned to fly from the *Invincible* direct to the main airport at Irakleío to collect the three remaining members of the CDC team, who were expected to touch down within minutes on the last leg of their long journey from Atlanta, Georgia.

The Flight Deck Officer was standing in front, and slightly to one side, of the helicopter, watching as the refuelling hose was detached from the inlet at the side of the fuselage. He checked to ensure that the hose was pulled well clear, then waved away the attending fire-fighters.

Above the deck, in his seat in Flyco – it was a comfortable black padded swivel chair adjustable in almost every direction, which was just as well bearing in mind how long Lieutenant Commander (Flying) or the Air Staff Officer spent sitting in it at a stretch – Roger Black peered downwards through the slanting windows, noted that refuelling had finished and called through to the bridge on the intercom.

'Officer of the Watch, Flyco. The refuelling's just finished, so we'll need launch wind across the deck in a few minutes.'

'Roger that. Turning starboard and increasing speed.'

On deck, the FDO unconsciously leaned against the heeling of the ship as it began its long turn to starboard and increased its speed, watching the helicopter pilot carefully. He acknowledged a signal from the cockpit, then beckoned to Richter, who picked up his leather bag and headed across the deck to where the FDO stood, stopping in full view of the Merlin's pilot. The two men waited for a signal, ensuring that the pilot was aware that his passenger was ready to embark, then Richter walked across to the side access door of the helicopter, ducking as he moved under the rotor disk, tossed his bag into the rear compartment of the Merlin and climbed in after it. He strapped himself in and waited for take-off.

The ship steadied on a south-westerly heading and began to pick up speed. Seated in Flyco, Roger Black checked the anemometer readout, waiting for the wind to move within limits for the launch. Although helicopters, and even Sea Harriers, can take off vertically in still wind conditions, they almost never do, simply because the amount of power required means that the payload – what it's carrying – is too low for the aircraft to achieve anything useful once it's airborne. Instead, Harriers use vectored thrust and a short take-off run to get airborne, and carrier-borne helicopters rely on wind gusting down the deck to increase the lift generated by the rotor blades.

Black nodded as the wind speed increased to the level he needed, and turned to the rating sitting beside him. 'Rotary wing – green deck for'rard.'

'Yes, sir. Rotary wing – green deck for'rard,' the rating repeated and flicked a switch.

On the Flight Deck, the FDO looked up towards the Bridge, saw the red light change to green and acknowledged. He gestured to the pilot and then waved four of his men in to the helicopter to remove the deck lashings. With ease born of long practice, the four ratings slackened and then removed the fabric belts – chains would be used in bad weather conditions – which secured the Merlin to the ringbolts studding the deck of the carrier. Then they trotted forward and stood in a line directly in front of the helicopter's cockpit, each man holding up the lashing he had removed.

The FDO ostentatiously counted each lashing, pointing at it with one of his illuminated wands as the aircrew in the cockpit watched, proving to the pilot that he was able to lift off when ready. Trying to launch an aircraft whilst any part of it is still attached to the deck of a ship is an extremely bad idea, and one that is absolutely certain to ruin everyone's day.

The pilot acknowledged, switched on his navigation and anti-collision strobe lights, and waited for the FDO's signal to take-off. Normally a ground marshaller handles the landing and take-off of helicopters and Sea Harriers, but there was nothing else going on anywhere on the Flight Deck, and the FDO liked to keep his hand in.

He raised the two illuminated wands from the 'parked' position – crossed in front of him below the waist – till they were outstretched fully at his sides, then raised them both slowly above his head, repeating the action as the pilot applied power and pulled up the collective lever that increased the angle of attack of the rotor blades to generate more lift. The noise of the Merlin's three jet engines increased to a steady scream and the aircraft rose very slightly, teetering gently from side to side on its landing gear, then rose into the air immediately above the deck.

As soon as the FDO was satisfied that the aircraft was established in the hover, he pointed his right-hand wand – the pilot's left – steadily out to sea and moved the left-hand wand in a semi-circle from outstretched left, over his head, to outstretched right. He watched as the Merlin moved off, landing gear retracting as it headed away from the ship into the dusk.

### Kandíra, south-west Crete

Tyler Hardin walked swiftly across the small hallway, which even with the light on was dark as the sun sank below the roof level of the neighbouring house. He climbed the stairs and stopped at the landing, then switched on the light and looked around.

As Gravas had already told him, there were two doors leading off the tiny landing. Both stood open. Hardin looked first in the spare bedroom, checking it more in hope than expectation for some sign of the flask whose existence he had deduced. As he had feared, he found nothing there, and moved across to the other room.

Hardin stopped at the doorway, reached around the jamb for the switch and flicked the light on. He looked into the bedroom before he stepped across the threshold, slowly taking in the scene. Belatedly, he remembered that he had a Polaroid camera somewhere in one of his cases, and should have brought it with him to record what he was now witnessing.

Before he approached the corpse, Hardin looked all around the room, checking under the bed, inside the single wardrobe and even on the two bookshelves, but found nothing that could possibly be the missing container. Only then did he look at the mortal remains of Spiros Aristides.

For three or four minutes, Hardin just stood and studied the shape on the bed. With the coming of dusk, most of the flies that had fed so greedily on the dead man's blood earlier in the day had vanished, but a few still remained, moving sluggishly across his chest.

Hardin's first thought was that Gravas had been somewhat conservative in his reporting. There was just so much blood everywhere, so much fluid, that it looked as if the Greek's body had been completely exsanguinated. Hardin had never seen a victim of Ebola in the flesh – few people had – but he had seen plenty of pictures, and in his opinion what he was looking at here was even worse, not least because the Greek had obviously died so quickly. From taking a drink in a bar to lying dead on his bed in less than twelve hours. Whatever this agent was, it was not only messily lethal but unbelievably rapid.

Hardin shook his head, and walked away from the bed without even touching Aristides's body. As he had told Gravas earlier, there was nothing he could do to isolate the causative agent without using the equipment that the rest of his team was bringing out. All he could say for sure was that Spiros Aristides was dead – self-evident to anybody who cared to look into that bedroom.

Much more important was to find the container that had held the agent that killed these two men.

Krywald had planned to leave the village in much the same way they had arrived, but as he and Stein made their way through the silent and darkening streets, he heard the sound of a helicopter approaching and immediately changed his mind. The two men had already discarded their gloves and masks, and now they pulled off their white coveralls and dumped them in an open trash can.

By the sound of it, the chopper was a big one, and Krywald guessed that it was probably ferrying supplies, equipment or maybe further personnel to Kandíra. Whatever its load, the aircraft would be the focus of attention for everyone trapped in the village, including the police officers manning the cordon, which meant the pair of them could probably slip away unnoticed.

They made their way towards the tents located near the main road – such as it was – leading into Kandíra, and stood back in the shadows for a few minutes, watching as the helicopter landed. It was a Royal Navy Merlin wearing light grey livery, and Krywald's guess had been right. It was carrying equipment, and three passengers – and both the goods and the people had begun their journey in Atlanta, Georgia. The remaining members of the CDC team had at last arrived.

As is usual in most of Europe, the prevailing wind came from the south-west, and the Merlin settled heavily onto the dusty ground with its nose pointing into wind and away from the cordon surrounding the village. The sliding access door to the rear compartment on a Merlin is located on the right side of the aircraft, which meant that nobody in the village or even manning the cordon could see when it was opened. Once the helicopter had landed, a few moments passed before anyone saw the newly arrived passengers approach from around the rear of the aircraft, keeping well clear of its spinning tail rotor.

Krywald and Stein waited until the helicopter's passengers had begun ferrying cases and equipment from the aircraft to the cordon, and a good two-way flow of people had been established. Then he and Stein stepped forward, waved their fake CDC identity cards towards one of the policemen, and walked across towards the helicopter. Stein was carrying the black case which contained the steel box. The two men slid around the rear of the aircraft, then simply continued walking away from the village and into the olive groves, where Elias was waiting in the hired Ford.

As they approached the lines of stunted trees, Krywald looked back. As he had anticipated, their departure had caused no interest whatsoever. Everyone was still transfixed by the helicopter, which sat, turning and burning, on the dusty scrub near the tents. Krywald grinned and carried on walking.


'That's odd,' Inspector Lavat remarked, as the three men approached the house where Nico Aristides had lived and died.

'What?' Hardin asked. He was moving very slowly in the biological space suit. The garment was undeniably cumbersome, and never intended to be worn by anyone out for a stroll. He was still wearing the Racal hood, because to have removed it would have meant going through the entire taping and checking procedure again, so he was sweating profusely.

'My police officer isn't here,' Lavat replied. 'I stationed a man outside each property.'

'A call of nature, perhaps?' Gravas suggested.

'Maybe,' Lavat said, 'but he should be somewhere close by. He wouldn't need to go far to find a convenient bush.' He gestured at the open countryside stretching in front of them.

'He'll be back in a few minutes, no doubt,' Gravas said. 'He's even left his radio on that window sill. Here, Mr Hardin, let me check you.'

Hardin stood quite still while Gravas prowled round him, visually checking every seam of the Tyvek space suit for any tears and ensuring that the tape was still in place at the American's ankles and wrists. Finally, Gravas examined the neck seal where the Racal hood was fitted, and then declared himself satisfied.

Hardin nodded his thanks and turned back towards the building. Like Spiros's house, and virtually every other property in Kandíra, it was small, white-washed and slightly scruffy. A narrow wooden door, painted in dark blue gloss, but heavily weathered and faded by the sun, gave access to the building from the street, and there was a steep flight of stone steps on the left side of the property that ascended to the first floor.

'Which floor, Inspector?' Hardin asked.

'The first,' Lavat replied. 'It's the only door up there. You'll need a knife to cut the seal on the door.'

'I have one here,' Gravas said. He took a small folding penknife from his pocket and opened the main blade. He walked towards Hardin, but stopped when he was a couple of feet away, then placed it on the ground and backed off.

Hardin stepped forward and picked up the knife. 'Thanks,' he said.

'Be careful with it,' Gravas said. 'It's very sharp.'

Hardin nodded, crossed the road and began to climb up the stone steps. At the top he paused before walking across to the door itself. Then he stopped and stared for a few seconds at the ripped fabric seal. One end had been nailed to the door and the other end to the frame, forming a symbolic rather than a literal or physical barrier, and the fabric had torn away from the nail in the door. Hardin walked back to the top of the outside stairs and called down to the street. 'Inspector?'

'Mr Hardin?'

'We have a problem here. Somebody has broken the seal. Someone has clearly entered this building since you and Dr Gravas were here.'

'What?' Lavat exclaimed, and started up the steps. He stopped a couple of treads from the top and stared across at the broken seal.

'This makes your missing police officer look more worrying,' Hardin said. 'Perhaps something has happened to him.'

Lavat nodded, turned back and started down the steps. 'I'll check,' he said.

Hardin put Gravas's penknife down on the low parapet, then opened the apartment door and stepped inside.

Ten minutes later he walked back down the stone staircase, laid the penknife on the ground and looked around. Gravas and Lavat were nowhere in sight, and he assumed they were searching the immediate area. He turned back to stare up at the house again just as Lavat walked around the corner.

'Any luck?' Hardin asked.

Lavat nodded briefly. 'Yes, we found him.'

'What did he tell you?' Hardin asked.

'Nothing at all,' Lavat's reply was low and angry, 'because he's dead. He's been tossed in a ditch like so much garbage, along with the bodies of two elderly locals. Dr Gravas is examining them all now.' Lavat paused and shook his head. 'This is turning into a massacre. It started out as a simple murder investigation,' he said, 'and we've now got five dead bodies, one of them a police officer. Two men killed by some germ, another two villagers and one of my officers slaughtered like animals by the same people who created that germ. I knew that young man personally. I've known him for three years and I'm the one who's going to have to tell his wife that she's a widow, and that's not a job I'm looking forward to.'

Lavat stared across at the space-suit-clad figure still standing in the middle of the street, his eyes moist and emotion choking his voice. 'You didn't find that missing container, did you?' he asked.

Hardin shook his head. 'No. There's nothing of that nature anywhere inside the apartment.'

'No,' Lavat said, 'because the bastards who killed my officer got here before us and took it away with them. But I'll find them. They must still be somewhere on this island, and if it's the last thing I do I'm going to track them down. I've already set the wheels in motion.' He turned as the doctor appeared behind him. 'Well?' he demanded angrily.

'They look like professional killings,' Gravas said, pulling off a pair of surgical gloves. 'The police officer was struck from behind, then somebody smashed his nasal bone upwards into his brain. That's a killing blow taught in certain schools of martial arts. They also crushed his larynx to stop him crying out. The two old men were basically strangled, but only after receiving crippling blows to their bodies.'

'I'm really sorry about this, Inspector,' Hardin said eventually into the long silence that followed the doctor's remarks, 'but we have to move on now. Dr Gravas, could you use the hand-sprayer, please?'

Gravas nodded and opened Hardin's bag, which he himself had carried from Spiros Aristides's house. The hand-sprayer it contained was fed with a bleach solution from an attached bottle. As Hardin stood in the middle of the street with his arms outstretched, Gravas walked all around him, spraying this solution liberally over the CDC investigator's Tyvek suit. As instructed, he started at the head, then worked his way slowly down to the American's booted feet.

The bleach was a high-concentration solution, which filled the still evening air with a stinging pungency.

'Normally we'd put this stuff in a biohazard bag and just dispose of it,' Hardin explained, as he pulled off the strips of tape to remove his hood, 'but we've limited equipment here on Crete and I've been very careful not to touch either body, so I intend to re-use this suit. That bleach solution will kill all known pathogens.'

Hardin bundled the suit into the biohazard bag Lavat had brought with him, added the hood and blower assembly, and closed the zipper. Lavat had a separate, smaller, biohazard bag, into which Hardin put both the pairs of surgical gloves he'd used, then sealed it. That bag and its contents would be destroyed by fire in due course. Hardin picked up the two biohazard bags and the three men began walking back towards the main street that ran through the village.

'So,' Gravas said, glancing back up the alley, 'no container.'

'No, so we have to assume that Nico had it in his possession and that whoever killed my police officer and then entered the property has now retrieved it. We also have to consider the possibility that Spiros found more than one container. We can be fairly certain that they opened one of them, but the fact that somebody has since been onto this scene . . .' Hardin suddenly halted, and Gravas turned to him curiously.

Something had been gnawing at Hardin's subconscious ever since he'd stepped out of the elder Aristides's house. Something he'd seen or heard that didn't seem quite right, but exactly what it was he hadn't been able to remember. Like a half-seen figure in fog, it had been too indistinct to discern but was equally obviously there. And suddenly he knew exactly what it was.

'God, I've been slow,' Hardin said. 'I should have realized back at the first house. I think you told me you closed his bedroom door after you, Dr Gravas?'

'Yes. I closed all the internal doors – it seemed a routine precaution.'

'But when I went upstairs, both bedroom doors were wide open. That means somebody else had access before I got there. I think we're up against somebody who knows exactly what's going on here and what they were looking for. And the fact that they're prepared to kill a police officer and two innocent bystanders tells me that the stakes are high, and are only going to get higher.'


## Lower Cedar Point, Virginia

A little after eight that evening Hawkins arrived at Lower Cedar Point and parked his car close to the water's edge, his watery pale blue eyes gazing across the Potomac towards Dahlgren and the setting sun. To the north there was a constant stream of traffic crossing the Harry W. Nice Memorial Bridge, which carries US 301 from Virginia to Maryland.

After a few minutes, the passenger door opened and he turned to greet the man who had telephoned him earlier. He was grey haired, big and bulky, and despite the warm weather was wearing a long black leather coat.

'John,' Hawkins said in brief greeting.

'CJ.'

'How did this happen?' Hawkins asked. 'I thought the wreck was too deep for divers to find it.'

'It should have been, but when the Lear was hit it looks like the pilot managed to retain some directional control and pointed the aircraft towards the nearest landmass, which happened to be Crete. That shouldn't have been a problem, because the water at that end of the Mediterranean is really deep, but unfortunately when the Lear finally speared in it was right between two islands about twenty miles south-east of Crete.

'Everywhere else in the area the seabed is far enough down that only really specialized equipment can reach it, but right where the Lear crashed the water's only about a hundred feet deep. It's not my field, but apparently that's pretty deep for a free diver using an aqualung, but it's not an impossible depth to reach as long as the diver knows what he's doing.'

'How sure are you that the right plane's been found?' Hawkins said after a few moments. 'There must be lots of wrecked aircraft at the bottom of the Mediterranean. What's your evidence?'

John Nicholson shrugged his broad shoulders. 'It's mainly circumstantial at the moment, but I think it's convincing enough. You remember the satellite watch we placed on the crash site?' Hawkins nodded. 'OK. A few days ago a work boat, which N-PIC later identified as a diving tender, was spotted in the area. In fact, it was anchored within a quarter of a mile of the original impact point. Only one image was available and that showed no activity – just the boat riding at anchor with nobody on board.'

'And from that it was inferred that there were divers underwater and at the wreck site? That sounds very thin, John.'

Nicholson nodded. 'I agree,' he said, 'but I did regard it as a wake-up call and requested N-PIC to take additional pictures there every time the bird passed overhead. There was no other activity for a couple of days, then another series of images all showing the same scene – the same diving tender in the same place. This time, we could see the diver as well, and he was hauling three aqualung sets back into the boat. My diving specialist tells me that using three aqualungs suggests either a very lengthy or a very deep dive, and the logical conclusion is that he went down deep. Very few divers will stay in mid-water, as the most interesting marine activity is usually on or just above the seabed.'

'It still sounds circumstantial to me,' Hawkins said. 'What you've got is a diving tender spotted in the area. That doesn't prove the diver found the wreck itself. In fact, we don't even know for sure that there's anything left to find after thirty years underwater.'

Nicholson nodded again. 'Yes, but there's more. The last frame received showed that one end of the rope he'd secured his aqualungs to was still in the water and there was almost certainly something else still attached to it.'

'Could have been a weight,' Hawkins suggested, 'or just another aqualung, maybe.'

'Yes, indeed it could,' Nicholson agreed, 'but I don't think so. N-PIC counted the aqualung racks visible on the tender, and that number matched the sets you can see in the pictures, so I don't think it was an extra lung. Furthermore, the diver cleated down the rope after he'd got the aqualungs up on deck. If all that was still in the water was a weight at the end of the rope, why would he bother to do that?'

Hawkins shook his head. 'I've no idea.'

'I think this diver found the wreck and retrieved something from it. The reason he didn't haul it straight into the boat was because he wanted to make sure that nobody was watching him.'

'In a diving tender out in the middle of the Mediterranean?' Hawkins's tone was mocking.

'You'd be surprised how many boats pass to and fro there,' Nicholson replied. 'Fishing boats, yachts, cruise ships, ski boats. If he'd found something he didn't want anyone to know about, it's logical that he would have had a careful look around before he pulled it on board.'

Hawkins nodded, reluctantly. 'OK, John. I concede that your scenario does make sense, though it is still entirely circumstantial. Because you're here talking to me, I assume you've already taken some action. What have you done to retrieve the situation?'

'I've sent a team out to Crete – in fact they should be there by now. I've briefed them to find and totally destroy the remains of the Learjet, after retrieving the case with the flasks.'

'And the file too, I hope?'

'Yes, and the file too.'

'What about this diver? Could N-PIC identify the diving tender? Can you trace the diver through his boat?'

Nicholson shook his head. 'I don't think we'll need to trace the diver.'

'Why not?'

'I checked the database before I called you, looking for any developments that might be related. There were two new entries that I think kind of tie everything together. First, this morning a Greek newspaper reported the death of a man called Spiros Aristides on Crete. He was an unlicensed diver. Second, the Centers for Disease Control in Atlanta have just responded to a request for assistance from the local Cretan medical authorities.'

Nicholson looked keenly at Hawkins, whose face now seemed paler in the fading daylight around the car. 'Why the CDC?' Hawkins asked. 'What was the nature of their problem? And what killed the diver?'

'A possible epidemic. The Cretans have reported that Aristides had probably been killed by Ebola, or some other kind of filovirus, but real fast-acting.'

Hawkins leaned back in his seat, and stared sightlessly through the windshield. 'So that's it,' he said at last. 'You're right. It's the only expla-nation that makes any kind of sense. This diver discovered the wreck, pulled out the case, then opened it up and found the flasks. And now he's dead because he opened a flask as well. Dear God, what a mess. I thought – I hoped – that after all this time we'd heard the last of it.' He shook his head. 'So what now? What secondary actions will you be taking?'

Nicholson didn't reply immediately, but glanced around the deserted area outside the car to check that they were still unobserved. When he spoke, his voice was low and almost sad. 'We – or rather I – have to pro-tect the Company, and America. I'm the only one left inside the Agency who knows exactly what happened, and why we had to do what we did. Under no circumstances can details of CAIP be allowed to leak out. That means I've had to take some hard decisions – and none, CJ, has been harder for me than this one.'

He reached inside his jacket and pulled out a small-calibre black automatic pistol with a silencer attached. He pointed it directly at Hawkins's chest.

'I'm truly sorry about this, CJ,' Nicholson continued, as the old man tensed and his face turned even paler, 'and you must believe this isn't easy for me. But I have to make sure there are no possible loose ends, and that means ensuring that all the agents involved in CAIP keep total silence. I'm afraid this is the only way I can be completely certain of that.'

For a long moment Hawkins stayed rigid, and Nicholson wondered if he might make a futile attempt to wrest the gun from his hands. Then Hawkins relaxed, seeming to accept the inevitable as he stared into the eyes of the younger man. 'You're probably right,' he said, 'but I would never have talked, you know. You don't need to do this.'

'You can say that,' Nicholson replied, 'but if they ever recovered the file they'd put you and the others under intense pressure. Your name and face would be splashed over the newspapers. You'd be publicly disgraced and humiliated. Then you might talk, just to explain what happened. I really can't take that risk. If you were in my position, you'd do the same.'

'Perhaps, perhaps not,' Hawkins muttered, then without warning swung a wild punch at Nicholson's jaw. The blow connected, but Nicholson had anticipated something of the sort and rode with it. He grabbed the older man's wrist with his left hand and forced his arm back. The pistol's aim barely wavered.

'This won't help, CJ,' Nicholson said, raising his voice and gesturing with the pistol. 'You know I have to do this, and it's up to you whether it's easy or hard.' Hawkins tensed again, and then relaxed, finally recognizing the futility of any attempt to overpower Nicholson: he was unarmed, twenty-five years older and seventy pounds lighter than his captor.

'I hate guns,' Hawkins murmured, slumping back into his seat.

'I can offer you a choice.' Nicholson reached into his pocket and tossed Hawkins a small twist of paper. In his safe at home, Nicholson kept a number of things he had acquired during his career with the CIA. One of them was a screw-top jar containing a dozen or so small brown pills obtained from Fort Detrick many years earlier.

Hawkins looked across at Nicholson, then undid the paper and stared at the pill.

'Just swallow it, CJ,' Nicholson said softly. 'I promise you it won't hurt. You'll just fall asleep. If you don't cooperate, I'll have to use this' – he motioned slightly with the silenced automatic – 'and that *will* hurt.'

Hawkins stared at his former colleague for a long moment, then across the Potomac at the last sunset he would ever see. 'You will take care of my wife, won't you?' he asked. Nicholson nodded as Hawkins took a last long look at the water in front of him, then swallowed the pill.

'That's why I was a few minutes late getting here,' Nicholson murmured, as Hawkins's eyes started to glaze over and his head slumped back in his seat. 'I already have.'

Three minutes later Nicholson checked for a pulse but found none. He got out of the car and strode off up the hill to where his own vehicle was parked. As he moved, he glanced at his watch, checking how much time he had before his second appointment of the evening – with a man named James Richards.

# Chapter 13

**Thursday**
**Réthymno, Crete**

It wasn't much of a hotel, but as far as Richter was concerned it was fine. He estimated he'd need a room for two nights, tops, and as long as the water was hot and the sheets were clean he was reasonably happy.

The Merlin had dropped him off at Irakleío the previous evening, and he'd hired a car – a blue Volkswagen Golf – and driven along the coast as far as Réthymno. The second hotel he'd tried had three vacant rooms, so he had picked the one that overlooked the hotel car park and hauled up his leather overnight bag from the Golf.

Richter didn't normally bother with breakfast, but it was included in the room price, so he walked down to the dining room just before eight and crunched his way through a slice of hard toast and an almost equally hard roll, washed down with coffee that actually tasted like it had been made from beans rather than powder.

Afterwards, he walked down the street to a souvenir shop and bought a map of Crete before collecting the Golf from the car park and heading further west along the main north-coast highway, destination Kandíra.

**Kandíra, south-west Crete**

'So, in summary, there are really two aspects to this outbreak that we need to address,' Tyler Hardin began. 'The first, the one that we the CDC team will be concentrating on, is to identify the pathogen that caused the deaths of these two men. Now that we have our equipment with us, I hope that we can achieve that fairly quickly.'

Hardin paused and looked round the tent that served as their makeshift base, set up by the main street that ran through Kandíra. His three CDC colleagues – Mark Evans, Jerry Fisher and Susan Kane – were sitting on collapsible chairs in front of him, mugs of coffee in hand and the remains of their breakfast scattered on the table behind them.

All were qualified doctors and Epidemic Intelligence Service officers, Fisher with eight years' experience, while Evans and Kane had only just completed their initial training at Atlanta. Hardin wasn't surprised to find that exactly half of his team were 'rookies'. The CDC had always believed that the best way to learn about investigating a sudden out-break of a disease was to just go out and do it. It was the ultimate form of 'on-the-job training'.

It was standard CDC procedure to deliver morning briefings before the field work started and this one was, in Hardin's opinion, probably the most important, because it was the first. He had talked to them briefly the previous evening, but all three had been exhausted both by their intense activity back in the States preparing for this operation and by the series of flights they'd had to endure to reach the island.

The last thing Hardin had wanted was to have tired and jet-lagged operatives messing with a Level Four Hot Agent, so as soon as they'd finished their evening meal he'd ordered them straight to bed – on camp-beds in the neighbouring tent – leaving it until late the next morning to brief them.

'The one piece of equipment we haven't got here is a scanning elec-tron microscope, but there's one in a research laboratory in Irakleío, which Dr Gravas tells me he has used in the past. Our investigation obviously has a very high priority, so we should be able to use that one more or less on demand. The most difficult part of conducting a micro-scopic investigation will be logistics. We're not very far from Irakleío as the crow flies, but getting there by road would take hours. Fortunately, we have some help there. Last night you arrived here by helicopter courtesy of the British Royal Navy aircraft carrier *Invincible*, which is standing off Crete specifically to assist us. I'm told her helicopters will be available to ferry us wherever, and whenever, we want to go. A liaison officer from the ship should be arriving here sometime this morning. He'll have a radio link to the *Invincible* and we'll be able to organize any helicopter flights we need through him.

'The second problem is the actual source of the infection. As I explained earlier, the evidence strongly suggests it was stored inside a heavily sealed container. If that is correct, we're dealing either with some bioweapon or with an unknown virus that has been discovered in the wild. And there's some other evidence that I'll discuss in a minute.'

Hardin glanced at his three colleagues in turn. 'In either case we are confronting something demonstrably deadly and almost certainly unfamiliar to us. You must take all the usual precautions in applying the rules for dealing with a potential Level Four Hot Agent. I know that's going to be difficult out here in the field, and we'll have to improvise, but it's essential that all of us exercise extreme care. Watch everything and everybody, and if you see anything that concerns you, stop the procedure immediately. Extreme caution is essential.

'My final point is somewhat unusual. I mentioned a container that I believe held this hot agent. What you should also know is that we haven't found it, nor expect to, simply because it seems somebody else has already removed it.' Hardin looked down at three astonished faces. 'When Dr Gravas realized Spiros Aristides might have died from some form of filovirus infection he took the basic precaution of closing all the doors before he left the house. When I subsequently entered, all the interior doors were standing open.

'Inspector Lavat had stationed a policeman outside the house to ensure that no one entered the property. When we questioned him, he was adamant that nobody had been in or out – except for the CDC personnel that he had been told to expect. What actually happened was that two men wearing white coveralls with the letters "CDC" stamped on them appeared at the house, showed him what appeared to be CDC identity cards, entered the building and then left a few minutes later.'

Hardin smiled mirthlessly, then explained what had happened at Nico's apartment. 'I myself believe that we're almost certainly dealing with either the raw material for a new weapon,' he continued, 'or even something that's already been weaponized, and we have to assume that these killers now have the container in their possession. We know there are at least two men involved because of the evidence of the policeman stationed outside the scene of the first death.

'One of these men was carrying a case, it seems, and it's no great leap of logic to assume that when they didn't find the container at Spiros's house, they went on to look in Nico's apartment. These men haven't been seen since, and their descriptions provided by the policeman himself aren't particularly helpful – Caucasian, mid-forties, average height, average build. One of them spoke Greek fluently but he wasn't a native-born speaker. We have to assume that they found the container and have now left Kandíra. It's a very small village, so if they were still here I'm quite certain we would know about it.'


### Réthymno, Crete

Hardin was quite right: Krywald and Stein were nowhere near Kandíra, and the flask was long gone. The steel case Aristides had recovered from the Learjet was locked in the larger suitcase they'd brought with them. They hadn't opened the steel case or even examined it except to confirm that it was the one they had been sent to recover. At his briefing, McCready had been most specific – they were under no circumstances to open the case or try to inspect its contents. They were simply to return it to the United States and hand it over to him personally.

Confirming they had found the right case hadn't been that easy. It had no markings of any sort, and its original leather covering had long since vanished. McCready's description of the case had, however, been extremely detailed, including its precise measurements and the types of locks and catch fitted to it. As soon as they'd driven a mile or so away from Kandíra the previous evening, Elias had stopped the hire car while Krywald compared the object they'd recovered with Nicholson's description, just in case they'd somehow picked up one that was only similar.

There hadn't been much doubt in Krywald's mind, though, even before he ran his tape measure over it – having never before seen a steel case with two locks and an over-centre catch to secure the lid. Even this cursory examination had convinced him that they'd found the right one.

Before Krywald went to bed that night, he sent an encrypted email to McCready, which simply advised him that phase one was completed. He suggested that they would probably complete phase two – the destruction of the wreck of the Learjet – the following day.

They slept late the next morning, the effects of their long journey catching up with both Stein and Krywald. Elias slept even longer –

being much less used to long-distance travel – and he didn't appear in the hotel dining room until gone ten-thirty. He spotted Krywald in a far corner of the room and walked over to him. The remains of a leisurely breakfast were spread across the table, and as Elias reached him Krywald pushed across a small wicker basket containing some rolls. 'There's coffee in the pot,' he gestured.

'Where's Stein?' Elias asked.

'He's out running an errand,' Krywald replied. 'As soon as he gets back, we need to go.'

'An early flight?' Elias asked, pulling out a chair and sitting down.

'What?'

'An early flight back to the States.' Elias said. 'I mean,' he glanced up at Krywald and motioned towards the black case sitting on the floor right beside the table, 'you've got the case, so that's it, isn't it? We can go home?'

Krywald grinned but shook his head. 'The job's not over yet. Getting the case was the most important thing, but we've still got some cleaning up to do, and that's where you come in. Best you don't eat too much, Mr Elias, because this afternoon you're going for a swim. A long, deep one, too.'

## Kandíra, south-west Crete

'We therefore have *two* hot zones to investigate and, equally obviously, two bodies,' Hardin continued. He glanced towards the rear of the tent where Dr Gravas was now standing alongside Inspector Lavat – again properly dressed in the uniform of a Cretan police officer – and listening with interest to the briefing. 'We have been helped considerably by the prompt actions of Inspector Lavat here, and his cordon around the village should have limited the possibility of the pathogen spreading.'

But even as he said these words, Hardin realized with a sudden sick feeling that in all probability the mystery virus had already been carried a considerable distance away from Kandíra. He just hoped that whoever had taken the container would have the good sense to keep it sealed.

'We'll proceed as far as we can using standard field procedures. By that I mean CRIEIPA.' Hardin pronounced it 'creeper', and Mark Evans nodded in recognition. 'I need hardly remind you what that involves, but for the sake of our visitors I'm going to anyway. First, *Containment* – that's pretty much been done already, thanks to our two colleagues here. The village has been cordoned off by the local police ever since Dr Gravas first suspected a filovirus. Almost nobody has been allowed in or out since then.

'Second, *Restriction of access*. The two hot zones have also been secured by the police, and nobody will be allowed access to either building unless vouched for personally by either Dr Gravas or Inspector Lavat. That's something of a stable-door reaction, given that both scenes have already been visited by unidentified men, but better security is now firmly in place. This restriction is primarily to avoid contamination of the scenes themselves, as I don't think there's much danger of any further outbreaks.' Hardin added with a smile as Jerry Fisher opened his mouth to challenge his statement: 'That may seem like a case of hypothesizing without data, but I'm basing my belief on what actually happened here so far.

'Four people entered the room where the first body was found on Tuesday morning, three of them wearing no protection at all, and they're all well and healthy after about forty-eight hours. Both the victims appeared to be completely normal at about midnight on Monday, but both were dead within twelve hours. That means we're looking for a hot agent that acts incredibly fast, but whose infective period is extremely short. Either that or the two victims ingested or perhaps injected the agent, though I can't imagine why they'd do that with an unknown substance.'

Hardin paused to take a sip of water: his throat was getting dry. 'OK, that's about as far as we've got to date. The next phase is *Investigation*. We'll start at the first victim's house, and begin with his body. We'll need to collect all the usual specimens – starting with blood, urine and stool samples, then whatever other specimens are indicated by the initial results. That will be followed by a full post-mortem, which I will undertake. Obviously I'll check for needle marks, just in case these two guys got their kicks by shooting up something they'd found somewhere, but I very much doubt if that's the case. I'll also want a full and thorough search of the house. Some traces of this agent might still be evident in the property, so look out for dust, unidentified liquids, smears, anything like that.

'If we can't find anything at that scene, we'll repeat the whole process at the second victim's residence. Until we've got some sort of handle on what this agent actually is, we're going nowhere. The last three phases – *Examination*, *Identification* and *Procedural Actions* – will have to wait until we know exactly what we're dealing with.'

Hardin looked up towards the back of the tent as the flap opened and another police officer entered, walked across to speak softly to the inspector, then handed him a slip of paper. Lavat glanced up at Hardin and stepped forward.

'You have a visitor, Mr Hardin,' he said, glancing down at the paper in his hand. 'A man called Richer – no, Richter. He's just appeared at the barrier across the main road and asked for you by name.'


## NAS Soúda Bay, Akrotíri, Crete

Stein braked the Ford Focus to a stop at the counter-weighted barrier guarding the main entrance to the Soúda Bay facility and wound down his window as the armed sentry approached.

'Good morning, sir. May I . . .?' the sentry started to inquire but stopped as Stein opened a small black leather folder containing his genuine CIA identification, and held it up in front of the soldier's face.

'The name's Stein and I have an appointment to see Captain Levy.'

The sentry looked carefully at the picture and then at Stein, then stepped back a pace, snapped off a rapid salute and scanned the paper attached to his clipboard. 'Yessir, Captain Levy at eleven-thirty. Have you visited here before, Mr Stein?'

As Stein shook his head, the sentry gave him crisp directions to the closest parking area and eight minutes later Stein walked into Levy's office.

Levy was tall, slim and coal-black, and one of two Company assets stationed at Soúda Bay. CIA officers do not normally wear a uniform of any description, but in some circumstances it is necessary, and NAS Soúda Bay was one of them. Like all US bases, Soúda Bay employs a number of civilian staff, but in the main they do fairly menial jobs. For several reasons the CIA needed an officer on the base in a position of some authority, and for the past two years Nathan Levy, Captain, United States Air Force, had officially been flying a desk here instead of the F-16 Falcons he had normally flown.

That, at least, was the official line. In fact, Levy wasn't a serving officer in the USAF, had never flown a Falcon – in fact, he had seen one exactly twice – and had no flying qualifications whatsoever. But he knew enough about aviation to hold a conversation without making a fool of himself, even with specialist aircrew, because he always pointedly refused to talk about his flying career, and nobody ever pressed him. A rumour had started almost as soon as he arrived on Crete that he had been involved in an accident that had killed his wingman, and that his desk job here was an attempt to stabilize him before getting him back in the air. Levy knew all about the rumour – in fact, he'd started it – and it suited his purposes very well.

'I'm Stein,' the visitor announced.

'I'm sure you are,' Levy said, 'but I'll still need to see some ID.'

Stein fished out his black leather folder again and passed it across to him. Levy studied it carefully, compared the number on the card with that on a signal resting on his desk, then closed the folder and handed it back. 'OK, Mr Stein. I've had a coupla signals from Langley about you, and they sent me a shopping list on the last one. The personal weapons were no problem. There are three of you so I've picked up three SIG P226s with silencers and two spare clips each; that's the SIG 220 variant with the fifteen-round magazine.'

'I know the weapon,' Stein said.

In fact, the 'shopping list' signal had instructed Levy to provide silenced personal weapons for Krywald's team, and to deliver another pistol of a very different sort, as well as a rifle that was even more unusual, to a hotel in Réthymno. Levy was going to give Stein an hour or so to get out of the area, then he was going to pick up the other two weapons in their innocent-looking cardboard boxes and deliver them himself.

Levy had been with the Company for a long time, and was used to the devious ways its personnel operated, but the current operation was a first, even for him. He had no definite knowledge of what exactly was going on, but the very nature of the weapons he had been instructed to procure allowed him to make an educated guess. Not for the first time in his career Levy wondered if he ought not to get out of the CIA and start working for an organization that applied higher moral standards to itself, like the Mafia or the Yardies, for example.

'OK,' Levy said, 'they've been sanitized. The serial numbers have been removed and even if somebody uses an X-ray machine to recover them, the trace will lead straight to the FBI.'

'Now that's a nice touch.'

'I've got plenty of plastic – I picked out four M118 demolition charges with a bunch of extra C4 added – but the detonators were a tad difficult. Real specialized items.'

'But you did get them?' Stein asked.

Levy nodded. 'Sure, I got them. Had to call in a coupla favours, and for sure that'll cost me somewheres down the road, but I did get them.' Levy reached down behind him, pulled up a large and apparently heavy red haversack and placed it carefully on his desk. Something in the haversack gave a metallic clunk as the fabric settled, and Stein smiled for the first time since he'd walked into the room.


## Kandíra, south-west Crete

Paul Richter leaned against the driver's door of the Volkswagen Golf and waited patiently in the late-morning sunshine. The car wasn't air-conditioned, and even with all the windows open, the heater set on cold and the fan going full blast, it had still been a long, hot, sticky and extremely slow drive down to Kandíra. He was hoping he could find out what Simpson wanted and get the hell out of Crete and back to the air-conditioned cool of the ship that same afternoon, or tomorrow at the latest.

He looked up as two men approached the barricade and walked over to meet them. One was very obviously a police officer, in uniform, and the other a middle-aged man wearing civilian clothes.

'Mr Hardin?' Richter asked, and Hardin nodded. 'My name's Richter, from the warship *Invincible*.'

'Oh, yes,' Hardin said. 'We've been expecting you.'

'You have?'

'We won't be needing transportation until this afternoon at the earliest, but we will certainly have specimens ready to send to Irakleío first thing tomorrow morning, so could we have a helicopter here by eight-thirty?'

'I think,' Richter said slowly, 'you have me confused with somebody else.' Light dawned as he remembered the helicopter squadron's outline briefing. 'I'm not part of the *Invincible*'s Air Operations team, if that's what you're thinking. He'll be coming out later today, by helicopter, and he'll be wearing a uniform and carrying a radio – neither of which I'm equipped with, as you can see.'

'Oh, OK,' Hardin said, and stared down at a piece of paper in his hand. 'So what can I do for you, Mr Richter?'

Richter reached into his hip pocket and extracted a slim wallet, which he opened and from it removed a laminated card. It identified him as a member of the British Medical Research Council and was one of a dozen or so cards Richter carried as a matter of routine. 'With the number of British tourists visiting Crete every year, we're obviously very concerned about this infection you're investigating,' he said. 'If you've time now, could you brief me on what your team has found out so far?'

Hardin smiled somewhat ruefully. 'So far,' he said, 'we haven't found very much, but I can give you at least some information. Look, the rest of my team members are waiting to get started on this. Could you wait a few minutes while I finish my briefing, and then I'll tell you what we know?'

Richter nodded his assent and followed Hardin and the police officer through the barricade and into a large canvas tent that had been positioned adjacent to the main street. Hardin waved him to a bench at a table situated towards the back of the tent, then five minutes later walked back in and sat down opposite him.

'One thing I'm not clear about, Mr Richter. You identified yourself as a member of the MRC, but you told me you'd come from the *Invincible*, which is a British Royal Navy warship. That I don't understand.'

'Both are correct,' Richter said easily. 'I'm a Lieutenant Commander in the Royal Naval Reserve and I was doing continuation training on the ship, but I'm also employed by the MRC as an investigator.'

Not too bad, Richter thought. One half of the statement was absolutely true, and the other completely false – normally he reckoned he was doing well if just one in three of the things he claimed had some basis in fact.

'You're not a doctor, then?' Hardin asked.

Richter shook his head. 'No, I'm just an investigator. I get sent out to look into reported cases of any kind of serious medical emergency or emerging disease. I collect the information, write a report and hand it over once I get back to Britain.'

'OK,' Hardin said, 'then I'll keep it as simple and non-medical as I can. First, have you ever heard of a filovirus?'

'I've heard of them, that's all. You're talking about Ebola and Marburg, right?'

Hardin nodded. 'Very good,' he said. 'We – that's the Centers for Disease Control – got involved because the local doctor, a man called Gravas who you'll meet soon, I guess, thought he'd identified a case of Ebola here on the island.'

'And had he?' Richter asked.

'Almost certainly not. I've been able to eliminate Ebola – or at least the two known strains which are called Sudan and Zaïre – because of the timescale involved. Even Ebola Zaïre, which is the most deadly variant, takes a week to ten days to kill its victim. Whatever this sucker is, it kills within hours.'

'Hours? Jesus!' Richter muttered.

'What Dr Gravas spotted did look remarkably like Ebola, because the gross effects of this agent are superficially very similar,' Hardin continued. 'We've found two victims so far, and both exhibited broadly the same symptoms. That's copious bleeding from every orifice, probably with convulsions, although that's a guess based upon a cursory inspection of the second victim. Internally, my belief is that we'll find that the majority of their organs have simply stopped working because they've been effectively drowned in blood. The actual cause of death may be simply blood loss, but I'll be able to confirm that later today.

'The other reason that I'm sure we're not dealing with Ebola is that the first victim apparently managed to call out literally minutes before he died. Ebola produces a dramatic effect on brain functions as the skull fills with blood, and in its latter stages the victim invariably goes into a deep and irreversible coma. No Ebola victim can utter a sound once the terminal phase is reached.'

Hardin's matter-of-fact delivery and the implications of what he was saying stunned Richter for a moment.

'So what is it then,' he asked, 'if it's not Ebola? And what level of lethality and infectivity are we talking about here?'

Hardin shrugged his shoulders. 'At this stage,' he replied, 'I have no idea. My gut feeling is that it could be some kind of unknown filovirus, but extremely fast-acting. I've only seen two victims so far and they're both dead, so to date its lethality has been exactly one hundred per cent, which makes this agent the species-killer to end all species-killers. Even Ebola Zaïre can only manage a lethality of around eighty to ninety per cent.

'The sole good news is that, whatever it is, it doesn't seem to be particularly infectious. Three people entered the bedroom of the first victim, without wearing any kind of protection, yet they're all still alive and healthy two days later.

'That suggests one of two things: either this agent isn't spread by airborne particles but by some form of body fluid transfer – blood, semen or saliva – or it can't survive for very long outside the victim's body. Maybe it decays if subjected to heat or light, or merely even exposure to the air. At this stage we just don't know, but I am now convinced we won't see an epidemic here on Crete. If that was going to happen, we'd already be piling the dead in the streets.'

'You don't paint a very attractive picture, Mr Hardin,' Richter said.

Hardin smiled briefly. 'I'm just trying to be realistic.' Then his face clouded. 'And there's something else you should know,' he added. 'At the first location I found evidence that the hot agent itself came from a small container, probably a vacuum flask, which suggests somebody had collected it and then stored it to use for research purposes.'

'Or,' Richter interrupted, 'to develop as some kind of bioweapon. And the other possibility is that it had already been weaponized. I take it from what you said that you didn't find this container?'

Hardin shook his head. 'No, there was no sign of anything like that at either location. And we've had a report of unidentified and unauthorized intruders at both hot zones: two men masquerading as CDC employees, one of them carrying a large case. At the second property they killed a police officer and two elderly villagers. We have no idea who these two men are or where they're from, but the conclusion is fairly obvious.'

Richter raised his eyebrows, then nodded, realizing immediately that his chances of getting back to the *Invincible* any time soon, with this investigation safely put to bed, were almost exactly nil. 'Yes,' he said, 'it looks to me like the original developers of whatever killed those two Greeks came back to collect their property.'

### Réthymno, Crete

In fact, Elias didn't get to dive that afternoon, simply because Krywald hadn't realized quite how long it would take to get where they were going and to get things organized.

Nicholson had spent some time trying to hire a boat for them on the island of Gávdos itself, to minimize the time they would take reaching the dive site. He finally gave up when it became apparent that the island had a population of less than fifty, virtually nothing in the way of infrastructure apart from a couple of tavernas, and the only form of motorized transport available was a handful of tractors used primarily for transporting goods, goats and tourists, but not necessarily in that order. He'd checked on Gavdopoúla, too, but as far as he was able to discover it was inhabited entirely by goats, so he had turned his attention to mainland Crete, picking Chóra Sfakia as the closest point to the dive site, and started again on the telephone.

Stein had left to make the pick-up at Soúda Bay as soon as he finished his breakfast. While they were waiting for him to return, Krywald checked the information 'McCready' had sent and then studied his tourist map. He wasn't pleased with what it showed him.

Chóra Sfakia was on the south coast of Crete, not all that far from Kandíra, in fact. The problem was the road, or lack of it. Looking again at the map, Krywald realized the distinct advantages of operating in a country like America or France, where the population understood the needs of the car. On Crete, it looked to him as if most of the roads were simply metalled goat-tracks, meandering from place to place as the whim of their original creators had inspired them.

There were only two ways to get to Chóra Sfakia, and he didn't like the look of either of them. The first option was to take the coast road and head west out of Réthymno as far as Vrýses and then turn left and follow the narrow and twisting mountain road through Káres and Ímpros down to the coast. The second route was probably worse: drive south from Réthymno on the main road towards Spíli, then turn right through Selliá and follow an even longer twisting road down to, and then along, the south coast of the island.

By the time Stein returned to the hotel, Krywald and Elias had packed overnight bags for the three of them and were waiting for him in a café along the street. As soon as Stein drove up they both climbed into the hired Ford. The steel case went with them, still securely locked inside the larger case: Krywald wasn't prepared to let it out of his sight now that they'd recovered it.

'Which way?' Stein asked, sliding the Focus into first gear and pulling away from the kerb.

'Head for Vrýses,' Krywald said sourly.

'Jesus,' Stein muttered. 'I've only just come from there. It's nearly as far as Soúda Bay.'

'Yeah? Well you should know the way, then,' Krywald retorted and lapsed into a sullen silence.

### Kandíra, south-west Crete

'The big question, of course, is where did an elderly Greek living in a tiny village on a small island in the eastern Mediterranean come across a sealed container filled with an unknown and totally lethal pathogen?' Richter asked.

Hardin shook his head. 'I have no idea. My involvement here is purely to identify the infective agent and to put measures in place to contain the epidemic, if there is one. Because this pathogen was apparently stored in some kind of flask, that makes it more a matter for the police. So let me introduce you to Inspector Lavat.'

Lavat wasn't that much help – not because of being obstructive in any way, but simply because he didn't know the answer. 'All I can tell you is that Aristides was a diver all his life, and according to the locals still used to go out diving most days, despite having no permit. He owned a day boat moored in the bay down below Kandíra.'

'Why would he need a permit?' Richter asked.

'The seabed round here is littered with wrecks. Some of them date back two or three thousand years and contain archaeological treasures that should be properly recovered by trained professionals. What the Department of Antiquities definitely doesn't want is a bunch of cowboy divers looting these wrecks indiscriminately and selling off whatever they've found. So all scuba divers must obtain a permit before they can legally put on an aqualung.'

'And this Spiros didn't bother, I suppose?'

'No, Spiros didn't bother. I understand that he frequently hauled up artefacts from the bottom of the sea and gave them to his nephew to sell. Nico's name came up a few times in police records hereabouts in connection with the unauthorized sale of archaeological relics to tourists who should have known better, but nothing was ever proved.'

'OK,' Richter mused, 'that might tie in with those Greek newspaper reports suggesting that Aristides found some kind of wrecked aircraft. Normally I don't believe anything I read in the papers but maybe this time there's a grain of truth in the story. He could have discovered something in a wreck on the seabed, then brought it home and opened it. What that still doesn't answer is exactly where he found it. Does anybody in the village know where he went diving recently?'

'No,' Lavat replied, 'if anybody knows, they're not telling – or at least not telling me. These outlying villages have no respect for the law, so the chances of any of the locals confiding in a police officer are virtually nil.

'I've looked at Aristides's boat,' Lavat continued, 'but found nothing of interest. There was nothing on board that shouldn't be there, apart from his diving gear, of course. I've checked his navigation charts, too, but none of them has any positions marked, nothing to indicate where he had been. I suspect he probably knew this area so well that he never bothered about using charts – he just kept them aboard as any other responsible boat owner would do.

'So if you're going to go out looking for the source of this pathogen, Mr Richter, I wish you luck. The Mediterranean covers about two and a half million square kilometres. Which bit are you going to start with?'

Richter smiled slightly. 'It shouldn't be that difficult. If Aristides found this container while he was diving, the location has to be some-where fairly close to Crete. You said yourself he only had a day boat, so he had to be able to motor out to his chosen site, carry out his dive and then get back to Kandíra that evening. Even if he was spending the night away from home – say at Irakleío – he would still have the same kind of constraint. He would need to get back to port somewhere the same day as he sailed. His boat probably has a maximum speed of about ten or twelve knots, so assuming he motored out to sea for five hours or so, that gives a radius of fifty, maybe sixty, miles maximum from the coast of Crete.'

'That's still a huge area – probably fifteen to twenty thousand square kilometres.'

'Yes,' Richter nodded, 'but again I can reduce it. Unless Aristides was using fairly sophisticated diving equipment, he couldn't have gone below about one hundred or maybe a hundred and fifty feet. A lot of the seabed around Crete is much deeper than that, which eliminates most of the surrounding area. And if he was hauling up archaeological relics from the seabed he'd want to be safe from prying eyes, even when he got back into harbour. He lived in Kandíra, and my guess is he used only Kandíra as his base. That means I'll be concentrating on possible sites lying to the south and west of this end of Crete.'

'You seem to know quite a lot about diving, Mr Richter.'

'It's been a hobby,' Richter said shortly.

Lavat was eyeing him curiously. 'You're also raising the kind of ques-tions that I wouldn't expect from a medical investigator. I believe you told Mr Hardin that you worked for the British Medical Research Council?'

'I have got another job,' Richter replied.

Lavat nodded. 'I assumed as much. And are you now going to try and find where the Greek discovered this pathogen that killed him?'

'Yes,' Richter said, 'I am definitely going to find the source of those germs. And I'm really sorry that you lost a police officer over this business.'

## Chóra Sfakia, Crete

In fact, the mountain road wasn't anything like as good as Krywald had hoped, but it was better than he had feared, so they reached Chóra Sfakia by mid afternoon. It wasn't a big place, and locating the diving supplies shop was easy. Finding the owner, or at least somebody to open the door so that they could collect the equipment Nicholson had booked for them, proved much more difficult.

The Spanish have the word *mañana*, but there's no word in the Greek language that conveys quite the same sense of urgency.

This realization dawned on Krywald when the shop's proprietor, a lanky, bald and burnt-brown Greek Cypriot named Monedes finally turned up a little after five-thirty, weaving from side to side as he made his unsteady progress down the street. He smiled happily at Krywald and Stein and belched at them an unwholesome mix of stale garlic and *tsikoudia* – the lethal Cretan distilled spirit made from the residue of the wine-press and containing some thirty-seven percent alcohol by volume.

Monedes clearly spoke nothing but Greek, and frankly Krywald was surprised he could still remember any language at all after the prolonged and largely liquid lunch he had obviously enjoyed. Stein therefore handled the negotiations, such as they were, in that language.

'You have a booking for us, I hope, in the name of Wilson? A boat and some diving equipment?'

Monedes stared at him as though through a haze. 'A booking?' he echoed as he leaned against the shop doorway while fumbling with a large bunch of keys.

'Wilson. The name is Wilson,' Stein repeated with as much patience as he could muster. 'The booking was made by phone from America.'

Monedes's face cleared somewhat, but it was only because he had finally found the right key. 'Come in, come in,' he said cheerfully, turning the key in the lock and pushing open the door. The Cypriot staggered over to the counter and lurched behind it. 'What can I get you?' he asked as he reached down and pulled up a glass bottle half-full of a clear liquid with a very faint bluish tinge. The label identified it as 'Raki', an alternative name for *tsikoudia* – though not related to the Turkish intoxicant of the same name.

217

Stein waved the bottle away and repeated his question, but Monedes appeared totally engrossed in removing the top.

'We need a boat and some aqualungs,' Stein said.

'I have aqualungs,' Monedes giggled. 'Lots of aqualungs. You've come to the right place.' He finally unscrewed the bottle cap, smiled at the two men, put the neck of it to his lips and took a gulp. Then he slammed the bottle back on the counter, gazed unsteadily at Stein for about a minute, pointed towards the open door with his left hand and slowly toppled sideways.

'Shit,' Krywald growled as the Greek hit the floor. 'That's all we needed right now.'

Stein stepped forward to check that Monedes was still breathing, then rolled the unconscious man onto his side into the recovery position. 'He'll have the mother of all hangovers when he finally wakes up.'

'Yeah, well that's *his* problem. *Our* problem is that we still need to acquire a boat and some scuba equipment for Elias.'

'That's not really a problem. We can pick it up in the morning,' Stein said. 'Look, it's too late for him to do any diving today anyway. We can go find a hotel, get back here first thing in the morning and we'll still have the job done by lunchtime. That means we can be out of here tomorrow afternoon and on our way back to the States tomorrow night.'

Krywald considered this for a moment. 'Yeah, I guess so,' he nodded. 'Go fetch Elias and the car, and we'll see what we can find here.'

# Chapter 14

'Hullo, John,' Jayne Taylor murmured, as Westwood pushed open the outer door to the office of the Director of Operations (Clandestine Services) and walked in.

'Good morning, Jayne. You're looking good.'

As she invariably did, in fact, Westwood thought, and wondered again at the rumours that periodically surfaced about the precise nature of the relationship between Walter Hicks and his personal assistant. Jayne Taylor's coal-black hair and huge brown eyes had inspired more than one fantasy even in Westwood, who had a wife he adored and two children he doted on, though this mental image crumbled almost immediately he included the lumbering figure of Walter Hicks.

'Thank you, kind sir.' Jayne Taylor smiled back at him. 'You can go right in – he's expecting you.'

Westwood headed across to the inner office door, knocked and entered.

'Hi, John. Take a seat and grab a coffee.'

Hicks gestured towards the conference table where another man was already sitting. He was wearing a 'Visitor' tag so Westwood knew immediately that he wasn't Company personnel.

'Frank, this is John Westwood. He's the head of the Foreign Intelligence Staff here at Langley, and he'll act as your CIA liaison officer for the duration of this investigation.'

'What investigation?' Westwood asked.

'All in good time, John,' Hicks said. 'Right, this is Detective Delaney of the Washington DC Police Department, who's actually heading up this case.'

Delaney was slightly overweight, had lost most of his hair and was perspiring gently even in the air-conditioned cool of the office. 'The name's Frank, Mr Westwood,' he said, clambering to his feet and extending his hand.

'And I'm John,' Westwood replied, before sitting down opposite him.

'OK,' Hicks said. 'John knows nothing about this yet, so perhaps you could fill him in on why you're here, Frank.'

'Sure.' Delaney placed his arms squarely on the table in front of him. 'Yesterday two former employees of the Central Intelligence Agency died in mysterious circumstances. One was certainly murdered and the other died as a result of a drug overdose, but we're reasonably sure it wasn't either an accident or suicide.'

Westwood pulled a cup and saucer towards him and reached out for the coffee pot. 'Who were these two men?' he asked.

'The man who was clearly murdered was James Richards. He was a widower who lived alone in a small community called Crystal Springs – that's just south of the old Route 66, about twelve, fifteen miles west of DC. He had a small house in a quiet area and none of his neighbours seemed to know him well. Certainly none of them knew he was ex-CIA: they all seemed to think he'd been involved in some kind of communications business.'

Westwood poured his coffee and took a sip.

'Richards was found this morning by a neighbour who had noticed that his front door was slightly ajar. She knocked, but got no reply and went inside. She found Richards lying beside the fireplace in his lounge, his head stove in and blood everywhere. She screamed and ran out to dial nine one one.' Delaney was warming to his theme. 'Now obviously Richards was murdered – that's not in dispute – and he died yesterday evening. The initial medical report suggests around ten to ten-thirty local time – not earlier than nine and not later than midnight. What bothers us were some anomalies at the crime scene.'

Delaney held up a slightly podgy hand and began ticking off points on his fingers in turn. 'First, he had a non-fatal bullet wound inflicted by a small-calibre weapon on his left upper arm, but none of his neighbours heard anything resembling a gunshot yesterday evening, though all of them we've interviewed were at home when Richards must have died. That means whoever pulled the trigger was using a silencer, which is not a common accessory for any burglar to carry. If they carry any firearm at all, it's usually a snub-nosed revolver or a small automatic – the extra length of a silencer just makes a pistol more cumbersome and a lot more difficult to conceal.

'Second, as far as we've been able to check, nothing was taken. Richards had a few nice pieces of hi-fi and video equipment and couple of expensive cameras plus around a thousand bucks in cash right there in his living room, and the perp just left them and walked away.

'Third, we found no evidence of a break-in. As far as we can tell, the perp came right through the front door, which means Richards let him into the house himself. So pretty obviously he knew his attacker.'

'So maybe a falling-out between friends?' Westwood hazarded.

'Possible, but we think that's unlikely,' Delaney said. 'People don't usually go calling on their buddies carrying silenced pistols unless they've got a real serious attitude problem.'

'The weapon didn't belong to Richards?' Hicks asked.

'No, sir,' Delaney replied. 'Richards had a couple of pistols in the house, with permits, naturally. Neither of them had been fired for some time, and neither had a silencer fitted. That's another anomaly – the pistols were found in a drawer in the desk in his lounge, but as far as we can see Richards didn't go anywhere near the desk. If the killer had been a burglar or someone else he didn't know and trust, we would expect him to try to pick up one of those weapons just as a precaution.

'No,' Delaney said firmly, 'what we're looking at here is a murder committed by someone Richards knew well and trusted enough to let into his home late in the evening. It looks like the perp pulled the gun on him and he fought back – that's how he picked up the wound in his arm. Then the killer finished him off with the fireside poker.'

'Why use the poker?' Westwood asked.

'Probably didn't want to risk a second shot. Even a silenced weapon makes some noise, but nobody would hear him crushing Richards's skull with a poker unless they were right there in the room with him.'

'What about the bullet that wounded Richards?'

Delaney shook his head. 'The perp took it with him. It went right through the victim's arm, but missed the bone. We found a hole in some wooden panelling where we guess the guy who pulled the trigger dug it out and took it away. Our best guess is it was probably either a twenty-two or a point-two-five-calibre weapon, certainly no larger than a thirty-two, but that's about it.'

As Delaney fell silent, Walter Hicks leaned forward, looking at Westwood. 'Right, John, I know what you're thinking. You're wondering why the murder of a former CIA employee would bring the Washington DC police to the Company, right?'

Westwood nodded. Hicks was sharp, and that had been almost exactly what Westwood had been thinking as Delaney completed his account of the crime.

'If it was just the murder of James Richards, we wouldn't get involved at all. Granted, there are some peculiarities about the murder itself, but in the normal course of events there's no way we would become involved in what seems purely a police matter. What has brought us together here is the second death on the same day. Right, Frank, it's your ball – you run with it.'

'OK,' Delaney said. 'The second death could possibly have been suicide, but we don't think so. The victim's name was Charles Hawkins. He retired from the Agency a couple of years before Richards and lived with his wife – her name's Mary – in Popes Creek on the edge of the Potomac, a few miles south of DC. It's the same house he owned when he was an Agency employee. They had three children, now all grown up and living away from here. That's the background.

'Late last night a guy out walking his dog at Lower Cedar Point – that's just south of the Nice Memorial Bridge on the Maryland side of the river – noticed a car parked near the water, and figured that the man sitting behind the wheel was just sleeping. He came back with his dog a half-hour or so later and the car was still there, with the driver slouched in exactly the same position. The dog-walker peered in and couldn't see any signs of life, so he knocked on the window and then tried the door when he got no response. The door wasn't locked.

'Having had some training as a paramedic, this guy felt for a pulse but couldn't find one. He closed the car door, walked to the nearest phone and dialled for an ambulance. When the meat wagon arrived the paramedics tried for a pulse as well. After confirming that the driver was dead, they checked his identity. They found his driver's licence, noted his home address and requested a black-and-white to go tell his wife the good news.

'And that's when we got involved, because when the squad car arrived at Popes Creek, they found that Mrs Mary Hawkins was also deceased. She'd died of a drug overdose, same as her husband, but in her case it certainly hadn't been self-induced. There were bruises all over her where somebody had knocked her about, then forced a pill down her throat.'

'Could have been a domestic?' Westwood interjected. 'Maybe Hawkins killed his wife then killed himself in a fit of remorse. It's been known to happen.'

Delaney nodded. 'Certainly has. However, when one of the neighbours saw Charles Hawkins driving away from his home at around seven-thirty that evening, Mary Hawkins was waving him goodbye from the front door. Hawkins never returned home, but around ten minutes after he'd left, another neighbour spotted an unknown male arrive at the Hawkins residence. Mrs Hawkins let him inside, so presumably she knew him. Nobody, as far as we know, saw this unsub – the unknown subject – leave.'

'Anybody get a description of this guy?' Westwood asked.

Delaney nodded. 'Yes, but it's not going to help a lot. White male, six feet tall, dark coat.'

'That's it?' Westwood asked, incredulous.

'That's it,' Delaney echoed. 'It's a quiet, good-quality area. People don't scrutinize what their neighbours are doing, or what their visitors look like. We're lucky we've got somebody who saw the unsub at all, otherwise we'd be looking at a murder–suicide scenario pretty much like the one you sketched out.'

'Right,' Walter Hicks said, 'you see the pattern. With Richards it's been by deduction, but in the case of Mrs Hawkins by direct observation. The killer – my money's on a single perpetrator – was known to two of his victims, and by implication was also known to Charles Hawkins. There were no marks of violence on Hawkins's body, so we presume that the only way he was persuaded to swallow the tablet that killed him was by the perp holding a gun to his head.'

'What was in the tablet? Were Hawkins and his wife killed with the same substance?'

Delaney shuffled through the papers in front of him on the conference table and pulled out a single slightly crumpled sheet.

'OK, we're still waiting for some final tests to be completed, but the initial results suggest that both the Hawkins swallowed the same poison. The last time I talked to the toxicologist he was waiting for the X-ray crystallography results, but in his opinion it was a vegetable alkaloid. He thinks it was probably a highly concentrated form of coniine.'

'Never heard of it,' Westwood said.

'It's the active principle in hemlock,' Delaney said. 'You know, what the ancient Greeks used when they wanted to take the night train.'

Westwood looked puzzled for a second or two, then nodded. 'You mean, commit suicide?'

'Yup,' Delaney replied.

Westwood glanced up at Hicks, who'd just lit a cigar. He was trying to cut down, as he told anyone who asked him, but as far as Westwood could see he was smoking fewer, but much larger, cigars than before, which probably meant his nicotine intake was pretty much the same as it had always been.

'OK, Walter,' Westwood said. 'I see that there's a pattern, and it's probably more than a coincidence that two ex-CIA employees have been killed on the same day, but what exactly is my role in all this?'

'Just what I said at the start of the meeting, John. Liaison. Frank will be handling the strictly criminal aspects of this investigation. What I want you to do is dig back through the old files here at Langley. Identify all the cases that Hawkins and Richards worked on together, just in case what we're looking at here is some kind of revenge killing spree – a guy assassinating Company agents who were involved in some operation that went wrong, or even went right.'

'Not quite so many of those, Walter,' Westwood said with a smile.

Hicks just looked at him. 'Smart answer,' he muttered. 'And, while you're doing that, identify everybody else who was involved with these two guys, just in case we can stop any other retired employees getting themselves knocked off.'


### Kandíra, south-west Crete

Tyler Hardin heard the throb of the Merlin's rotors as it swept over Kandíra on its way back to the *Invincible*. It had, he assumed, just brought the Operations Officer who would liaise with the ship to provide flights as and when required. What he did know for certain was that the man who'd called himself Richter was now on board the helicopter and returning to the *Invincible*.

The Brit was a puzzle. Hardin knew very little about the British Medical Research Council, but what he did know didn't fit at all with what Richter had been saying. The MRC was certainly involved in research – that was, after all, what the letter 'R' stood for – but not at all the kind of research that Richter had referred to. Hardin had never heard of the MRC sending out field investigators to the site of a medical emergency and, if they had done, he was certain that they would be qualified doctors. Sending a lay person to investigate a complex medical crisis would be completely pointless.

No, he was quite satisfied that Richter was nothing whatever to do with the MRC, but was obviously some kind of investigator of considerable importance, otherwise they would not be ferrying him about the Mediterranean on board a British warship. No doubt, Hardin mused, he would find out the truth eventually.

Mark Evans stood on the opposite side of their makeshift mortuary table. The two men, wearing Tyvek biological space suits and Racal hoods for safety, had set up a trestle table in the smaller, spare bedroom of Aristides's house, simply because Hardin didn't yet want to risk moving the corpse out of the building. Downstairs, Fisher and Kane were beginning an exhaustive search of the property, looking for any remaining trace of the infective agent.

Once Hardin's instrument boxes had been brought upstairs, they'd picked up Aristides's body and carried it carefully from the room in which he had died, laid it flat on its back, and prepared to go to work.

In broad terms, a hot autopsy – meaning the dissection of a potentially biohazardous corpse – is performed in very similar fashion to a normal post-mortem, but a range of additional precautions are put in place to protect the personnel involved. In a hospital or morgue, the body is placed on a specially designed mortuary trolley called a pan, incorporating a trough underneath to catch any fluid or other debris that might drop from the corpse and contaminate the floor. Additionally, the body is encased in at least two biohazard bags, both of which remain completely sealed until the autopsy itself is about to commence.

The procedure will be carried out on a stainless-steel autopsy table, its upper surface made of either mesh or perforated steel. Above the table, below banks of high-wattage fluorescent lights, several microphones will be suspended to enable the pathologist to provide a running commentary.

Unless the body is considered to be dangerously contaminated, full biohazard suits will not usually be worn. Although they provide the ultimate protection, they are cumbersome and uncomfortable, making it difficult to carry out the delicate procedures required. The tendency of the face masks to mist up doesn't help either.

Instead it is usual for the mortuary staff to wear three layers of lighter protection: over the normal scrub suits worn in operating theatres they wear surgical gowns, and over the gowns plastic waterproof aprons. Their hair is then covered with surgical caps, and their theatre shoes have plastic or paper covers fitted.

The delicate areas most vulnerable to infection are the eyes, nose and mouth, so plastic safety goggles will be worn, and a surgeon's mask made of biofilter material designed to trap biological particles. The hands are arguably the most likely parts of the body to become infected, due to the sharp instruments used, so at least one and usually two pairs of surgical gloves will be worn, with an additional pair of heavier rubber kitchen gloves over them.

The prosector or pathologist who physically performs the postmortem examination also wears a stainless-steel chain-mail glove over his non-dominant hand. This is essential, because most accidental injuries are to the hand that isn't holding the surgical saw or scalpel. Over this, a rubber kitchen glove will be worn to provide a better grip.

Tyler Hardin looked around the spare bedroom and shrugged. The contrast between the gleaming and totally equipped mortuary suites in the States where he normally conducted his autopsies and this small and scruffy bedroom could hardly have been greater.

# PANDEMIC

## Réthymno, Crete

Mike Murphy opened his eyes to look at the travelling alarm clock sitting on the small bedside table. For a few moments he had absolutely no idea where he was. Then recollection and awareness returned. It was late afternoon, the room was bright with the sun slanting through the windows, and he found he'd slept for well over twelve hours.

For a few minutes he just lay there, listening to the noises of the hotel and the sound of the traffic on the road outside, then he swung his legs off the bed, walked into the bathroom and turned on the shower. While he waited for the water temperature to rise to a level he considered acceptable, he opened his small case and pulled out his washing kit, then stripped off, tested the temperature and stepped into the cubicle.

Once he'd dressed, he unconsciously mirrored the actions Roger Krywald had taken late the previous evening, switching on his laptop computer and using his mobile phone to log on to a classified and unlisted service provider in America to check for any messages from Nicholson.

There was only one: a confirmation that phase one of the operation had been completed, and that the other group – named the First Team by Nicholson – had already located and recovered the case. Murphy had no idea what was in the case, and he had no interest in finding out. His orders had been extraordinarily simple: he was to retrieve the case from the First Team, and then eliminate all members of that team.

Nicholson had included two other pieces of information. The first was a note of the real names, aliases and descriptions of the three members of the First Team, and details of the hotel they had been booked into. The second was a reminder to Murphy to expect a delivery at his own hotel imminently.

Fifteen minutes later Murphy descended the stairs to the lobby and crossed to the desk clerk. 'My name's White,' he said, producing a genuine American passport bearing that name, but which had never been anywhere near the US State Department. 'I'm expecting a couple of packages to be delivered here. Some camera equipment, a tripod and so on.'

'Yes, sir,' the clerk replied, in heavily accented English. 'They arrived earlier this afternoon.' He reached down behind the desk and lifted up two heavy boxes. 'Here you are.'

'Thanks,' Murphy said. 'Do I need to sign for them?'

The clerk shook his head. 'No, sir, they were delivered personally by your friend.'

Murphy had no idea who his 'friend' might be, nor again had the slightest interest in finding out. He remained one of the least curious people one could ever encounter, concerned only with the essentials necessary to get a job done. He nodded his thanks, picked up the two packages and returned to his room.

### Kandíra, south-west Crete

'How many autopsies have you performed since med school, Mark?' Hardin asked.

Evans lifted his eyes from Aristides's corpse and met Hardin's questioning gaze.

'Exactly or approximately?'

'Exactly.'

'None at all,' Evans said, and Hardin could see a smile forming on the younger man's face.

'OK,' Hardin reached out to switch on the portable tape recorder. 'I'm the prosector here and you're my assistant, so if there's anything you don't understand I'll talk you through it. Now, normally a body would arrive at the dissection table on a gurney and contained inside a couple of biohazard bags. After weighing the cadaver we'd unzip those, lift the body onto the table and have the bags themselves destroyed. We'll consider that stage to have already been reached – so, what's next?'

'Observation?' Evans replied. 'The external exam.'

'Exactly,' Hardin nodded. 'Never forget, a pathologist spends most of his time just looking and examining, and that's particularly important once you're doing investigations out in the field. There may well be indicators on a body, on its clothing or in the surroundings, that you'd never get to see in a morgue, simply because in a normal autopsy absolutely all you've got to work with is the body itself. So tell me, what do you see?'

Evans looked down at the table. 'We have a white Caucasian male,' he said, 'aged about sixty-five to seventy, deeply suntanned over his whole body apart from the groin, where the skin is noticeably lighter. There are no apparent indications of external injury to the anterior surface of the body, but large quantities of blood are evident. The subject appears to have bled from eyes, ears, nose and mouth . . . and possibly from the penis.'

'To save us turning the body over right now, Mark, Dr Gravas has already confirmed that he's bled from the anus as well. OK, let's get a couple of snaps. We'll take pictures at each stage of the procedure: meaning right now; then after the external examination is complete; after the chest cavity has been opened, and a couple of shots of each organ as it's removed.'

Evans stepped around to the end of the trestle table, raised a Polaroid camera to take one picture of Aristides's body from the feet up, then another from the head down, and finally one from each side, the camera whirring as each print was ejected. He put the prints and the camera back on a small chest of drawers and returned to the table.

'Right,' Hardin said. 'We'll clean him up now and then do a full external.'

Evans picked up a plastic bucket half-full of water, which contained a couple of cloths that Hardin had found in Aristides's kitchen. Wringing out one of them, Evans started to remove the heavily encrusted blood from the Greek's body, the water in the bucket turning deep red almost immediately. Once the front of the corpse was clean, they turned it over and washed the back as well. Then they started the external.

Working together, the two men carried out a minute examination, starting at the top of the Greek's head and working down to the soles of his feet. They were looking for cuts, bruises, punctures, needle marks, abrasions or any other external injuries, in fact anything unusual, such as a swelling, discoloured skin or evidence of broken bones. Once they'd finished the anterior surface, they turned the body over and repeated the process on the posterior.

'OK,' Hardin said aloud, for the benefit of the tape recorder. 'We can find no evidence of any recent external injury or trauma. There are several old scars, one badly healed, but none appears to have any bearing on the cause of death.

'The unusual features are the signs of bleeding from all orifices. An initial inspection shows that bleeding from the eyes, ears, nose and mouth has been caused by seepage of blood from the smaller vessels. The eyes in particular are very red, and most of the veins in the eyeballs appear to have ruptured.' He paused as Evans took three more pictures. 'Right, I'll open him up now.'

Hardin took a scalpel firmly in his right hand, first checked that Evans was standing well clear of the table, then slid the blade into the tanned brown skin at Aristides's right shoulder. He ran the blade diagonally across and down the chest until he reached the sternum, then shifted his stance slightly and continued to cut all the way down to the top of the pubic hair, skirting around the navel. Then he extracted the scalpel, inserted it in Aristides's left shoulder and completed his initial Y-shaped incision.

The scalpel had cut deep, slicing through the skin and subcutaneous fat, but had not penetrated far enough to reach the ribs, so Hardin bent forward and began deepening the incisions and cutting under the skin until he was able to reflect – or lay back – the three sections of skin and flesh and expose the ribcage. The upper section covered most of Aristides's face.

Evans took more pictures, then Hardin picked up his pair of lopping shears and severed all the ribs on both sides of the body until he was able to lift out the chest plate and the central part of the ribcage, exposing the contents of the abdomen. He passed the chest plate to Evans, who placed it on the floor beside him on a rubberized sheet Hardin had laid out for that purpose. Evans used the camera to take two more shots, and then Hardin began dictating his report again.

'Initial incision completed, chest walls reflected, ribs cut and chest plate lifted away.'

Only then did he and Evans lean forward and peer cautiously into the open red maw exposed before them.

'Goddamnit, Tyler,' Evans muttered. 'What the hell is that?'

## Réthymno, Crete

In his hotel room, Murphy locked the door and jammed a chair underneath the handle as an added precaution, then opened the two packages in turn. He'd told Nicholson he'd need a rifle and a personal weapon, and he'd suggested using non-US manufactured arms, just in case he was forced to abandon them at the scene. As soon as Murphy opened the bigger package he realized that Nicholson had taken him precisely at his word.

It contained a *Snayperskaya Vintovka Dragunova* sniper rifle in 7.62mm Soviet calibre, complete with a bipod rest. Externally similar to the ubiquitous Kalashnikov, the Dragunov has a greatly extended barrel giving it an overall length of just over four feet, a ten-round magazine only one-third the size of the standard Kalashnikov unit, and an unusual cut-out stock incorporating a pistol grip. Normally the weapon is equipped with either the PSO-1 telescopic sight or the NSPU-3 night sight, which incorporates an image-intensifier, but this one was fitted with an under-barrel laser sight of a make Murphy didn't recognize, and a Bushnell telescopic sight. Belt and braces, he thought.

Murphy hefted the weapon in his hands. It felt solid and familiar, which was unsurprising as he had used one of these twice in the past. He switched on the laser sight and, after checking that he was unobserved, aimed the rifle through the window at the building opposite. Clearly visible in the absolute centre of the sight was the tiny red spot, which showed where the laser marker was being projected. Whoever had sighted-in this rifle knew their trade.

He laid the Dragunov aside, careful not to damage the box it had arrived in. He was going to have to transfer the weapon down to his car, and he could hardly walk through the hotel lobby carrying a four-foot sniper rifle in his hand.

The second box contained a spare pistol magazine, twenty rounds of 7.62mm Soviet ammunition for the Dragunov, a box of fifty rounds of 9mm Parabellum bullets, and a pistol that Murphy at first didn't recognize. It looked like a Ruger P85 but the hammer design was completely different, so it took Murphy a few moments to place it. It was a most unusual choice: a Daewoo DP51, manufactured in South Korea since 1993, and a good, reliable weapon.

Murphy pressed the release on the left side of the butt and extracted the magazine, opened the box of ammunition and loaded thirteen rounds, then picked the spare magazine out of the box and loaded that as well. There was also a screw-on silencer for the pistol, which he slipped into his jacket pocket.

With his personal weapon now loaded, Murphy smiled slightly. It would certainly be difficult to attribute the forthcoming assassinations of three CIA agents to any one nation, not if a Russian sniper rifle and a South Korean pistol were the weapons used. And probably the last nation that anyone might consider responsible would be America.

### HMS *Invincible*, Sea of Crete

Despite his confident assertions to Inspector Lavat, Richter hadn't underestimated the magnitude of the task facing him. Trying to locate exactly where the Greek had been diving was going to take luck as well as determination, but he did have both a plan and a secret weapon – the Agusta Westland Merlin HM Mk 1 ASW helicopters carried by the *Invincible*. But first he had to talk to Simpson.

The Merlin landed on three spot and the noise of the three jet engines diminished slightly as the pilot dropped the collective lever all the way down and the aircraft's weight settled onto its landing gear. Flight Deck personnel walked forward as soon as directed by the FDO and lashed the helicopter to the deck. Only then was the rear door of the Merlin slid open and the sole passenger – Richter – allowed to climb out.

He walked across the Flight Deck, opened the door into the island and climbed the stairs up to Flyco. As he had expected, Roger Black was in the chair and controlling the deck, but Wings was standing behind him, gazing down as maintainers swarmed around the Merlin which now sat on the deck below, engines silent, rotors stationary and folded back into the parked position.

'That was quick, Paul,' said Commander (Air). 'Is there anything you should be telling us?'

'Possibly, sir,' Richter replied. 'But first could I have a word in private?'

Wings looked somewhat startled, but nodded. 'There's nobody in the Bridge Mess at the moment. Would that do?'

'Fine.' Richter turned and led the way down the stairs. The Bridge Mess is a small dining room located directly below Flyco, and is only used to provide meals for officers who need to spend long periods of time on the bridge and, because of their duties, can't leave it to go down to the Wardroom to eat. Typically, it's used by Commander (Air), Lieutenant Commander (Flying) and the Air Staff Officer.

Richter slid open the door and entered, Commander (Air) right behind him. The two men sat down facing each other across the table.

'This is all very mysterious, Paul. What's going on?'

'At this moment, I'm not absolutely certain,' Richter said, 'but what I can tell you – for your ears only at the moment – is that there are two dead Greeks lying in a tiny village called Kandíra on the south coast of Crete. All the indications are that one of them found a sealed container somewhere which he took home and opened, with the help of the second Greek, his nephew. Within twelve hours both men were dead, killed by a really fast-acting pathogen.

'That's the overall picture, but there are several aspects of the situation that worry me. The Greek who found the container was a professional diver. Open-source information from a couple of Athens newspapers claim that he had found the wreck of an aircraft on the seabed somewhere near Crete. The obvious conclusion is that he found the container in that same wreck.'

'When did he find this aircraft?'

'No more than a day or two before he died, I think. That's the first anomaly. What was a deadly pathogen doing in a wrecked aircraft lying on the bottom of the Mediterranean? According to the CDC expert who's on the scene right now, whatever killed those two men so rapidly makes it far more lethal than any other known virus. And the fact that it was in a sealed container suggests that either it was being transported to a secure laboratory for investigation or it was heading the other way.'

Commander (Air) nodded. 'You're suggesting it was some kind of biological weapon that had already been developed?'

'Exactly, and whether it's a natural agent or some kind of developed bioweapon is irrelevant – the essential fact is that this agent is lethal.

'My next concern is that there's been some third-party involvement in the situation. I've told you about a sealed container, but that was merely deduced by the CDC man because the item itself is missing. It seems that two unknown men entered both scenes to retrieve the evidence before the CDC expert got there.

'My principal worry is that whoever retrieved it did so with the intention of using it somewhere else. We could be looking at some form of terrorist activity, and the men involved are clearly ruthless. They killed a police officer stationed outside the second property and dumped his body in a nearby ditch, along with those of two elderly villagers.'

Wings' intense expression turned to one of shock. 'Yes,' he said, 'the killings obviously add a different dimension to the situation. What assistance do you want from us on the *Invincible*?'

'Three things, sir. First, a secure communications channel so that I can talk to my section in London. Second, the use of a Merlin first thing tomorrow morning. I want to use its dunking sonar to try to locate the wrecked aircraft that the Greek found. Third, and assuming we manage to find this aircraft, the help of the ship's diving officer to go down and investigate it.'

# Chapter 15

**Thursday**
**Kandíra, south-west Crete**

The two men stared down into Spiros Aristides's chest cavity.

'There's a hell of a lot of blood in there,' Evans said. 'I've never seen anything like it before.'

'Me neither.' Hardin shifted his gaze from the body to Evans's face. 'I've never encountered it, thank God, but I only know of one virus that can do this.'

'Which is?'

'Variola.' The single word cut across the room like a knife, stunning Evans.

'Smallpox?' he echoed, taking an inadvertent step backwards. 'But that's been eradicated, has been for years.'

The last recorded victim of naturally occurring variola, the smallpox virus, was a hospital cook in Somalia named Ali Maow Maalin who contracted the disease on 27 October 1977, and who survived. The last ever smallpox infection was reported about a year later, when three members of a family named Parker contracted the disease in Birmingham, England: two of them died. But this outbreak apparently occurred because of viral spores escaping from a small laboratory in the building where the first member of the Parker family to be infected – Janet, a medical photographer – worked. The researcher whose room had probably been the source of the infection was later found dying, an apparent suicide.

Hardin nodded at Evans. 'But this isn't smallpox, unless it's a completely unknown strain,' he said, gesturing at the body. 'No pustules, no sign of any damage to the skin at all. No, this is something very different.'

But there was no denying the truth of what Evans had said.

Normally, the chest cavity of a corpse being autopsied contains virtually no blood, and what there is almost invariably results from the gross assault on the body carried out by the pathologist when opening up the cavity itself. All of the organs there contain blood, of course, but the cavity itself should contain none.

Inside Spiros Aristides's opened-up chest there was blood visible everywhere.

'Right,' Hardin said. 'The cavity appears to contain at least one pint of blood, and it is still fairly fluid. This long after death it should have clotted, which suggests we might be dealing with some kind of haemorrhagic fever virus that has attacked the platelets. On initial external examination the organs appear normal.'

'Should we take a sample of blood from here for bacterial examination?' Evans asked.

Hardin nodded. 'Yes. I don't yet know where all this blood came from, so a sample might help. If it came from the heart or the lungs, there's a good chance of contamination by various kinds of airborne bacteria, so take a sample from the femoral artery as well, if you can, for comparison.'

Evans nodded, easily filled a syringe with blood from the Greek's abdomen, then parted Aristides's legs so that he could reach the site of the femoral artery in the groin. He mounted a needle on a forty-millilitre syringe and slid it into the artery. As he eased the plunger out he was rewarded by a small amount of deep red liquid. Removing the lids from two small containers of brown blood-culture liquid, he injected the blood samples into them and carefully labelled each one correctly. If there were any bacteria present in the blood they would develop inside the containers, thus enabling them to be observed and identified.

Once Evans had finished his bit, Hardin selected another scalpel and reached into the chest cavity. 'I'm now removing the heart,' he said to the tape recorder. He began severing the arteries and veins that surrounded it, then cut away the supporting membrane. He pulled the vital organ free, studied it for a few moments and then handed it carefully to Evans. Beside the younger man a selection of large stainless-steel bowls stood ready on the sideboard, and he placed the heart into one of them for dissection later.

'The heart appears normal on external examination. I'm next removing the lungs,' Hardin continued, then reached back into Aristides's chest cavity, cutting carefully with the scalpel until he could free them. 'They're heavy,' he said, as he picked them up using both hands. 'Five gets you ten they're oedematous – full of blood,' he added as he passed them across to Evans who was already holding out a steel dish ready to receive them.

'OK,' Hardin said, 'we'll look at those later. Now we come to the smelly bit – the small intestine.'

Coiled and convoluted, the small intestine is held in place by the mesenteric membrane, itself a part of the peritoneum, the skin which lines the abdomen in all vertebrate animals. Hardin cut away the membranes securing the small intestine to the abdomen, then severed both ends of it. Immediately a pungent odour filled the room which both men could smell even through their Racal hoods, and a grey goo – called chyme and consisting of partially digested food – began oozing out of the lower end of the intestine.

Evans looked down at the chyme as Hardin wrestled the coils into the large steel dish he was holding. 'Is it my imagination, Tyler, or is this chyme darker than usual?'

Hardin stopped and looked closely at the severed end of the intestine. 'It varies from individual to individual and a lot depends on diet, but you could be right. We'll wash it out later and take some samples for toxicological examination.'

Hardin started working on the liver next, using his scalpel to separate it from its various blood vessels, and placed it in a steel dish. 'More smells,' he said, as he turned to the membranes supporting the stomach and large bowel. He removed the stomach first, then cut through the rest of the membrane supporting the large bowel, severing the end of the rectum as close as possible to the anus, and also cut away the urethra and bladder. All these pelvic organs Hardin removed together, then used his scalpel to separate them. The bladder and urethra he placed in one steel bowl, and the large bowel into another one.

'I won't bother about the testicles,' Hardin said. 'I still don't know what killed him, but I'm quite certain it wasn't some form of venereal disease.'

The final organs left in the abdomen were the kidneys, and Hardin swiftly removed them. 'Right,' he said to the tape recorder. 'The abdomen is empty apart from the residual blood, with all organs removed. External examination suggests that the lungs, and possibly the liver and kidneys, contain fluid of some sort, probably blood, which again is consistent with death caused by some form of viral haemorrhagic fever. OK, Mark, just the brain to remove and then we can start looking at the organs themselves.'

In a mortuary suite, the head of a cadaver is placed on an H-shaped head block made of hard rubber which facilitates the opening of the cranium using a Stryker saw. Hardin had neither a head block nor a power saw, so he had to improvise.

He arranged three small sandbags – sand was plentiful enough around Kandíra – in a U-shaped pattern to support Aristides's head, then picked up a fresh scalpel to be sure of a sharp blade. He pushed the tip of the scalpel into the fairly thin skin above the right ear and kept on thrusting it in until it made contact with the bone of the skull. Then, pressing hard, Hardin ran the blade over the top of Aristides's head until he reached the top of his left ear, so separating the scalp into two sections. He seized the front half of the scalp and pulled it forward over the dead Greek's face, then pulled the rear half backwards, thus exposing the top of the skull.

A Stryker is a power saw fitted with a small and very sharp reciprocating blade. It screams when in use and fills the air with an unpleasant odour: an amalgam of burnt bone and blood. The mortuary attendant whose job it is to open the cranium will begin and end the cut at the forehead, often leaving a small notch to allow the calvarium or cranial cap to be accurately replaced after the autopsy has been completed. Hardin wasn't even slightly bothered about whether or not the calvarium could be refitted neatly: all he was interested in doing was getting into the skull and removing the brain.

In the absence of a Stryker saw, Hardin had selected the next best thing – a short-bladed bone saw. He had to be careful using it, because all he wanted to achieve was to cut through the bone of the skull itself. He didn't, if he could possibly avoid it, want to cut into the dura mater, the tough membrane that lies directly below the bone and encases the brain. With Evans holding the sides of the skull firmly, Hardin started at the forehead, cutting with swift, sure strokes once the blade had started to bite. Then he and Evans changed positions, Evans wielding the saw on the left-hand side of the skull while Hardin held it firmly. It took over twenty minutes to complete all the cuts necessary.

Normally the calvarium is freed from the skull by inserting a bone chisel into the incision made by the saw and twisting it, repeating the process all the way round the skull until the cap loosens and can be lifted off. Hardin preferred to use a broad-bladed screwdriver with a T-shaped handle, and had the calvarium freed in a couple of minutes.

He and Evans carefully examined the grey dura mater, and Hardin pressed it experimentally a few times, testing for any excessive pressure in the skull that might be caused by leaking blood vessels. Hardin had heard of autopsies on Ebola victims where so much blood had leaked into the brain that the dura mater had bulged outwards as the calvarium had been removed and in one case, possibly apocryphal, the pressure had allegedly been sufficient to rupture the dura itself, sending a lethal stream of Ebola-rich blood spraying across the floor of the pathology suite.

'It looks and feels normal to me,' Hardin finally announced, reaching for a pair of blunt-ended scissors to cut away the dura mater. He first used a pair of forceps to pinch a small section of the dura, then cut into it with the scissors. A few drops of blood leaked out, but that was all. Hardin nodded in satisfaction and cut away the rest of the dura mater, revealing the surface of the brain, the cerebral cortex.

'The brain appears normal on first examination,' Hardin said, again speaking to the tape recorder. 'OK, Mark, this is a bit fiddly, and you'll need to help me. Can you just lift the frontal poles for me so that I can cut through the olfactory nerves? Good: that's it.' Hardin eased his scalpel down the anterior of the brain. 'Right, now I'll sever the optic nerves and we'll take a look at the pituitary stalk.

'The pituitary reveals no apparent abnormalities,' Hardin announced, a minute or two later. 'Now I'll detach the tentorium cerebelli and then we can remove the roof of the cerebellum. OK, that's fine.' Working more quickly now, as the daylight outside began to fade, Hardin cut the remaining nine pairs of cranial nerves, and waited while Evans collected a sample of cerebrospinal fluid in a pipette. Then Hardin cut through the lower medulla oblongata and the vertebral arteries, and gestured to Evans. Evans wrapped both hands around the brain and moved it gently from side to side. That freed it enough to allow him to ease it backwards out of the skull, exposing the spinal cord, which Hardin severed to free the brain completely. Evans removed it from the skull and placed it carefully in the last steel dish on the sideboard.

'OK,' Hardin said. 'I think the answer lies in the blood and in the lungs. Let's see what we can find here.'


## Chóra Sfakia, Crete

It was still low season for tourism in Crete, which meant the first couple of hotels Krywald stopped the car outside were firmly closed. The next one he found was open, but full, but one around the corner, on the northern outskirts of the town, still had four rooms free. As Stein booked three of them, Krywald parked the car on the street outside, the hotel having no private car park. Then the three men carried their few bags inside and took the lift up to the second floor.

Stein and Krywald took for themselves the two rooms closest to the lift and staircase, though on opposite sides of the corridor, while Elias's lay four doors further down the passage. Once they'd dumped their luggage, Krywald – still carrying the case containing the steel briefcase – summoned them to the nearly empty bar next to the reception desk to discuss their plan for the next day.

'As long as that drunken bum Monedes is even halfway sober by then we should be OK,' Krywald said. 'All he has to do is give us the scuba gear, tell us where the boat is kept and give us the keys to get it started. After that he can drink himself to death for all I care.'

Stein nodded agreement, then turned to Elias. 'You're familiar with boats, I guess?'

'If you're a diver, it pretty much goes without saying,' Elias confirmed. 'You spend a lot of time sitting around in them.'

'I appreciate that, but can you navigate and so on?'

Elias shook his head. 'I don't have any formal qualifications, no,' he said, 'but I reckon I can handle the sort of boat provided tomorrow without any problems. But I figured that one of you two would be qualified.'

Krywald gave a short laugh. 'Nope,' he said, 'our talents lie in different directions. But all we have to do is get the boat out of the harbour and find our way out to the spot where this Greek diver found his wrecked aircraft. McCready supplied us with the exact co-ordinates, and we've got two GPS units right here. There we drop anchor, you get suited up and go over the side. You do your stuff on the bottom and we're out of here.'

Elias put down his coffee cup and looked at Krywald inquiringly. 'McCready was a bit evasive about that. When you say "do my stuff", what exactly do you mean?'

Krywald glanced briefly at Stein before replying. 'Apart from the contents of the steel case I've got right here, that wrecked aircraft is the last possible link to a covert Company operation run in the 1970s. You don't need to know what it involved – in fact, I don't know all the details myself – but if any information about it came to light today it would reflect badly, very badly, all round. McCready's orders are most specific. The case goes back to Langley for disposal, and all traces of the aircraft must be obliterated. I'll deal with the case: the aircraft is your job.'

For a long moment Elias just stared at him. 'You mean I've got to blow it up?' he finally demanded.

'The boy's quick,' Krywald commented drily. 'Spot on, Mr Elias. You just drop yourself down to the bottom of the sea, plant some plastic on board the wreck, light the blue touchpaper and get the hell out of there.'

'But I don't know anything about explosives,' Elias's voice rose.

'You don't need to.' Krywald glanced round the bar to make sure nobody could overhear them. 'When he went out earlier this morning Stein collected enough plastic explosive to sink half of Crete. All you have to do is put some charges in the wreck, snap the end off each of the pencil detonators and then get yourself back up to the boat. The fuses are pre-set for three hours so as to give us plenty of time to get clear. We could well be on our way back to Réthymno before the big bang occurs.'

'I don't like the sound of it,' Elias said. 'Suppose something goes wrong. What if the fuses are faulty and the explosive goes off while I'm still in the water?'

'Roger told you our talents lie in different directions,' Stein replied. 'I'm an explosives expert, so I know detonators and I know plastic. I've already checked the stuff we've been given and it's good. The fuses are the latest models – pencil fuses safe down to five hundred feet – and I guarantee this plastic won't blow for three hours.'

Elias nodded, looking far from convinced. He stood up. 'Look, I'm going to take a walk. After being stuck in that damn car all day, I need to clear my head. We're going to eat somewhere here?'

Krywald glanced across the road, where three restaurants were clearly preparing to open. 'One of those places should be OK, so get back here by eight. We don't want to eat late, and if you're diving tomorrow you should get a good sleep tonight.'

Elias nodded agreement and walked out of the bar.

'You have any problems at Soúda Bay?' Krywald asked, as he and Stein stepped into the lift.

Stein shook his head. 'No. The plastic's OK and they really are three-hour detonators.'

'Bit of a surprise, that,' Krywald murmured. 'I wouldn't have put it past McCready to have doctored them to take out the three of us while we're bobbing around in the goddamn ocean. You get the weapons as well?'

'Sure did. Three SIG P226s with silencers and two extra magazines each.'

'Nice,' Krywald said.

Inside his room, Stein handed one of the weapons over. Krywald worked the action a couple of times then slammed a fully loaded magazine into the butt. 'No serial number,' he observed.

'No. They've been sanitized. I don't know how he did it,' Stein said, 'but our Captain Levy told me that a trace on these weapons will lead straight to the Fibbies.'

'No kidding? That'll really piss off the Bureau if they ever find out.'

Stein loaded a second pistol and tucked it into the rear waistband of his trousers. 'You want me to give the other one to Elias?' he asked.

'Are you out of your fucking mind? He's just an analyst. If he wasn't a qualified diver he'd still be pushing paper round his desk at Langley. The last thing we do is give him a gun to play with. Christ knows what he'd do with it.'

# PANDEMIC

## Kandíra, south-west Crete

'Mr Hardin?' Inspector Lavat called up the stairs.

'I'm here,' Hardin replied, from above.

'I've got the floodlights you asked for. Do you want them now?'

'Yes, please, Inspector. It's starting to get a bit dark.'

Outside, the sun was sinking towards the western horizon and although it was still demonstrably daylight, the shadows were lengthening as evening approached.

Lavat climbed up the stairs with a mains-powered portable floodlight in each hand. He stopped on the landing, outside the door of the spare bedroom, put the lights down on the floor and squinted into the room. The first thing he saw was the eviscerated corpse of Spiros Aristides, chest cavity gaping open and the top of the skull grotesquely absent.

Like most other policemen, Inspector Lavat had been required to attend occasional autopsies in the course of his duties, but he had never been able to view a dead body with anything like the clinical detachment exhibited by doctors and pathologists. And the sight of the mutilated corpse in the incongruous surroundings of a spare bedroom in a Cretan village house was doubly disturbing. The two figures crowded into the small room behind the corpse didn't help either, the orange Tyvek suits and Racal helmets reminding Lavat uncomfortably of aliens from a low-budget science-fiction film.

Hardin looked up at him as Evans stepped out onto the landing and picked up the floodlights. He positioned them in opposite corners of the bedroom, pointing the bulbs upwards to give reflected rather than direct light.

Hardin followed Lavat's gaze to Aristides's body. 'We'll be tidying the cadaver up later, once we've finished the organ examination.' He then noticed that Lavat looked distinctly uncomfortable. 'Are you feeling all right, Inspector?' he asked.

Lavat nodded, though feeling the bile rise, his face noticeably paler beneath the suntan. 'It's just the—' He got no further, but turned away and headed swiftly down the stairs and out of the small house.

'Is he OK?' Evan asked.

'I think so,' Hardin replied. 'We get so used to this kind of thing' – he gestured to the corpse – 'that we tend to forget other people rarely get to see it.'

Evans nodded. 'Right, what's next?'

'We'll start with the heart, and we'll do the lungs last,' Hardin said. 'I think they're going to be the most interesting.'

Mark Evans had earlier moved the steel dishes containing Aristides's organs over to one side of the room, and had placed a wooden board on the top of the chest of drawers, which they could use for the dissections. Wood is not the ideal surface for such an operation because it retains traces of whatever was placed on it previously, and obviously if the organs are potentially 'hot' the wood itself becomes a source of infection. But they hadn't been able to find anything else more suitable, so both the board and the trestle table on which the Greek's body lay would be burnt as soon as Hardin had completed his autopsy.

Evans weighed the steel bowl containing the heart on the portable scales he had fetched out of one of the CDC boxes. He then placed the heart itself in the centre of the wooden board, before weighing the bowl and subtracting that figure from the total to calculate the weight of the heart itself. Hardin studied the organ carefully for several minutes, prodding it around so that he could visually check its entire surface.

'The heart appears externally normal, and the weight falls within the usual range,' Hardin announced for the tape recorder. 'I'll now begin the dissection itself.'

Evans watched as Hardin took a fresh scalpel and expertly slit open the organ. He looked closely into each chamber of the heart, then turned his attention to the coronary arteries, cutting them open so that he could examine their inner surfaces.

'The interior appears normal. There's some furring of the coronary arteries, but on the whole the heart looks healthy, particularly for a man of this age. For each organ we'll be carrying out histological and toxicological examinations, so I'll take samples now.' Hardin leant forward and cut four roughly one-inch squares from the heart muscle.

Evans passed over two stock jars – small specimen containers pre-filled with formalin, a clear liquid that's a highly poisonous preservative – and dropped one segment into each. He labelled both with the name of the deceased, the date and the source of the tissue, then added a red stick-on note reading simply 'HISTOLOGY'. These samples would be examined under a microscope to try to detect any changes to the individual cells that might have been caused by a fatal disease. Privately, Hardin thought histology would reveal nothing of significance, but it was normal procedure.

The other two segments he put into what are known as 'tox jars' – plastic containers that don't contain any preservative because that would destroy any toxins present in the specimen. On each of these he affixed a label bearing the word 'TOXICOLOGY'. He would repeat this entire process as each separate organ was dissected.

'Right,' Hardin said, 'I don't think there's anything else we can learn from studying the heart, so we'll move on to the liver.'

Evans removed the dissected heart from the wooden board and replaced it in its steel bowl. After they'd finished the autopsy, all the organs would be sealed into plastic bags and placed in one of the two chest freezers provided for them by the Cretan Ministry of Health. Final disposal would almost certainly be by burning, probably in a sealed incinerator at a local hospital.

The two men had already established a working routine – first weigh; then external examination; dissection; internal examination; take samples for specialist histological and toxicological examination – followed by discussion, conclusion and verbal notes spoken into the tape recorder.

'The liver shows some signs of cirrhosis, but at a comparatively early stage, and certainly not life-threatening,' Hardin said as Evans removed the organ in question from the cutting board in front of him. 'Probably cheap Cretan wine. Normally the liver appears bright and shiny, but in this case it's dull and a fairly dark red. The organ contains rather more blood than would be normal, and there are some signs of blood weeping from the minor vessels of the liver, which is most unusual and could be indicative of haemorrhagic fever.'

The spleen is one of the likeliest places in the body to find the infectious particles characteristic of victims of this type of virus, so Hardin examined that organ with particular care, and again cut out several pieces for further examination. He checked the stomach, small intestine and large bowel, then took samples of both the contents and the structure of each section of the digestive tract. As Evans had spotted during the autopsy, the contents of each were noticeably darker than usual.

Aristides's bladder and rectum were next sectioned and examined; both showed clear evidence of blood inside them, which served to confirm what the external examination of the body had indicated – the Greek had bled from every orifice. The kidneys, like the liver, appeared basically normal, but again showed signs of weeping blood vessels.

Hardin then turned his attention to the brain. There were no obvious external signs of anything abnormal there, but when Hardin bisected it laterally the two men spotted the same indications of weeping capillaries and veins. 'It's the same thing, Mark,' Hardin said. 'The minor blood vessels in particular show signs of seepage through the walls. That's a classic sign of Ebola or some other viral haemorrhagic fever, caused by the damage done to the endothelial cells that line the blood vessels.'

'But you still don't think it's actually Ebola?' Evans asked.

'It's definitely not Zaïre or Sudan, which means that if it is Ebola it's a new and unknown strain,' Hardin replied. 'The effects on the body itself, and on the organs we've examined so far, are certainly consistent with the early to middle stages of an Ebola infection, or the terminal phases of an attack by Lassa Fever. That's an arenavirus not a filovirus, of course, though the whole family – apart from the commonest form, lymphocytic choriomeningitis, which is a Level Three Agent – are still classed as Level Four Hot Agents. But nothing we've seen up to now could actually have caused death. Discomfort and pain, yes, but not death itself. Something else must have killed this man.'

Hardin took samples from six areas of the brain for further investigation, then wiped down the cutting board while Evans replaced the brain in the steel dish. 'The brain appears generally normal, apart from the same sort of capillary bleeding that we've noted in the other internal organs.' Hardin watched as Evans lifted the large steel dish containing Aristides's lungs, placed it on the scales to be weighed and wrote down the result.

Hardin positioned the lungs on the board and for a few moments just looked down at the specimen while Evans weighed the steel dish and calculated the actual weight of the organs.

'They're *heavy*,' Evans said, showing Hardin the sheet of paper on which he'd written down the two figures. 'Well outside the normal range.'

Hardin nodded. 'Full of blood, I suspect. OK, external examination first.' He studied the lungs for some minutes, noting carefully their colour and feeling their texture as well as he could through the multiple layers of gloves he was wearing. 'The lungs appear larger than normal for a man of this age, but that is probably a function of his lifestyle. Divers, like athletes, tend to develop larger lungs than most people. Their colour is darker than normal, and there is evidence of external bleeding from both major and minor vessels on the outer surface. This is a subjective observation, especially through these damn gloves, but his lungs feel very pulpy, as if the alveoli are full of fluid.'

He took a fresh scalpel, positioned the tip of the blade carefully at the top of the left lung, and slid it down smoothly. The two halves of the lung separated and almost fell apart and, with a rush, about half a pint of blood slopped over the board and onto the rubber sheets that covered the floor.

'OK,' Hardin said, 'now we know what killed him.'

## Réthymno, Crete

Murphy waited until dusk had fallen before carrying the Dragunov down the hotel's back stairs and stowing it in the boot of his hire car. As a precaution, he'd removed the loaded magazine, but would keep that with him at all times. With the weapon stored out of sight, and with the Daewoo still tucked into the rear waistband of his trousers under his light summer jacket, Murphy left the hotel car park and moved away down the street.

To a casual observer, he would have looked like any other aimless tourist out for his pre-dinner stroll, but Murphy actually had a specific destination in mind. He'd already picked up a hotel map of Réthymno and, despite not yet having Nicholson's go-ahead, had decided to reconnoitre the area where he was likely to find his targets.

When Murphy reached the hotel where Krywald, Stein and Elias were staying, he glanced up and down the pavement and then selected a café on the opposite side of the street. At a table offering a clear view of the hotel, he ordered a beer, then opened his copy of an American car magazine.

He didn't anticipate actually spotting any of his three targets – he knew they were somewhere else on the island completing the second phase of their tasking – but Murphy had always found, in his grisly trade, that time spent checking out his area of operations was never wasted. There was no such thing as too much preparation.

Despite his apparent absorption in his motoring magazine, Murphy was actually figuring the angles. His major problem was to be facing three CIA agents. The fact that they were fellow Americans and CIA employees didn't bother him in the slightest: what concerned him was the reaction of the remaining two once he'd eliminated the first one.

They were going to be operational agents, probably armed and certainly experienced. If he were to simply set up his sniper rifle and shoot the first target as he walked out of the hotel, Murphy knew the other two would then do their best to hunt him down. He'd be lucky to escape with his life if he didn't account for all three. No, what he needed here was cunning and a couple of *accidents*.


## HMS *Invincible*, Sea of Crete

There were no private cubicles or anything like that in the Communications Centre on Five Deck, next to the Operations Room, and Richter was particularly keen that anything he said on the telephone to Simpson should be heard by Simpson and by no one else. After discussion with the Communications Officer, Richter retreated to his cabin on Two Deck and waited for the crucial call to be patched through to him there.

Once the telephone rang, Richter picked up the receiver. Behind the crackles he heard a voice. 'Commander Richter? This is the CommCen – we're connecting you now. Go ahead, sir.'

There was a loud click, followed by a moment of echoing silence, then a distant voice spoke. 'Richter? Richter? Can you hear me?' Simpson's voice was faint, but perfectly clear.

'Yes.' Richter sat down on his day bed. He'd made some notes while he was waiting for this call to be connected, and he scanned them quickly.

'Where are you?' Simpson asked.

'Right now,' Richter said, 'I'm in my cabin on board the *Invincible*, and the ship's still holding position a few miles off the north coast of Crete.'

'And what have you found out?' Simpson demanded. 'It had better be good to justify all this buggering about with secure lines.'

'It's not good,' Richter said. 'In fact, it's bad. What caused the deaths of the two victims here on Crete is, in the opinion of the CDC specialist, either an unknown but naturally occurring virus, or a manufactured bioweapon. Whatever it is, it kills its victims within about twelve hours of infection, and so far it's proving one hundred per cent lethal.'

'How does he know?'

'He doesn't. He's just making assumptions based on the evidence that's available to him.'

Richter explained concisely what Hardin had found in Kandíra, the American's deduction about the sealed container, and finally the suggestion that Spiros Aristides might have found the virus in the remains of a sunken aircraft.

'That's all a bit circumstantial,' Simpson said. 'There could be other explanations.'

'Like what?' Richter demanded. 'The corpses are real enough, and they certainly didn't die from old age or heart attacks. Something got inside them that left them spewing blood like a lawn sprinkler. And there's something else.'

'What?'

'Two men entered both properties in the village and almost certainly took away the container that held the virus, and they killed a policeman and two villagers to do it. They're probably working for the people who created whatever was in that container, and came to Crete to retrieve their property. What worries me is what they're going to do now they've got the stuff back.'

'Did anybody get a description?'

'Yes,' Richter replied, 'but it won't help much. Caucasian, average height, average build. You won't get much of a photofit from that.'

'So what leads have you got?'

'Right now,' Richter said, 'only one. Most of the water round here is too deep for free diving, which limits the number of places where the

Greek could have discovered the aircraft. I'm plotting possible locations on a navigation chart and I've requested a Merlin to get airborne first thing tomorrow morning to try to locate the wreck using its dunking sonar. Once we've found it, I'm going down to take a look.'

# Chapter 16

**Friday**
**Chóra Sfakia, Crete**

Monedes still wasn't completely sober when Stein and Elias pushed open the door of his shop just after nine that morning, but at least he was upright. Stein guessed that the previous night he'd probably slept right where he'd fallen over, behind the counter. That was fortunate because it meant that he hadn't locked the door and, according to a hand-written notice taped to the shop window, it wasn't supposed to open until ten.

Monedes regarded the two men through red-rimmed and bleary eyes that held no sign of recognition whatsoever. Stein handled the negotiations with a certain inevitable feeling of déjà vu.

'You have a booking in the name of Wilson, for a day boat and some diving equipment? It was made from America this week?'

Monedes nodded and swallowed, his face grey, then reached under the counter. For a second Stein wondered if he was reaching for the bottle of *tsikoudia* and a 'hair of the dog', but instead he pulled out a red loose-leaf binder, placed it carefully on the counter, and began flicking through it.

'Wilson?' he muttered, as he searched the pages. 'Yes, here it is,' he said at last. 'A day boat, one aqualung set with four spare bottles. Plus a wetsuit, mask, fins, weight belt and everything else. The suit is for you yourself?' he asked, looking at Stein.

'No, for my friend.' Stein gestured towards Elias.

Monedes looked Elias up and down. 'No problem,' he said, and led the way towards a door at the rear. The two Americans followed and found themselves entering a room lined with shelves groaning under the weight of various pieces of diving equipment.

Monedes said something to Stein, who turned to his colleague and pointed at the shelves. 'He says you can help yourself,' Stein explained, guessing that either bending down or reaching up might be beyond Monedes's capabilities in his present fragile state.

Elias was in his element here. He selected a black neoprene two-piece wetsuit complete with hood, and added separate bootees and gloves. The aqualungs were stored in racks at the back of the room, and Elias checked the demand valves on three sets before he declared himself satisfied with one of them. He picked out four full compressed air cylinders as spares, weighing them by hand, then added demand valves, air hoses and mouthpieces to them. He chose a weight belt and a couple of dozen weights, a stainless-steel diving knife and calf sheath, a depth gauge, a compass, a one-hundred-metre coil of thin cord and another one-hundred-metre coil of orange polypropylene rope and a lead weight to anchor it. Then he selected fins, a mask, snorkel, a life-saving inflatable jacket, two powerful underwater torches, and a large string bag – as was used for collecting specimens – to complete the outfit.

Monedes watched Elias's progress around the storeroom with a certain weary detachment. He turned to Stein as Elias added the last items to his growing pile. 'Your friend knows what he's doing, and he's going deep, I think.'

Stein nodded without comment, then bent down to help Elias carry the equipment out to the car, parked right outside the door. While Elias was stowing the last item in the boot, Stein headed back into the shop. 'The hire fee should already have been paid?' he inquired.

Monedes nodded. 'Yes, by American Express, but I will need your passport as security.'

Stein didn't demur – he was carrying three completely genuine American passports in different names – and he immediately handed over the one bearing the name 'Wilson'.

'Can I see your diving permit?' Monedes asked, as something of an afterthought.

Stein stared at him and shook his head. 'What diving permit?'

'You should have got a diving permit from the Department of Antiquities if your friend is going to dive here in Cretan waters. I am supposed to see it before I supply you with any equipment.'

Stein's face cleared. 'No, he's not,' he said, thinking on his feet. 'We're diving well away from Crete – that's why we need the boat.'

Monedes still looked doubtful, so Stein passed over a handful of notes. 'If anybody should ask you,' he said, 'perhaps you can confirm that you *have* seen our permit.'

Monedes looked at the notes in his hand and nodded slowly. 'Yes,' he said, pushing them into his hip pocket, 'perhaps I can.'

Stein grinned. 'And the boat?' he asked.

Three minutes later their car was pulling up alongside a nearby jetty. Twenty minutes after that Krywald and Stein were sitting side by side on a bench in a grubby but sea-worthy blue-painted open wooden boat about fifteen feet in length. They watched as Elias started the inboard diesel engine and slowly began to manoeuvre the craft through the harbour and out to the open sea.

## HMS *Invincible*, Sea of Crete

The previous evening Richter had spent nearly two hours poring over a selection of navigation charts of the waters surrounding Crete. But he'd spent a few minutes preparing his criteria before even looking at them. He had decided to eliminate all areas within half a mile of the coast of Crete or any other inhabited islands, on the grounds that an aircraft wreck so close to the shore would have been discovered long before. He had also excluded all stretches of water greater than one hundred and fifty feet – fifty metres – in depth because of the difficulties of anyone diving that deep without specialized equipment.

What surprised him was how small – not large – an area that left to be searched. At his self-imposed half-mile cut-off point, there were virtually no locations around the Cretan coast where the water was less than one hundred metres deep. About the only possible areas on the coast itself were the two north-facing bays at the western end of the island – Kólpos Chanión and Kólpos Kissámou – but Richter was fairly certain Aristides hadn't been diving in either of them.

Quite apart from anything else, both inlets contained popular holiday resorts, so anybody diving there would easily become the focus of numerous pairs of eyes and binoculars, not to mention cameras, and a man who earned his living by illegally recovering ancient artefacts from the seabed would hardly want such a large and attentive audience to witness his activities. No, on balance, Richter decided that Aristides would have been diving somewhere else.

But there were numerous small islands around Crete itself, most of them uninhabited because they were simply too small to be developed, so the shallower water close to their shores was a definite possibility. Richter had already marked several of these, starting with Andikíthira and finishing with the Gávdos–Gavdopoúla pair.

Privately, he put his money on three strong contenders: Paximáda in Órmos Mésaras, south-west of Agía Galíni; Chrýsi and its much smaller companion Mikronissi lying to the south of Ierápetra, though this area lay some way outside his theoretical radius of fifty to sixty miles from Kandíra; and finally the area extending between Gávdos and Gavdopoúla. The outside bet would be the Koufonísi group located south of the Stenon Konfonisou at the eastern tip of Crete. That was too far for Aristides to reach in a day and still get back to Kandíra, but it was still a possibility if the diver had spent one or two nights somewhere in the area.

With his target areas established, Richter had worked out a route that would allow the Merlin to check the chosen sites in the most logical order in terms of speed. With *Invincible* still loitering out to sea north of Réthymno, he decided that the first site to investigate would be Andikíthira lying north-west of the western tip of Crete, followed by Gávdos and Gavdopoúla, and then Paximáda. Then probably a refuel, although that depended on the amount of time they would spend searching at each location, the Merlin having a top speed of over 160 knots and an endurance in excess of four hours.

If refuelling was necessary, they'd fly north, straight over the Cretan mainland and back to the *Invincible*, undertake the long transit south-east to Chrýsi and Mikronissi, then a short flight east to Koufonísi and then back to the ship. If by that stage they'd found nothing, Richter was going to have to think again.

'And we're looking for what, exactly?' Lieutenant Commander Michael ('Mike') O'Reilly was the 814 Naval Air Squadron Senior Observer – known inevitably as 'Sobs' – and he'd elected to fly this sortie when he'd heard the Merlin wouldn't just be acting as an airborne taxi cab. They were in the Rotary Wing Briefing-Room on Two Deck, where the met officer had finished his spiel a few minutes earlier, and Richter had just outlined the route he intended the Merlin to take.

'A wrecked aircraft on the seabed,' Richter said. 'Probably an executive jet of some sort – a Lear, Falcon, that sort of size – and it's been at the bottom of the sea for a while, probably ten years or more. It was apparently shot down, so it's almost certainly going to be severely damaged.'

'Shot down – how do you know? Who by? And whose aircraft was it?'

'That's three questions,' Richter replied, 'and the three answers are: it was in the newspaper; no idea and no idea.'

'In the newspaper?' O'Reilly grinned broadly. 'Is that where you spooks get the information you need? It's hardly Echelon or Carnivore, is it?'

Echelon is a communications intercept programme operated jointly by the American National Security Agency and Britain's Government Communications Headquarters, and with contributions from Australia, New Zealand, Canada and elsewhere. It routinely monitors all telephone calls, emails and fax transmissions originating or terminating within its operating area, searching for specific words and phrases. Carnivore is a broadly equivalent programme, but run on a much smaller scale and operated by the Federal Bureau of Investigation in the United States.

Richter smiled back at him. 'Sometimes open-source information proves just as valuable, Mike, and in this case I've no option but to rely on it because it's all I've got. And you're just a touch out of date anyway – the cutting-edge communications intercept programme now running is the National Reconnaissance Office's Blue Crystal, not the National Security Agency's Echelon.'

'Blue Crystal? Never heard of it,' O'Reilly replied.

'I'm delighted to hear that,' Richter said. 'If you had, I'd have had to shoot you. Now, do you think you can find this bloody aircraft for me?'

'Of course,' O'Reilly said. 'Finding needles in haystacks is our speciality. Let's get going.'

## Kandíra, south-west Crete

'He died of what?' Inspector Lavat doubted the truth of what he'd just heard.

'He drowned,' Hardin repeated. 'Aristides drowned in his own blood. The actual cause of death was respiratory failure as his lungs filled up with blood. This is a type of pulmonary oedema that's often called Adult Respiratory Distress Syndrome or ARDS. It's the commonest cause of death in patients suffering from an attack by an arenavirus like Venezuelan Haemorrhagic Fever, Brazilian Sabia Virus or Lassa Fever.'

'I've heard of Lassa Fever,' Lavat said, 'but not the other two. So Aristides died of something like Lassa Fever – is that what you're saying?'

'No, or at least not Lassa or any of the other known arenaviruses, because those all act quite slowly. The victim first complains of a headache and muscle pains, which gradually get worse, then he gets feverish and starts vomiting, has diarrhoea and begins bleeding from the gums. Occasionally those affected suffer haemorrhages in the whites of the eyes. Their blood pressure falls dramatically, they go into shock, and in the later stages they suffer convulsions and lapse into unconsciousness.

'In the final stages many display a massive swelling of the head and neck and decerebrate rigidity – a condition that freezes the body into a contorted posture as the higher brain functions are lost. Some suffer from encephalopathy – that's an inflammation of the brain – and those who do usually lapse into a coma with severe convulsions.'

'I'm a little out of date,' Dr Gravas said, 'but I think I've read about some kind of treatment for Lassa Fever.'

'Yes,' Hardin said, 'there is a treatment now, though it's still somewhat experimental, and the drug – it's called ribavirin – must be administered as early as possible after the diagnosis has been made if treatment is going to be successful.'

Gravas nodded slowly. 'In this case,' he said, 'I doubt very much if ribavirin or anything else would have helped, given the sheer speed of the infection. In some ways,' he added, 'from what you're saying it looks as if Aristides died from a hugely accelerated form of an arenavirus – what you might almost call a kind of "Galloping Lassa"?'

Despite himself, Hardin smiled. 'That's not a bad way of putting it, Dr Gravas. He did die of ARDS, and although a lot of the classic symptoms of Lassa were absent in Aristides's case, and the kind of severe bleeding he presented is rare, we can call it that for the moment.'


## ASW Merlin callsign 'Spook Two', off Andikíthira, Sea of Crete

The Spook Two callsign hadn't been Richter's idea, but Mike O'Reilly had thought it amusing enough to suggest using it for communications on a discrete frequency between helicopter and ship, and Wings had raised no objections. If they had to talk to Soúda Bay or any outside controlling authority, they would instead use the aircraft's side number.

The transit to Andikíthira had taken only a few minutes in the Merlin flying at one hundred and forty knots and by ten-thirty local time the aircraft was in the hover just over a mile to the east of that tiny island. Andikíthira is arguably the most isolated speck of land in the Aegean and is inhabited by a population of about fifty people living mostly in the port of Potamos at its northern end.

Potamos boasts one of almost everything: one policeman, one telephone, one doctor, one teacher and one monastery. But there's no bank or post office, and the only way on or off the island is by a ship that stops there once a week on its journey to Crete from the much larger island of Kíthira, lying a few miles to the north-west. Running water and toilets are either scarce or unavailable, depending on the time of year. There is a café and a restaurant, and about ten rooms available for tourists sufficiently determined to spend time there.

The island's chief claim to fame is the celebrated 'Andikíthira Mechanism', which was pulled from the sea just off the island in 1901 and is now on permanent display in the Greek National Archaeological Museum in Athens. The fragmentary remains of a highly complex object fabricated from bronze around two thousand years ago, it appears to have been designed as an astronomical clock, and is unique in that no equivalent device is known of until the time of the Renaissance. Hence it has been argued that this mechanism was the progenitor of all subsequent timepieces.

None of this, however, was of the slightest interest to Richter, or to any of the other men aboard the Merlin. All they were concerned about was locating the wrecked aircraft as soon as possible.

The pilot had used the flight control system to auto-transition the helicopter into the hover, and was now flying the aircraft hands-off, waiting for further instructions from Mike O'Reilly, who was the senior officer and therefore the aircraft captain. And O'Reilly wasn't saying much presently because his entire attention was concentrated on the displays directly in front of him. Below the helicopter a cable snaked vertically downwards into the blue of the Aegean and at the end of it dangled a Flash lightweight folding acoustic dipping sonar from Thales Underwater Systems which was capable of searching depths down to two thousand feet. It was the data received from this sonar which O'Reilly was analysing.

'Anything yet?' Richter leaned closer to Sobs in the cramped rear compartment, still trying to get used to the slight warble in his voice caused by the throat microphone.

He had spent nearly a thousand hours flying Sea Kings before he had made the jump sideways to train on Sea Harriers, but he had always sat in one of the front seats, so what went on in the aircraft's darkened rear compartment was a complete mystery to him. Essentially, the observer in the back of a Merlin fights the aircraft. He tells the pilot where to go and what to do when he gets there, and not for nothing are ASW helicopter pilots referred to as 'taxi drivers'. That was one reason why Richter himself had switched to fixed wing: he had quickly got tired of sitting twiddling his thumbs and looking out at different-coloured bits of various oceans while the guys in the back had all the fun.

O'Reilly dragged his eyes away from the display and began hoisting the sonar body from the water. He glanced sideways at Richter. 'Yes, there's quite a lot of stuff down there, but we can eliminate most of it for reasons that I won't bore you with. I've marked three contacts that I'd like to have another look at, but first we should do a general survey of all the waters around the island.' O'Reilly checked to make sure that the sonar body was inboard. 'Pilot, jump three five zero, distance two thousand yards.'

'Roger that,' another voice spoke on the intercom, and Richter sensed the increasing vibration as the pilot wound on the power and the Merlin began to climb out of its hover.

## Between Gavdopoúla and Gávdos, Eastern Mediterranean

It became obvious fairly quickly that Krywald was not a natural sailor. The water in the harbour was almost flat calm, but outside the protection afforded by the jetties it became fairly choppy. By the time they were a mile or so off-shore Krywald was looking distinctly green, his eyes fixed determinedly on the distant horizon and his replies faint monosyllables to anything either of the other two men said.

Elias wasn't drawn to Krywald, but he sympathized with him. The gulf that exists between somebody who is seasick and someone who isn't is enormous. It's said that there are two stages in the condition: in the first you're afraid you're going to die, but in the second you're afraid you're *not* going to die. And the only truly infallible cure for *mal de mer* is to go and sit under a tree.

But they were now a long way from anywhere Krywald was likely to find a tree. Elias glanced back over his shoulder towards the rocky outline of Crete, around eighteen miles distant and still just visible through a slight heat haze, then gazed ahead at the open water.

Before starting up the engine back at Chóra Sfakia harbour, Elias had taken the only chart he could find in the boat and marked on it the co-ordinates 'McCready' had supplied to Krywald. The position indicated was pretty much mid-way between the two islands of Gavdopoúla and Gávdos, so Elias didn't think they'd have any trouble finding it. They were even then passing abeam Gavdopoúla, the smaller and more northerly of the two islands, so the chart was now almost superfluous. Elias realized he could navigate the rest of the way just by using his eyes.

On the chart itself, which lay on the wooden bench seat in front of him, Elias had placed one of the two GPS units that Krywald had supplied. As he gazed down at the squat black box, which looked something like an over-sized mobile telephone, he noticed the co-ordinates in the display change. The boat was moving steadily south-south-west at about eight knots: Elias glanced at his watch and calculated that they should reach the dive site within about thirty minutes.

In fact, this estimate was slightly pessimistic, and just under twenty-two minutes later Stein headed to the bow of the boat to toss the concrete block serving as an anchor over the side. Elias watched as the rope vanished over the gunwale, waiting for the tell-tale slackness that would signify that the anchor had reached the seabed, then instructed Stein to cleat the rope down and switched off the engine.

The open boat swung gently around in a circle, its bow now secured by the anchor rope. Elias checked the GPS once again, cross-checking it with the co-ordinates provided, then pulled off his shirt and shorts to reveal a pair of black swimming trunks. He next attached the lead weight to the end of the polypropylene rope and measured out lengths of it using an old diver's trick – from the average man's left shoulder to his out-stretched right hand was about three feet or one metre.

Using this crude but surprisingly accurate method, he identified the depths at which he wanted the four extra aqualung cylinders to be located, and swiftly secured them in turn to the rope. He then lowered the weight, the rope and the cylinders over the side and tied down the rope securely to a set of cleats on the port-side gunwale. It was crucial to his own survival that the compressed-air cylinders were located at the correct depths, so he took extra care in paying out exactly the right amount of rope before securing it.

Ten minutes later Elias zipped up the jacket of his wetsuit, shrugged the aqualung onto his back, secured the weight belt around his waist and checked all his equipment twice, from the knife strapped to the calf of his right leg to the mask pushed up to rest on his forehead. Then he turned to Stein. 'I don't like this,' he said.

'I know you don't, but it's really very simple. Once you've found the aircraft, all you need do is position these charges, activate the detonators, and get back up to the boat. Then we're out of here and on our way back to the States.' Stein bent down and opened the neck of the rucksack he'd placed on the seat beside him. He pulled out a plastic-covered packet and tossed it from hand to hand. 'This is what's called an M118 Composition Block Demolition Charge,' Stein explained. 'Usually they contain four half-pound sheets of C4 plastic explosive, and they're normally used as cutting charges to slice through steel bridge supports, building girders or metal beams, that kind of thing. These are a bit bigger in fact, each containing about six kilos of plastic, because we don't want anything left intact down there.'

Elias looked uneasily at the packet as Stein offered it to him. 'How stable is it?'

'Very,' Stein replied. 'Watch this.'

He hefted the package of explosive in his hand a couple of times, then smashed it down on the wooden bench with all the force he could muster. The explosive flattened out slightly, but otherwise didn't react in any way. Elias had instinctively crouched down low in the stern of the boat, but gradually eased himself back to an upright position.

'You can hit this stuff with a hammer or even fire a bullet into it, and it still won't do a goddamn thing,' Stein continued. 'You have to use a detonator. Good reaction time there, though it wouldn't have done you any good. If this baby had gone off you could use the biggest bit left of this boat as a toothpick.'

'Christ,' Elias said. 'Don't do things like that. What's this C4 stuff made of anyway?'

'Basically, it's RDX,' Stein said, 'with a polyisobutene plasticizer added. The C4 looks like uncooked pastry, and you can perfectly safely mould it into pretty much any shape you want, which is why the military use it so frequently. It's got a shelf-life of years, and it's cheap, reliable and goes off with a hell of a bang.'

'And underwater?' Elias asked. 'Is it waterproof, or what?'

Stein nodded. 'Water doesn't affect it at all. Now the detonators are real easy.'

He reached again into the rucksack and pulled out a plastic box about the size and shape of a child's pencil case. He opened this and pulled out a long thin object, itself similar in size to a pencil. 'This is a three-hour detonator,' he explained. 'Normally C4 is triggered by an electrical detonator powered by some kind of battery or current generator, but in these circumstances we obviously can't go that route.

'This detonator has a battery installed at the end you insert into the explosive, with two contacts that will actually carry the current. All you have to do is snap the end off each detonator, right here where the metal is pinched in. That allows sea water to seep inside and starts a chemical reaction which slowly eats away at a membrane about halfway down the detonator itself. Behind that membrane is a water-activated switch: once the membrane's pierced, the switch completes the circuit to connect the battery, and everything goes bang.'

## Kandíra, south-west Crete

There was little that Inspector Lavat could usefully do to assist Hardin and his team in their search for the hot agent: police work had no place in the purely medical and epidemiological investigation of the two deaths. Though he realized that the investigations were inextricably linked, he was far more concerned with the murder of his own officer, and he frankly wasn't sure how best to identify the killers.

As a routine precaution, he had instituted a watch at all ferry ports and all three airports on the island, but the description his cordon police officer had provided was so vague as to be almost useless. The man was over at headquarters in Irakleío, trying to help build up a photofit picture of at least one of the two suspects, but Lavat wasn't optimistic about the likely result of that.

The roadblocks were still in place, although village residents were now being allowed to move into and out of Kandíra. All outsiders were still being refused entry. Lavat had just completed a tour of the perimeter of the village, checking that his officers were still manning the cordon and that they had an adequate supply of drinking water at their posts. Then, because it was, even by Cretan standards, a very hot day, he'd himself taken shelter from the sun in one of the tents erected near the main road entering the village.

He was sitting with his second glass of water when Theodore Gravas appeared at the entrance flap. Twenty minutes earlier they'd both stood at the barrier to watch as the light grey Merlin sent from the *Invincible* had lifted off from some waste ground outside the village – bound for the laboratory in Irakleío with the organ samples Hardin had extracted from Spiros Aristides's body.

'Found anything yet?' Lavat asked, as Gravas sat down on the other side of the table.

The doctor shook his head. 'I've just been talking to Hardin. They've found nothing in Spiros's house so far. They've taken swabs from the floors, doors, walls and so on, but the Americans seem to believe the causative agent either wasn't there to be found or it's been dissipated since and is now so scattered that they won't be able to find it.'

'So what's their next move?'

'Hardin's people have just started on Nico's apartment. Since that scene hasn't had the same amount of traffic as Spiros's house they may get lucky there. Otherwise, our best bet to find the agent is in the blood and tissues of its victims, so we'll have to wait and see what Irakleío can uncover.'

## ASW Merlin callsign 'Spook Two', off Andikíthira, Sea of Crete

The second location O'Reilly directed the pilot to lay almost directly north of Andikíthira and around two miles off-shore. Here again, he lowered the sonar body into the water and began an active sweep of the seabed below them and further around the eastern and northern coasts of the small island.

Metallic objects, especially large metallic objects, are not uncommonly found on the floor of the Mediterranean Sea. This area was a birthplace of civilization and was always the principal route for commerce between Europe and North Africa, besides being the location of several naval and air battles in the wars of the twentieth and previous centuries. And shallow waters – in oceanographic terms the Mediterranean is considered a shallow sea – are often the scene of the most violent storms, which have claimed numerous victims over the years.

While it wouldn't be true to suggest that the seabed is littered with wrecks, there were certainly more than either Richter or O'Reilly had expected. Their first two sonar scans had between them located no less than forty-eight separate large metallic objects on the sea floor extending to the east and north of Andikíthira, and when O'Reilly carried out his third scan, to the north-west of the island, he identified a further nineteen.

'Jesus,' Richter said, doing the arithmetic in his head, 'that's sixty-seven contacts in all. You said your speciality is finding needles in haystacks, Mike, but if we have to dive on all of these we're going to be here for weeks.'

O'Reilly shook his head. 'You won't have to. We can carry out a lot of filtering first to discriminate between old shipwrecks and the remains of a fairly modern aircraft. Look, I may be teaching you to suck eggs, but ships are big and aircraft are comparatively small. So, the first thing is to eliminate all returns over a certain size, simply because unless you're looking for a Jumbo Jet, the wreckage would be just too big.

'Second, when a ship sinks it tends to stay all together in one piece, being a very heavy and robust piece of engineering, specially designed to spend its life on the water. Aircraft need to fly, obviously, so their construction is much lighter and hence weaker, and they tend to break up on impact with the water and get scattered over quite a wide area.

'So what I'm looking for is not a single piece of wreckage, but a number of small pieces that are lying in more or less the same area. Now,' O'Reilly gestured at the display in front of him, 'applying those fairly simple parameters to these sixty-seven contacts, we can immediately eliminate fifty-two of them, which gets us down to fifteen altogether. Eight of these contacts are too deep for free diving, and three of them are less than half a mile out from the shore, so in fact we're left with only four possibles to check out.'

### Between Gavdopoúla and Gávdos, Eastern Mediterranean

David Elias descended slowly towards the bottom of the Mediterranean Sea, his left hand lightly encircling the anchor rope as he followed it down, his right hand clutching one of the two torches he'd chosen at the dive shop. The second torch was safely in the string specimen bag attached to his weight belt, along with the coil of thin polypropylene cord, the four M118 demolition charges and half a dozen pencil detonators, more than he needed but just in case he dropped some.

The water around him grew increasingly cold and dark as he swam deeper, but visibility was still good enough for him not to need to use his torch. Elias had no idea how long it would take him to find the wreck, and he would certainly need one torch, possibly both, when he did, so he was conserving his resources.

The bottom appeared suddenly, looming under him, and Elias checked his depth gauge as he slowed to a stop just above the seabed.

Eighty-three feet. Fairly deep, but not too deep. He pulled out the polypropylene cord, unravelled one end of it and secured it to the anchor rope just above its concrete weight. He needed to be able to find his way back easily to the rope, and then up through the water lying directly beneath the boat, because that was where his spare aqualungs were positioned, and if he couldn't locate them he would either die or be crippled when he surfaced.

Holding the still coiled cord in his left hand, Elias peered around him. He had no idea in which direction the wreck might lie, because the co-ordinates McCready had supplied were obviously only those of the Greek diver's boat up on the surface. The wreck itself had to be some-where close by, but it could lie in any direction around him. He first checked his compass, then kicked off the seabed and began swimming with lazy, energy-conserving strokes to the north, paying out the cord as he moved away from the concrete anchor.

### ASW Merlin callsign 'Spook Two', off Andikíthira, Sea of Crete

'That's certainly not it,' O'Reilly muttered, as he studied the image of the second of four possible wrecks. 'It's far too small, so I think it's prob-ably some kind of metallic rubbish that's been dumped from a passing ship. Maybe empty barrels or cylinders, or sections of pipe, something like that.'

Richter stared at the display immediately in front of O'Reilly, and then looked at the Senior Observer with an expression somewhat akin to amazement. 'You can deduce all this from that garbage?'

O'Reilly turned his head slowly to face him. 'I would hardly expect a mere stovie, especially a part-time stovie, to understand, Spook, but this garbage, as you call it, is the product of arguably the world's most advanced acoustic signal processing equipment, and I, as a leading exponent of such technology, can certainly deduce that what I'm look-ing at here are cylindrical objects. Look,' he pointed out an image on the screen, 'you see that? Quite clearly a regularly shaped object, round in cross-section and about one and a half metres long.'

Richter looked carefully, and frankly saw nothing like that, but refrained from saying so. 'It's not an aircraft then?' he said, feeling somewhat stupid.

'Of course it's not a bloody aircraft. OK, now we'll try the third site.' O'Reilly reeled in the dunking sonar body, then spoke into the intercom. 'Pilot, aircraft captain. Jump two three zero, distance one thousand five hundred metres.'

## Between Gavdopoúla and Gávdos, Eastern Mediterranean

Elias had found nothing by the time he reached the end of the one-hundred-metre length of the polypropylene cord, so he decided to try what he mentally called 'Plan B'. He'd worked it out in his hotel room the previous evening, but it had depended absolutely on the topography of the seabed.

If the bottom was fairly flat, and his progress outwards from the concrete anchor had confirmed that, he could use the cord itself to try to snag the wreckage. Using the anchor as the centre of a circle, he could start to swim around the perimeter, just above the seabed, and any projecting object would catch the cord. It wasn't a bad plan, and it was the only one he had apart from repeatedly swimming back and forth from the anchor weight on a series of different compass headings, so Elias looped the end of the cord around his wrist, ascended until he was about five feet off the bottom, and began swimming slowly counterclockwise.

He'd swum only about fifty feet when he felt a sudden tug on his left arm, but when he investigated the obstruction, it turned out to be just a rocky outcrop projecting some six feet above the seabed. No matter, Elias thought, that just proved the plan was working, so he lifted the cord over the rock, swam back out to the perimeter of the circle as defined by his cord, and started off again.

The sixth time it happened he found the Learjet's wing.

# Chapter 17

According to O'Reilly, the third site looked more promising: a scatter of metallic debris in a more or less straight line some one and half miles off the north-western tip of Andikíthira, and lying in only fifty feet of water.

'This could be it,' O'Reilly said. 'I can't get a clear indication of shape, but there are a couple of large objects that could be engines, a lot of smaller bits of dispersed debris, and one flat section that might be a piece of a wing.'

'OK,' Richter said, 'we'll check it out.' He turned towards the Merlin's rear compartment where Lieutenant David Crane, the ship's diving officer, had been sitting patiently ever since 'Spook Two' had lifted off the deck of the *Invincible*. 'Do you want the first dive?' Richter asked.

'Damn right I do,' Crane replied. 'Anything to get out of this paraffin budgie for a while.'

'The water's only about fifty feet deep. Do you need to wear a wet-suit?'

Crane shook his head. 'No. At that depth it's just as easy if I free-dive down for a quick look-see. If it is the plane we want I'll come back up and get properly suited-up.'

Richter helped Crane don the aqualung and weight belt, and then the diving officer sat in the open side doorway of the Merlin as it hovered about five feet above the surface of the Mediterranean, put on his fins and mask, and gripped the mouthpiece between his teeth.

'Ready?' Richter asked.

Crane nodded, gave the diver's 'OK' sign – circling his thumb and forefinger – then straightened up and dropped straight down into the circle of rotor-disturbed water immediately below the helicopter. He re-appeared briefly on the surface, waved an arm at the aircraft hovering above, then turned face down, lifted his legs and disappeared smoothly beneath the waves.

## Between Gavdopoúla and Gávdos, Eastern Mediterranean

The wing stuck straight up out of the sand on the seabed, reminding Elias of that black monolith on the moon in *2001: A Space Odyssey*. He unsnagged the cord from the side of the wing and looked carefully around him. Obviously he was in more or less the right place, but for the moment he couldn't spot the rest of the wrecked aircraft.

Well, Elias reasoned, Plan B had worked pretty well so far. He could use it to find the remainder of the wreck as well. He studied the wing for a few moments before looping the polypropylene cord over a broken spar. Then he swam away from the wing, paying out the cord as he went. Just before he reached the full extent of the rope, Elias noticed a vaguely mushroom-shaped object hovering above a pile of rocks and he stopped dead in the water.

Seconds passed as he peered carefully at the hazy object, before suddenly recognizing it for what it was – a diver's lifting bag, partially inflated, and attached to something on the seabed. It was then he realized that he had almost certainly found the rest of the aircraft.

Elias checked his watch, mentally calculating decompression times, then swam over to the lifting bag. The rope securing it, he saw at once, had been looped through two adjacent holes on the side of what was obviously an aircraft fuselage, covered in marine growth and barely distinguishable from the rocks around it.

He swam round to one end of the fuselage, peered inside and stopped short as the powerful beam of his torch revealed the three bodies sitting directly in front of him. Elias stared and shuddered, and immediately decided that he was as close to them as he was prepared to get. Fuck Stein's instructions about careful placement – he was now going to just arm the explosives, toss them inside the wreck and get the hell away from the grisly open tomb on the seabed.

Elias knelt down, pulled the string specimen bag around in front of him and extracted the detonators and the four demolition charges.

Conscious of the power contained in these objects, he followed Stein's instructions to the letter. Removing the diving knife from its calf sheath, he used the point of the blade to make a tiny hole at one end of each of the four charges.

Then he replaced the knife, opened the small plastic box containing the pencil detonators and pulled out four of them. He pushed the detonators deep into the plastic explosive through the holes that he had just made, then snapped the end of the first one. Nothing terrible happened, so he felt able to breathe again, and repeated the action with the other three. He tossed the four charges into the remains of the fuselage, without even waiting to see where they fell, then picked up his torch and began to follow the cord that would lead him back first to the wing, and then to the concrete anchor, and finally up to his aqualungs suspended beneath the boat.

Before, he had swum with lazy, energy-conserving strokes. But now, with the explosives planted and chemicals fizzing inside the detonators, he swam as fast as he was able, conscious that the clock was already ticking.

### ASW Merlin callsign 'Spook Two', off Andikíthira, Sea of Crete

Richter was still peering through the door of the Merlin when David Crane resurfaced. The pilot spotted the diver at almost the same moment, and swung the big helicopter to starboard to pick him up. From behind Richter, the aircrewman stepped forward and began paying out the winch cable, the orange lifting strap dangling from its end.

Seconds later, the aircraft was established in the hover some thirty feet above the surface of the sea. Crane waited until the metal hook on the cable had touched the water, earthing it, before swimming the ten feet or so to the lifting strap. He pulled the strap over his shoulders, settled it under his armpits, gave a thumbs-up signal and dropped his arms down beside his body as the aircrewman began hauling in the winch cable. Fifteen seconds later he was standing inside the rear compartment of the Merlin, water dripping everywhere, and removing his aqualung.

You can't converse in the back of a Merlin, or any military helicopter, because it's just too noisy, but as Richter looked inquiringly at Crane, the diver shook his head. As soon as the man had attached his safety harness and plugged his headset into the intercom, Richter asked him the question.

'What was it?'

'You might not believe this,' Crane said, 'but it was metal chairs and a couple of tables.'

'What the hell are we talking about here – some kind of mermaid's picnic?' O'Reilly demanded. 'What do you mean?'

'About twenty metal-framed folding chairs and two round tables,' Crane replied. 'Probably dumped from some pleasure-boat during a drunken party.'

'But no aircraft?' Richter pressed.

'No,' Crane reached for his towel. 'No aircraft.'

'OK,' Richter said, 'let's try contestant number four.'

'Right,' O'Reilly agreed. 'Pilot, Sobs. Jump one nine five, range three thousand five hundred metres.'


**Kandíra, south-west Crete**

Tyler Hardin was peering around the bedroom of Nico Aristides's rented apartment. His team had carried out a thorough search of the place and had found exactly what he had anticipated – only the kind of things one would expect to find in a property inhabited by a young single man.

They'd opened the wardrobes and cupboards and stared at clothes and shoes. In the living room they'd found an expensive sound system and dozens of CDs, a television set, a DVD player with a collection of disks, some pornographic. In the kitchen it soon became clear that Nico was no cook: the fridge contained only beer, and there was nothing in the cupboards apart from biscuits and various tinned and packet meals. What they hadn't found was anything that looked like the bottle or flask Hardin had deduced from the scanty evidence found.

Nico's body still lay in the bedroom. Hardin had initially considered performing a second autopsy, but the external condition of the young man's corpse was so similar to his uncle's that he decided it was pointless, because they were unlikely to glean any additional information. Instead, he'd given orders that both bodies should be collected as soon as possible for transferral to the mortuary in Irakleío. He had also instructed that the corpses be held in the mortuary indefinitely in case further tests were required.

If there were any clues at all to the identity of the agent that had slaughtered the two Greeks, they were most likely to be found in the swabs and samples collected from Spiros's house or in the tissue specimens removed from his body. All Hardin could do now was wait for the laboratory staff in Irakleío to complete their analyses.

In the meantime, with no indication whatsoever of any further cases of 'Galloping Lassa', there seemed no good reason for keeping Kandíra sealed off. Hardin shook his head in frustration and headed down the outside staircase to tell Lavat that his men could start taking down their barricades.

### Between Gavdopoúla and Gávdos, Eastern Mediterranean

'You didn't tell me that fucking aircraft was full of fucking bodies,' Elias almost screamed.

'Bodies?' Krywald asked weakly. He was still suffering, though his stomach had settled somewhat once the boat had come to anchor. 'What bodies?'

'There are three dead bodies inside that fucking aircraft,' Elias shouted. 'It was a hell of a shock. You should have warned me.'

'We didn't know,' Stein said firmly. 'McCready didn't tell us anything more about the aircraft than where to find it and what to do with it. I suppose we should have guessed there could be human remains inside.'

Elias angrily undid the buckles securing his aqualung and lowered it onto the wooden seat in front of him.

'OK,' Stein demanded. 'You planted the demolition charges?'

Elias nodded. 'Yes, no problem there. I did just as you said, and now all four are inside the fuselage.' He didn't add that he'd just tossed them inside instead of placing them carefully at intervals, as instructed.

Stein glanced over at Krywald, and received an almost imperceptible nod.

'That's very good, David,' Stein said, 'we couldn't have managed this without you.' He waited until Elias had turned away to begin unbuckling his weight belt, before he pulled out his SIG P226, racked back the slide to chamber a round, and in one fluid motion raised it to the back of Elias's head and pulled the trigger. The silencer muffled the sound of the shot to a dull cough, but the American's head almost exploded with the impact from a 9mm Parabellum round at such short range. His body slumped, lifeless, over the gunwale, half in and half out of the boat.

'Thanks again,' Stein muttered, pressing down on the de-cocking lever on the left side of the SIG's butt to drop the hammer into the safety notch. Then he replaced the pistol in the waistband of his trousers, stepped forwards, lifted Elias's legs into the air and watched as the body tumbled into the water and floated gently away from the boat. Elias's weight belt was still half secured around his waist, and Stein watched as his body began to sink slowly. Quickly he tossed the spare aqualungs and all the other impedimenta that the diver had used over the side, then hauled up the anchor, moved back to the stern and started the engine.

'I sure hope you know your way back,' Krywald muttered sourly, 'because I'm no sailor.' He briefly glanced over to where Elias's body had disappeared from view, a spreading cloud of blood already attracting fish.

'Neither am I,' Stein replied, 'but it shouldn't be difficult. Hell, we can almost see Chóra Sfakía from here. All I have to do is point the boat in that direction and stop when we get to the other end. Christ, if a guy got lost here he could just hang around and follow the ferry back to Crete. Even you could manage that.'


### ASW Merlin callsign 'Spook Two', off Andikíthira, Sea of Crete

Lieutenant Commander Mike O'Reilly leaned back from the display in front of him and shook his head. 'No,' he said, 'I don't think that's it either. These shapes are too regular and too similar in size. I think this is dumped cargo, or maybe pig-iron ballast, something like that.'

Richter had been leaning against one of the equipment racks to look over the Senior Observer's shoulder. He stood up as O'Reilly glanced at him and nodded agreement.

'You're the expert,' Richter said. 'If you say it's pig-iron, I'll believe you. To be honest, I think the most likely site for our wreck is somewhere to the south of Crete – Andikíthira's a bit of a long flog for a man in an open boat starting out from Kandíra. Anyway, that's the last likely contact around here – let's go and take a look at the Gávdos area.'

O'Reilly pulled a navigation chart from a cubbyhole and studied it for a few moments, measuring the angles and directions by eye. 'Pilot, Sobs,' he next instructed on the intercom, 'climb out of the hover and steer track one eight five, height two thousand feet.'

'How far is it?' Richter asked.

'By the shortest route it's about seventy nautical miles,' O'Reilly explained, 'but that means climbing way up over the mountains, talking to Soúda Bay and all the rest. So I'm taking us the pretty route instead. We'll head south, clip the western end of Crete and then transit directly to Gavdopoúla. It's the longer way round by about twenty miles, but in this baby that's less than ten minutes extra.'

Richter nodded and sat on a pull-down seat on the starboard side of the cabin. He looked at his watch and began figuring times and distances. It was almost midday, which meant they'd already spent nearly one and a half hours in their search with absolutely nothing to show for it. He just hoped that this next site would prove rather more interesting.

As the Merlin transitioned from the hover to begin its flight south towards Gavdopoúla, the chemical reactions within the pencil detonators on the four demolition charges scattered randomly through the cabin of the wrecked Learjet had already been running for a little over forty-three minutes.

### Central Intelligence Agency Headquarters, Langley, Virginia

John Westwood leaned back in his chair and stretched his arms up above his head. He seemed to have been in this building for hours, yet to have achieved remarkably little.

The theory Walter Hicks had floated at the meeting in his office the previous day had then seemed to contain obvious merit – someone might well want to take revenge if he had suffered because of some operation those two Company men had been involved in – but the more Westwood examined the records, the less likely this scenario appeared. The obvious objection was the timing. Both Richards and Hawkins had left the CIA over ten years earlier – Hawkins had been retired for nearly thirteen years – and it seemed inconceivable to Westwood that anyone bent on revenge would wait around for over a decade and then kill two men *and* a woman on the same day.

There was one possible explanation that he was still tossing around in his mind. The reason for the killer's delay might simply be because he had been locked up all that time in a prison somewhere. But even that theory didn't make a lot of sense. The three killings were so markedly different in execution. One victim had been shot, then beaten to death with a poker, but the other two had been forced to swallow poison capsules.

Somebody coming to seek revenge would more likely want to be physical about it. They would want to make their victims suffer physically for whatever grievance had been done to them in the past. Forcing somebody to swallow a poison capsule that would produce unconsciousness in a matter of seconds didn't really count as 'suffering' in Westwood's book.

And besides, all the evidence suggested the killer was known to both his male victims and to Hawkins's wife as well. If the perp – or the unsub, to use Detective Delaney's phrase – was a man the CIA had sent to prison years ago, it seemed inconceivable that Richards would have opened the door to him. And why on earth would Mary Hawkins have let the man so readily into her house?

Quite possibly Charles Hawkins had met his killer by appointment, which implied that the two men knew each other quite well. If that was the case, it probably explained why the deaths had occurred in the sequence they did. With Hawkins lured out of his house the killer would have a window of opportunity to eliminate Mary Hawkins, while she would be there alone. Hawkins would be the next victim, already sitting alone in his car by the Potomac, waiting for his wife's killer. Then Richards would follow. Maybe the unsub had originally intended to eliminate all his victims with poison capsules, but his plan had been thwarted when Richards fought back.

The only scenario to make any sense was that the killer was somebody known to all three victims – Richards, Hawkins and Hawkins's wife – and that probably meant somebody who had once been, or perhaps even still was, an employee of the Central Intelligence Agency.

## ASW Merlin callsign 'Spook Two', Sea of Crete

As the Merlin rounded the south-western end of Crete and passed due south of Palióchóra, Mike O'Reilly changed frequency on his UHF box and glanced over at Richter. 'Let's see if Ops Four is awake,' he said, pressing the transmit button.

'Fob Watch, this is Spook Two.' There was absolutely no response. 'He's probably got his face full of sandwiches and coffee,' O'Reilly muttered, and transmitted again. 'Fob Watch, Fob Watch, this is Spook Two.'

There was a click, a short burst of static, and then a clearly puzzled voice responded. 'This is Fob Watch. Say again your callsign.'

'This is Spook Two. We're an ASW Merlin from Mother in transit from the western edge of Crete to Gavdopoúla, level at two thousand feet on the Regional Pressure Setting. We're presently two miles south of Palióchóra, heading one five zero and we'll be holding at least two miles clear of the coast until we return to Mother. Have you any traffic for us?'

'Negative, Spook Two, and good afternoon, sir.' The Air Operations Chief Petty Officer – 'Ops Four' – had obviously recognized the 814 Squadron Senior Observer's voice. 'I have nothing known at this time. The next scheduled flight isn't due here until around fifteen hundred this afternoon.'

'Roger, Fob Watch. We'll be carrying out anti-submarine exercises in the vicinity of Gavdopoúla, and we'll check in again when we climb out of the area.'

Forty minutes later the Merlin was sitting in the hover some two miles off the eastern coast of Gavdopoúla, and the dunking sonar body was on its way down.

## Central Intelligence Agency Headquarters, Langley, Virginia

John Westwood was worried. Worried and puzzled. On his desk in front of him lay the analysis report of the poison used to kill Charles Hawkins and his wife. As Detective Delaney had said the day before, the lethal agent in question had been confirmed as coniine, a toxic vegetable alkaloid derived from the hemlock plant.

Westwood was puzzled because there were literally thousands of common poisons more readily available, and even the complier of the analysis report had never previously encountered the use of coniine – at least, not since the days of Socrates, who himself had been executed using a preparation of hemlock.

Coniine, which is more accurately described by its chemical designation 2-propyl piperidine, is one of the simplest and most toxic of the vegetable alkaloids – with a fatal dose for human beings amounting to less than zero decimal two of a gram. In its pure form it's a colourless and slightly oily liquid with an unpleasant smell and bitter taste. The source plant – hemlock – has a long history of medicinal use, having been employed by the Arabs as well as the Greeks as a sedative and painkiller, but always with the greatest care because of the very small difference between a therapeutic and a lethal dose.

The coniine that had killed Hawkins and his wife was highly concentrated. Taking hemlock first causes stimulation – it's related to nicotine, another vegetable alkaloid, and has a similar initial effect – followed by depression of the nervous system, then loss of feeling in the limbs, drowsiness, paralysis and ultimately death after perhaps an hour – not unconsciousness in seconds. Whoever had chosen coniine had selected an unusual and rare poison, in sufficiently concentrated form to produce a dose that would be almost immediately fatal.

This was not easy to achieve, and suggested a fairly well-equipped laboratory staffed by experienced doctors and technicians. From his time in the Company, Westwood knew that private laboratories willing to turn out lethal poisons were somewhat thin on the ground, at least in America, so that possibly meant Fort Detrick was involved.

Fort Detrick is the current home of USAMRIID, the US Army Medical Research Institute of Infectious Diseases, located in the foothills of the Catoctin Mountains in western Maryland. Officially and actually,

USAMRIID is part of the US Army Medical Research and Materiel Command and is the principal research laboratory of the American Biological Defense Research Program. Fort Detrick contains one of the only two Biosafety Level 4 laboratories in America, intended to assist its personnel in the fight both against naturally occurring viruses or other pathogens, and in combating the biological weapons – bioweapons – manufactured by foreign regimes.

That's the official story at least, but Fort Detrick has a secret and murkier past – and present. One of the conundrums of scientifically developing counter-measures to biological weapons is that you need to have a supply of the bioweapon you're seeking defence against. So Fort Detrick holds – and has always held – stocks of a vast range of such agents including anthrax, botulinus toxin and so on. But developing antidotes or inoculations against them is only half the story.

Predicting how your enemy might modify anthrax, say, is something of a guessing game, and the only practical way to produce counter-measures to modified biological agents is to modify them yourself in order to develop more efficient strains, and then to develop effective antidotes. By default, therefore, Fort Detrick itself has to be constantly involved in the biological warfare business.

Although the CIA is officially forbidden to engage in assassinations, at numerous times in the past this rule has been relaxed sufficiently for attempts to be made to eliminate certain people whose intentions seemed diametrically opposed to those of the Agency. A classic example was Fidel Castro, who survived four CIA-sponsored attempts to assassinate him using poisons, supplied by the scientists at Fort Detrick, and at least the same number of attempts using alternative methods.

The first attempt employed regular poison pills, but the agent chosen to administer them couldn't get anywhere near Castro. The second time they tried a scatter-gun approach, supplying a mixed bag of goodies, which included a poison pen, a cigar impregnated with botulinus toxin – one of the most lethal substances known to man and nowadays most notorious by being associated with ageing Hollywood stars trying to remove their wrinkles – and various substances containing biological agents. This attempt, delegated to a Cuban dissident living in Havana, also failed, of course.

The third time round, organized crime figures working under

contract to the CIA identified a Cuban employed in a restaurant favoured by Castro, who was prepared, for a fee, to poison the Cuban leader's food. Poison pills were duly supplied, but by the time the plan came together Castro had switched his affections to a different restaurant.

A year after the Bay of Pigs fiasco, the Company tried yet again, once more resorting to their contacts within organized crime and providing poison pills. This time the Cuban dissident agreeing to make the attempt wanted his payment in kind – demanding weapons and radio equipment instead of money. This was supplied to him by CIA front companies operating out of Florida before the assassination attempt was due to be made. Once again the attempt failed, and it's possible that the Cuban never even tried to get near to Castro, once he'd received what he wanted.

All that showed clearly how the CIA was not averse to developing and utilizing lethal substances. So maybe the coniine used here had come from a secret chemical weapon stockpile somewhere within the Company itself. If so, Westwood's earlier deduction about the possible source of the killer was probably justified.

What he wasn't sure about was where to go from there. If the killer was indeed a Company employee, he would certainly have covered his traces well. Even with his high-level security clearance, Westwood knew that there were areas on the CIA database that he himself was unable to access, and anyway he had no idea at all where to start looking for the source of the poison. He even toyed with the idea of just entering 'coniine' in the database search field to see what the system generated, then quickly decided not to. If the unknown assassin was still an active CIA agent, he could have left tripwires within the system to alert him if anybody started digging too close to him.

Reluctantly, Westwood turned his attention back to the personnel records, searching for some link between James Richards and Charles Hawkins that made any kind of sense in the context of their deaths.

## Off Chóra Sfakia, Crete

Stein and Krywald were only about four miles off Chóra Sfakia when they spotted the helicopter approaching from the west. At first it was just a curiosity to them, nothing more, but when it descended into the hover over the area of sea lying between Gavdopoúla and Gávdos, Stein began to worry.

'That looks to me like an ASW bird,' he murmured, peering southwards through a small pair of folding binoculars, 'but I can't identify it for sure. It could be a Sea King or one of the new Merlins.'

'Who uses them primarily?' Krywald asked. With every mile they'd covered in their approach to Crete, he had been feeling a little better, considerably cheered by the prospect of stepping onto dry land.

'If it's a Sea King, almost anyone,' Stein replied, still studying the helicopter. 'It's a very good aircraft and a hell of a lot of nations operate them – Germany, Canada, Spain and Egypt for starters – and any of those could have warships in this area. If it's a Merlin, Britain and Italy are the most likely.'

'What's it doing?'

'From here I can't be certain, but it looks as if it's transitioned into a hover, so it's probably using its dunking sonar.'

'You think they're looking for the Learjet?'

'I doubt it. It's probably just doing regular anti-submarine exercises. And even if it is looking for the wreck, those charges are going to blow real soon now.'

## ASW Merlin callsign 'Spook Two', between Gavdopoúla and Gávdos, Eastern Mediterranean

Just over thirty minutes after the Merlin had begun its dunking sonar search, O'Reilly suddenly leaned forward, staring intently at the display in front of him.

He then glanced up at Richter who was trying to peer over his shoulder. 'This looks more like it,' O'Reilly said. 'A cylindrical object about thirty feet long which could well be part of an aircraft fuselage – it's big enough for that – plus two flat plates, one right next to the cylinder and the other a short distance away and standing vertically upright.'

'Wings?' Richter queried.

'That's my guess,' O'Reilly said. 'One still attached to the wreckage, the other torn off by the impact with the sea. I've also got two very strong returns from fairly small objects, which I assume are the engines. This is the best candidate we've located so far,' he added, 'but it's deep, around one hundred feet.'

Richter looked at him. 'OK, Mike, on a scale of one to ten, where do you reckon this contact scores?'

O'Reilly thought for a moment. 'At least a seven,' he said, 'maybe eight.'

'That's good enough for me.' Richter turned towards the rear of the helicopter. 'David, get suited up.' Turning back to the Senior Observer, he added, 'Mike, we'll have to use the life raft, and we'll need a buoy to mark the precise spot. Can you position the aircraft as near as you can to what you think is the fuselage?'

'No problem.' O'Reilly did some swift calculations. 'Pilot, jump one three five, seven hundred yards.'

As the helicopter climbed away from the hover, Richter joined Crane at the rear of the cabin and began pulling on a wetsuit.

### Central Intelligence Agency Headquarters, Langley, Virginia

John Westwood snapped the file closed. He got up from his chair, stretching his arms and rubbing his eyes, then paced the office carpet for a few moments. He had come in fairly early that morning, and ever since then he seemed to have done nothing but either stare at text on the computer screen or plough through dusty operation files.

Hicks had been adamant there were answers to be found somewhere within the vast CIA database of information, and equally firm that he expected Westwood to find them, although not at the expense of his normal work. But 'cracking the Walnut', as Hicks had somewhat dismissively termed this operation, had not proved as easy as at first supposed.

Westwood had initially searched the database to identify those cases and operations in which either Charles Hawkins or James Richards had participated. That had eventually produced a list he had output to his laser printer, but that, of course, was just the start. Once he'd identified the operations in which the men were involved, he was obliged to read through all the case files as well, and that was where his problems really started, just because of the sheer volume of data he was trying to analyse.

James Richards and Charles Hawkins had both worked in the Operations Directorate for almost their entire professional careers, a total in Richards's case of over thirty years. Hawkins had transferred to Administration for the last five years of his time at the Agency, but that still left twenty-eight years' worth – over one hundred and twenty operations involving one man or the other – to be scanned and assessed.

Westwood had read through the first three operation files on screen, but then decided to get the original paper files out of storage, because he suspected that the electronic versions were somewhat abbreviated, and besides some of the scanned documents were actually quite difficult to read. Also, he was still concerned about leaving an electronic trail of opened files running visibly through the CIA database. Hauling the originals up from the archives might therefore be a whole lot better for his long-term health prospects.

It would have been worth it, he thought, if after all this work he'd actually found something, but the search had turned up nothing. He'd just in fact finished reading the last case file of all, had filled a couple of dozen pages with hand-written notes, but the eventual result was a neat round zero. Nothing found in any of the files linking these two men could, by any stretch of the imagination, have led to their deaths. There had to be something else – something he was missing.

### Between Gavdopoúla and Gávdos, Eastern Mediterranean

Richter and Crane stood shoulder to shoulder next to the open starboard-side door of the ASW helicopter and checked each other's equipment. Below the hovering Merlin, the surface of the Mediterranean was churned into spray by the down-wash from the massive rotor blades, so the buoy, attached to a lead sinker by a one-hundred-and-fifty-foot rope that they'd dropped five minutes earlier, was being blown all over the place.

They were going deep, and so would need something on the surface as support. Richter nodded to O'Reilly, then he and David Crane stepped back out of the way as the Senior Observer and the aircrewman manhandled a bulky fabric-covered bundle over to the door. O'Reilly seized a lanyard on the side of the bundle and, as the aircrewman pushed, he tugged it.

The bundle dropped straight down and, with a loud hissing sound audible even over the beat of the rotors and the roar of the jet engines, it burst open, as bright orange air cells filled rapidly with compressed air from the bottle secured on the life raft.

The raft floated briefly upright on the sea below the helicopter, but almost immediately the rotor downwash began blowing it aside. Crane moved forward and stepped out of the doorway, keeping his legs straight as he plummeted into the Mediterranean. He submerged, then reappeared, swam a few strokes, grabbed the safety line attached to the life raft and began towing it towards the buoy.

The pilot moved the Merlin about fifty yards away to make it easier for Crane to tow the raft. Once it was secured, the helicopter moved directly over the raft again while O'Reilly and the aircrewman began lowering the rope to which Crane and Richter had secured the aqualung sets. Below them, still buffeted by the downwash, Crane struggled to heave them into the raft. Once the last set was on board the fragile craft, the helicopter again moved a few yards away.

As soon as the Merlin was clear of the raft, Richter stepped out and dropped into the sea. Entering the water was a mild but very pleasant shock. It had already been hot inside the Merlin, and both he and Crane had got a lot warmer very quickly once they'd pulled on their wetsuits. The water was cooler than the air, and Richter immediately felt more comfortable as he surfaced and looked round for Crane. Above him, the helicopter peeled away to his left. There was nothing else the aircraft could do, so O'Reilly had decided earlier to land it on Gavdopoúla and wait there, rotors running, until the two men resurfaced after their dive.

Richter reached the life raft just as Crane had finished securing the end of the aqualung rope to it. Together the two men lowered the weighted end of the coil down into the sea beneath them, their extra sets of breathing apparatus vanishing into the depths, to hang suspended beneath the raft.

'You ready?' he asked, and Crane nodded. 'Keep your eyes on me, please,' Richter added. 'It's a long time since I've done any diving, so if I start doing something stupid, just stop me.'

'You bet.' Inserting their mouthpieces, both men ducked beneath the surface, lifted up their legs and began their descent. Richter led the way, mainly so Crane could keep watch on him, following the path of the anchor rope attached to the buoy.

As they descended deeper, the light gradually faded, the azure of the surface water giving way slowly to darker shades of blue and finally almost to grey as they reached eighty feet down. When the seabed loomed up quite suddenly, Richter halted his descent by abruptly grabbing the buoy rope. As Crane drifted down beside him, the two men gazed around them.

The dunking sonar had already provided an extremely accurate position for the wreckage, so the buoy had been dropped as close to it as possible. Nevertheless, Crane, like Elias before him, had come well prepared. As Richter waited, Crane reached into the pouch attached to his weight belt and withdrew a roll of thin but very strong nylon cord. He expertly tied one end of it to the buoy rope about ten feet off the bottom then, after making sure Richter was still beside him, began to pay out the cord as the two men swam westwards.

Just over a minute later they halted again on spotting the ghostly shape of the Learjet wing, one end driven deep into the seabed, looming in front of them. The Merlin crew had dropped them virtually on top of the wreckage they were seeking.

Richter turned to Crane and gave the 'OK' sign. The two men then moved on, beyond the wing, searching for what was left of the aircraft's fuselage. Crane held a rough plan drawn on a waterproof board, showing the relationship between the sonar returns detected earlier on the seabed. He checked his compass again, tapped Richter's right arm and led the way across the murky grey sea floor. Less than two minutes later Crane spotted the lifting bag that Spiros Aristides had attached to the major section of the Learjet's fuselage.

Meanwhile, inside the wreckage and tucked well under the seats where Elias had tossed them, the chemicals inside four pencil detonators were slowly eating their way through the membranes that protected the water-activated switch and the battery. When Crane spotted the lifting bag, the detonators had already been live for a little over two hours and twenty-five minutes.

# Chapter 18

'Mr Westwood?' The gruff voice on the telephone was unmistakable.

'Good morning, Frank,' Westwood replied. 'You have some news for me, I hope?'

Detective Delaney's chuckle echoed over the telephone line. 'More like no news, I guess. We've done the usual house-to-house in Crystal Springs, where James Richards lived, and we've also pretty much taken his property to pieces.

'Basically, nobody saw anything unusual, nobody heard anything. Three neighbours – smartasses after the event – claim to have seen a suspicious-looking character lurking near Richards's house early that evening. The composite description gives us a black Caucasian male between five seven and six two in height, weighing between one-twenty and one-ninety pounds, clean-shaven with a full beard, wearing a black or tan or blue overcoat. It's just possible there's a description of this unsub in there somewhere, but I wouldn't count on it.

'Our forensic guys managed to lift just over four hundred full and partial prints, mainly latents but a few visuals too, from the lounge and hall of Richards's home. Three hundred and eighty-five of these were left by Richards himself, and all but four of the rest were deposited by his neighbours. The four remaining were glove prints, not fingerprints. Fine quality leather, the techs tell me.

'We found faint traces of mud on the lounge carpet, but it could have come from pretty much anywhere in that area, maybe even from Richards's own garden. We also picked up seven head hairs that didn't come from Richards or any of the neighbours we've interviewed. All the lab can say so far is that they came from a Caucasian, probably male, dark hair turning grey. So until we find ourselves a suspect, they're as much use as tits on a boar-hog.'

'And Hawkins?'

'Pretty much the same scenario,' Frank Delaney continued. 'At his house, two partial glove prints – the same fine quality leather – and several indistinct glove marks on Mary Hawkins's throat and arms. Three hairs from the same source as those picked up in Crystal Springs, so at least we now know that the killings are related. Traces of mud on the carpet, but that definitely came from the street right outside Hawkins's house. There was no other physical evidence inside the property that couldn't be accounted for.

'The third crime scene was Hawkins's car. We found glove marks on the passenger-side door handle, one gloved hand-print on the dash-board and the same on the outside of the passenger door window. We also found a single hair on the headlining on the passenger side, just above the door – from the same source as the others. But nothing else. The one deduction we could make from finding that hair, apart from proving that the same unsub committed all three murders, is that he's probably fairly tall, which supports the Popes Creek neighbour's description of an unknown male seen entering the Hawkins's residence. But, basically, we got zip. Whoever this guy is, he's a pro.'

As Delaney had been speaking, Westwood had jotted down a few notes, and once the detective finished he scanned over them. 'That's not a lot to go on, Frank,' he said finally.

'Tell me about it,' Delaney muttered. 'You got anything from your end? Any idea about motive?'

'Nothing yet,' Westwood replied. '*Nothing* about this business makes a hell of a lot of sense right now. I'm checking through all the files but I can't think of any reason why somebody would need to go around killing *retired* CIA officers.'

'Beats the shit out of me, too,' Delaney growled. 'If our boys come up with anything else, you'll be the first to know. And you find out any-thing, you tell me – otherwise, don't call me, and I won't call you.'

'Got it,' Westwood replied, and put down the phone.

# PANDEMIC

## Between Gavdopoúla and Gávdos, Eastern Mediterranean

They swam slowly with easy, energy-conserving strokes towards the hollow shell of the Learjet's fuselage. Richter stopped at the rear end, beside what had once been the tail-plane and engine nacelle, and looked closely at what was still visible of the registration number. Someone – presumably Spiros Aristides – had cleaned off some of the marine growth, so the letter 'N' could clearly be seen.

Richter gestured to Crane for the waterproof board and pencil, and he passed them over. Richter pointed at the letter 'N' and wrote down 'USA'. Then he cleaned more growth off the fuselage, looked again at the registration number and copied it onto the board below the word he'd just written. With this, he could initiate a check through the Federal Aviation Administration database and then positively identify the aircraft. That was probably the single most important piece of information he was likely to collect from the wreckage.

The forward end of the fuselage was a mess. The entire cockpit had been torn away, either on impact with the surface of the Mediterranean or during the aircraft's subsequent plunge to the bottom of the sea, so the front of the passenger cabin gaped wide open.

Due to the depth of water, there hadn't been the huge amount of colonization in and around the wreckage that would have occurred if the plane had crashed at a shallower level, but there was still enough marine growth to soften the edges of the torn metal and obscure the shape of whatever objects remained inside the cabin.

The two men switched on their torches before peering cautiously inside. It was pretty much as Spiros Aristides had explained it to Nico in the village bar. The dancing torch beams illuminated five aircraft seats, the sixth having apparently been ripped away from the floor, probably on impact with the water.

Two of these seats were unoccupied, but all the others held disintegrating human skeletons, strapped in. Richter was no anatomist, but from the size of their skulls he guessed that all three victims were male. On the cabin floor, between the two rows of seats, he spotted a bulky black object, and a pile of what looked like tools and instruments beside it. Richter swam cautiously over and examined it more closely. The black object seemed to be an empty doctor's bag and, on prodding the pile beside it, Richter was able to identify an array of forceps, tweezers and scalpels.

It wasn't therefore a great leap of reasoning to deduce that at least one of the corpses nearby had been a doctor, but that didn't help Richter work out why the aircraft had been shot down in the first place. And he was quite certain that it had been blown out of the sky: the traces of the missile that had virtually torn the port engine from its mounting were unmistakable to his trained eyes.

He moved slowly and carefully through the cabin, ensuring he didn't snag his aqualung hoses on anything sharp. Apart from the doctor's bag, whatever clues there were to the identity of the three corpses had probably long since vanished, so Richter realized that he was almost certainly wasting his time. The bodies were now little more than skeletons, and while a forensic pathologist might identify their sex and age from their bones, and even come up with their names if their dental records were on file, there was virtually nothing he could do down here in the dark at the bottom of the Mediterranean.

The cabin floor was covered in debris and marine growth, so even slight movements by either diver caused eddies of sediment to rise in clouds from the floor, reducing visibility. But Richter persevered in searching anyway, and found exactly nothing until he got right to the back of the cabin. There was a scattering of debris against the rear bulkhead and, prodding at it more in hope than expectation, he was rewarded by a tiny silvery gleam. He stretched out his gloved hand to grab at it. It was bigger than he had expected, heavier too, and of a vaguely familiar shape.

Gripping the object firmly in his left hand, Richter reached down to his right calf and pulled his diving knife from its rubber sheath. When he hit his discovery smartly with the back of the blade a chunk of marine encrustation fell off, and he knew immediately what it was. He put it carefully into the mesh bag attached to his weight belt and was again prodding the pile of debris when Crane tapped him urgently on the arm, gesturing towards the front of the cabin.

Richter looked at him, and Crane waved again towards the rent in the fuselage. He took off and swam swiftly in that direction with Richter following. The diving officer swung round in a tight circle, grabbing hold of the edge of one of the seats and pointed under it. Richter stopped beside him and looked down.

During his first few months of employment with the Foreign Operations Executive, Richter had spent a considerable amount of time attending various training courses that enabled him to recognize and handle proficiently most types of modern handguns, sub-machine-guns and assault rifles, and so on. At the same time he'd also been taught to identify a wide variety of explosive devices, both improvised and manufactured, while receiving a basic instruction in fuses and detonators. So he had no difficulty at all in recognizing the two M118 Composition Block Demolition Charges lying side by side under the seat, despite their unusually bulky appearance. Only the pencil detonators sticking out of them were new to him.

## St Spiridon Forensic Laboratory, Irakleío, Crete

The samples flown from Kandíra to Irakleío by Merlin were of two very different types. The majority were specimens of tissue gathered during the autopsy on Spiros Aristides, which had been whisked straight into the medical section of the laboratory for histological and toxicological analysis. The rest were a motley collection of dust, fluff and soil samples gathered from inside the dead man's house or from the ground immediately outside it, plus swabs and scrapings from the walls, doors and furniture of his living room and bedroom – even the whisky bottle and glass that he had presumably drunk from before lying down on his bed. The medical samples were immediately subjected to a battery of well-established tests, while the glass and bottle were dusted for fingerprints and the sediment in them analysed, but about all the laboratory could do with the dust and other bits was to scan them through the microscope.

So that's exactly what they did. Starting with the scrapings from the walls and doors and most of the furniture, they found nothing. The fluff revealed nothing either, and nor did the soil samples, at least when scrutinized through a conventional light microscope. But when the laboratory technician used a scanning electron microscope to examine the scrapings collected from the old oak table in Aristides's living room, she noticed something she'd never seen before.

Before calling her supervisor over, she tried a technique she'd employed previously with some success on similar samples, and prepared another specimen for examination in the SEM. When she looked carefully at this second image, she was frankly astonished.

### Central Intelligence Agency Headquarters, Langley, Virginia

Pacing up and down in front of his desk, Westwood looked for inspiration. The logic of the situation seemed undeniable, and he was now feeling in agreement with Walter Hicks. Two men had been killed on the same day in the same area, and there seemed to be only three linking factors. First, eyewitness and forensic evidence strongly suggested that both victims had known their murderer. Second, it seemed probable that the same perpetrator had carried out both crimes, as subsequently confirmed by Delaney's forensic evidence. Third, the only thing that seemed to connect the two victims was their years of service in the Operations Directorate of the Central Intelligence Agency.

But Westwood had found nothing at all in the case files that he had studied so diligently to provide any kind of a motive for these murders, especially so long after both men had retired from the Company. But the fact that the killings had happened meant there had to be a motive, so Westwood had presumably just missed it.

Was there, he wondered, any other way to look at the evidence – some piece of lateral thinking that would enable him to consider the data he had extracted from a different perspective? And time was now getting short. Walter Hicks hadn't been riding Westwood so far, but he would certainly be expecting some results fairly soon.

'Time,' Westwood muttered to himself, pacing the carpet while wondering whether another shot of caffeine would help pummel his brain into action. *Time.*

Suddenly he stopped short. Time? That *would* be another way of looking at the data. A timeline of both men's careers side by side. Westwood forgot all about getting himself another cup of coffee and returned to his desk.

He took a fresh sheet of paper and wrote 'RICHARDS' and 'HAWKINS' in capital letters at the top of it. Then he checked the two deceased agents' personnel files and on the left-hand side of the page below the name he wrote the month and year that James Richards had joined the CIA – August 1958.

For a few moments Westwood just sat and stared at the date: nearly half a century ago. What possible relevance could there be in such ancient history? He shook his head, picked up James Richards's personnel file and began scanning through it, recording the start and finish dates of every course, every posting and every operation that the man had been involved in. When he'd finished, he did exactly the same for agent Charles Hawkins.

### St Spiridon Forensic Laboratory, Irakleío, Crete

'What is it?' the supervisor asked, peering over the technician's shoulder at the image on the screen. You don't *look* through a scanning electron microscope: the samples being examined are held in a vacuum chamber and the 'viewing' is carried out on a closed-circuit television screen positioned beside the apparatus itself.

Typically, the SEM offers a range of magnifications from about fifteen up to around two hundred thousand, allowing progressively finer and finer details of the object to be observed. The sample needs to be very carefully prepared to withstand the vacuum inside the chamber, and also has to be modified to conduct electricity because the sample is scanned with a stream of electrons, not light waves. This process is usually done by coating it with a very thin layer of gold.

Once made ready, the specimen is placed carefully on a small tray attached to the inside of the door of the vacuum chamber, the door itself is then closed and sealed and the air pumped out. Once a vacuum has been created, a gun at the top of the microscope fires a beam of electrons downwards through a series of magnetic lenses, which focus the beam on a very tiny area.

That spot of energy is then moved backwards and forwards across the surface of the sample by a series of coils: this is the 'scanning' part of the SEM. As the beam hits the specimen, secondary electrons are dislodged from its surface. These are counted by a detector, which sends the information to an amplifier, and the final image that appears on the screen is created by counting the electrons emitted by the sample.

'I don't know,' the technician replied. 'It looks like some kind of a spore, but not one I've ever seen before.'

'Where did it originate?'

'I found it in the scrapings from the dining table in the house belonging to this man Spiros Aristides – the index case.'

The black-and-white image of a handful of spherical objects appeared on the screen – because the SEM uses electrons the image will never appear in colour, although printed images often have false colour added. The detail generated by the equipment was remarkable, but even with a magnification of one hundred and fifty thousand there was, frankly, little to see: just a collection of tiny spore-like items.

'Actually,' the technician said, swiftly readying the electron microscope to receive the second specimen, 'that wasn't what I wanted you to see.' As soon as the vacuum had been dispelled she unlocked and pulled open the airtight door, then removed the first specimen and replaced it with the second one. 'When I saw those things, I wondered if they were lying dormant. So I added a small amount of water to a second sample, prepared that for the SEM and then examined it too. This,' she finished, as the screen came to life, 'is what I wanted you to look at.'

The supervisor leaned closer, his mouth dropping open in astonishment. The microscopic spherical objects were still there, but all, without exception, had burst open and the sample was now a mass of what looked like virus particles, but not, the supervisor noted immediately, with the characteristic thread-like shape of a filovirus.

'Well, the good news is it's definitely not Ebola or Marburg,' he said. 'The bad news is that I don't know what it is. If I had to guess, I'd say it was some kind of bovine virus. The only thing I've seen that looks anything like it is BLV – Bovine Lymphotrophic or Leukaemia Virus – but that makes no sense at all. That virus only infects cattle and it's very slow-acting: it attacks the lymph glands and can eventually cause cancer. There's no way that it can kill a healthy human being in less than twenty-four hours.'

# PANDEMIC

## Between Gavdopoúla and Gávdos, Eastern Mediterranean

For Richter, time seemed to have stopped. He hung motionless in the water, figuring the angles. He could see the two demolition charges under the seat in front of him and he knew perfectly well that if either or both of them exploded the biggest remnant of his body anybody might subsequently find would be a tooth.

Naturally, that worried him. What also worried him was the fact that the charges he could see appeared to have been tossed into the cabin at random: for a proper demolition job they should have been placed in strategic locations to ensure the total destruction of the aircraft. The casual manner in which they had been dumped suggested that possibly there were others scattered under the seats, in the piles of debris, or even outside the fuselage.

They now had, he realized, exactly two choices: they could quickly search the cabin and try to locate and defuse all the charges before they went off or they could get the hell out of there. It wasn't a difficult decision for him.

Richter whirled round and gestured upwards with his thumb. Crane nodded and the two men immediately swam out of the gaping hole in the front of the cabin and headed back along the thin cord Crane had paid out towards the detached wing. With imminent death lurking in the dark waters behind them, they moved as quickly as they could.

They passed the Learjet's wing, and began to swim even faster, following the cord towards the lead anchor and the rope that led to the buoy up on the surface. Crane spotted it first, braked abruptly and began swimming upwards, his left hand grabbing and then encircling the rope. Richter was right behind him all the way.

In the wreckage of the Learjet, the four pencil detonators had been active for a little over two hours and forty minutes, so the remaining thickness of membrane separating the switches and batteries from the sea water could now be measured only in microns. Making chemical-activated detonators has never been an exact science, because there are so many different circumstances that cannot be factored in. The water depth and hence the pressure, the water temperature, and even the force used to snap the end of the pencil and initially arm the detonator: all could affect the time elapsing before the device would explode. The fuses Stein had collected from Soúda Bay were of good quality, pretty much state of the art, but still they were going to blow some minutes before the full three hours were up.

Richter and Crane deliberately slowed their pace as they ascended – going up to the surface too fast kills more divers than almost anything else because it doesn't allow the absorbed nitrogen in the blood to come out of solution gradually. Crane had arranged aqualung sets at twenty and then at ten feet below the surface, and Richter slowed himself even further as they approached the lower of the two sets. But Crane waved him on, and they stopped together just ten feet below the surface, seizing hold of the buoy cable.

Crane started his stopwatch, then checked his dive watch. He then consulted a dive table printed on a plastic board attached to his weight belt and made some swift calculations, working out how long they'd been submerged and at what depths. These two factors would determine the length of time they had to spend decompressing before they could surface safely. Once he'd arrived at an answer, he did the whole check over again.

At this point Crane wrote 'WHAT THAT?' on the waterproof board and passed it across to Richter, who had just opened the air valve on one of the two aqualung sets attached to the buoy cable and swapped mouthpieces.

Richter took the pencil and scribbled 'BOMB' in reply, then added 'WHEN SURFACE?' below it. Crane checked his stopwatch and wrote '6 MIN'. Richter wrote: 'TOO LONG – GO UP IN 4'. The diving officer at first shook his head, but both he and Richter ascended as soon as four minutes had elapsed, clambered into the life raft and tore off their masks.

'You shouldn't fuck around with decompression tables,' Crane warned, adding 'sir' as a grudging afterthought. 'It's too dangerous.'

'Not half as dangerous as getting your head blown off by fifty pounds of plastic,' Richter retorted.

'We were down at about one hundred feet for over thirty minutes,' Crane said. 'We should have decompressed for nine minutes at ten feet. I cut two minutes off that time, which is dangerous enough, and you lopped another two minutes off that, meaning we surfaced four minutes too early.'

Richter grinned at him across the life raft. '*You* could have stayed down there,' he said.

'Not fucking likely,' Crane replied. 'What were those packages?'

'They were modified demolition charges. Normally they're made up of four half-pound sheets of C4 plastic explosive, so each one contains just under one kilo, but the ones down there looked a lot bigger, maybe a couple of kilos or more. C4 is very efficient and you really don't want to be around when it goes off.'

'Are we safe here?' Crane asked.

'No idea,' Richter replied. 'It depends how much explosive's actually been placed in that wreck. I spotted just two charges, but there could easily be others scattered in the debris or under the fuselage. Where's that fucking chopper?'

The Merlin had meanwhile landed on a stretch of flat ground at the south-east end of the island of Gavdopoúla, scattering a dozen goats in its descent, and Mike O'Reilly had since been watching the life raft carefully through binoculars. As soon as he saw the divers surface, he turned and instructed the pilot to take-off. Seconds later the helicopter lifted into the air and made straight for their position.

The Merlin had covered most of the distance towards the two men when the sea around them erupted and boiled.

### Central Intelligence Agency Headquarters, Langley, Virginia

Westwood closed Hawkins's file and picked up the paper on which he'd noted down the briefest possible summaries of the lives of the two dead former CIA agents. In fact, he'd had to use three sheets of paper to get all the dates down, because of the long careers both men had enjoyed with the Company. He leaned back in his chair and began comparing the two records, year by year.

Strangely enough, although both men had worked in the Operations Directorate, their paths didn't seem to have crossed all that often. They'd attended two courses together, fairly early in their careers, but as far as Westwood could see they had never worked together on a single operation of any sort. But if Hicks's theory was correct, the record had to be wrong, or at least incomplete, so Westwood studied the dates again.

Then he noticed something he hadn't expected. In mid 1971 both men had taken sabbaticals, each being away from the Agency for just under twelve months. The dates of their absences were not an exact match, but both started and ended within a week of each other. Westwood had been looking for operations, not vacations – and it was only when he compared the timelines side by side that he saw the coincidence. Only perhaps it wasn't just a coincidence.

He drummed his fingers on the desk impatiently. This wasn't what he had been hoping to find, but it was something. Maybe they'd gone off on vacation together, hunting or the like, and something had happened during that period, something that had, over thirty years later, sent a man after them with a gun. God, that was thin, but it was the only patch of ground Westwood had so far uncovered, so he had no option but to start digging.

He picked up the internal telephone, dialled down to the Registry Archives and asked them to send up all the leave and sabbatical request records for the calendar years 1971 and 1972.

## ASW Merlin callsign 'Spook Two', between Gavdopoúla and Gávdos, Eastern Mediterranean

The pilot of the Merlin instinctively hauled back on the collective and the control column, pulling the helicopter up into the air and away from the huge plume of spray and water rising from the sea in front of him.

'What the hell was that?' O'Reilly demanded as the aircraft lurched violently.

'An underwater explosion. It looked to me like a depth charge going off, just like in those old Second World War films.'

'Fuck,' O'Reilly muttered. 'Can you see our two divers?'

'Not yet,' the pilot replied. 'The water's disturbed as hell. The life raft's been holed on one side, and I can't see anybody near it.'

The pilot tilted the nose of the Merlin downwards again and acceler- ated towards the partially submerged orange raft. He was still about fifty yards away when O'Reilly spotted a shape in the water directly below them.

'Back up,' he ordered. 'Body in the water – there's someone down there. Aircrewman, ready with the winch.'

The pilot immediately swung the helicopter into a tight left-hand turn, scanning the surface below as the Merlin turned away from the focal patch of disturbed water and the swamped life raft. 'Got it,' he said, dropping the aircraft closer to the sea. 'Right two o'clock at thirty yards.'

The side door of the helicopter had been left open throughout the flight, there being no other way of keeping the rear compartment at a reasonable temperature. O'Reilly was now hanging out of it, looking down, and as the pilot's position report echoed in his ears, he spotted the figure again. A black-clad body, no aqualung, no weight belt, floating limply and face down on the surface of the sea.

O'Reilly didn't hesitate. He took off his headset, unclipped his safety harness, then removed his boots and flying overalls. He put his safety harness on again, then pulled the loop attached to the end of the winch cable over his shoulders and secured it under his armpits. 'Lower me,' he shouted to the aircrewman, then stepped out of the Merlin's door to dangle at the end of the cable.

The pilot didn't even bother engaging the flight computer. He just drove the helicopter down towards the surface, coming to a hover about fifteen feet above the waves as O'Reilly began to drop downwards, the winch cable paying out above his head. The Senior Observer entered the water about six feet away from the floating body, and with two swift strokes he was beside it. The harness had two loops, one for the aircrewman himself, and a second for the person to be rescued. O'Reilly grabbed one arm of the body, swiftly looped the harness over its head and under the other arm, then gave an urgent gesture to be raised.

Almost immediately, he felt the cable tighten as the winch took the strain. With a jerk he was lifted clear of the water, the body rising with him. But O'Reilly guessed they were wasting their time. He had felt a total lack of movement in the body as he'd positioned the harness around it, so he was virtually certain that the man was dead.

The only thing he didn't know for sure was whether he had his arms round David Crane or Paul Richter.

## Chóra Sfakia, Crete

Stein wasn't making too bad a job of nosing the boat into the harbour, though he didn't have anything like the same level of skill as Elias. Krywald had almost recovered from his nausea by the time they entered the harbour, though he still looked unwell as he stood in the bow, mooring rope in hand. Suddenly they heard a dull rumble somewhere out to sea behind them.

Stein said nothing, concentrating on giving the boat just the right amount of reverse thrust to stop its forward motion. He switched off the engine as soon as Krywald had stepped safely onto the jetty and looped the mooring rope over a bollard, then took up the stern mooring rope to finish securing the boat. Only then did Stein check his watch. 'Two hours fifty-five minutes, as near as makes no difference,' he murmured. 'I told you those were good detonators.'

'Yup.' Krywald stepped back into the boat and picked up the black case containing the steel one they'd retrieved what seemed like weeks ago from Nico Aristides's apartment in Kandíra. 'OK, that's pretty much the end of it as far as we're concerned. Let's find the car and then get the hell off this island.'

## Kandíra, south-west Crete

Tyler Hardin had attached a note with Inspector Lavat's mobile phone number to the samples he had sent to the Irakleío forensic laboratory so that he could be contacted as soon as any results were obtained. He was in conference with his team in one of the tents when Lavat entered, telephone in his hand. 'For you, Mr Hardin,' the inspector announced.

The American took the phone and pressed it to his ear. 'Hardin,' he said shortly, and then he just listened for three minutes. 'Thank you,' he said, and added, 'I'd like that in writing, please. Thank you again.'

Snapping the telephone closed he handed it back to Inspector Lavat. 'Well, this case gets stranger by the minute. That was Irakleío. They're still analysing the specimens but they seem to have found something in the samples taken from Spiros Aristides's house.'

'A filovirus?' Susan Kane inquired.

Hardin shook his head firmly. 'Definitely not,' he said. 'They found what looked like spores of a completely unknown type, which is interesting enough, but when they added some moisture to the sample, the spores burst open and released virus particles. Lots and lots of virus particles.'

'Could they identify it?' Kane asked.

'That's the interesting bit,' Hardin said. 'It appears to be of an unknown type, at least on examination using the electron microscope, but what it seems to resemble more than anything is Bovine Leukaemia Virus.'

There was a brief silence as the CDC personnel absorbed this information.

'That,' Jerry Fisher said slowly, 'makes no sense whatsoever. BLV only attacks cattle, and it's really slow-acting. As far as I know there's never been a case of the virus having any effect whatsoever on a human being, and even if it did, it would probably cause a cancer gestating over a period of years. What it definitely couldn't do is kill two healthy men within twelve hours.'

'They didn't say that it *was* BLV,' Hardin pointed out. 'They just said it looked more like BLV than anything else they've got recorded in their database. I've said it before: I think we're dealing here with a brand-new virus, something that works like a filovirus or an arenavirus – a cross between Ebola and Lassa Fever, say – but a hell of a lot faster. Dr Gravas's tag of "Galloping Lassa" is actually pretty close to the mark.'

## Central Intelligence Agency Headquarters, Langley, Virginia

John Westwood hadn't found anything yet, but what he had *not* found was concerning him.

His search through the Company vacation and sabbatical requests for 1971 and 1972 hadn't helped, simply because neither Hawkins nor Richards had, according to the records, either submitted a request for a sabbatical or taken one. That directly contradicted what their personnel records had stated, and suggested to Westwood that he was on the right track.

Both men, it now seemed clear, had been involved in some kind of covert operation starting in mid 1971. An operation so covert that all details of it had been expunged from their personnel files and the bland 'sabbatical' reference substituted in its place.

Westwood picked up the telephone, intending to contact the Registry Archive to request copies of all operation files active between July 1971 and July 1972, but then he hesitated and replaced the receiver.

He'd wanted to avoid using the CIA computer system where possible, but this time he couldn't see any other way to get the information he needed. He turned now to his computer keyboard and initiated a search of Walnut specifying the same parameters he'd intended to request from the Archive. There were, viewing the search results, hundreds of entries, far more than he could possibly search through if he wanted to get any other work done. There was an obvious way to reduce the total to a manageable number, so he specified a search within the results he'd generated, and added the names 'Hawkins' and 'Richards' to its parameters.

That search produced only two results: both men had been assigned to operations in mid July 1972, immediately after they'd returned from their supposed 'sabbaticals'. Westwood swiftly checked the details of each operation, but neither was highly classified nor in any way contentious, and he was more sure than ever that it was during late 1971 and early 1972 that he should be looking.

And then Westwood realized what he was overlooking, and what he was doing wrong. The CIA computer database is a secure source of information, and data entered into it has to conform to certain basic rules. One of these is that even if a file is sealed, the file date, file name and the names of the responsible CIA officers are hard-coded into the database, and cannot be deleted – a basic security measure – even if everything else has been sanitized. Westwood had so far been looking for active operations, and hence active files. With a sense of growing excitement, he entered the names 'Hawkins' and 'Richards' again, but this time specified sealed and inactive files only.

Then he sat back and watched as the computer monitor displayed a single file name, with a date in July 1971, and the names of six senior CIA agents. Two of those names were Charles Hawkins and James Richards.

# PANDEMIC

## ASW Merlin callsign 'Spook Two', between Gavdopoúla and Gávdos, Eastern Mediterranean

The aircrewman expertly spun O'Reilly round, grabbed the back of his harness and pulled him into the rear compartment, paying out cable from the winch as he did so. As soon as O'Reilly's feet touched the floor he clipped his safety harness to a nearby strap, then stepped out of his loop harness and bent over the black-clad body lying face-down in the helicopter's rear compartment.

Together, O'Reilly and the aircrewman turned the body over. For a second the pair just stared down at the bloody and unrecognizable mess that had once been a human face, then O'Reilly seized the top of the diver's wetsuit hood and pulled it off. His probing fingers felt for a pulse in the neck but found nothing.

The aircrewman was saying something, but O'Reilly couldn't hear him over the noise of the rotors and engines. He pulled on a headset, and immediately the din dropped to a more bearable level. 'What?' he said.

'Who is it?' the aircrewman asked him again, and O'Reilly gazed down at the still figure lying on the floor.

'I don't know,' and O'Reilly realized that he really didn't. It wasn't Crane – the ship's own diving officer was markedly taller than this man – and Richter's hair was very fair. The body in front of him was average height and had light brown hair. And as O'Reilly looked more carefully he realized something else. This man had been shot, shot in the head. 'I don't know,' O'Reilly repeated, 'but I'm sure it isn't either Crane or Richter. So who the hell is it? And where the hell are *they*?'

As he spoke these words, the pilot's voice echoed in his headset. 'I can see two others in the water, left eight o'clock at fifty yards.' O'Reilly immediately felt the Merlin lift and turn to port and moments later the helicopter was again in a hover and he found himself looking straight down at Richter and Crane in the sea below him. Four minutes later, the two men were also standing drying off in the rear compartment of the helicopter, looking at the body of the unidentified diver sprawled on the floor.

## Central Intelligence Agency Headquarters, Langley, Virginia

John Westwood stared at his computer screen with a certain amount of satisfaction, not to say déjà vu. It was all, he realized, slowly coming together. The amount of stuff his search had extracted from the database was very limited, but at last he had something he could show to Walter Hicks.

On the screen in front of him was revealed a very brief entry. The filename was 'CAIP', which he immediately recognized from his earlier, unofficial searches for details of the Learjet crash. The file's initiation date was 3 July 1971, and the names of the six senior Company agents responsible for conducting this operation were Henry Butcher, George Cassells, Charles Hawkins, William Penn, James Richards and Roger Stanford. No details of the operation itself were listed, or even the geographical area in which it had been conducted, although Westwood could take an intelligent guess at that, because of the one other piece of information provided by the system. As soon as Westwood had seen the filename he had predicted what the final part of this entry would be. The last line on the screen displayed the note: 'Cross-reference: N17677. Access prohibited. File sealed July 02, 1972', and the security classification 'Ultra'.

It was clear to him that in mid 1971 the CIA had become involved in some kind of highly covert operation, probably in the eastern Mediterranean. Whether this operation had succeeded or failed Westwood had no idea, but what he did know was intriguing enough. Almost exactly one year to the day after CAIP had been initiated, and one month after the State Department-owned Learjet registration N17677 had plunged to the bottom of the Mediterranean, well away from the area that was subsequently searched for the wreckage, the operation file had been sealed and all possible details expunged from the database.

For a few minutes Westwood just stared at the data in front of him. He knew that a sealed file could always be unsealed – it was not an irreversible process. All that was required was the agreement and approval of the officer who had sealed it, or that of a higher-ranking officer in the same department or one of the Company's senior officers – a supergrade – to over-ride the sealing order. Granted, that could take some time to achieve, especially with an old or large and complex file that might have to be read first by a number of senior officers to determine its suitability for unsealing, but it was certainly possible.

Westwood didn't know the exact procedure he would have to follow to get this file opened, but it wouldn't take him long to find out. There were a couple of things he could do before he went that route, however, and he could initiate them immediately.

First, he called up the sealing instruction and checked the authorization. Inevitably this would consist of a bunch of initials – the CIA, like most large organizations, is more or less governed by acronyms – but when the brief entry suddenly appeared on the screen, Westwood didn't, for a moment, recognize it because it was something he'd never seen before within the CIA. When he did recognize the acronym, he whistled softly and sat back in his seat. In that instant he knew the file was going to *stay* sealed, no matter what he or anyone else tried to do about it.

The other thing he could try was quite simple. He called up the directory listing for the CAIP file and requested details. This displayed additional information that included the date each file was created, and last modified, and crucially its size. He scanned down this list until he reached 'CAIP', read the figure beside the name and noted it down. He changed directories and repeated the process with the 'N17677' file. He then made a short telephone call to the IT section, just to confirm what he already knew.

Westwood still didn't know the significance of any of this, but at least he had a little more to go on. It looked as if, the moment the wreckage of the Learjet had been found, somebody had begun taking steps to ensure the permanent silence of all the former senior CIA agents involved in CAIP. There were six names on his list and he knew already that two of them were dead: he obviously had to take immediate action to check on the others.

Westwood dialled the Registry and asked for the personnel files on Henry Butcher, George Cassells, William Penn and Roger Stanford. He also, more or less as an after-thought, requested any files relating to CAIP and to the Learjet registration N17677, though he very much doubted if the Registry Archive staff would find anything there.

## ASW Merlin callsign 'Spook Two', between Gavdopoúla and Gávdos, Eastern Mediterranean

'I presume that was what kept you?' Richter asked, gesturing towards the body lying on the floor of the Merlin.

O'Reilly nodded. 'I spotted the body in the water as we approached the site of the explosion, and ordered the aircraft to reverse course so we could carry out a rescue. Turned out we were a little too late for *this* guy though. And while we were sorting him out, we had the chopper facing away from where you two were bobbing around, so we didn't see you.'

Richter nodded and stepped over to the corpse. He looked down for a few moments at the shattered face, then lifted and turned the head slightly before lowering it. He bent down to pick up the wetsuit hood from the floor where O'Reilly had dropped it, and examined it carefully. 'You were definitely too late,' he said. 'This man's been shot in the back of the head with a large calibre pistol or maybe a rifle. It looks to me like there might be some powder burns on the wetsuit hood, which would suggest a pistol, but it's hard to tell on the neoprene.'

'Has he been dead long?' O'Reilly's experience of dead bodies was extremely limited: the corpse on the floor was the first he had ever seen in the flesh, so to speak.

Richter shook his head. 'Not long,' he decided. 'The body's limp and still warm, which means rigor mortis hasn't set in yet. Something's been feeding on what's left of his face but if he'd been in the water for long he'd be in a much worse mess. My guess is he was alive just a few hours ago, certainly this morning.'

O'Reilly shuddered slightly. 'Any idea who he was?'

'I've never seen him before,' Richter replied, 'but I can make a guess. I think he was the diver who placed the explosives that have just blown the remains of the Learjet into a million pieces. Presumably there was a falling-out among the team members, or maybe they just figured he was expendable. Either way, I suppose you could say the body's evidence, so we'd better get it ashore and let the Cretan police sort things out.'

O'Reilly nodded somewhat abstractedly, then turned and gave instructions to the pilot. Seconds later the Merlin began to climb out of the hover and moved forward, heading towards the southern coast of Crete.

'Where should we take him?' O'Reilly asked. 'Irakleío?'

Richter shook his head. 'No, go to Kandíra. I've already spoken to a police inspector there called Lavat about this wreck, and I think he's more or less in charge of the investigation from the Cretan end. Whoever that diver was,' Richter jerked a thumb towards the rear of the aircraft, 'it doesn't take a rocket scientist to work out that he was probably one of the bad guys responsible for killing the policeman at Kandíra, so I guess Lavat would be only too pleased to get him, dead or alive.'

'OK,' O'Reilly said, and instructed the Merlin pilot to make for Kandíra. As the helicopter changed course slightly for the western end of the island, Richter and Crane finally began pulling off their wetsuits.

'What's in there?' Crane pointed at the string bag containing the encrusted debris Richter had found in the wrecked aircraft.

'I'll show you.' Richter pulled it out and laid it on the floor of the cabin. He took his diving knife and rapped at it sharply with the back of the blade. The encrustation fell away, coming off in chunks like the shell of a walnut, to reveal a stainless-steel Colt revolver.

'I found this inside the Learjet,' Richter said. 'Remember, guns, like cars and aircraft, carry serial numbers, and through that number you can trace at least the first registered owner. I'm guessing, but I think that the Learjet and the Colt will both turn out to have been owned by the American Central Intelligence Agency, which will kind of add a new dimension to the cause of this little epidemic we have here on Crete.'

# Chapter 19

Friday
Central Intelligence Agency Headquarters, Langley, Virginia

As Westwood had expected, the Registry Archives came up with two 'no trace' responses to his request for files relating to CAIP and the crashed Learjet, but they had no trouble finding the personnel records for Henry Butcher, George Cassells, William Penn and Roger Stanford respectively.

It took Westwood under three minutes to learn that Cassells, Penn and Stanford were all dead: Penn in an automobile accident and the other two of fully documented natural causes. Henry Butcher, though, was still alive, but only just. According to a note in his file, he lay in a coma in a hospital in Baltimore, Maryland. Helpfully, the same note also listed the hospital telephone number and the name of the doctor – George Grant – who was treating him.

Westwood got through to Grant almost immediately, which was something of a surprise. He decided to use his real name rather than some pseudonym that he might subsequently forget at a crucial moment. 'My name's John Westwood,' he began. 'I believe you're treating a former colleague of mine called Henry Butcher?'

'That's right,' Grant replied.

'May I ask how he is?'

'You'll appreciate, Mr Westwood, that I can't disclose confidential medical information over the telephone. All I can tell you is that Mr Butcher is very ill.'

'I understand that,' Westwood replied. 'Would it be possible for me to visit with Henry at the hospital?'

'Certainly,' Grant said, 'though I can't say whether or not he'll be conscious, or even recognize you if he is.'

'Even so,' Westwood said, 'I'd like to make the effort.' In fact, he really did have to make the effort – Henry Butcher, no matter what his mental state, was the only living link to CAIP that Westwood had been able to uncover so far, and he definitely needed to see him, if only to confirm that he couldn't provide any further information about that operation from the seventies.

'Very well. At your convenience, Mr Westwood. We have no set visiting hours for patients who are seriously ill.'

'Thanks. I'll be up there this afternoon,' Westwood said, and rang off.

## Kandíra, south-west Crete

As soon as the Merlin touched down, Richter jumped out and headed across to the tents erected beside the road. Though Inspector Lavat wasn't there, he appeared within minutes, attracted no doubt by the sound of the helicopter.

'Mr Richter,' he said as soon as he saw the Englishman, 'we meet again.' He didn't sound or look surprised.

'Hullo, Inspector. I've got a present for you.' Richter led the way back towards the helicopter. 'We're in a hurry, so I'll keep this short. We found the aircraft that Aristides had been diving on, and—'

'How do you know it was the right aircraft?' Lavat interrupted.

'Because of what we found there and what happened after we found it. It was a Learjet, and there were three bodies inside it. There was pretty much nothing else visible after about a quarter of a century at the bottom of the Mediterranean, but fortunately my diving partner spotted some explosive charges inside.'

'Old ones?'

Richter stopped as he reached the Merlin. 'No, brand new. They blew a minute or so after we reached the surface, so there'll be nothing at all left of the wreck now.' The door of the helicopter was open, and Richter pointed inside. 'We picked up this guy floating in the water right above the aircraft wreckage. He wasn't killed by the explosion. He was shot through the back of the head. I'm guessing he was the diver who planted the charges.'

Lavat peered curiously into the helicopter. 'I presume he was what the Americans would call an expendable asset – just like my police officer,' he said bitterly.

Richter nodded. 'He might have been a local man hired for the job, or maybe some low-level operative flown in especially to perform the demolition. Either way, if you can identify him you might get a lead to the other people involved. Unfortunately,' Richter added, 'you certainly won't be able to use a photofit picture – the bullet that killed him came out pretty much through his nose, and it took most of his face with it.'

Ten minutes later, leaving the unidentified corpse zipped inside a body bag and awaiting road transport to the mortuary at Irakleío, the Merlin lifted into the air for a short transit over the mountains back to the *Invincible*.


### Outside Petres, Crete

'Are you OK?' Stein asked, as he swung the hired Ford around another of the seemingly endless bends on the road between Chóra Sfakia and Vrýses. They'd covered about half the distance up to the main road running along the north coast of the island, and were now just outside Petres.

Krywald didn't look at all well. His skin still possessed the greenish pallor that Stein had noticed in the boat, assuming it was just seasickness, and his eyes were bloodshot.

'Yeah,' Krywald muttered. 'Just being in that goddamn boat half the day and then on this fucking road, it's enough to make anyone feel sick.'

'You want to stop for a while?'

The other man shook his head. 'No, let's get back to the hotel, collect the rest of our stuff and get the hell out of here.'

'OK.' Stein changed down and accelerated past a pair of goats that were apparently also heading for Petres. 'But if you feel you wanna throw up, give me a call ahead of time, will you?'

Krywald nodded, then sneezed. Two minutes later he sneezed again.

# PANDEMIC

## HMS *Invincible*, Sea of Crete

As soon as the marshaller had waved in the deck crew to begin lashing the Merlin to the tie-downs on the deck, Richter climbed out of the aircraft. He waved a brief acknowledgement to David Crane and Mike O'Reilly, who had agreed to sort out the diving equipment for him. He then hurried across the Flight Deck to the island and let himself in through its steel watertight door, still carrying his mesh bag containing the pistol and the diving officer's waterproof board bearing the registration number of the Learjet, and climbed swiftly up the stairs to Flyco.

Wings was sitting in his usual seat, watching as Roger Black supervised the shut-down of Spook Two, and he turned as Richter entered Flyco. He glanced at the bag in Richter's hand and stood up. 'Success?' he asked. 'You found what you were looking for?'

Richter smiled briefly. 'I'm not entirely sure. We found the wrecked aircraft and I took a note of its registration number, but we didn't find a lot else, because somebody contrived to blow up the wreckage before we had a chance to do a proper survey. I recovered a pistol from the aircraft cabin, and the chopper then picked up a dead body as well. That's the short version, but Mike O'Reilly can give you chapter and verse, because he saw everything from the comfort of the Merlin while Crane and I were being tossed around after the explosion.

'With your permission, sir, I'd like to signal my section in London to start tracing action on the aircraft remains and the pistol, and then I'll probably have to return to Crete at fairly short notice. Whoever placed those charges – or rather ordered them to be placed – is almost certainly still somewhere on Crete, and I'm planning on locating him before this ship leaves the area. Crane and I could very easily have died in that explosion, so I've got a score to settle.'

## St Mary's Hospital, Baltimore, Maryland

John Westwood pushed through the double swing doors leading into the hospital reception area. He attracted the immediate attention of the harassed receptionist by the simple tactic of pushing his way to the head of a line of people and pulling out his CIA identification. Six minutes later he was following George Grant, a short, overweight African-American, down a long white-painted corridor.

As Dr Grant halted beside a large window set in the left-hand wall and simply pointed through it, Westwood peered into the room beyond and saw a slight, grey-haired figure lying motionless on a bed. Pipes and wires connected his inert body to an array of monitoring equipment and machines whose purpose Westwood could only guess at.

'Mr Butcher is comatose,' Grant explained. 'That means he's deeply unconscious almost all the time. He enjoys very occasional and invariably short periods of partial lucidity, but the prognosis is terminal and he will certainly die within months, perhaps even within days.'

'What exactly is wrong with him?'

Grant glanced appraisingly at Westwood. 'As I thought I had explained, Mr Westwood, I cannot divulge any detailed medical information except to members of Mr Butcher's immediate family.'

'Actually, Doctor,' Westwood produced his CIA identification, 'I think you can. There's a possibility that Mr Butcher knows information that can be classified of national importance. I require to know what is wrong with him – the exact prognosis. If necessary I can obtain a warrant, which will compel you to disclose any and all information relating to Henry Butcher, but that would take time, so I would far rather you assisted the Agency without my having to resort to legal compulsion.'

'No need for the big guns, Mr Westwood,' Grant replied, studying the folder Westwood was holding out to him. 'Now I know who you are, I'm perfectly happy to help in any way I can. I don't suppose you want the full medical diagnosis, so in summary what Mr Butcher is suffering from is a rare form of cancer that primarily affects the central nervous system. He's in the terminal stages of that disease now.'

'How long has he got?'

Grant shook his ample shoulders. 'God knows,' he said, 'and I do mean that literally: only God knows. If I had to provide a forecast I would say anything from six weeks to three months, but that really is just a guess. He's breathing by himself, his heart is in reasonably good condition and we're feeding him intravenously. Eventually the cancer will take him, but until it does he's likely to endure.'

Westwood nodded and looked again at the still figure lying on the other side of the glass. 'What about his family? Do they come to visit him?'

'His wife is dead, and as far as I know he's had no visitors at all since he became my patient about five months ago.' Grant glanced at the information contained on a clipboard he'd taken from the slot in the door. 'His next of kin is listed as his brother, but I've never seen him here.'

For a few moments Westwood debated arranging to have a police officer or a junior agent stationed outside Henry Butcher's door, but after another glance through the partition he decided that would be a complete waste of time. 'You mentioned some periods of partial lucidity,' he said. 'Are these frequent?'

Grant shook his head. 'If you're hoping to question him I'm afraid you'll be disappointed. The last time he showed any signs of consciousness was over three weeks ago, and he was barely aware that he was in a hospital. I would be very surprised if he came round long enough to recognize anyone, so any kind of detailed questioning is almost certainly not going to be feasible.'

Westwood nodded. 'I understand that, but two things, Dr Grant. First, please don't allow Mr Butcher any visitors apart from his immediate family and next of kin. If anyone else attempts to enter his room, please have them detained on my authority. Secondly, just as a precaution, could you arrange to have a tape recorder positioned by his bed. If he recovers consciousness, no matter how briefly, get someone to record anything he says and then let me have the tape.' Westwood was clutching the smallest of all possible straws.

Grant nodded. 'Is there anything special we should be listening for?'

'No, just record everything. Right, thank you, Dr Grant. It was worth the journey here just in the hope I could have talked with him. I'll give you my direct line number at the Agency and if by any chance he should come round or his condition changes for the better, please contact me immediately.'

'I can almost promise you he won't improve,' Grant replied, taking Westwood's card, 'but I'll certainly advise you of any change in his condition.'

## HMS *Invincible*, Sea of Crete

Richter was in his cabin on Two Deck drying his hair after taking a shower when there was a knock on his door. He slid it open to find a Communications rating standing there with a buff envelope stamped 'SECRET', and with Richter's name printed on it.

'Sign here if you would, sir.'

'Thanks. Could you wait a moment, please?' Richter scrawled his signature on the form attached to the clipboard. He ripped open the envelope and extracted the signal that had been sent from Hammersmith via the Secret Intelligence Service. The message was brief and to the point.

FAA REPORTS LEARJET MODEL 23 REGISTRATION N17677 RETIRED FROM SERVICE IN USA IN 1979 PRESUME RINGER. COLT REPORTS PISTOL SERIAL NUMBER ISSUED TO STATE DEPARTMENT PRESUME CIA. INVESTIGATION APPROVED.

Richter put the message back in its envelope and watched as the rating re-sealed it. 'Destroy it, please,' he instructed, and slid his cabin door closed.

For Simpson to approve further investigation was one thing, but Richter had no clear idea about what to do next. Because of the weapon found inside the wrecked Learjet's cabin, and the duplicated aircraft registration, it was a reasonable guess that the jet had once been a CIA asset. What he didn't know was what it had been doing over the eastern Mediterranean, or where it had been before that, where it was going to or what it had been carrying. Nor did he yet know what had killed Spiros Aristides and his nephew, or why somebody now believed the mere existence of the wreck was so dangerous that it had to be completely destroyed.

Richter had just finished dressing as he heard his name called over the tannoy system. 'Lieutenant Commander Richter is requested to report to the Commander.' Three minutes later he knocked on a door, waited for the gruff command to enter, then stepped inside the cabin.

The Commander on a Royal Navy aircraft carrier is the Executive Officer, the most senior Commander on board, second in command and responsible for discipline and for the smooth running of the ship. He didn't, Richter noticed, look too pleased with life, and he didn't ask his visitor to sit down.

'Richter,' he began flatly, 'I'm not happy about your conduct on board this ship. Since you arrived you've flouted the rules on more than one occasion. I understand that your so-called diversion to the Italian airfield was nothing more than a ruse to get you ashore overnight, but this last incident is intolerable. This ship isn't here just for your personal convenience. We could have lost a very expensive Merlin helicopter, not to mention an even more expensive crew, through your unauthorized activities.'

Richter just stared at him. 'Is that it?' he asked after a few seconds.

The Commander spluttered. 'Are you being insubordinate?'

'Almost certainly,' Richter said, 'but I've got better things to do than stand here and listen to you waffling on. You need to get a grasp on the facts of life. I'm not a member of this ship's company – in fact, I'm no longer even a serving naval officer – and I take my orders from another organization.'

'I'm fully aware of that,' the Commander said, his normally russet face darkening a couple of shades, 'but while you're on board this ship you're still subject to naval discipline and you will obey orders and accord proper respect to senior officers.'

'I will do whatever I have to do,' Richter retorted, 'to complete tasks set for me by my section. If that means I have to flout naval discipline and ignore orders that you or anybody else on this ship issues, then that's what I'll do. If you don't like it, that's tough. If you feel like taking the risk, clap me in irons, but until then, I've got work to do. I'd like to do so with your cooperation, but if you want to make an issue of it I can probably get a very specific directive from their lordships at the Admiralty telling you exactly what to do. Your choice.'

For several seconds the Commander stared at Richter in silence, then finally he spat: 'Get out of my sight.'

'I was just going anyway.' Richter turned and walked from the cabin, heading for the CommCen. He had a signal to send off to Simpson right away.

## Central Intelligence Agency Headquarters, Langley, Virginia

'So what have you got, John?' Walter Hicks asked. The two men were sitting in Hicks's comfortable office, the inevitable coffee pot on the table between them and the usual cloud of blue smoke rising towards the ceiling from Hicks's cigar.

'If I'm completely honest, Walter,' Westwood replied, 'the answer has to be "not a lot". As you instructed, I've been liaising with Detective Delaney, but so far the crime scenes haven't been much help to us. All Delaney knows for sure is that it was the same perpetrator who killed Richards and the Hawkins couple. That was confirmed by some dark hairs belonging to the same individual found at all three crime scenes. All the analysts can tell is that they come from the head of a Caucasian, probably male, and were turning grey. That includes about thirty per cent of the adult male population of America, so it doesn't narrow our search a hell of a lot.

'The house-to-house in Crystal Springs – where James Richards lived – turned up a bunch of mutually contradictory descriptions of an unknown male who may, or more probably may not, have had anything to do with the murder there. The description of a man seen entering the Hawkins's residence at Popes Creek by one of the neighbours is probably the only genuine eyewitness account we have, but it's so vague it's almost completely useless. It states white male, around six feet tall, wearing a dark coat. About the only thing we know for sure is that we're not looking for a black female dwarf.

'As far as Delaney and his men can establish, nobody saw Hawkins arrive at Lower Cedar Point, or noticed him sitting there in his car, and no one saw any other person approach his vehicle, apart from the guy who found him, of course.'

'So the short version,' Hicks said, 'is that these murders were all committed by the same man, but nothing in the forensics can be used to track him down. But once any suspect's in custody, what Delaney's found so far can be used to confirm whether he's the killer?'

'In a nutshell, Walter.'

'OK, sounds as if the leg-work investigation is pretty much dead in the water unless Delaney can come up with a new eyewitness. What about the other side of the coin? What did you find out from the files here at Langley?'

'As I said, not a lot. I've already trawled through mountains of files for any combination of factors that could possibly link Hawkins and Richards. I've found only one, and it's old and pretty tenuous. It also seems to have been a deep black operation that was highly classified.'

'That's interesting,' Hicks said. 'Go on.'

Westwood glanced down at his notes. 'OK, on the third of July nineteen seventy-one a file was opened on an operation called "CAIP". That's spelt Charlie, Alpha, India, Papa. The senior agents tasked with running it were Henry Butcher, George Cassells, Charles Hawkins, William Penn, James Richards and Roger Stanford. According to our records, that is the only operation that ever involved both Hawkins and Richards working together.'

'What was CAIP intended to achieve?'

Westwood shook his head in frustration. 'I've no idea,' he admitted. 'The file was sealed just under a year later, and was then classified "Ultra". And this is where it starts to get interesting. I've been through the Registry and the Archives and there's no hard copy of anything relating to CAIP to be found anywhere: no files, not even any record of the destruction of a file. It's as if CAIP never happened, so somebody – I'm guessing the same person who killed Hawkins and Richards – did a very thorough job of expunging all traces of that operation. The only thing he couldn't achieve was to eliminate the basic file details from the computer system, simply because of the way the database itself is set up. But he did the best he could: he protected the file from random searches. The only way you can get to see what little information there is, is if you type in "CAIP" and nothing else. Wildcard searches don't work. You do see what this means, Walter?'

Hicks nodded. 'Whoever offed these two former Company agents probably still works right here at Langley. That's very disturbing, John.'

'Tell me about it. Oddly enough, I think I now know why our Mr X killed Hawkins and Richards. There are no details of anything to do with CAIP on the computer apart from what I've told you, but there was one other piece of information. CAIP is cross-referenced to a file called "N17677". I checked that file as well, and guess what? It was started in

June nineteen seventy-two, classified "Ultra" and sealed on exactly the same date as CAIP – the second of July seventy-two.'

'And N17677 is what, precisely?'

'It's the registration number of an aircraft – a Learjet 23 to be exact – which went missing over the eastern Mediterranean in June that year. The file itself was sealed long before the search for the aircraft's wreckage was abandoned.'

'So what's the link to CAIP?'

'I don't know, but I'm guessing that CAIP, whatever the hell it represented, was a covert op somewhere in the eastern Mediterranean and the crashed Learjet was bringing out some of the agents involved. The only problem with that hypothesis,' Westwood anticipated Hicks's obvious question, 'is that there's no record of any Company personnel dying during that period, anywhere in the world. But if this joker can sanitize our records the way he did with CAIP, losing a few personnel files wouldn't prove that difficult a trick.'

'OK,' Hicks said, 'let's do this the easy way. Get those files unsealed and see what the hell CAIP is all about. Who authorized the sealing anyway?'

Westwood smiled and shook his head. 'I've already checked that, Walter, and we're going nowhere with it. The authorization was POTUS.'

For a moment Hicks just stared. 'POTUS?' he echoed.

Westwood nodded. 'POTUS – as in President Of The United States. That file was sealed by the authority of the White House. And before you ask, Walter, I checked the Learjet file as well – that was sealed by the same authority.'

'Jesus,' Hicks muttered. 'This is serious stuff, John. There's no way that we're going to be able to get the White House to unseal these files. I've never even heard of any President authorizing the sealing of a Company file, but there obviously had to be a real good reason.'

'And unsealing would be a waste of time anyway, Walter,' Westwood said. 'Another thing I did was check the file sizes. The CAIP and N17677 files are both around fifteen kilobytes in size, which means they're effectively empty. Whoever did the actual sealing made absolutely certain that nobody would ever be able to discover anything, even if they did get them unsealed. They deleted everything in each file, then sealed them both. The IT guys tell me fifteen kilobytes means the file will contain a title and pretty much nothing else. Almost no text at all, certainly nothing usable.'

For a few moments Hicks said nothing, just puffed on his cigar and gazed out of the window with unfocused eyes. 'OK, John,' he said, 'what you've told me makes sense, despite the lack of any hard data. But I'm worried about how those files were sealed – the authority, I mean. The White House getting involved kicks this whole matter to a much higher, and much more dangerous, level. I'm also concerned that whoever orchestrated these recent killings might still be working here at Langley. So tread carefully, John.'

Hicks stubbed out the remains of his cigar and drained the last of his coffee. 'I've a couple of other questions, though. First, why did your Mr X wait until now before he decided on killing Hawkins and Richards? And what about the various other agents involved?'

'Let me answer your second question first. As soon as I found the CAIP reference, I checked the personnel files of the other four senior agents listed as part of the operation. Cassells and Stanford died of perfectly natural causes and William Penn got killed a few years ago in a car accident in Ohio.

'The last man listed is Henry Butcher, who's lying in a coma in a hospital in Baltimore. He's apparently dying of a rare cancer that attacks the central nervous system. I've even been over to see him, and talked to the doctor looking after him. I'm told he's got a few months, maybe only a few weeks, to live, and the chances are he won't recover consciousness. Even if he does, the doctor thinks any kind of questioning would almost certainly be a waste of time. So I'm afraid that's another dead end.

'Now the reason our Mr X started his killing spree is something else. This information came from a public domain source posted on Walnut. Some time last week a Greek diver named Spiros Aristides, living on the island of Crete, found the wreckage of a small jet aircraft on the seabed. It was down deep, around one hundred feet, and it apparently took him several expeditions to locate the remains of the cabin. He noted part of the registration number, and was overheard in a local bar talking about his find.

'Then things start to get weird. Twelve hours later, both the diver and his nephew were found dead, because of some kind of real fast-acting pathogen. The local papers picked up the story, and one of our assets there sent it to Langley. Now, three things puzzled me. First, the newspaper reported the wreckage as being found close to Crete. That meant that the crash occurred a long way from the area originally searched back in seventy-two, so the aircraft itself had either drifted well off-route or was on a covert flight when it went down. Second, according to the diver, the wreckage showed signs of battle damage, suggesting it had been deliberately shot down. Third, we suspect that the same Greek found something in the wreckage containing a virus or chemical that subsequently killed himself and his nephew.'

Hicks nodded slowly. 'Yes, I can see where you're going with this. The reason Mr X killed Hawkins and Richards is because the aircraft wreckage had finally been found. There must have been something in the wreck that would blow the lid clean off operation CAIP, and he wasn't prepared to chance any surviving Company men being questioned about it.' He paused. 'But what I still don't buy is the timescale. The file on CAIP was closed over thirty years ago, and the world has changed a hell of a lot since then. Why is it so important to eliminate the only people who knew about it?' Hicks paused again, then added, 'Five gets you ten that this guy has already got a team en route to Crete to take care of that wreckage.'

### Chaniá, Western Crete

Stein screeched to a halt by the roadside a mile or so outside Chaniá and leapt out of the car. He ran round to the passenger door, wrenched it open and virtually dragged Krywald out.

'Jesus, Roger,' he grumbled, as Krywald vomited onto the edge of the tarmac. 'What the hell's the matter with you?'

'I dunno,' Krywald replied weakly. It was the third time Stein had had to stop the car since they'd left Chóra Sfakia. Each time Krywald had thrown up, his vomit laced with blood. Quite apart from that, he looked awful.

'I've got to get you to a hospital,' Stein muttered. He'd said the same thing twice before, but each time Krywald had dismissed the suggestion. This time he just nodded faintly and slumped back into the passenger seat.

Stein sat down behind the wheel, pulled out a map and glanced at it quickly, then started the engine and accelerated away. 'The closest hospital is at Chaniá,' he explained, 'and that's where I'm gonna take you, right now.'

Again all Krywald did was nod, and Stein realized just how sick his companion must be feeling. 'Did you eat something – shellfish or something that I didn't have?' But even as he asked, Stein knew what the answer would be.

The three men had eaten dinner together the previous evening and shared only a light breakfast that morning, and on each occasion the food had been nothing other than bland. He and Krywald were seasoned enough travellers to avoid any dishes that might cause them problems abroad. They'd been careful to make sure that Elias stuck to simple food as well, not wanting any problems until after he'd completed the crucial dive.

When Krywald shook his head, Stein persisted. 'You drink something, then?'

'A coupla beers last night, same as you. Coffee this morning. That's all.'

Stein looked over at him. 'Well, you've sure as shit caught something,' he muttered.

Krywald's face wore a scared and hunted look that Stein had never witnessed before. He'd worked with him half a dozen times previously, and Stein well knew that his partner wasn't scared of anything or anyone. 'What is it?' he pressed.

Krywald turned to look over at him. 'The case,' he said, his voice wavering weakly. 'I took a look in the case this morning. I think I must have caught whatever killed those Greeks.'

'Oh, shit,' Stein muttered, unconsciously leaning away from Krywald and pressing his foot down harder on the accelerator. 'What did you find in it?'

'That's the stupid part,' Krywald said, his voice now so weak that Stein had to concentrate hard to hear what he was saying. 'There's a classified file, and spaces for twelve small flasks – but it contained only four. Three of them are still sealed and somebody's cut one of them open. I didn't touch the flasks . . . just looked through the file.'

'What was in it?' Stein asked, overtaking three cars apparently travelling in convoy.

'Medical stuff.' Krywald was breathing very slowly. 'I didn't understand too much of it. The file title read "CAIP", and I've still got no idea what that stands for. I only looked,' he added, 'in case it contained something we needed to know about before we handed it over to McCready – and there was.'

'What?' Stein asked.

'This CAIP thing,' Krywald muttered. 'You have to read it, Dick. I've been with the Company ever since I left college, and I've never read anything like it. For starters, it was classified "Ultra", and I've never seen a file with that classification outside the secure briefing-rooms at Langley.' Krywald broke off and coughed, clutching a handkerchief to his mouth. When he pulled it away, the handkerchief was stained bright red.

'You OK?' Stein asked, immediately aware of how stupid this question was.

'Of course I'm not OK,' Krywald wheezed. 'Listen to me. If that file ever gets made public, it could destroy the Company.'

'What?' Stein inadvertently jerked on the steering wheel, swerving the car across the fortunately empty road. 'Christ, Krywald, that file's over thirty years old. Whatever the Company was doing back then can't be important today. So what the hell's in it?'

Krywald shook his head. 'You have to read it but, believe me, I'm not exaggerating. It could shut down the Agency and maybe even topple the US administration.' Krywald fell silent, slumped back in his seat.

Stein wondered if his colleague's ramblings were some kind of a side effect of whatever he was suffering from. But Krywald had always been outstandingly level-headed, so Stein realized he was going to have to read the file himself to try to make any kind of sense of what the man was now saying.

'There must have been some kind of infectious agent inside the case,' Stein suggested after a few seconds. 'Something you didn't even notice – like dust, a liquid, something?'

'There was some powder on the cover of the file,' Krywald said, 'but I blew it off before I opened it.'

*Bingo*, Stein thought, but said nothing further. Eighteen minutes later, having removed the SIG pistol from Krywald's waistband and the two spare magazines from his pocket, Stein helped him through the double doors of the hospital and watched helplessly as his partner was rushed away for emergency treatment.

## Hammersmith, London

'Oh, shit,' Simpson muttered, and tossed the signal flimsy over to the Intelligence Director, who stared at it in incomprehension.

'What's the problem?' the ID asked, having read it through to the end. 'OK, the signal's from Richter. He's explained what happened when he dived on the wrecked Learjet, he's acknowledged your instruction to investigate further and he's confirmed he'll take care of it, so presumably that's exactly what he'll do.'

'It's not what the signal says,' Simpson snapped, 'but what it means. I don't like the way Richter takes care of things. Buildings get destroyed, aircraft get blown up, and the body count gets higher the more pissed off he becomes. And as somebody's just detonated a bunch of plastic explosive directly underneath his little rubber boat, I'm guessing that he's *very* pissed off right now.'

'You're exaggerating.'

'Yes, I am, but not a lot.'

'He's under your orders, so he'll do what he's told.'

'You wish.' Simpson laughed mirthlessly. 'He was supposed to be under my orders out in Italy. I instructed him – not once but several times – not to touch Lomas. Six minutes later Lomas was lying on a gravel drive while two Italian policemen tried to shovel his intestines back inside his abdomen. Don't talk to me about Richter being under my orders.'

'Well,' the Intelligence Director suggested, 'if he's such a loose cannon, then get rid of him. Give him to the Italians. I'm sure they'd be only too happy to stick him in the *oubliette*, so to speak.'

'No way.' Simpson shook his head. 'For all his faults, Richter's probably the most useful man I've got – and I'll tell you why. He's like a Rottweiler with attitude. Once he gets his teeth into a problem he simply never lets go until he's fixed it.'

'But if he won't follow your orders?'

'I can live with that, as long as he gets the job done – which he always has up to now. Of course, the day may come when he'll outlive his usefulness and then I'll have to get rid of him, permanently, but until then I'm prepared to cope with the problems he causes.'

'But what he did to Lomas—'

'What he did to Lomas,' Simpson interrupted again, 'was a hell of a lot less than I'd have done if I'd had the same chance. And Richter was probably right: all the Italians would do is stick Lomas in a nice comfy safe house for a year or two, give him three square meals a day, and ask him politely if there's anything he'd like to tell them. From what we know of that bastard they'd get the square root of sod all out of him. And anything they did get would probably be disinformation that they'd then spend months wasting their time checking out.

'In fact, Richter may actually have done us a favour. While Lomas is recuperating and dependent, the Italians are probably more likely to get something useful out of him. They can fiddle with the drugs, feed him a little sodium pentothal or scopolamine, and give him the third degree while he's still woozy. All Richter has to worry about is what Lomas will do once he's recovered.'

'He'll go after Richter, you mean?'

'Like a shot. Richter, of course, is looking forward to that. He doesn't like unfinished business.'


## HMS *Invincible*, Sea of Crete

'*Invincible, Invincible*, this is Fob Watch, over.'

'Fob Watch, *Invincible*, you're loud and clear. Go ahead.'

'*Invincible*, this is Fob Watch with a transport request, and a message for Lieutenant Commander Richter. Ready to copy? Over.'

'Ready to copy.'

'Roger. Message reads as follows. "From Tyler Hardin, CDC, to Lieutenant Commander Richter, HMS *Invincible*. Third suspected case reported within last few minutes. Subject is surname Curtis, first name Roger. Nationality, American. Profession, reporter. Status, emergency admission to Chaniá hospital. Request helicopter transport from Kandíra to Chaniá ASAP. Suggest Richter accompanies." Message ends.'

'Fob Watch, *Invincible*, all copied. Listen out this frequency for aircraft callsign and estimate for Kandíra. Out.'

The communications rating pulled off his headset, read over what he'd written, then handed it to the duty Communications Officer who scanned it quickly. 'Three copies,' the officer said crisply. 'One for Air Operations, one for Commander Richter, and file the other.'

Just over thirty minutes later an 814 Squadron Merlin was sitting on two spot, rotors turning and waiting for the ship to steady on a flying course. Richter, back in civilian clothes, was the only passenger. Beside him was his leather overnight bag, in the inside pocket of his jacket was an Enigma T301 mobile phone, and tucked in the rear waistband of his trousers was a Browning 9mm semi-automatic pistol.

# Chapter 20

Westwood had just arrived back in his office when his outside line rang.

'Mr Westwood? It's George Grant, from Baltimore.'

'Dr Grant. I didn't expect to hear from you so soon. Has something happened?'

'Yes. I'm afraid Mr Butcher died about an hour ago,' the doctor replied.

Westwood realized immediately that his last possible straw had just vanished. 'Isn't that rather sooner than you were expecting?'

'Frankly, yes,' Grant said, 'but, as I told you, in these cases our expectations are only very rarely accurate. Some patients last a lot longer than we anticipate, others die much sooner than expected. I said as much to his brother too.'

'His brother?' Westwood asked.

'Yes, John Butcher came to visit just a couple of hours after you left, and his brother Henry slipped away soon after he had gone. And before you ask me, Mr Westwood, I did confirm his identification. I checked his driver's licence, and I had the ward nurse keep an eye on him all the time he was in the room with our patient.'

Despite Grant's reassurances, Westwood immediately recognized the lethal hand of Mr X, tying up yet another loose end. 'Can you describe this John Butcher, please?' he asked.

'Certainly. He's a big man, around two hundred pounds, red-brown hair and a full beard.'

'Thank you.' Westwood jotted down the brief description, which was probably that of a man wearing a simple disguise. 'One other thing, Dr Grant. Can you please arrange for an autopsy on Henry Butcher? And as soon as possible?'

'I *can*,' Grant said, surprise evident in his voice, 'but it's most unusual in any case where there's no doubt about the diagnosis. May I ask why?'

'Yes, you may. I have good reason to believe that Henry Butcher may have been murdered, most likely poisoned.'

There was a brief stunned silence across the line as Grant absorbed the implications. 'That's absolutely unbelievable,' he replied finally. 'This patient was comatose and terminally ill. What would be the point in murdering a dying man? And who did it? His own *brother*?' His voice rose the better part of an octave on the last word.

'All that's classified information, Dr Grant, but I'd be very surprised if the man who identified himself as John Butcher was any relation to your patient.'

'Very well. I'll contact you when I get the results.'

As soon as he put the phone down, Westwood pressed buttons on his computer keyboard and brought up Henry Butcher's personnel file, accessing details of his family. Butcher's wife had died some years earlier, and his next of kin was listed as his brother – John James Butcher – with an address in Idaho. Westwood noted down the telephone number and then dialled it. His call was answered almost immediately.

'Mr Butcher?'

'That's me. Who's calling?'

'My name's Westwood, Mr Butcher, from your brother's old company.'

Westwood heard a wheezing chuckle. 'Spare me the covert crap, Mr Westwood. I know Henry was a spook. Now, what can I do for you?'

'I've some bad news, I'm afraid, Mr Butcher. Your brother Henry died today in his Baltimore hospital.'

There was a short pause before John Butcher replied. 'Well, that's a relief, I guess. He had no quality of life left. Not for a while, really.'

'When did you last see your brother, Mr Butcher?' Westwood asked.

'Oh, 'bout six months ago, I reckon. Didn't seem too much point to go on visiting him. He never even knew I was there.'

Two minutes later Westwood replaced the receiver. He'd been fairly sure before he'd made that call, but now there was no possible doubt. Somebody still working at Langley was making sure that all the details of CAIP, and any possible witnesses, would be dead and buried for ever.

### Merlin 'Whisky Tango'

The crew of the Merlin had been pre-briefed earlier in the day for the sortie. They hadn't known exactly when they were due to fly to Kandíra but, as the duty HDS crew, they had expected to make that journey at least once. The aircraft had been kept fully fuelled and waiting on two spot, so the crew were been strapped in and ready for engine start less than ten minutes after the message had been received from Fob Watch.

The short delay had been caused by Richter himself. As soon as he'd read the message from Tyler Hardin, he'd guessed that the 'sick journalist' mentioned was almost certainly one of the men who had entered the two properties in Kandíra. As far as could be deduced, the sole source of the infection that killed the two Greeks had been carried in a container that had been removed from Nico Aristides's property by the two intruders. The only way anyone else could become infected was by immediate access to that container. Therefore this supposed 'journalist' had to be one of the intruders.

Richter had quickly done three things before walking across the Flight Deck and climbing into the back of the Merlin. First, he'd drawn the Enigma phone from the CommCen – the T301 uses high-level encryption to provide secure communications with other users of the equipment on normal GSM networks, and Richter knew his section had several handsets available.

Next he'd signalled Simpson, giving him the mobile number and requesting encrypted facilities be enabled at Hammersmith. He also asked for the assistance of a Secret Intelligence Service asset on Crete, and specified a recognition procedure. He'd classified the signal 'Secret' and gave it the precedence 'Military Flash', thus guaranteeing that Simpson would receive it within the hour.

SIS maintains a fairly large team at Irakleío, mainly employed in monitoring radio transmissions from the Middle East and nations of the former USSR. Richter knew there had been at least two men posing as CDC officers in Kandíra, but there could easily be a whole opposition team involved, so he wanted back-up.

The last thing he'd done, therefore, was to draw the pistol and thirty rounds of ammunition from the *Invincible*'s armoury.

# PANDEMIC

## Réthymno, Crete

Richard Stein was a desperately worried man. He'd seen the state of the bodies of Spiros and Nico Aristides, and he'd just spent a couple of hours sitting in a closed car next to Roger Krywald while his partner coughed up blood as his condition steadily worsened. The unknown biological agent that had killed the two Greeks was probably now going to kill Krywald, and Stein knew for certain that it was sitting – silent, lethal and invisible – in that case in the back of the hire car.

But its location wasn't his problem. His anxiety was that maybe it was all around him right now, in the air, in Krywald's blood smears on his jacket lapels – maybe even on the adjacent seat his partner had been sitting in. To say that he was terrified it might attack him too was considerably understating the case.

As soon as he'd propelled Krywald through the doors of the Chaniá hospital, Stein had pulled off his blood-stained jacket and tossed it into the back of the Ford. He climbed back into the car and gunned the engine, ignoring the speed limits as he headed east for Réthymno and the illusory sanctuary of the hotel. He stopped twice on the way back: once to buy petrol and the second time to purchase a pack of large black trash bags.

The moment he arrived at the hotel, Stein locked the car carefully, leaving the case that Krywald had been guarding so assiduously inside it. He grabbed the room key from the desk clerk, virtually ran up the stairs to his room and locked the door behind him. He tore off all his clothes and dumped them unceremoniously into one of the trash bags. He tied the neck of it with a double knot, then stuck the bag inside another one and secured that as well. After that he walked straight into the bathroom and under the shower.

Having read somewhere that bacteria and viruses thrive in warm conditions, he set the temperature control firmly on 'cold', turned the tap on full and stood, shivering and teeth chattering, under the flow for five minutes, soaping his hair and whole body repeatedly. Then he brought the temperature up to warm and washed himself again, before climbing out and putting on fresh clothes.

Twenty minutes after he'd rushed up the stairs, Stein was again on his way out of the hotel, surgical gloves on both hands and holding the black bag containing his clothes at arm's length. He walked a few yards down the street, found an open trash bin and lobbed the bag inside. Then he pulled off the gloves and threw them in as well.

Only then did he relax and start thinking clearly again. He stood on the pavement for a few seconds, then headed a hundred yards further down the street, sat down at a café table and ordered a coffee while he worked out what he was going to do next.

Stein barely noticed the short dark man sitting at a café table on the opposite side of the street, his head bent over a magazine, but the man had already positively identified him.

And Murphy was puzzled. His orders had listed three CIA agents, and now he was sitting looking at just one of them, so where the hell were the other two? And had they already completed phase two? He'd have to contact Nicholson as soon as possible and try to find out what the fuck was going on.

### Merlin 'Whisky Tango', over Crete

Tyler Hardin stood with Dr Gravas at the edge of the landing site as the Merlin settled onto the dusty open ground. He had brought a bulky bag with him, which Gravas helped him lift into the rear compartment of the aircraft. Once Hardin and the Cretan doctor had strapped themselves in and pulled on their headsets, the helicopter lifted off and headed north towards Chaniá.

'What's in the bag?' Richter asked.

'My biological space suit and air filtration unit,' Hardin replied. 'I'm not going anywhere near this Curtis character without all the protection I can get.'

'How do you think he became infected?'

Hardin looked at him quizzically. 'I think you know the answer to that as well as I do, Mr Richter,' he said. 'Whatever this mysterious agent is, it at least doesn't seem to be particularly infectious. Nobody else who entered either property in Kandíra has suffered any ill-effects, so my obvious conclusion is that Curtis was one of the two intruders, and that he recently opened the container.

'Our latest information from the lab in Irakleío says that in the scrapings from Aristides's dining table they found some microscopic spore-like objects, and when these are subjected to moisture, they rupture to release what look like virus particles.'

'What kind of a virus?' Richter asked.

'That's the puzzle. We were expecting a filovirus or perhaps an arenavirus, purely because of the effects of the agent on the two bodies. But according to the senior supervisor at the lab, this agent looks more like BLV than anything else.'

Richter looked blank, so Hardin took pity on him. 'Bovine Leukaemia Virus.' He enunciated the words slowly. 'It's a fairly common infective agent that attacks cattle, often causing cancer. Anyone genuinely working for the Medical Research Council, even as a consultant, would at least have heard of it. So I think we can drop the MRC fiction, don't you, Mr Richter? You're obviously some kind of investigator, which is why I suggested you come with me to Chaniá to look at this American, but you're certainly not employed by the MRC.'

'OK,' Richter said, 'I admit it. It just seemed a convenient persona to adopt in the circumstances. So tell me about this virus – if it's not very infectious, why has this American suddenly been attacked by it?'

'I think the answer lies in the spores,' Hardin explained. 'As far as we can tell at this early stage, the spores themselves are reasonably inert, but the moment they become moist they rupture. I'm only guessing, but I think this guy Curtis probably opened the container and breathed some in, or maybe even got the spores on his fingers before touching his face. The moisture present in the mouth or on the mucous lining of the nose would be enough to make them open up and for the infection to start.'

Richter nodded. 'But you still don't know what this virus is?'

'No. As I said, it apparently *looks* like BLV but that obviously has to be a coincidence. BLV is specific to cattle and it's also a slow-acting virus. What we have here is something that works like Ebola or Lassa Fever, but infinitely quicker. Spiros Aristides died by drowning: his lungs filled with blood.

'This virus seems to attack the endothelial cells in the blood vessels and the platelets. The result is leaking blood vessels, and blood that won't clot. It starts with those vessels with the thinnest walls – typically the eyes and mouth – then gradually other organs are attacked.

The gross effect is that the victim will begin to bleed, and the blood will just keep on pouring out through the walls till eventually he will die from fluid filling the lungs, as Aristides did, or maybe simply from massive blood loss.'

'What can you do about it?'

'Nothing,' Hardin said shortly. 'As far as I can see, there is no possible treatment at this stage. Oh, we could inject an agent that would make the blood clot once it leaves the body, but if the internal blood vessel walls are still leaking, that wouldn't help us much. Remember that Ebola has been known since the late nineteen seventies. It works very much like this new virus, but nobody has yet come up with any kind of a treatment. If somebody catches Ebola, all the medics can do is stick him into a secure biological isolation facility and wait for him to either die or recover. Most victims die,' he added, with a faint sad smile.

In the long silence that followed, the note of the helicopter's engines changed slightly and Richter glanced out of the side door. They were in descent towards a patch of open ground at the edge of Chaniá, and he spotted a white vehicle waiting in the road close by. Gravas pointed towards it. 'I asked the hospital to send transport to pick us up,' he said.

Two minutes later the aircraft was on the ground, the Merlin's rotors a solid blur above their heads as they climbed out of the rear compartment and strode across to the minibus.

### Réthymno, Crete

Stein had made up his mind. He'd been employed by the Company for a long time, and he knew the importance that the Agency attached to the success of its every mission. He couldn't just give up and walk away from the assignment: if he did, he'd be looking over his shoulder for the rest of his life. He had to deliver the case they had retrieved to McCready, but he was also determined not to take any unnecessary personal risks in doing so.

The first thing he had to do was hire another car. The Focus might be fine, might be uncontaminated, but he wasn't prepared to chance that. He'd hire a car, transfer the suitcase containing the steel case to it, and leave the Ford right where it was currently parked. That was step one.

Then he'd go back to the hotel and use Krywald's laptop to email McCready to arrange his pick-up from Crete. He could still be on his way off this island within twenty-four hours, easy.

He dropped some coins onto the table, stood up and headed back up the street towards the hotel.


## Chaniá, Crete

Richter wasn't interested in actually seeing Curtis, or whatever the man's real name was, for himself – he was quite happy to leave that to the expert, Hardin – but he was interested in knowing how he'd arrived at the hospital and what address, if any, had been given to the reception staff. Like every other foreign language apart from Russian, Greek was – quite literally in this case – all Greek to Richter, but with Gravas standing beside him to translate, he had no trouble in finding out what he wanted to know.

'This patient Curtis,' he asked, 'did he arrive here by himself?'

'Oh, no,' the receptionist volunteered eagerly. 'He was very, very weak, coughing and choking and with blood all over his face. He could hardly stand, so his friend had to almost carry him in here. We put him on a trolley and took him straight into one of the examination rooms – down the corridor there.'

Richter glanced in the direction she was pointing. 'This friend of his,' he asked, 'did he give you his name?'

The receptionist flicked back through a loose-leaf binder and ran a well-manicured finger down the hand-written entries. 'Yes,' she said. 'Here we are. He gave us Mr Curtis's details, and the address of the hotel they're staying at here in Chaniá. His name was Watson – Richard Watson.' She wrote both the names and the address of the hotel on a slip of paper and passed it over the desk.

'Can you remember what this Mr Watson looked like?'

The receptionist thought for a few seconds, then shook her head. 'I'm sorry,' she said. 'We were all so concerned about Mr Curtis that I don't think any of us paid too much attention to the other man.'

'That was easy, Mr Richter,' Gravas said as he turned away towards the corridor where Hardin was waiting.

'Far too easy,' Richter grunted. 'I'll bet this Watson character just gave her the name of a hotel he drove past on his way to the hospital, and Curtis and Watson are certainly going to be aliases. Wherever these two jokers have been staying I'm reasonably certain it isn't Chaniá. But at least it gives me somewhere to start.'

## Réthymno, Crete

The new car, which Stein had hired by using some of his own documents rather than those issued by the CIA, was a light blue Seat Cordoba. He'd wanted a saloon car – he'd actually asked for a 'sedan', which had just confused the booking clerk – because he had no intention of sharing the new vehicle with the steel case containing the flasks and their lethal contents. Though it might not make any practical difference, he wanted that case securely locked in the trunk, not sitting right behind him in the luggage compartment of a hatchback.

Stein drove the Seat into the half-empty car park at the back of his hotel and slotted it conveniently into the space next to the Ford Focus. He first glanced round the car park to ensure that he wasn't being observed, then pulled on a pair of surgical gloves and swiftly opened the boots of both vehicles.

Unfortunately, Stein hadn't looked around thoroughly enough. Mike Murphy wasn't actually in the car park itself, but was sitting in his own hire car about eighty metres up the street. He'd been waiting there for over an hour, using a set of compact but powerful binoculars to watch the Ford that Nicholson said had been originally hired by Krywald and Stein. He hadn't expected Stein to turn up in another vehicle, and Murphy wasn't quite sure now which car the American would be using, so he carefully noted the number and colour of the Seat as he continued observing Stein's activities.

His problem was that he was facing the fronts of the two cars. He could see that Stein had opened the boots of both vehicles, and was moving between the two, presumably transferring something from one to the other. But from his vantage point he couldn't identify what the American was shifting.

The black case was right where Krywald had left it earlier. Stein gingerly stretched out an arm to seize the handle, then lifted the case and placed it carefully inside a black rubbish bag, which he quickly sealed. Then he took another bag and repeated the procedure. With the outer one secured as well as he could make it, he carried it over to the blue Seat, dropped it into the boot and slammed the lid shut. He next pulled Krywald's briefcase and his own overnight bag out of the boot of the Ford, leaving his blood-stained jacket inside it, then secured the boot lid and finally pulled off and discarded his gloves. He wasn't intending to touch the case again, or even open the boot of the Seat, until he was ready to climb into whatever aircraft McCready would arrange to fly him off Crete.

In his hotel room, Stein put Krywald's briefcase on the desk and opened it. Then he stopped dead and backed away. The CAIP file that Krywald had been so insistent Stein should read was sitting right on top of the laptop computer. Obviously after he'd removed it from the steel case, he'd decided to keep it readily available so he could refer to it again. And sitting beside the laptop was a small stainless-steel flask, heavily sealed and with a faded label on its side.

For perhaps half a minute Stein just stared at the briefcase, remembering what Krywald had said earlier. There had been some sort of dust or dirt on the file cover, which his partner had brushed away with his hand, and that was why he was now lying in intensive care in the hospital at Chaniá, and there might still be some of the stuff lurking on or in the file, or elsewhere inside the briefcase. But Stein had to get the file out of there in order to make use of the laptop – because that was the only way he could contact McCready in the States.

He backed away further and sat down on the bed, his eyes still fixed on the open briefcase. Then he realized something that he had forgotten. When he and Krywald had entered those two houses in Kandíra, at least the first one of them had to have been full of virus particles, yet neither he nor Krywald had suffered any ill effects at that stage. And, Stein rationalized – unwittingly reaching almost the same conclusion as Tyler Hardin – the reason that they were not infected was that they had been wearing gloves and masks. Obviously the contaminants, whatever the hell they were, couldn't pass through the fabric or rubber.

Actually, Stein wasn't correct in the full detail of his deduction, because when active the virus particles could easily penetrate the comparatively coarse fabric of a mask, but that didn't matter now. The fact was that wearing a mask and gloves prevented any of the virus spores from coming into contact with the mucous membranes of the nose or mouth. The only risk was therefore to the eyes.

Stein got up off the bed and rummaged round in his case, finally pulling out a mask and surgical gloves, which he swiftly put on. Still cautious, he closed the lid of the briefcase slowly and carefully, so as not to disturb anything, and carried it through into Krywald's adjoining room. There, he placed it on the bed and opened it to face away from him. He then reached over the lid and used both hands to carefully remove the file and place it beside the briefcase. He did the same for the laptop and its power adaptor, the cable to connect it to the mobile phone, the phone itself, and finally the flask. Then he closed the briefcase and put it on top of the free-standing wardrobe in one corner of the room. He wouldn't touch it again and, as far as Stein was concerned, if some Cretan chambermaid spotted it and took it home with her, that was her lookout. He had his own almost identical case in the room next door, and everything could now go in that.

His most pressing need was for the laptop. Stein crossed into the en-suite bathroom and picked up a couple of small towels, then returned to the bed. He thoroughly wiped the external surfaces of the computer, always moving the towel away from him, then opened up the laptop and did the same to its screen and keyboard. He put the machine to one side, and in turn cleaned the power adaptor, all the leads and cables, the mobile phone, and the steel flask, just as carefully.

The file proved more difficult, but Stein did what he could, wiping the cover carefully before he opened it. Inside he could see no sign of anything that looked even slightly like the dust Krywald had described. Finally he picked up all the items and returned to his own room. He put everything down carefully on the desk, then closed and locked the connecting door: he wouldn't be entering that room again.

Stein plugged in the laptop computer and switched it on. He attached the mobile phone via the data cable and waited while the operating system loaded, then opened up Outlook Express and dialled the unlisted service provider they were using back in the States.

There were no emails waiting for Krywald, so Stein closed the connection and began composing his own message. It wasn't a long email.

He briefly advised McCready that the Learjet had been destroyed and that David Elias's body had been consigned to the deep. He assumed that Krywald had already told McCready that they'd retrieved the steel case from Kandíra, but he confirmed this information anyway. Then he explained how Krywald had opened the case, despite most explicit operational instructions, and was now lying in a critical condition in the Chaniá hospital.

When he'd finished he used the PGP encryption program to scramble the text, re-dialled the server and sent off the message. And all he could do then was wait for McCready to respond.

## Central Intelligence Agency Headquarters, Langley, Virginia

John Westwood spent some time jotting down notes on a piece of paper, trying to work out the criteria that had to apply to Mr X, which wasn't easy because he still didn't have a hell of a lot to go on.

What he knew for sure was that the unknown killer had to have been working for the Agency by 1971, and probably for at least a couple of years before that to have acquired sufficient experience to become involved in Operation CAIP. But he wasn't listed as one of the senior agents, all now dead, so it had probably been one of his first assignments. The other thing Westwood deduced was that he was either still employed by the CIA or had a very close associate who was. And because Mr X seemed determined to eliminate *anyone* who knew anything at all about CAIP, the 'associate' idea didn't really fly. Finally, he knew the man must be based at Langley or somewhere very close, because that area was where he was doing his killing.

The numbers bothered him. The Central Intelligence Agency employs just over twenty thousand full-time non-clerical staff, plus a virtually unlimited number of part-time specialists and consultants, as well as contract agents – normally just hired for one specific assignment because of their specialist knowledge or abilities – and regular support staff. With that large an organization, finding just one man was going to prove extremely difficult, but as far as Westwood could see it was the only avenue still open to him.

He nodded to himself at the realization, then rang the Personnel

Department. 'I need the names and departments of all CIA agents who joined the Agency in or before 1969, and who are still employed by us, but who are not currently on overseas assignments.'

There was a slightly stunned silence. 'Do you have any idea how much work that's going to take? I'm not even sure we can manage it.'

'I'm sure you'll find a way,' Westwood replied firmly. 'Just imagine I'm the head of a department, and that it's real urgent.'

'You *are* the head of a department.'

'So I am,' Westwood said. 'That should make it easier for you. And it *is* real urgent.'


### Réthymno, Crete

About an hour after Stein had sent off his email message to McCready, Mike Murphy was back in his hotel room, sitting at the desk and logging on to the same classified server, requesting a SITREP on the activities of the First Team.

He didn't have long to wait. Thirty minutes later he logged on again, downloaded, decrypted and then read the brief reply from America: 'Phase two complete. Elias dead. Krywald critically ill in Chaniá hospital. Stein has steel case. Recovery of case now Priority One task. Elimination of Krywald and Stein is Priority Two. Immediate executive action approved at your discretion.'

'OK,' Murphy muttered, and smiled as he shut down the laptop. 'Time to get this show on the road.'


### Chaniá, Crete

Richter's mobile rang as he was leaving the hospital. 'Hullo.'

'This is Mickey Mouse,' the quietly cultured voice said into his ear, and Richter immediately identified the first part of the recognition signal he himself had specified to Simpson.

'Summer Lightning,' Richter replied, giving the correct but completely unpredictable response.

'Charles Ross. I'm your friendly local representative. How can we help you?'

'Paul Richter. What phone are you using?' Richter moved off the pavement and well out of the way of any passers-by.

'Regular Nokia, I'm afraid,' Ross replied. 'We don't have all the facilities here we'd like, if you see what I mean.'

That was an irritation, nothing more. Encrypted phones only work if both parties are using them: as Ross only had a regular GSM mobile, Richter knew he would have to be circumspect in what he said and how he said it.

'First, I need to trace two Americans who have been staying here on the island. Their names are Roger Curtis and Richard Watson, and they've probably been here for a week or so.'

'Hotel or apartment?'

'Most likely a hotel,' Richter replied. 'They've probably also hired a car somewhere, and maybe a boat as well. They were planning to do some diving.'

'Deep diving with a somewhat explosive aviation connection, you mean?' Obviously Ross had been well briefed by SIS London, or per-haps had even heard direct from Simpson.

'Exactly. I've just heard that Curtis is hospitalized at Chaniá, and he's not going to be coming out for a while, maybe not ever, so I really do need to trace Watson.'

'OK,' Ross drawled, 'I'll get my people to look into it. Anything else you need?'

'Yes, as soon as you have a location for Watson, we need to meet so that we can pay him a visit. There are some things I need to discuss with him urgently.'

### Réthymno, Crete

Richard Stein had read more classified operation files than he could remember, but this CAIP business was a first for him.

It wasn't actually the file's contents that had alarmed him, because he frankly understood almost none of it. The whole file was full of detailed notes about medical procedures and inoculations, and the reactions from patients to those procedures. That part looked reassuringly harmless.

But at the very back of the file was an 'Executive Summary' of CAIP which pre-dated by about nine months all the other material contained in the file. This six-page summary explained in some detail exactly what CAIP involved and what it was intended to achieve. That bit was obviously what Krywald had read, and when Stein finished reading the last page, he knew exactly what his partner had meant – and he hadn't been exaggerating. If anybody outside the Central Intelligence Agency found out what CAIP was meant to achieve, Stein really could see a backlash of public opinion forcing the closure of the Agency. The fact that CAIP had been wound up over thirty years earlier meant nothing at all. Even if CAIP were to be made public in a hundred years from now, the result could well be the same.

Almost without conscious thought Stein took a pocket knife and sliced through the corner of the summary, removing it from the tag that had secured it to the file. Those six pages were dynamite, and he wondered if he could use them somehow to buy his safety and his freedom. After a moment, he folded them twice and shoved them to the bottom of the very back document pocket of his briefcase.

The actual mechanics of CAIP had been technically simple, barely even meriting the description of 'operation'. There had been no enemy, no resistance and no danger, in the conventional sense of the words. But the casualty figures made very impressive – or very distressing – reading, depending entirely upon the point of view of the reader.

At last Stein understood exactly why McCready had been so insistent that the aircraft must be completely destroyed, and why recovery of the case containing the file and remaining flasks was so vital.

He also realized there were two reasons why McCready had expressly instructed that the case be passed to him unopened. First, anyone who opened the case was clearly exposing himself to the deadly agent that lurked inside it. Roger Krywald knew that now, but it was far too late for him. The second reason was the file. Anyone reading the file and finding out what CAIP stood for, what the operation had comprised, became an immediate threat to the CIA itself.

Stein could guess exactly what kind of action McCready might take to eliminate that threat. And as Stein's last message had already confirmed that Krywald had opened the steel case, there could be little doubt that either Krywald or Stein, or maybe both of them, had read at least some of the incriminating file. Stein wished, briefly, that he'd taken a look at the file before he'd sent that message to McCready. But it was too late for that now.

No doubt there was already an assassination squad located somewhere on Crete, ready and waiting for an executive instruction to eliminate him. Since they had arrived on the island, neither he nor Krywald had bothered taking the usual precautions, simply because their task had seemed to be nothing more than a simple clean-up operation.

His knowledge of CAIP changed all that. He was going to have to start watching his back, remain aware of everything and everyone, otherwise he was likely to become just another statistic. Stein reached for the pistol in the waistband of his trousers, extracted the magazine and checked that it was fully loaded, slid it back into the butt of the SIG and worked the slide to chamber a round.

It would be a novel experience, he thought as he tucked the pistol back under his jacket, to be the prey rather than the hunter. He just had to ensure that it wouldn't be a terminal experience.


## Chaniá, Crete

The hospital staff at Chaniá had been very confused when Roger Krywald stumbled in through their doors. None of them had ever seen a case like this before. The American was bleeding from almost everywhere, but had no apparent external injuries. He was fast becoming delirious, and weakening steadily from loss of blood.

In the absence of any better ideas, they put him in a side-ward, placed a large sign on the door forbidding entry to anyone not directly connected with the patient's treatment, stationed an orderly outside to ensure this prohibition was enforced, and immediately started barrier nursing procedures. Nobody would go near him who wasn't wearing theatre scrubs, a waterproof apron, rubber boots, mask, protective goggles and two pairs of surgical gloves, one over the other. And as soon as they emerged from the side-ward they changed out of these garments, which were immediately bagged for disposal by burning. It wasn't quite as effective as an isolation ward, but the best they could manage in the circumstances.

The first thing the nursing staff did with the patient was cut the clothes off him and double-bag them for destruction by fire. With Krywald lying naked on the bed on a waterproof mattress covered by a thin cotton sheet, one doctor again checked his body for any lesions or other signs of violence, while a second ran his vital signs. What he found was pretty much what he could have predicted: weak pulse, low blood pressure, yet a surprisingly strong heartbeat.

They set up two saline drips, one in each arm, and because Krywald was beginning to thrash about they secured his wrists and ankles to the bed frame with soft fabric straps. He was in this condition, one of the doctors still in attendance, when Hardin and Gravas arrived.

When the orderly barred their access to the side-ward, Gravas quickly explained that his companion was an infectious diseases specialist, and needed to talk to the attending doctor immediately. As the orderly turned to rap on the glass window in the door, Hardin unzipped his bag and began pulling out his biological space suit.

As soon as the door opened, Gravas motioned to the orderly to move well clear as the doctor stepped out into the corridor. 'My name is Gravas,' he said, 'and with me here is an American specialist from the Centers for Disease Control in Atlanta. We believe this patient is suffering from the same viral infection that has already killed two men in the village of Kandíra.

'It's vital that you treat him as if he is highly contagious. I can see that you've already started barrier nursing, but you should also ensure there's no physical contact between the nurses and doctors involved.'

Hardin gestured that he was ready to have his biological suit sealed. 'Now,' Gravas said, 'Mr Hardin will enter the ward and examine the patient. Have you been recording his pulse and respiration?'

The Cretan doctor nodded. 'Since he arrived, his pulse has grown weaker and his blood pressure has been falling steadily. When I first saw him, he was delirious, and now he's unconscious.'

Gravas translated for Hardin's benefit. The American checked that his battery-driven blower was firmly attached to his belt, with the HEPA filter in place, then pushed open the door and stepped inside.

## Réthymno, Crete

Stein again checked the server for messages, though in view of what he now knew about CAIP he thought it unlikely that McCready would provide him with any way off this island outside a pine box. So he wasn't particularly surprised when he found nothing waiting for him.

He had to decide what to do now. Krywald was dying, might already be dead, and there was no way Stein was going to go back to the hospital to check on him. He also was going to have to be careful about leaving his hotel. McCready would almost certainly have sent a cleaner, perhaps even a team of them, to Crete, so it was possible that one was already sitting on the opposite side of the street watching the hotel entrance through the telescopic sight of a silenced sniper rifle.

Stein was going to have to use the rear entrance, maybe even wait until after dark before he could leave safely. The only other possibility was to exit in the middle of a large party of tourists, but the hotel currently didn't seem to have enough guests to make that a viable option.

Even when he got out, he wasn't sure where he could go: he couldn't return home without undergoing extensive facial surgery. But, no matter. Stein had always liked Europe, and he had funds salted away in various banks around the world so, while he wasn't exactly a rich man, he could certainly live fairly comfortably on his assets. And, if things got tight, he could always try peddling his knowledge of the inner workings of the CIA to some of the more anti-American European intelligence services – like the French, for example.

## Chaniá, Crete

'They're based in a hotel in Réthymno,' Ross explained as soon as Richter answered his mobile. 'I'm still in Irakleío, but I'm leaving in five minutes. I suggest we meet there in the town. Where are you now?'

'Right, I'm in Chaniá at the moment,' Richter replied, 'but I've got a room booked in Réthymno. How about we meet at my hotel?'

'Fine,' Ross said, 'give me the address.'

Richter's hire car, he belatedly remembered, was still over at Kandíra, so he hailed a taxi. After a short argument over the fare – the driver hadn't liked the idea of charging it on the meter, but Richter could be very persuasive when he wanted – he was en route to Réthymno along the main north-coast road.

# Chapter 21

**Friday**
**Chaniá, Crete**

Mike Murphy actually passed Richter's taxi on its way east towards Réthymno, as he himself approached the outskirts of Chaniá in his Peugeot. He had decided to take care of Krywald first, just in case the American staged some kind of miraculous recovery from whatever bug had attacked him. What he couldn't do was just wait around until Krywald died: Nicholson had been emphatic that there were to be no loose ends when Murphy left the island.

He left his car in a public parking area outside the hospital, headed in through the double doors and across to the receptionist. After some slight language difficulties, he was given directions to the ward where 'Mr Curtis' was confined.

But when he glanced in through the window while walking down the corridor under the suspicious gaze of the orderly standing outside, Murphy realized that his presence was probably both superfluous and pointless. Superfluous, because Krywald was quite obviously, even to untrained eyes, on the point of death, and pointless because there was no easy way he could get anywhere near the patient. At least, not from inside the building.

Ignoring the orderly, Murphy carried on along the corridor without breaking stride. A side-ward two doors down from Krywald's was empty and, after a swift glance around to check that nobody was watching, he pushed open the door and stepped inside. The room had a small bathroom attached, with just a toilet and a sink, and hanging from a rail was a light blue hand towel. Murphy grabbed it, stepped back into the main room and walked across to the window. He pushed it open, dangled the towel partly outside, then pulled the window closed to hold the towel in place. Now he had a useful marker.

For a few seconds Murphy peered out of the window, staring across the scrubby grass of the small and unused internal quadrangle towards the side of the building opposite, then he exited the side-ward and retraced his steps to the front entrance.

Two minutes later, outside the hospital, he headed quickly over to where he had parked his car. He opened the boot, reached inside and pulled his overnight bag towards him. Quickly checking that he was unobserved, he unzipped it and removed the Daewoo DP51, sliding it into the waistband of his trousers. He'd left the pistol in the boot just in case he'd had to pass through a metal detector to get access to the hospital. He felt around again inside the bag until his fingers touched the smooth cylindrical shape of the silencer: that went into his inside jacket pocket.

Murphy closed and locked the boot, turned back towards the hospital, but didn't approach the main doors. Instead, he walked around to the other side of the building, striding confidently as if he knew exactly where he was going, and made his way through a service entrance located over on the left-hand side of the hospital complex.

He possessed a good sense of direction and, once inside, followed a passageway leading to his right. It was lined on both sides with doors marked with signs in Greek, and more or less paralleled the corridor he'd followed in the main building. He had to push open half a dozen doors before he found what he wanted. The seventh door along stood slightly ajar and inside he glimpsed piles of dirty laundry: sheets, towels, gowns and other garments heaped everywhere.

He'd encountered nobody in the passageway, so it was the work of just a few moments to step inside, grab a slightly discoloured white surgical coat and slip it on over his jacket. There was no name tag, no convenient stethoscope to dangle around his neck, but Murphy wasn't concerned. All he wanted was something that made him look more as if he officially belonged, and in a hospital nothing works better than a doctor's white coat.

Another few metres along, the corridor ended in a T-junction. There, on his right, was what he'd been hoping to find: an unlocked door giving access to the small quadrangle that lay between the ward block and the utility wing.

On the other side of the patchy grass Murphy spotted the light blue towel moving slightly in a gentle breeze, then counted the windows positioned to the right of it, working out which one belonged to the room in which Krywald was being treated. He pulled the Daewoo pistol out of his waistband, checked that the magazine was fully loaded, then slammed it back in place. He screwed the silencer firmly onto the barrel, racked the slide back to chamber a round, set the safety catch, and replaced the pistol out of sight.

Only then did he step out and begin moving confidently along the perimeter of the quadrangle.


### Réthymno, Crete

'Understand we've got a bit of house-breaking to attend to?' Ross asked.

'It's a hotel rather than a house, but otherwise yes,' Richter replied. 'I hope you're good at picking locks,' he added, 'because I'm not.'

'All part of the basic training,' Ross nodded. 'It's part of the kit they give you when you join: exploding briefcase, Walther PPK, bullet-proof Aston Martin, that kind of thing.'

'Really?'

'No, not really,' Ross replied, 'but I have done the course, so unless this hotel is a lot more secure than most you find on Crete, it should be easy enough to get into their rooms.'

The two men had arrived at Richter's hotel almost simultaneously, going through the same recognition procedure in the street outside it as they'd followed during their previous telephone conversation. Ross was tall and slim with dark hair greying at the temples, and with a square, somewhat aggressive-looking moustache. He'd been here on Crete for two years, and now that his Greek had become pretty fluent he was confidently expecting a posting notice from SIS almost immediately, which would send him off to some other country where the locals spoke any language but Greek.

'The Royal Navy's much the same,' Richter confided, as they took chairs at a table outside a street café. 'The moment you're competent and comfortable in any job, they immediately post you somewhere else. So how did you locate the Americans' hotel?' he asked.

'It wasn't that difficult,' Ross replied. 'Some of the biggest and most expensive hotels employ their own computerized booking systems, while the really small ones don't bother with anything except telephone or fax reservations. So if they'd been staying in a hotel at either end of the spectrum it might have been awkward, but we guessed they'd probably go for a middle-priced place. The majority of the hotels on the island use the same central reservations system, and we've needed to hack our way into that several times before. It's not difficult, because the information contained isn't particularly sensitive or confidential.'

Ross switched to Greek to order two coffees from the waiter who had appeared beside their table, then continued in English. 'We searched for the names you gave me and came up with nothing, but in the circumstances that wasn't entirely surprising. Then we searched for any two American men who were not part of a large group travelling together, but were staying in the same hotel. That generated fewer matches than you might expect; only about a dozen, probably because it's low season here now. Finally we narrowed it down to just seven names.

'We then sent men out to check with the hotels those seven men were registered at. Four were in Irakleío itself, so it didn't take long to get the results. The first two men were a pair of elderly widowers doing Europe, and the other two were very obviously gay lovers. So unless the CIA has started recruiting poofs to do its dirty work, the two men you're looking for have got to be among the last three we identified – Roger Clyde, David Elias and Richard Wilkins. All three are staying right here in Réthymno. I know you're only looking for two men,' Ross added, 'but these three are apparently travelling together. Is it likely there might there be a third man involved?'

'That,' Richter brooded, 'could well make sense. When we located the wreck, the chopper picked up a body from the water. He'd been shot in the head and my guess is that he was a specialist diver who'd been recruited just to plant the explosives. Once he'd done his stuff, the others just blew his brains out.'

The waiter returned with their coffee and Richter paid the bill. 'And the hotel they're using?' he asked.

'It's just up the road,' Ross replied. 'We can go as soon as you're ready.'

## Chaniá, Crete

Tyler Hardin took a final look at the motionless figure, with wires and cables connecting him to a bank of monitoring equipment, then shrugged his shoulders and stepped over to the door of the side-ward. As he'd explained to Richter in the helicopter from Kandíra, there was no known treatment for the virus that was attacking the patient called Curtis. The American's pulse was markedly weaker than when Hardin had last checked it only a few minutes earlier and his blood pressure was now so low it was frankly miraculous that he was still alive. What blood remained in his veins and arteries was gradually seeping out of his ears, eyes, nose and mouth and, even though Hardin could neither see nor measure it, also into his abdominal cavity and internal organs. The man was dying in front of his eyes and Hardin was powerless to do anything to stop it.

He stepped out into the corridor, pulling the door closed behind him. Gravas and the orderly were waiting outside, and kept well away from Hardin's space-suited figure. Both were wearing surgical gowns, rubber boots, masks, gloves and protective goggles.

'Is he dead yet?' Gravas asked, his voice slightly muffled.

'No,' Hardin replied, 'but it won't be long now.' He turned back towards the side-ward and suddenly caught a glimpse of movement outside the external window beyond, which faced onto the grassy quadrangle. He fell silent and stared for a moment, then turned back to Gravas. Perhaps it had just been a bird flying past.


The instant the figure in the bulky orange suit had turned towards him, Murphy had ducked down below the level of the window sill. He didn't think he'd been spotted, and all he had to do now was finish the job.

He edged carefully upright against the concealing wall, then peered briefly through the adjacent window. The orange-clad figure was still out in the corridor, talking to two others wearing green surgical scrubs, but the ward itself was empty apart from the motionless figure of Roger Krywald.

For a moment, Murphy peered down at the bed inside, wondering if the man was already dead, if he was endangering himself for no purpose. But then he noticed Krywald's left hand twitch, and realized he had no option. He leaned back again, pulled out the Daewoo pistol and slipped off the safety catch, concealing the weapon behind his body and pointing it at the ground.

When he checked the ward again, the three figures out in the corridor had now moved away slightly, so Murphy knew that this was about the best chance he was likely to get. The window in front of him was armoured glass, designed to prevent any violent patient from jumping through it. Murphy knew he wouldn't be able to knock a hole in it easily, even with a rock, but it would offer almost no resistance to a 9mm Parabellum bullet.

Stepping slightly away from the wall, he aimed his pistol through the window at Krywald's still form. When he squeezed the trigger, the pistol coughed once, and a neat hole appeared in the window, surrounded by concentric rings of shattered glass. A brass cartridge case span through the air, as the second round was chambered by the recoil action, and Murphy watched Krywald's body shudder with the impact.

He sighted and fired again, this bullet striking Krywald's chest within two inches of the first wound, then ducked down below the level of the window, his eyes scanning the ground. Murphy picked up one cartridge case, then found the second, and put them carefully into his jacket pocket. He slid the pistol back into the rear waistband of his trousers, under his jacket, crouched low until well clear of the side-ward windows, then he stood upright and headed calmly back the way he had come.

He'd been out there in the grassy quadrangle for less than ninety seconds, and the first of his Priority Two tasks was successfully completed.

### Réthymno, Crete

'Are their rooms likely to be kept guarded?' Ross asked. The two men had moved further down the street and were now standing about a hundred yards away from the hotel.

'There's no reason why they should be,' Richter said. 'My guess is that we found one of the three already shot by his companions after he'd completed the diving for them, and another is dying in the hospital in Chaniá. That just leaves contestant number three, the guy who gave his name as Richard Watson at the hospital, and who's probably shitting himself in case he might be infected with the same bug that's killing Curtis. So my guess is that guarding his room will be the last thing on his mind. He'll be looking for a way off this island really fast, and it's even possible that he may already have left.'

'So you reckon we can just walk in?'

'I hope so,' Richter muttered.

'OK. I'll go up first and inspect the lock. Unless there's a problem, I'll open the door and check out the room. You'd better stay in the hotel lobby as a look-out.'

'Fine with me,' Richter said.

'And we're looking for what, exactly?' Ross let the question hang in the air.

'That,' Richter confessed, 'is the awkward bit. I really don't know. And there may be nothing there to find anyway if our third man has already legged it. Whatever it is, it's got to be reasonably small if it can be pulled out of a submerged plane wreck and carried to the surface by a solo diver. So it's probably a small box or chest, and possibly they've already put it in a briefcase or suitcase, that kind of thing.'

'OK,' Ross said grimly, 'let's do it.'

### Chaniá, Crete

Shrill alarms from the cardiac and EEG monitors echoed along the hospital corridor as Krywald's heart stopped beating. Hardin span back towards the door of the ward and wrenched it open. He registered instantly the flat lines running across both ECG and EEG displays and knew immediately that the patient was dead. There was obviously no point in considering resuscitation, so Hardin walked across to the left of the bed and switched off the equipment. Instantly the alarms fell silent.

Though expecting it since he'd first stepped into the patient's room, it was, like every other death he'd witnessed in his career, still something of a shock to him. He stepped closer to the bed and stared down at Curtis's body. On looking more closely, he spotted the two open wounds in the left side of the patient's chest. Bullet wounds were something he rarely saw, but Hardin had not the slightest trouble identifying them.

He swung round as quickly as the space suit would let him, searching for the assailant who he suspected, for an instant, might still be hidden somewhere in the ward with them. Then he saw the two rings of broken glass in the window with the bullet-holes in the centre of them, and realized that the killer had struck from outside.

He stepped across to the window and cautiously peered through it, but the grassy quadrangle was deserted. Whoever had killed the mysterious Curtis had already made good his escape.

### Central Intelligence Agency Headquarters, Langley, Virginia

'Is that Mr Westwood?'

'Yes, Dr Grant,' Westwood recognized the voice immediately. 'You've got the autopsy results already?'

'No, no. The procedure won't be completed for another half-hour or so, and then we'll have to wait for the toxicology results. But I thought you'd be interested to know that you were right. Henry Butcher was murdered.'

Westwood's reply didn't sound even slightly surprised. 'But how do you know that if the autopsy isn't finished?'

'Simple,' Grant replied. 'After we last talked, I made a point of examining Mr Butcher's room and the equipment contained in it. As you probably noticed, he was receiving saline solution through an intravenous drip, and I noticed a tiny discolouration in the bottle. Saline solution is, of course, completely clear. So I checked the seal on the bottle and found a puncture, the kind that could be made by a hypodermic needle. I immediately had the contents analysed, and the lab found traces of a vegetable alkaloid.' Grant paused, as if in triumph.

'Thank you, Dr Grant,' Westwood said. 'I'd like to hear the final analysis result when you have it, but my guess is that you'll find Butcher was killed by a dose of coniine. That seems to be our mystery man's preferred modus operandi.'

# PANDEMIC

## Réthymno, Crete

Richard Stein had decided on two things. First, he wasn't going to wait around any longer than necessary in the hotel at Réthymno, which meant he had to sneak out the back way, climb into his hire car and, as they say in the old westerns, get out of town. He was reasonably certain that neither McCready nor anybody else could have linked the Seat to him, because he'd paid for it using cash, and the credit card that the hire company had swiped as security had come from the private stash of documents that he always carried with him.

The second priority was to make a final check of any emails waiting for him on the server in America, just in case there was anything he could use. Just moments after he logged on, he sat reading an email from McCready with an escalating feeling of disbelief.

It didn't exactly say *come home: all is forgiven*, but it certainly sounded like the next best thing. The message specified a route for him off Crete, courtesy of the US Navy, or at least a US Navy frigate that was even then approaching the island from the west, after a helicopter pick-up from the coast the following afternoon. McCready expressed his brief regrets about Krywald, then reiterated that the steel case should remain sealed for Stein's own protection. Stein had no problem with that request, but he was surprised that McCready had apparently decided not to eliminate him immediately. And he reckoned he'd be safe enough on a US Navy vessel – McCready surely couldn't have suborned the entire crew – and if he felt unhappy about things once he got on board, he would probably have the chance to leave the ship and get himself ashore somewhere in Europe.

The trick, however, would be climbing into that helicopter without getting his brains blown out. Stein wasn't stupid, so he realized immediately that McCready's arrangement meant that the following afternoon his location would be both known and fixed, giving an ideal opportunity for a sniper to take him down. Clearly he would have to take extreme precautions in checking out the rendezvous well before the chopper arrived.

In the meantime, there was nothing to stop him getting out of this hotel and finding somewhere else to spend his last night on Crete.

*

Ross and Richter entered the hotel at more or less the same instant that Richard Stein shut down his laptop computer. Richter turned left and walked into the coffee shop where he found a vacant seat that offered a good view of the lobby, lifts and stairs. He watched as Ross strode across to the two adjacent elevators. As he waited for the lift to arrive, Ross dialled a number on his mobile phone and then slipped it into his jacket pocket.

Richter's phone rang – a new unit supplied by Ross for the duration of this operation. He picked it up and answered it. 'Richter.'

'Ross. Loud and clear.'

His voice *was* exceptionally clear through the lightweight hands-free headset that he had donned just before entering the hotel. It would allow him to keep in constant contact with Richter, while leaving both hands free to carry out his searches.

Just then the lift arrived, and Ross stepped inside. Richter watched as the doors slid closed. 'Going up,' Ross muttered, and seconds later Richter clearly heard the sound of the elevator doors sliding open. 'Third floor,' Ross said. 'I'll start with 301.'

The hotel booking computer system had shown the three American guests as occupying one single room on the third floor, number 301, and on the other side of the corridor two adjoining rooms with connecting doors, numbers 306 and 308.

'Roger.' Richter glanced around the lobby. 'Clear at this end.'

The hotel doors had key-locks, rather than the more modern, and more difficult to crack, electronic card-locks. Ross knocked firmly on the door of 301, calling out 'Room Service' in Greek, but received no response. He checked up and down the corridor, then knelt beside the door and studied the lock. 'Standard three-lever, by the looks of it,' he murmured into the headset microphone. 'Shouldn't be a problem.'

He took a small leather pouch out of his jacket pocket, unzipped it and extracted two thin stainless-steel tools. He slipped one into the lock and exerted slight turning pressure on the barrel with his left hand, then slid the other, L-shaped tool inside and began probing for the tumblers. After a few moments there were three faint but distinct clicks, and suddenly the lock began to turn.

Ross opened the door a crack, again checked the corridor in both directions, then slipped into the room. 'I'm in,' he announced. In the lobby below, Richter heaved a sigh of relief. 'It looks like the occupant is still booked into the hotel,' Ross continued. 'The room's tidy and the bed's been made up, but there are clothes folded over the back of the chair and' – Richter faintly heard the sound of a door opening – 'in the wardrobe as well. Also, there's an empty overnight case on the suit-case stand.'

'Any idea whose room it is?' Richter asked.

'There's nothing on the overnight case,' Ross replied. 'No labels apart from the airline baggage reclaim chits. Oh, hang on. There's a book here on the bedside table. Yes. This room appears to be occupied by David Elias. He's obviously paranoid about people nicking his paperbacks, so he's stuck a label on the inside front cover: David H. Elias, with an address in Virginia. Likely a Company man, eh?'

'Almost certainly,' Richter said, 'but my guess is Mr Elias is no longer with us. He's probably the diver they brought over to plant the explo-sives, and what's left of him is now helping the Cretan police force with its inquiries.'

'Makes sense,' Ross said. 'The two professionals would logically be the ones to take the adjoining rooms.'

'This third man,' Richter observed, 'was probably never considered a full member of the team. He was just some poor sod who got sucked into this mission because he happened to be a qualified diver.'

'Bit of a cliché, the third man, especially bearing in mind who we both work for,' Ross replied. 'Right, that means I'm probably wasting my time hunting for your case in here. I'll now try number 306.'

'Just be careful.' Richter resumed his scrutiny of the lobby.


Decision now made, Stein had spent ten minutes stuffing his clothes and other personal gear into his carry-on overnight bag, and the com-puter, its accessories and the file into his briefcase. Then he shrugged on his lightweight jacket, picked up the SIG P226 and tucked it, the silencer still attached, into the rear waistband of his trousers.

He picked up his carry-on bag with his left hand – he wanted his right hand free in case he needed to use the SIG, which meant he was going to have to make two journeys to carry down both his overnight bag and the briefcase. He walked across to the door and listened carefully. Then he opened it, looked swiftly up and down the corridor, pulled it closed and set off towards the rear stairs leading to the car park.

Almost immediately after Stein had vanished down the back stairs, Ross shut the door of room 301 behind him. He stopped outside number 306, knocked firmly and again announced himself as Room Service. When he got no reply he pulled his lock-picking kit out of his pocket and got busy. Two minutes later he was inside.

'More or less the same story in here,' he reported. 'The room's obviously been recently occupied, though there don't seem to be any clothes or personal effects. But there's a briefcase still sitting on the end of the bed.'

'That might be it,' Richter said. 'Better check it out.'

For a few seconds Richter heard nothing, then two faint clicks. 'Right,' Ross said, 'the briefcase wasn't locked. I've just opened it and lifted the lid. Inside there's a laptop computer, a red file marked – oh, that's interesting.'

'What?' Richter demanded.

'The file is classified "Ultra". I've never seen an Ultra before.'

'Neither have I,' Richter murmured. 'What's the filename?'

'No name, just the initials "CAIP" – that's Charlie Alpha India Papa. There's also a mobile phone, various leads and cables, and a small vacuum flask.'

'What, for his coffee?'

'No.' Ross sounded preoccupied. 'This one's small and light, and it's been very heavily sealed.'

'Shit,' Richter said. 'Charles, is the seal broken? Please check very carefully.'

There was a silence that seemed to stretch into minutes. 'No,' Ross finally replied, 'the seal's intact. The top's covered first with red wax and that's got a tight-fitting wire mesh securing it.'

'OK, whatever you do, don't break that seal. The chances are that flask contains the same stuff as the one the Greek diver cut open in Kandíra. It killed both him and his nephew.'

'No problem there,' Ross muttered. 'I'm putting it back in the case right now.'

'Before you do, are there any letters or numbers or symbols on the flask itself?'

'Yes,' Ross replied, holding up the flask and peering at it carefully. 'It's got a plain white label with "CAIP" written on it, and below that a figure ten.'

'CAIP again? What the hell does it mean?'

'No idea,' Ross replied, his full attention now concentrated on the contents of the briefcase. He didn't hear Stein slide his key into the lock, or the faint noise as the American turned the door handle.


Richard Stein stepped into his hotel room, intent on simply picking up the remainder of his stuff and getting the hell out of Réthymno. The first thing he saw as he entered was a stranger bent over his briefcase and pawing through its contents.

When Ross heard the sound of the door behind him, he stood up and spun round to face the interruption. Stein took in the scene before him in an instant. The sight of an intruder, already ransacking his briefcase, wearing a headset obviously linking him to an accomplice somewhere outside, added up to only one thing: this man had to be a member of the clean-up squad McCready had sent to Crete to eliminate him.

Before Ross could say a word, Stein pulled out the silenced SIG automatic pistol, sighted down the barrel and pulled the trigger. The single bullet hit Ross square in the chest, slicing straight through his heart. He dropped to the floor, killed instantly.

Stein stepped forward warily, with gun-hand extended, conscious that there might be another assassin in the bathroom. He checked both rooms thoroughly before bending over Ross's body, looking for the weapon he was sure he would find there.

He discovered instead a mobile telephone, and pulled it out of the dead man's inside jacket pocket. Ripping out the hands-free lead, he studied the display. The line was still open, so he pressed the 'end' button to cancel the connection, then used redial to display the last number called. He didn't recognize it, but he didn't expect to, but he did note that it was a Cretan mobile number. That confused him for a moment, because he'd been expecting to see an American number, but then, he rationalized, the clean-up team would probably be equipped with local mobiles.

He tossed the phone aside and ran his hands over Ross's body. He repeated his search, then sat back, puzzled. An unarmed member of a clean-up team – that didn't make any sense. So who was this guy? He pulled open the dead man's jacket and examined the label sewn inside it. That only puzzled him even more.

Stein shrugged and stood up. He was probably never going to find out anyway, but it was time he was somewhere else. He slammed down the briefcase lid, snapped the catches shut, picked it up and walked out of the room. He pulled closed the door behind him and jogged lightly away down the corridor.

# Chapter 22

**Friday**
**Réthymno, Crete**

Richter heard what he thought was a cough in his earpiece and ignored it, but then the crash as Ross's body hit the floor told him that something had gone badly wrong. He said nothing and listened acutely, but the sounds he now heard made no immediate sense – a rustling noise, a door opening, a couple of footsteps. Next heavy breathing and then Ross's phone was abruptly switched off, which told him pretty much all he needed to know. Obviously contestant number three had returned to his room. The more he re-ran the sequence of sounds in his mind, the more that cough had sounded like the report of a silenced pistol.

Richter started to move: out of the coffee shop and across the lobby to the main stairs and lifts. Not running, because that could attract unwanted attention, but moving quickly and smoothly. He ignored the lifts – they would just be too slow – and took the stairs. As he reached the first floor, he stopped dead.

Apart from two tiny chambermaids, arms full of linen, he had seen nobody else using either the stairs or the lifts since his colleague had ascended to the third floor. That meant there had to be a back staircase, something neither he nor Ross had investigated earlier. Hindsight was always a wonderful comfort.

On the first-floor landing, Richter looked in both directions. About ten feet away, he spotted a notice in red lettering screwed to the wall, and ran over to study it. It was an emergency evacuation plan, in four languages, complete with a diagram of the hotel's entire floor layout. A fire escape and rear staircase were indicated at the end of the right-hand corridor.

Richter turned and ran, crashed through the fire doors at the far end and began scrambling as quickly as he could down the stairs. As he

357

reached the bottom and pushed open the outside door, he was just in time to see a light blue Seat saloon – maybe a Cordoba or a Toledo – swing left out of the opposite side of the car park and accelerate hard along the adjoining street and out of sight.

Richter pulled a small notebook and ballpoint pen out of his pocket and made a brief note, then headed back inside the hotel and climbed the stairs to the third floor. The door to room 306 was closed and had automatically locked. Unlike Charles Ross, Richter had no lock-picking skills, but he was in no mood to wait around for somebody with a pass-key. He stepped back from the door and kicked it hard, with the flat of his foot, right above the lock. The door creaked but held firm.

The third time his foot hit it, the door crashed open and Richter stepped inside, his Browning 9mm pistol cocked and safety catch off, held out in front of him in the classic two-handed combat grip. He saw Ross lying motionless on the floor at the foot of the bed and stepped across to him. One glance at the surprisingly small dark red stain in the centre of his chest told the whole tale, but Richter checked for a pulse anyway. Two minutes later he left the room, went down the stairs and out through the lobby.

He crossed the street to a café, sat down at a table and ordered a coffee from the waiter. He then pulled out his mobile phone and note-book, checked the emergency contact number Ross had given him earlier for the duty SIS officer and dialled. A voice answered on the second ring.

'This is Summer Lightning,' Richter said. 'I need a clean-up team at the hotel in Réthymno. Mickey Mouse didn't make it.'


### Central Intelligence Agency Headquarters, Langley, Virginia

John Westwood was pleased at the speed with which the Personnel Department managed to generate the information he wanted, but unpleasantly surprised by the number of names on the list. Over two and a half thousand people fitted his initial criteria, and he knew he'd have to whittle that number down considerably before he could start any kind of a detailed investigation.

He picked up the internal phone and dialled Personnel. 'Thanks for the listing,' he said, 'but I need to apply some filters to reduce it to a manageable size. Using the information you've supplied as a base, eliminate all agents known to be currently on vacation outside the continental United States, also those who are hospitalized, and any known to be incapacitated. By that I mean people recovering at home from a broken leg or in long-term care, that kind of thing. Some guy who rang in last Tuesday claiming he had a migraine doesn't count.'

Thirty minutes later a new print-out lay on his desk, but there were still just over eighteen hundred names left, far too many to make a search feasible.

Westwood pondered for some time before he applied the next obvious filter, simply because he wasn't sure he was wise to do so. He had no idea exactly where the killer was based, but wherever it was it had to be within fairly easy reach of the state of Virginia. Instinctively, Westwood thought Mr X was probably sitting in an office in the same building at Langley as himself right then, but that was an assumption he certainly couldn't rely on.

So he made his decision and called Personnel again. 'Now eliminate all those based outside Washington, DC, Maryland and Virginia,' he ordered.

After four hours of successive filters, he had whittled the listing down to fifty-seven people, and couldn't think of anything else to reduce the number any further. So now it was just down to footwork, checking the personnel file of each agent in turn.


**Réthymno, Crete**

Three minutes after he'd terminated his call to the duty SIS officer, Richter's mobile rang.

'This is Tyler Hardin, Mr Richter, and I've got some news for you.'

'Let me guess,' Richter said. 'The man calling himself Curtis is dead?'

'Correct, but that isn't the news I think you'll want to hear. Curtis was going to die anyway: maybe this afternoon, maybe tonight, but he certainly wouldn't have seen tomorrow. No, the news is that somebody wasn't prepared to wait for this pathogen to take its course. The virus didn't kill Curtis – someone with a pistol did that.'

Richter wasn't often lost for words, but that stumped him for a moment. 'Let me get this straight,' he said. 'Curtis was unconscious, even comatose, and due to die within a few hours, no matter what, and somebody still felt they had to eliminate him? That makes no sense.'

'Tell me about it,' Hardin replied, 'but there's no doubt about what happened. I've just pulled two nine-millimetre slugs out of the victim's chest, and the local police have taken them away for testing. I'll let you know what they come back with, if anything.'

'Thanks, Tyler. I wish I could say I knew what the hell is going on here.'

Hardin laughed briefly. 'Join the club.'

## Western Crete

Stein knew he was running for his life. He was still uncertain exactly how he stood with McCready, but he guessed that he was now a disposable asset and that McCready would have him killed as soon as he'd handed over the crucial file and the flasks. That was one problem.

Another problem was the dead man he'd left behind him in the hotel at Réthymno. He had no idea who he was, but the label inside his jacket had been sewn there by a tailor in London's Jermyn Street and, although far from conclusive, it did at least suggest that the man was a Brit.

Whoever he was, Stein guessed that by now the Cretan police would have been called in and furnished with a description of Stein himself, and maybe even a photofit, by the hotel desk clerk. So he was going to have to rigorously avoid making eye contact with the local cops until he could get off this island.

The mystery dead man also meant that he dare not risk trying to catch a passenger ferry or regular airline flight out of Crete, because the police would be watching out for him at all the ports and airports. It was looking more and more likely, therefore, that he was going to have to accept McCready's highly suspect offer of a helicopter flight to the US Navy frigate. That didn't please Stein at all.

In fact, about the only good news in his life right then was that at least he still felt fine, so he presumed that his rudimentary precautions earlier had prevented the lethal virus from infecting him. In the circumstances that was a very, very small consolation.

Stein had no clear idea where he was heading, except away from Réthymno. He'd swung the rented Seat out of the hotel car park as quickly as he dared, just in case the dead man's colleagues might guess where he was heading. He hadn't seen anyone as he'd accelerated away, but that didn't mean that somebody hadn't spotted him leave.

Within minutes of driving away from the hotel he'd joined the main north-coast road and headed west towards Chaniá. If he was going to take a chance on the pick-up McCready claimed to have arranged, at least Chaniá, or even somewhere further west, meant a shorter distance to drive the following afternoon. The email had specified a pick-up point north of the road heading to the coastal area, beyond Plátanos, on the extreme west side of the island.

## Réthymno, Crete

Martin Fitzpatrick, the SIS officer Richter had been told to expect, turned up within twenty minutes and sat himself down heavily next to Richter at the café. He'd been out on the road when he'd been briefed by the duty officer over a secure radio circuit, and had broken every speed limit ever imposed to get to Réthymno.

Richter explained briefly what had happened, and that Ross was dead. Just as he finished, they heard the whine of police sirens getting closer. Richter guessed that somebody passing had peered into room 306 and seen Ross's body lying on the floor.

'I think the shit's about to hit the fan,' Fitzpatrick murmured. 'I'd better get over there and try to calm things down. I think I can assure the local fuzz that this is an entirely external matter, not involving anyone local, apart from poor old Charles Ross, and he's in no position to make a fuss.'

'One thing before you go.' Richter pulled out his notebook. 'I'm fairly sure the guy we're looking for is driving a blue Seat saloon, and I've got a partial plate number. It's almost certainly a hire car, rented within the last three or four days. Can you ask your police friends to get me the whole plate number and then issue a watch order for both the vehicle and occupant. I don't want this man approached, however. He's running and he's likely to shoot first, and second, and not bother asking any questions. What I want to know is where he's located now. He's almost certainly left Réthymno, but he's likely to have checked in to a hotel somewhere else. If they can find out where he is, even where his car's parked, I'll handle it from there.'

Though it was a bright sunny day, something about the way Richter uttered those last few words sent a chill up Fitzpatrick's spine. 'When you say "handle it", can I assume this renegade American won't be bothering us here any more?'

'You assume correctly,' Richter said, his face hard and unsmiling. 'I brought Charles Ross into this mess, and now he's dead because he was doing his job. That makes his death my responsibility, at least by implication. The man who killed him won't just walk away from this, that I can promise you.'

Just then two police cars arrived outside the hotel opposite and squealed to a halt, their sirens dying away in a discordant duet. Four officers scrambled out and ran into the hotel entrance. Murder's a fairly rare crime on Crete, and Richter assumed they were all eager to take a good first look at the victim.

'Right,' Fitzpatrick concluded, 'I'll see what I can do. Can you hang on here until I've got things sorted out across the road?'

Richter nodded. 'Until you find me this bastard's location, I've got nowhere else to go.' As Fitzpatrick crossed the street towards the hotel, he heard Richter summon a waiter and order another cup of coffee and a *baklava*.


## Between Kolymvári and Réthymno, Crete

Mike Murphy had just passed the north-bound turning for Georgioúpoli, heading back towards Réthymno, when he spotted the light blue Seat Cordoba travelling in the opposite direction. Murphy had extremely good eyesight and immediately recognized the Seat's registration number. It helped that he'd been expecting to see the car, having been copied Stein's pick-up instructions by Nicholson.

He did nothing until the Seat had got about a quarter of a mile behind him, then he hauled the Peugeot round in a U-turn and floored the accelerator pedal. He didn't know exactly where Stein was going, but he figured that the target was on his way to a new location somewhere on the western end of the island, and closer to where the helicopter would land the following day. Murphy guessed that Stein had the case and file with him, and the easiest option was to follow his target and find out where he was going next. Then he could choose his moment for eliminating the man and completing the job.

But Stein was a fellow professional, and would certainly be constantly watching his mirrors. The traffic was light, which didn't help, so once Murphy had got close enough to double-check the Seat's registration number, he dropped back steadily until he was about five hundred yards behind. There he hovered, close enough to keep visual contact with the Cordoba but hopefully too far behind for Stein to become aware of his presence.

The problem came when the Seat approached the turning for Máleme, in now thickening traffic. Murphy found himself sandwiched between two tour buses and the lorry that they were slowly overtaking, and by the time he could clearly see the road ahead of him again, the blue Seat was no longer in sight.

Murphy accelerated hard, just in case Stein had increased his speed, but by the time he reached the junction for Kolymvári he knew that his quarry must have pulled off the road earlier, probably heading into Máleme.

He cursed, swung the Peugeot off into Kolymvári and then back onto the main road, heading east. He'd just have to check every possible turning and hope that he spotted the Seat again before Stein dumped it.

### Central Intelligence Agency Headquarters, Langley, Virginia

John Westwood had been shelving the vast majority of his regular work ever since the briefing he'd attended in Walter Hicks's office, but he'd now reached the point where he had to stop trying to track down the shadowy figure lurking behind the deaths of James Richards, the Hawkins couple and now Henry Butcher, and do some real work.

The killing of Butcher had to some extent brought the current phase of the investigation to an end. Butcher had been the last CIA officer known to be involved in Operation CAIP. It was a reasonable assumption that there would be no more killings, simply because nobody else currently or previously employed by the Company knew about CAIP. Apart from the killer, of course, and Westwood was still determined to find him, one way or the other.

But there was simply too much other important stuff piling up in his in-tray for him to ignore it any longer. Some of it he could pass on to his deputies and assistants, but most of it he couldn't: he was a head of department here and he had greater responsibilities than just tracking down Mr X.

Once he had the personnel files on the remaining fifty-seven possible suspects delivered to his office, he put them straight into his wall safe and locked it. He'd start reading through them the following morning, hopefully with a clearer pair of eyes after a good night's sleep – and with less subconscious pressure if he could manage to clear some of the routine stuff that was awaiting his attention.

So he pulled his in-tray towards him and got to work.


### Máleme, Crete

Murphy's deduction had been correct: Stein had pulled off the main north-coast road and headed into Máleme. He drove around for a few minutes, getting a feel for the layout of the town, located on the south coast of Chaniá Bay, then stopped on the western outskirts.

He found a tiny hotel well away from any of the usual tourist areas and paid in cash, in advance, which avoided him having to use any personal documentation. He booked two nights' bed and breakfast, though he knew he would be leaving early the following afternoon. He wasn't prepared to wait around in the hotel's tiny lobby after being forced to vacate his room in the morning.

As a precaution, he parked the Seat in a car park a couple of hundred yards down the road and carried his two bags the short distance back to the hotel. The room he chose was on the first floor at the rear, right next to a circular metal fire escape that ran down from the top floor to the ground, in case he needed another way out in a hurry.

He debated for a while about getting rid of the Seat, just in case it had been spotted back in Réthymno, but he decided not to. He would only have to use it for one more journey, the following afternoon, and he believed he would be exposed to far more risk of being identified if he tried to hire or steal another car.

Stein plugged the laptop and the mobile phone into power sockets for recharging. He might well have to use one or the other the following day after he'd left the hotel. Then he jammed the back of a chair under the door handle, stripped off and ran a bath. He took the SIG into the bathroom with him, just in case.

## Réthymno, Crete

Forty minutes later Martin Fitzpatrick walked back across the street and sat down next to Richter. 'We make progress,' he said. 'They had to get it cleared with their powers that be, which is why it took so long, but they'll be taking no further official action over the incident. If anyone pushes them they're going to claim that it was accidental death. Ross was entitled to carry a firearm in certain circumstances, although we both know he wasn't armed today, so the official position will be that it was an accidental discharge with no third-party involvement.'

Fitzpatrick pushed a piece of paper across the table. 'They've tracked down the full registration number of the Seat. You were right: it's a Cordoba and it was hired a short while ago here in Réthymno by an American tourist called George Jones.'

Richter nodded. 'That's a new name, of course, but I've no doubt it's the same man.'

'Right. The Cretan police have put out a watch order for the car itself, but a hands-off instruction for the driver, as you requested. As soon as anybody spots it I'll let you know. Where are you going to be for the rest of the day?'

'Right here in Réthymno,' Richter said. 'I've got a room at a hotel about half a mile up the street. I'm going to hire a car this afternoon so that I'm able to get moving immediately, but until I hear from you, I'll be staying at that hotel. I'll have the mobile Ross gave me switched on at all times.'

Fitzpatrick stood up and extended a hand. 'Good to meet you,' he said. 'Just a shame about the circumstances. I'll be in touch.'

As the SIS officer walked away, Richter's mobile rang.

'Richter.'

'Tyler Hardin,' the voice said. 'I don't know if it's much help to you, but I've been passed a preliminary report about the weapon used to kill Curtis.'

'Wait one,' Richter murmured, putting the mobile down on the table. He pulled a ballpoint pen and notebook from his pocket and prepared to write. 'Go ahead,' he said.

'OK, Curtis was killed by two bullets from a nine-millimetre weapon, presumably a pistol. The local forensic laboratory has only been able to state what weapons within that calibre didn't fire them.'

'Which were?' Richter asked.

'OK, this isn't my field, so I'm reading from a list here. The two bullets I pulled out of Curtis's chest had six grooves and a right-hand twist, like those fired by just about every other 9mm pistol that's ever been built. The weapons that couldn't have fired them include a Glock; Steyr; some of the Czech CZ models; Heckler and Koch; most of the Russian pistols like the Makarov and Tokarev; most Chinese pistols; Colts; and the old Luger. Colts have six grooves but a left-hand twist in the rifling, and all the others have a different number of grooves, usually four, or a strange barrel shape like the hexagonal thing on the Glock. Does any of that make any sense to you?'

'Yes,' Richter said. 'It makes perfectly good sense, but it doesn't help much. It just means whoever killed Curtis wasn't helpful enough to use some kind of more unusual weapon that could help me to identify him.'

### Máleme, Crete

Stein sat down on the edge of the rather hard bed and looked at the map that he'd spread out beside him. The laptop computer was perched next to the bed on an upright chair, the screen again displaying the email he'd received earlier that day from McCready. He'd read the text at least half a dozen times and still wasn't sure about it.

It was just about possible that McCready was prepared to play it straight. The single, and unquestionable, advantage that Stein had was actual possession of the steel case containing the flasks and the Company file. To recover those items, he believed McCready would go to almost any lengths, so he was fairly certain that a helicopter from the US Navy frigate would appear at the pick-up point specified. What he wasn't sure about was who else might have been told to turn up at that rendezvous, and what their orders might be.

The problem was, Stein couldn't actually see what other options he had. Before he'd shot that unknown man in his hotel room, there had been at least a chance he could have tried slipping away from Crete by air or ferry, but the killing had precluded that. The Cretan police would by now have both a good verbal description of him and a copy of his passport photograph, since the hotel clerk in Réthymno had photo-copied all three of their passports as they'd checked in. The fact that the name on that passport wasn't the same as the one he was currently using was, in that context, irrelevant. If the police had done nothing else meanwhile, they would at the very least ensure that all the port and air-port officials would have his picture sitting on view right in front of them.

One alternative he had considered was to hire or steal a boat and sail it up towards the Greek mainland. But Stein knew that his own abilities fell far short of what was required: just getting that open boat back to Chóra Sfakia after the dive had taxed him to the limit.

So, despite the inevitable risks, he really had no option but to turn up at McCready's rendezvous. He'd be sure to get there early, take every possible precaution, and watch his back as best he could. If he even made it as far as the chopper, he'd feel safe. Until then, Stein was going to be living on his nerves.

## Réthymno, Crete

Sitting in the hotel bar late that afternoon, a coffee cup, a bottle of water, a glass, two mobile phones and an unopened novel arranged in front of him, Richter had come to broadly the same conclusions as Stein, and for pretty much the same reasons. The Cretan police were probably not as efficient or as organized as some other European forces, but they'd had plenty of practice in locking down all the regular routes off their island.

The only way Richard Watson or George Jones, or whatever his real name was, could get off Crete was if somebody arranged some kind of a clandestine pick-up for him, and that probably meant either a boat or a helicopter. Fortunately, Richter was in a pretty good position to do something about either option – or, to be exact, he wasn't, but HMS *Invincible* was. Richter mused for a few minutes, then made his decision. He'd pissed off the Commander in a fairly big way, and was reasonably certain that any obstacle that man could place in his path he would, so the obvious option was to request what he wanted from their lordships at the Admiralty, through Hammersmith.

Richter reached for the Enigma mobile he'd collected on the ship itself and dialled a London number. It took him nearly five minutes to reach and brief the duty officer, and another two minutes before he heard Simpson's less than amiable tones in his ear.

'Now what, Richter? And who's this man Ross you've managed to get killed? I've had Vauxhall Cross bleating on about him for the last hour.'

'I didn't get him killed, Simpson,' Richter snapped. 'Charles Ross was the man the local Six office loaned me, mainly for his language and lock-picking skills. Unfortunately, he encountered the last of these three Americans I've been chasing. The Yank was armed: Ross wasn't. The outcome was entirely predictable.'

'Not by you, apparently, Richter.'

'I can't tell the local Six people how to conduct their business. We had one pistol between us, and as I was acting as the downstairs man, it seemed more appropriate that I should be carrying.'

'So you say. My guess is that Vauxhall Cross will want you grilled and served up on a platter once you get back here. First Lomas, now this man Ross – and in less than a week, too. That's a pretty unimpressive record even by your standards.'

'I don't give a toss what Vauxhall Cross – or anyone else, for that matter – thinks of me. I'm trying to do a job over here – like you instructed, if you remember – and I'd manage it a lot better if you climbed off my back and gave me some real help instead of bitching about what's gone wrong.'

'Watch your mouth, Richter. What help do you want now anyway? Another Six man to act as a bullet-catcher?'

'No.' Richter ignored the jibe. 'I want a series of orders sent to the *Invincible*.'

'Why ask me? You can probably see the bloody ship from where you're sitting now. Just use the phone or a radio or something.'

'It would be better if these orders were official, from the Admiralty. I had a slight run-in with the Commander earlier, and I think I'd encounter fewer problems and more cooperation if the instructions came from above.'

Simpson's chuckle echoed in the earpiece. 'You seem to have a real knack for losing friends and failing to impress people, Richter. So, what do you want the ship to do for you?'

'Just some basic surveillance. This last American agent's running scared. His picture's soon going to be plastered across the walls at all the ferry ports and airports, and every local cop will have a photograph in his pocket. The only way he's going to get off Crete is if somebody organizes a pick-up from a US Navy vessel or even a submarine. My guess is that the rendezvous will be somewhere on the western end of the island. So I'd like the *Invincible* to move station from her present location out towards the west, and then plot every boat or aircraft that looks like it's heading for a landfall at that end of Crete.'

'Then what? You want it shot down or sunk as well?'

'You're joking, I presume. I just want it tracked, and as soon as the landfall location can be established, I want to know about it.'

'Sounds a bit of a long shot to me, Richter. Even if the ship spots a chopper on radar, by the time they inform you and you find your car keys and drive to wherever it's intending to land, the chances are it will already have picked up your man and headed back out to sea.'

'It is a long shot, as you say, but right now it's pretty much all I've got, unless the local plods can eyeball this comedian's car pretty soon. If they can, that changes everything.'

'OK, I'll set the wheels in motion. And, Richter, try and keep the body count down from now on, will you? No doubt this American agent's going to come to grief if you've got anything to do with it, but if you could leave at least some of the local population still standing when you've finished whatever the hell you're doing I'm sure the Cretan tourist board would be grateful.'

'Ever thought about a career on the stage, Simpson?' Richter pressed the button to disconnect.

## Central Intelligence Agency Headquarters, Langley, Virginia

John Nicholson wasn't exactly worried, but he was certainly concerned. He had realized that the killings of C. J. Hawkins and James Richards – he was hopeful that Henry Butcher's death would be attributed to natural causes, and Mary Hawkins's elimination was irrelevant as far as he was concerned – would result in a police investigation. He was also aware that it wouldn't take the local police long to deduce that the same perpetrator had been responsible for all the deaths. Discovering that the only solid link between the elderly men was their previous employment in the Central Intelligence Agency would, he reckoned, take them longer, hopefully a lot longer, to establish. Nevertheless, sooner or later the police would make this connection and some kind of an internal inquiry would be certain to follow.

He'd meanwhile done what he could to monitor the kind of activity that an investigation was bound to generate, although there was already almost nothing that anybody could find. The hard-copy files had been removed from the Registry and shredded; he'd done that himself over thirty years ago, as a junior agent acting on the specific instructions and with the written authorization – which had later been destroyed as well – of Henry Butcher, who had been the ranking agent responsible for CAIP. The electronic records in the Walnut database had been purged as far as possible and the file entries – the only data that couldn't be removed – had been sealed under the signature of an authority that would be absolutely impossible to breach.

Nicholson was therefore satisfied that the only information anyone would now be able to find would be the name of the operation, the names of the senior agents responsible for it, and the registration number of a crashed Learjet. Even Sherlock Holmes himself would have had a job deducing much from such paucity of data.

But still he'd set some tripwires, the first of them now nearly thirty years old – automatic triggers that would be pulled by anybody accessing particular electronic files, or inputting specific keywords into Walnut's search facility, or even requesting certain hard-copy files from the Registry. Each tripwire would tell him the date, time, nature of the request or search string and, most importantly, the name of the originating agent for each occurrence, and all such information was recorded in a log file to which only he had access.

Ever since the Learjet had been found, Nicholson had been checking the log file on a daily basis, and wasn't unduly surprised when one name kept on appearing, since logic suggested that a single agent would be instructed to look into the implications of the deaths. Therefore he'd been able to pinpoint the date on which the internal investigation had started, and to a large extent been able to follow the subsequent thought processes of the investigating officer.

He checked his office computer that afternoon and scanned the log file again. Westwood's last request, for nearly sixty personnel files, showed that, far from the guy's investigation dying a death due to lack of data, as Nicholson had hoped, it seemed to be hotting up.

He knew John Westwood by sight, but that was all, their respective divisions being sufficiently diverse to ensure that their professional paths hadn't crossed. He knew little about the man, but if he continued probing, it was possible John Westwood might have to meet with an accident, and soon.

### HMS *Invincible*, Sea of Crete

A little under two hours after Richter's call to Simpson, the ship's propeller revolutions increased slightly and the carrier began a slow transit towards the west, in company with its Royal Fleet Auxiliary supply ships and two escorting frigates. In the Air Operations Department, Ops 3 began calculating an outline flying programme for the following day. The new orders from the *Invincible*'s operating authority specified a high level of surface, sub-surface and air surveillance of the Mediterranean to the west of the island of Crete, paying specific attention to any surface or airborne contacts that might make landfall on the island.

This was the kind of activity that the ship had frequently carried out during exercises, but had only rarely employed in a real world environment. Ops 3 had already decided that the Sea Harriers could help out as well, running CAP to supplement the coverage of the ship's own radars and those of the escorting frigates and the ASaC Sea Kings and ASW Merlins.

The supplementary orders were unusual too: any possible landfall location was to be advised immediately to a secure mobile telephone, which only a handful of people knew was in Paul Richter's possession.

### Máleme, Crete

Once he'd lost sight of Stein's car, Mike Murphy had spent several increasingly anxious hours trying to find it again.

On the assumption that Stein intended to spend the night in Máleme, he guessed the American would choose one of the anonymous town-centre hotels and more easily lose himself in the crowds, but despite checking every single hotel car park, and all on-street parking areas, he saw no sign of a blue Seat Cordoba.

So he widened his search area to include the outskirts, but it was almost ten that night before he finally struck lucky. He heaved a sigh of relief when he eventually spotted the Seat at the rear of a hotel, in a car park that served two neighbouring hotels also.

His immediate problem was deciding which establishment Stein had checked in to, and at that time of night there seemed no easy way to do it. Unless Stein was propping up the bar in one of them, which seemed foolhardy and extremely unlikely, Murphy reckoned he was going to have to wait until the morning.

But he decided to take a look anyway. All three hotel bars were open, doing a modest trade, but nobody who looked even slightly like Richard Stein was in any of them. Ten minutes later, Murphy walked out of the third one he had investigated and went back to his car. There wasn't much more he could do that night. Stein would certainly have used a false name, so even if he could devise some way of getting a look at all three hotel registers there was no way he could confirm whether or not Stein was a resident.

Murphy was pragmatic by nature. With no obvious way of finding his target that night, he hauled his overnight bag out of the back of the Peugeot and checked himself in to the middle hotel of the three establishments. Ensuring that the room he'd been given overlooked the rear car park, he went down to the bar and ordered a beer and a bar snack in lieu of the dinner he'd been forced to miss that evening.

Just an hour after locating the Seat, Murphy climbed into his hotel bed, his travelling alarm clock set for six-thirty in the morning. He intended to be up and dressed long before Stein appeared in the car park below to reclaim his vehicle.

# Chapter 23

George Pallios had been a police officer on Crete for almost his entire adult life. He'd been born in Chaniá, shared a small apartment in the town with his wife of six years and their two children and, when he thought about it at all, he guessed he would eventually die there. Always having wanted to become a police officer, from the day he first donned the uniform he had done his best to live up to the standards he knew were expected of him.

It therefore had genuinely been something of a shock to realize that these standards included a certain amount of blind-eye activity in return for envelopes containing notes of fairly high denominations, but it hadn't taken him too long to get comfortable with the idea. After all, most of his fellow officers seemed happy to do exactly the same thing.

He'd also got used to not having to buy meals or drinks whenever he was in uniform. Most bar and restaurant owners were only too pleased to receive occasional visits from a local police officer – as a useful reminder to their clientele to behave – so they were more than happy to offer a beer or a glass of raki in exchange. Any proprietors whose hospitality was less forthcoming tended to find that their calls for assistance were answered tardily, or not at all.

Life, in short, was pretty good most of the time. The worst part of his job, Pallios decided, was the night-shift. The streets were more or less deserted and almost everywhere was closed while the island slept. With no bars open where he could enjoy a glass or two, nothing much to look at in the towns apart from parked cars and closed doors, and an occasional sleep-walking goat on the country roads, Pallios sat behind the wheel of his patrol car and cruised slowly around, fingers tapping out tunes from one of the local radio stations.

Where he drove was up to him, so long as he covered a specified minimum mileage. Tonight he'd started just after midnight in Chaniá and decided to spend some time cruising the tangle of roads linking Chaniá, Soúda and the Akrotíri peninsula. That yielded nothing of interest, and by three-thirty Pallios was driving out of Chaniá again and heading west.

He drove slowly through the towns he came to, alert for any sign of trouble because, despite his relaxed and accommodating attitude, Pallios was, at heart, a lawman and he took his job seriously. Galatás, Plataniás and Geráni: all were quiet. He skirted the edge of Máleme and drove on out to Kolymvári, arriving there a little after five. He debated then about following the main road to its natural end at Kastélli, but decided not to. He'd check Kolymvári and Máleme, then head back to Chaniá and call it a night.

He reached Máleme at six and began a slow sweep through the town, passing the hotel where Stein had left his hire car at six-twenty. If he'd been much earlier, he probably wouldn't have spotted the blue Seat Cordoba or at least realized it was blue because it would have been too dark to see the colour.

In the early-morning light Pallios instantly noticed the vehicle as his eyes swept the car park of a small hotel on the outskirts, but he didn't immediately react in any way. He drove on past the hotel without changing speed and continued around the next right-hand corner. There he stopped the car and switched off the engine. On a clipboard secured to the dashboard were several sheets of paper comprising current watch notices, warnings and other instructions. Pallios was certain one of them had mentioned a blue Seat.

He flicked through the pages and then stopped at the one he sought. He memorized the registration number, but also noted the instruction – underlined and in bold type – not to approach the car or its driver. Pallios took a small pair of binoculars out of the glove box, climbed out of his patrol car, locked the door, checked that his pistol was loaded and the holster flap unclipped, and moved slowly back down the silent street towards the three adjoining hotels.

Reaching the corner, he paused and visually checked up and down the street before continuing. He stopped again about seventy metres short of the car-park entrance, staying on the opposite side of the street and well out of sight of the hotel windows. There he raised the binoculars to his eyes and looked carefully at the front of the Seat Cordoba. Then he nodded in satisfaction, turned and retraced his steps.

Three minutes later Pallios was a little over half a mile away, microphone in hand and describing the exact location of the parked car to his control room.

### Réthymno, Crete

At six fifty the SIS mobile phone beside Richter's bed began playing the theme tune from the television series *Morse*. Not for the first time he wished he could remember to change the tune to something – anything – else.

'We've found the Seat,' Fitzpatrick informed him. 'It was spotted by a police officer in Máleme about half an hour ago in a hotel car park.'

'Nobody was in it, I presume?' Richter asked, waking up fast.

'No. Following his orders, he didn't approach it to feel the bonnet or anything to see if it had been there all night, but he confirmed the registration number. It's definitely the car that this Watson or Jones character hired in Réthymno yesterday.'

'What else has been done so far?'

'Nothing at all. The orders were most specific: no approach to either the car or the driver. Once he was satisfied it was the right car, the cop just climbed back into his patrol car to radio in his report and drove away.'

'Right,' Richter reached for a notepad, 'give me the details.'

### Máleme, Crete

Murphy had settled his hotel bill in advance, explaining that he would have to leave very early in the morning. By six fifty-five he was sitting in the Peugeot, his bags stowed in the boot. The night before he'd positioned the car with an unobstructed view of the rear of the three hotels. That way, he would be able to spot Stein the moment he left his hotel to enter the car park.

He couldn't see the Seat itself, which was out of sight behind a Renault Espace and a Volkswagen Transporter, but he reckoned that was less important than covering the hotel exits: he wanted to be able to start his car and get mobile the moment Stein appeared. He planned to follow him as he drove away, then take him down somewhere quiet, recover the case and the file, and then get the hell off the island.

It was cool so early in the morning, and Murphy ran the engine for a few minutes to get the heater working. Then he switched it off and settled down for what could be a very long wait.

## HMS *Invincible*, Sea of Crete

It was quite amazing just how many surface contacts there were around the western rim of Crete, even that early in the morning. Most of them, as the Surface Picture Compiler knew, were fishing boats, ferries, yachts, power boats, ski boats and a host of other types of pleasure craft that were heading out into the mirrored blue waters of the eastern Mediterranean to take advantage of yet another beautiful day.

The orders the SPC had been given were quite specific: he was to track and report any surface contacts that appeared to be heading for a landfall anywhere on the western coast. Theoretically, that meant he could disregard all those contacts heading away from the island, but the problem, as he'd realized almost immediately, was that the vast majority of those contacts were at some point going to turn round and head back the way they'd come, for lunch, a refuel, change of passengers, an overnight stop or whatever, so actually he was having to track almost everything that moved.

Since coming on watch he'd been keeping a personal written tote, listing the track number he'd allocated to each contact through the computer system, the location where the radar had first detected it, usually within a few hundred metres of leaving whatever port it had departed from, and its approximate heading. That way, he hoped, he could effectively eliminate all those surface contacts that simply sailed from some Cretan harbour, headed out into the Mediterranean, and then turned round and came back again.

But what he was really looking for were the unknown contacts, those vessels appearing on his radar screen from far out to the west, and especially the bigger ones that might carry a helicopter. Just after seven that morning, he spotted another one. This contact wasn't yet being detected by the ship's radar, but had been fed into the system by secure data-link from one of the two ASaC Sea Kings established in holding patterns some fifty miles to the west of the *Invincible*. It was heading almost due east, on a track that, if unchanged, would take it to a point just to the south of Crete. And it was big – much bigger than most of the stuff buzzing about the waters near the *Invincible*. As he'd done dozens of times already, he allocated a track number to the new contact and reported it to the Principal Warfare Officer at his console in the centre of the Operations Room.

'PWO, SPC. New track number two three one, bearing two six two range one hundred and twenty miles, heading zero nine five. Source is ASaC data-link.'

'SPC, PWO, roger. Maintain tracking. Report any changes of heading and when the contact reaches range fifty.'

'Aye, aye, sir.'

The SPC bent over his display again, checking that every contact on his screen was wearing a computer-generated label of some sort, but the main focus of his attention was on the new track. Every sweep of the timebase around the radar screen showed it very slightly closer, and it was, the SPC thought, almost exactly what he'd been told to watch out for.

And he was quite correct.

### Máleme, Crete

Richard Stein woke up at seven-thirty, climbed out of bed and walked straight across to the window overlooking the car park at the rear. He pulled back the curtain a fraction and looked out carefully at the cars, at the adjacent streets and the adjoining properties, and saw absolutely nothing that seemed out of place. He shrugged, checked that the chair still jammed the room door, headed into the bathroom and took a shower.

Just after eight he sat down to a light breakfast in the hotel's small dining room, then went back up to his room and again viewed the car park. People were now moving about the streets, and two couples that he recognized from breakfast were loading suitcases into the boots of their cars – a white Opel and a light grey Fiat – but nobody else was visible anywhere near the building.

Stein switched on the laptop and the mobile phone and logged on to the server back in the States. There were no further messages for him or Krywald, so he shut both down and packed them away into his brief-case. The pick-up McCready had arranged was for fifteen twenty that afternoon, which meant he had about six hours to kill before the ren-dezvous, and Stein had no intention of going outside until he had to. He had no desire to spend the day cooped up in this hotel, but he realized his chances of being recognized would be far greater out in the open.

He took a paperback novel from his overnight bag and lay down on the bed to try to read it, but his mind kept wandering and he found him-self re-reading the same page over and over again. Every few minutes he got up to open the door to his room and check up and down the corridor, and inspected the car park below his hotel room window. The only disturbance was the chambermaid who came in to tidy his bed and clean mid-morning. Stein never let her out of his sight the whole time she was in the room, the SIG – minus its silencer – grasped loosely in his hand underneath the novel.

At twelve fifteen he again checked both the car park and the corridor, then headed down to the dining room, bought himself a buffet lunch and was back up in his room just before one.

By one twenty he had packed his few belongings into his overnight bag and put it on the bed beside the crucial briefcase. He glanced at his watch, mentally calculating times and distances, and took a last look round the room and in the bathroom to make sure he hadn't forgotten anything. Before he left the hotel room, he again spent some time peer-ing out of the window from behind the curtain, checking that nothing seemed out of place. Stein then picked up his bags, moved quietly along the corridor to the rear of the hotel, opened the emergency exit door and climbed down the metal fire escape to the car park. At ground level, he again checked all round him, then crossed the street and strode off down the road towards the car park where he'd left his Seat.

He was about twenty yards from the Cordoba when he noticed that an old Cretan, wearing a filthy hat and ragged coat, was working his way through the car park, checking the garbage bins. Bent and bowed with age, he was moving slowly as if in pain, a plastic bag clutched in his right hand. Stein registered him briefly, and then ignored him. That was a mistake.

Stein used the central locking to open the boot, put both his bags inside and slammed the lid shut. As he straightened up, he felt more than saw a swift movement to his right. He span round, grabbing for his pistol, but he was far too slow. His world exploded in a sudden blaze of stars and lights and he slumped to the ground, car keys and pistol both spinning from his hands.

Murphy had been concentrating on the rear exits of the hotels. He'd seen the old Cretan wander off the street into the car park but, just like Stein, he'd disregarded him, not least because the old man had been hanging around there for most of the morning. He hadn't even seen Stein because his target had approached not from one of the hotels but from the opposite direction, and had thus been hidden behind parked vehicles.

He was suddenly aware of an engine starting, then saw the rear of the Seat Cordoba swing out towards him, its reversing lights on, and immediately the car moved swiftly away and bounced out of the car park, accelerating rapidly down the road.

Murphy cursed – how the hell had Stein slipped past him? He span the starter, slipped the Peugeot into first gear, and pulled away from the kerb. He reached the main road in seconds and swung his car right to follow the Seat. As he straightened up and accelerated, he gave a puzzled frown. He was almost certain he had seen two people in the Seat. But Elias and Krywald were both dead, so who the hell was in the car with Stein?

### South of Zounáki, western Crete

'I need you to check some names,' Richter spoke into the Enigma mobile. He'd got through to Hammersmith three minutes earlier and briefed the Duty Officer – Simpson not being in the building – on developments overnight. Now he had the fat red file open on his lap, and he was about to read out the names of senior personnel he'd found listed inside the front cover.

'I imagine these are all CIA agents,' Richter said, 'so I suggest you make an initial check with Langley. OK, their names are James Wilson, Jerry Jonas, Henry Butcher, George Cassells, Charles Hawkins, William Penn, James Richards and Roger Stanford.'

'This *is* important, is it, Richter? I mean, you do know you're right at the top of Simpson's current shit list, and if he thinks you're just fannying about down there on Crete he'll crucify you when you get back here.'

'Yeah, yeah,' Richter said. 'Don't worry, I've already had the bollocking. Just run that check, will you?'

'And what's your source for these names? Are they important?' Richter gave him a brief summary of what he had discovered so far. 'Right, you've convinced me. All you have to do now is convince Simpson. I'll get those names across to Langley this afternoon.'

'One more thing. Do me a favour and run a check on the name "CAIP", and see if it's in anybody's database. I'll give you a call later today.'

'You've got it.' The Duty Officer broke the connection.

Richter switched off the mobile phone – he didn't want it ringing while he questioned 'George Jones' – placed it on the dashboard and glanced around outside the car, which he'd parked a little way off the road leading south from Zounáki to Nterés. There were no houses, vehicles or people anywhere within his view. He turned slightly to look behind him.

Stein, sitting on the rear seat, was at last showing signs of coming round, having been unconscious for the better part of an hour. Richter had tied his wrists together using plastic cable ties, then secured them to the grab handle above the right-hand passenger door. Stein's arms were pulled uncomfortably upwards as his torso slumped forwards, but Richter wasn't bothered about his comfort. As far as he was concerned Stein was already dead: it was just a matter of when he'd actually stop breathing. But he had wanted to ensure that the American agent was completely immobilized.

Stein lifted his head, his eyes blinking slowly as he looked around him. The first thing he saw was Richter staring back at him, and the second thing he noticed was the muzzle of a 9mm Browning Hi-Power pointing at his head.

'Try to move,' Richter growled, 'and you'll never move again.'

'Oh, shit.' Stein's voice was low and racked with pain. 'You were that goddamn old man I saw working the street.'

Within ten minutes of the call from Fitzpatrick, Richter had been sitting in his Renault Clio hire car holding eighty miles an hour, en route from Réthymno to Máleme. As he'd reached the outskirts of the town he'd seen an old man shuffling along in the gutter and hauled the car to a stop. Using a selection of hand gestures and the handful of Greek words that he'd picked up since he'd arrived on Crete, he'd managed to do a convenient deal. The old man's hat and coat in exchange for enough money for him to have an overcoat custom-made for him in London, unlikely though that possibility might be.

Having no idea when his target would leave the hotel, Richter had spent hours wandering about in the vicinity of the car park where he had seen the blue Seat. He had been seriously wondering if the American calling himself Watson or Jones was going to stay in his hotel all day, when he had at last spotted the man himself approaching the vehicle.

'Did McCready send you?' Stein suddenly asked from the back seat.

'Who's McCready?'

Stein leaned back in the seat, easing the pressure on his aching arms. For a moment he said nothing.

'I just asked you a question,' Richter said. 'Who's McCready?'

Instead of answering, Stein studied him curiously. 'You're a Brit,' he decided.

'Full marks for deduction,' Richter said, 'but you still haven't answered me and I'm not a patient man. Tell me, who's McCready?'

Stein shook his head. 'McCready doesn't matter,' he muttered. 'He was just our briefing officer back home, and I was kinda expecting him to have sent a welcoming committee here, after all the fuck-ups.'

'Fuck-ups like killing the unarmed man in Réthymno? That kind of thing?'

'Listen,' Stein said, 'I'm real sorry about that. He looked to me like he was going for a weapon.' Richter just stared at him, saying nothing. 'I'm sorry,' Stein repeated. 'I thought he was carrying. And who are you, anyway? Who are you working for?'

'That's none of your business.'

But Stein shook his head. 'It might be,' he said. 'Are you a cop, or what?' Still Richter didn't reply. 'OK, then I've got nothing to tell you,' Stein added, finality in his voice.

What the hell? Richter thought. Whether or not this American knew who employed him probably didn't matter.

'OK,' he said, 'I work for British Intelligence. I presume you're with the Company?'

Stein nodded, an expression of relief on his face. 'OK, then, great. We're on the same side.'

'No fucking way,' Richter snapped. 'Any "special relationship" ended the moment you fired your pistol in Réthymno. Your itchy trigger finger killed a senior British SIS officer.'

'I told you, that was an accident.' Stein's face grew pale as the implications of his action dawned on him. 'I didn't know who he was, I swear.'

'You might be telling the truth,' Richter said, 'but I don't see it that way, and neither will SIS.'

'What are you going to do with me?'

Richter paused for a few moments before replying. 'I haven't decided yet. A lot depends on what you're prepared to tell me. What was your function in this operation?'

'I was only the linguist,' Stein said, deciding to dumb down his role. 'I speak fluent Greek, which was needed to get the job done. Look, I've about had it with this op. My partner's as good as dead and I'm hauling around a file I don't understand and a bug that'll kill you in under a day. You work for an allied intelligence service, so if you want that fucking case and the file, you take 'em. Just let me get the hell out of here.'

'It's not that easy,' Richter said, 'and I've still got some questions. Who else was in the team?'

For a moment Stein didn't reply, apparently considering his options.

Richter leaned slightly closer to him, and his voice, when he spoke, was frigid with menace. 'Let me explain things. You have exactly two options. You talk to me, answer my questions, and there's just a chance you can walk away from this. Clam up on me, and you're just so much dead weight. I'll haul you out of the car right now and put a bullet in your head. Is that clear enough?'

Stein looked at the Englishman, and didn't for one second doubt that he meant exactly what he'd said. He gave a brief shrug. 'OK,' he said, 'the diver was a guy named David Elias. He was an analyst, not from Operations, and he was only along because we needed somebody who could dive deep enough to place the charges.'

'And once he'd done that he became expendable, right?' Richter demanded.

'McCready's orders.' Stein paused. 'We didn't like it at all, but—'

'But you killed him anyway? Just like that police officer in Kandíra? And the two old villagers?'

Stein nodded reluctantly. 'Krywald killed the cop,' he said, 'not me.'

'Who else was involved? And what's your real name?'

'It's Richard Stein. There were just the three of us. The guy in charge was Roger Krywald.'

'And the briefing?' Richter pressed.

'Just the bare minimum to get the job done,' Stein muttered.

'What exactly did the briefing officer tell you?'

'We had to fly to Crete, locate some guy called Aristides, recover the case from him and destroy the wrecked aircraft.'

'Did he explain why?'

'No, he didn't. You know about CIA covert ops, don't you? He just told us it was classified Cosmic Top Secret and real urgent – Priority One. Recovery of the case and its contents was paramount; all other considerations were secondary.'

'How were you supposed to be getting off the island?' Richter changed tack.

'McCready arranged a helicopter pick-up for me this afternoon out to the west of Plátanos.'

'And the big question,' Richter said, 'is what's in those flasks?'

'I didn't look inside the case,' Stein explained, 'but Krywald mentioned there were only four of them although the case has spaces for twelve. He said one of them had been opened. I can't tell you what's in them because I don't know, but it's something fucking dangerous.'

Stein decided in that instant to say nothing about the file summary he'd found. 'Krywald looked through the file, and so did I, but it didn't mean a hell of a lot to us. Just a bunch of letters and memos and real long words. We worked out it involved some kind of operation in Africa, but that was about all. Krywald reckoned that the stiffs in the aircraft were a bunch of scientists who'd pulled some kind of lethal bug out of the rain forest, to develop it as a biological weapon.'

That made sense to Richter. It was an open secret that despite America's official stance on biological and chemical warfare, to develop antidotes requires possession of the biological agents themselves. Of necessity, therefore, America has always possessed a huge variety of bioweapons, so extracting a new virus out of the rain forest so as to develop an antidote for it was indeed a likely scenario.

At that very moment Mike Murphy was little over two hundred yards away from the blue Seat, his Peugeot hire car tucked off the road and well out of sight. He was lying prone on the dusty ground, peering through a pair of compact binoculars up the hill towards the Cordoba from the shelter of a stunted bush. Beside him was the long cardboard box containing the Dragunov SVD sniper rifle, and as soon as he'd worked out what the hell was happening up there, he was planning on using it.

He'd picked up the Seat within a couple of minutes of the vehicle leaving the hotel car park in Máleme and he'd followed it easily enough as the driver picked up the main road and headed west. What he hadn't anticipated had been the Seat turning off the road at Tavronítis, and Murphy had had to close the gap between the two vehicles quickly so as not to lose sight of his quarry.

He'd been a quarter of a mile behind the Seat as it left the village of Zounáki. The moment he'd seen the other car pull off the road, Murphy had turned his own vehicle around, driven a short distance back and parked out of sight. He'd opened the boot, grabbed the Dragunov and run to the top of the gentle hill in search of what he'd hoped was a good vantage point.

He'd just settled down to watch the Seat when the driver's door opened and a man climbed out, glanced around him, then opened the right-hand rear passenger door and leaned inside. A few seconds later he'd closed the door and climbed back into the driver's seat. Murphy had braced himself, wondering if he was going to drive away, which would mean a hard run down the hill back to his Peugeot, but there was no sign yet of the Seat's engine starting.

Murphy hadn't even got a decent look at the man – he'd still been focusing his binoculars when the stranger had climbed out of the car – but he was certain he'd never seen him before. What he'd registered was a fair-haired male, and that was about all. Having had some previous experience of John Nicholson's operating methods, for a brief while Murphy wondered if he'd been set up, whether Nicholson had sent somebody else to help Stein get off the island, but a few moments' thought told him this idea was a non-starter. So that really left only one possibility: some other intelligence organization had somehow got involved, and they had got to Stein before Murphy could complete his contract.

So what should he do about this newcomer? Eliminating an American agent was bad enough: killing an agent of a foreign intelligence service could prove disastrous, especially when he had no idea which one of them was involved. The last thing Murphy wanted was to spend the rest of his life looking over his shoulder for an assassin sent after him by the SVR or Mossad.

Ideally, Murphy needed to email Nicholson to advise him of the changed situation and to request advice, but there was absolutely no way that he was going to have the luxury of doing that. Sooner or later, either Stein would emerge from the stationary car or it would drive away and Murphy would follow it again, until Stein did get out. Whatever scenario, Murphy had no option but to kill Stein and eventually probably the stranger as well.

Then another thought struck him. Killing Stein was his remaining priority-two task. His highest priority was recovering the case and the file. He'd been assuming all along that Stein would have both items with him, but what if the stranger had kidnapped Stein and the case and file might be stuck in a hotel safe or even locked up inside another car? Maybe the killing of Stein would just have to wait a while.

\*

'So where's the case?' Richter demanded.

'It's in the trunk of this car,' Stein replied. 'Krywald opened it and he got infected, so I've wrapped it in a couple of garbage bags. I swear there's nothing you can say or do that will make me open it up for you. You want it, you take it. You open it up, and in twelve hours you'll be dead.'

'I don't want to open it,' Richter said, 'just make sure it's really there. I'll free your arms, and then we'll go and check it together.' He opened the door and slid out. Moving round the car, he opened the rear passenger door and reached in with a knife to slice through the cable tie securing Stein's bound wrists to the grab handle. Then he seized the American agent and pulled him out of the back seat. They stepped around to the Seat's rear and Richter popped open the boot.

'That's it,' Stein nodded towards a bulky oblong object wrapped in heavy-duty black plastic. 'I suggest you leave it right where it is.'

Richter nodded, but nevertheless reached into the boot and grabbed the black plastic object, lifting it a few inches. Stein stepped back immediately, panic written all over his face.

'OK,' Richter said, 'I believe you.'


Murphy stared through his binoculars, watching the two men intently. Then he grunted in satisfaction, opened up the cardboard box beside him and hauled out the Dragunov. He spread the bipod legs, inserted the magazine, switched on the laser sight, and in one fluid movement hauled the rifle into his shoulder and chambered a round. He looked through the Bushnell scope towards the Seat Cordoba and the two men standing beside it.

The black-wrapped object sitting in the trunk had to be the case, just because of the way Stein and the stranger were reacting to it, and if the case was in the trunk, then for sure the file must be there too or somewhere else in the car. That meant Murphy could complete his remaining priority-two task, killing Richard Stein, and get rid of the other man at the same time.

Murphy picked his target, the Bushnell variable-power telescopic sight seeming to pull the two men towards him. He made a conscious effort to control his breathing, and then gently squeezed the trigger.

# Chapter 24

**Saturday**
**South of Zounáki, western Crete**

For a few seconds Richter just stared at the innocent-looking black plastic bag in the open boot of the Seat Cordoba. It could have contained almost anything – a week's worth of garbage, a collection of old clothes, even a dismembered corpse – but everything that he could imagine, even a corpse, would have been better than the invisible and utterly deadly pathogen that he knew was inside it.

Something had been nagging away at Richter's subconscious, since he'd started talking to the US agent. It was something Stein had said, or had maybe not said, and it had eluded him until this precise moment.

'You said that Krywald was as good as dead,' Richter said, 'but in fact he died yesterday, in the hospital at Chaniá.'

'I didn't know that,' Stein replied. 'He was pretty far gone when I took him to the emergency room, but there was no way I was going to go back to check on him.'

Richter was watching Stein closely and, as far as he could tell, the man was telling the truth. This confirmed a nagging suspicion he'd entertained ever since Hardin explained how Roger Krywald had died.

'The virus didn't kill him,' Richter continued. 'Somebody punched a couple of nine-millimetre slugs through his chest, and I had that down to you.'

Stein turned pale, and shook his head decisively. 'It wasn't me. Look, if I'd wanted to take him out I could have shot him by the side of the road somewhere. But I didn't go back to the hospital just to kill him.'

'So who did then?' Richter wondered.

'I don't know,' Stein said, 'but my guess is that McCready has sent a cleaner here to Crete. He'll have orders to take out all of us, recover the case and get it back to the States.' Even as he said the words, Stein glanced around nervously, conscious how the two of them were standing exposed on open ground. 'We should get the hell away from here. We're like two ducks in a shooting gallery.'

Richter glanced round quickly, then back towards Stein and suddenly saw a tiny red mark appear in the middle of the American agent's chest. It signified a laser sight, almost certainly attached to the barrel of a sniper rifle.

He reacted immediately. The sniper was going to save him a job. He took one step back towards the car, then shoved Stein sideways and ran off towards the driver's side of the Seat.

At precisely the moment Mike Murphy squeezed the trigger, Stein stumbled, lost both his footing and his balance, his arms still lashed together in front of him, and fell sprawling to the ground. The bullet that Murphy had aimed missed him completely, but drilled a neat hole through the right-hand side of the Cordoba's boot lid then smashed into a rock some twenty yards beyond, ricocheting off it and into the distance.

As he leapt into the driver's seat, Richter glanced in the interior mirror. He spotted the bullet hole in the boot lid and he'd already seen the spray of debris from the rock as the 7.62mm bullet had struck it. He didn't need any particular expertise in trigonometry to estimate the position of the gunman: the sniper was located behind him and on higher ground.

Richter was armed. He had the 9mm Browning drawn from HMS *Invincible*'s armoury, and he also had the SIG he'd liberated from Stein after knocking him unconscious. But only a fool or a hopeless optimist would even consider tackling a sniper with a couple of pistols. Richter's only option now was to put some distance between himself and the unknown assassin. The Seat's engine screamed as he started it up, then he floored the accelerator pedal in first gear and powered the car away and up the gentle slope, weaving from side to side to present his adversary with a more difficult target.


Two hundred metres away, Murphy cursed fluently and brought the sights of the Dragunov back to bear on the target area. It was now time to finish the job, but the moment Murphy steadied his weapon and sighted through the Bushnell again, he realized that might not be so easy.

The Seat was already in motion, gathering speed fast as its unidentified driver accelerated up the road. The boot lid was still up, preventing Murphy from seeing through the rear window, and the driver was weaving about to make sighting difficult.

Murphy moved the Dragunov over slightly, looking for Stein. His primary target had already scrambled to his feet, and was running as fast as he could towards what little cover the area afforded: a group of rocks and a few stunted trees standing over to the right. Stein could wait, he decided in an instant. The fact that his hands were tied meant that he was unarmed, so Murphy could track him down later and finish him off at his leisure. What he had to do first was stop the Seat.

Murphy swung his rifle barrel to the left, located the tarmac road through the telescopic sight and moved the muzzle up an inch or two. The blue Seat had already moved almost a hundred yards since he'd fired the first shot, but was still easily within range. Murphy concentrated on it, noting how the vehicle still swung from one side of the road to the other, and settled his aim not on where the car actually was, but where he calculated it would be in about a second. Only then did he squeeze the trigger.

The shot missed, or at least had no apparent effect, and he fired again almost immediately, and then again – the semi-automatic action smoothly reloading the weapon each time he fired. The car was by then over three hundred and fifty yards away, and gathering speed quickly. The result of his third shot was immediate, though. The Seat lurched, lost momentum, then slid off the road to the right, coming to rest in a cloud of dust almost broadside-on to where Murphy lay hidden. He guessed he'd either hit the mystery driver or burst a tyre.

Murphy watched the vehicle intently through the telescopic sight, finger caressing the trigger, waiting to see if the driver emerged, but after two minutes there was still no movement. He couldn't even see the man's shape behind the wheel, but he knew he still had to be inside the car. Murphy nodded in satisfaction: obviously he was badly wounded or maybe even dead. Just to be on the safe side, he sighted carefully and fired another round through the left-hand side front door, below the level of the window where the bullet was bound to strike him if he was crouching across the front seats.

Then he turned his attention to the point where Stein had been heading, and quartered the area of ground with his telescopic sight. Wherever the American agent had hidden himself was unfortunately invisible from Murphy's vantage point. He would therefore just have to do it the hard way.

He left the Dragunov where it was – it was far too cumbersome to be useful at close-quarters – but ejected the loaded cartridge and removed the magazine, which he placed in his jacket pocket for safety. He then took out the Daewoo pistol, chambered a round, slipped off the safety catch, and began to walk down the hillside towards the road.

Stein crouched behind a small cairn of boulders, well out of sight of the hill from which he knew the shots had originated – he'd seen the bullet plough through the Seat's boot lid and strike the ground beyond – and kept worrying at the plastic cable ties round his wrists with his teeth. If he could get his wrists free he would no longer be helpless. He would then be able to fight back, even if the only weapons to hand were sticks and rocks.

With a sudden stabbing pain in his jaw, his teeth finally snapped together as the tie parted, freeing his arms. He peered around the cairn of rocks he was hiding behind, checking the whole area. The Seat was about two hundred yards away, and off the road. Its engine was still running, since he could just make out a whisper of smoke from its exhaust. He presumed the Englishman was either dead or badly wounded, so guessed that the sniper would be coming to attend to him first. He again checked the hill to his left, but saw no signs of movement. On the other hand, the sniper could sneak down to the road out of sight on the far side of the hill, then cross straight to where Stein was hiding.

He looked around desperately for any kind of weapon. He seized a fallen branch and hefted it in his hand. The end of it was slightly rotten, but he guessed it could still strike a killing blow, if he got the chance. Then he looked back, towards the hill. Still nothing visible, but he knew the sniper had to be coming for him.

In the last few seconds Stein had worked out a kind of plan, but it all depended on what he saw when the sniper did come into view. If he was carrying his rifle, Stein would just have to take his chances in a close-quarter fight, though he had no illusions about how successful he would be using his broken branch against a man carrying both an automatic pistol and a rifle. But if the sniper was carrying only a pistol, then Stein was going to run – and he knew exactly where.

He stared around, but there seemed nowhere better to hide, no better place to wait for the assassin's arrival. And he had to wait for him to appear before he could begin to run. Stein desperately considered other possible options, but he saw none. To the north of the handful of trees and rocks in which he was hiding the land lay flat and open. If he tried to run across that way he'd be cut down from behind in an instant, and in any case he was half-expecting the sniper to approach from that direction. He rubbed his hands to remove some of the sweat on his palms, took a firm grip of his improvised club, then did his best to blend into the rocks and dirt around him.

Murphy paused for a few seconds as he reached the road, scanning the terrain in all directions. It had taken him only seconds to get down to level ground, and Stein couldn't have broken cover in that short a time without still being in sight. That meant his quarry must still be hiding in the same place.

He jogged across the road, heading for the small group of stunted trees into which he'd seen Stein run only a few minutes earlier, then stopped and again surveyed his surroundings. He decided to circle round slightly and approach the same trees from the east. But at that moment he saw Stein break cover and start to head away from him to the south. Immediately he realized what the other man was trying to do.

Stein had seen him coming and froze for an instant. He'd moved swiftly around the other side of the pile of rocks, gratefully putting their solidity between himself and the approaching assassin. And then he'd leapt to his feet and started running, hard, towards the road which led south, every pace taking him closer to the blue Seat Cordoba, which still sat motionless with its engine idling.

If he could only reach the car, he would have some kind of a chance because he knew that the Englishman had both his SIG and a Browning Hi-Power, and with either weapon Stein could confront the sniper on more equal terms.

He just had to get there in time.


Murphy stood irresolute for under a second. The effective range of an automatic pistol is generally accepted as between fifteen and thirty yards: heroes who can snap off a shot and bring down a man at fifty yards exist only in the fevered imaginings of Hollywood film directors. When Stein had started to move he was about sixty yards away – therefore already well out of pistol range. Murphy realized he had two choices: he could pursue him and hope to run him down before he reached the Seat, or he could get back behind the telescopic sight of his Dragunov and pick him off before he got that far.

It wasn't a difficult decision. Murphy snapped off two quickly aimed shots in Stein's general direction, neither of which got within fifteen feet of the fugitive, then turned away and ran back towards the hill where he'd left the Dragunov.

Thirty seconds later he slammed the magazine back into the rifle and cycled the action to chamber a round. Pulling the stock of the weapon into his shoulder, while struggling to control his breathing, he peered through the Bushnell sight for the running target. It looked as if Stein was now less than fifty yards from the Seat.

Murphy sighted quickly and snapped off a shot. He didn't see the impact point but it must have passed close to Stein's left side because he lurched suddenly to the right, then continued running towards the car. Murphy sighted again carefully, then squeezed the trigger.


A small rock about ten feet in front of him and just to the left suddenly shattered and sent razor-sharp stone splinters in all directions. At that instant Stein knew that the sniper had gone back to use his rifle. He also realized he was as good as dead.

The agent wasn't in bad physical condition – he worked out at the local gym twice a week back home – but he'd always concentrated on upper-body exercises. Track and field had never been his strong point, so even the run up the slight slope to the parked Seat had exhausted him. But when a bullet screamed past him he found extra reserves of strength to accelerate.

And he very nearly made it. He was less than twenty yards from the Cordoba when a 7.62mm round from the Dragunov smashed into his left thigh. It splintered his femur and sent him tumbling and screaming to the ground.

## HMS *Invincible*, Sea of Crete

The contact that the Surface Picture Compiler had labelled track two three one had continued heading directly towards Crete. By early afternoon it was only some fifteen miles off the coast, but it had been identified several hours earlier.

One of the CAP Sea Harriers had been instructed to descend to low level and take a quick look at it while the contact was still around fifty miles off the Cretan coast. The pilot had then radioed the *Invincible* to report that the ship was an American frigate, and the Ops staff had noted its identification number.

When it reached twelve miles off the coast, the frigate slowed and began loitering. Just before fifteen hundred local time one of the *Invincible*'s Merlins, working as part of the Ripple Three ASW screen, reported activity on the frigate's flight deck. Minutes later a helicopter got airborne from the American vessel, climbed up to five hundred feet and began heading towards the western tip of Crete.

In the Operations Room on board the *Invincible*, air contacts are the responsibility of the Air Picture Compilers, and the moment the American helicopter launched it was allocated the label H (for 'helicopter') 17. As soon as its track was established – it appeared to be heading directly towards Plátanos – the APC called to advise Ops 3 of the helicopter's projected landfall. Ops 3 noted the details and immediately dialled the number of the mobile phone he'd been given earlier.

But instead of the ringing tone he expected, he heard a pre-recorded message in Greek which he guessed meant that the mobile was either switched off or outside range of a cell. He tried again, then shrugged and gave up. He had no other way of contacting Richter, except to try calling him a few more times over the next half-hour.

At fifteen ten the helicopter began to descend west of Plátanos, until its radar return was lost in the ground clutter. Eight minutes later the helicopter re-appeared, again climbed up to five hundred feet, and headed west back towards the frigate. As soon as it had landed on board, the American ship turned towards the north-west and increased speed to twenty knots, heading away from Crete.

## South of Zounáki, western Crete

Murphy gave a grunt of satisfaction as, through the Bushnell scope, he watched Stein tumble to the ground. He slipped the magazine out of the Dragunov, pulled out his pistol and jogged down the hill towards the road. He could hear Stein screaming when he was still a hundred yards away. Murphy slowed to a walk as he approached the Seat, moving carefully and deliberately, his pistol held ready in a loose two-handed grip. He could bring it up into aiming position in under a quarter of a second.

Stein had managed to crawl another few yards towards the car, but was still about ten yards away when Murphy stopped moving and gazed down at him over the sights of the Daewoo.

'Make it easy on yourself,' Murphy called out, raising his voice over the noises the man on the ground was making. 'Answer a couple of questions and it'll all be over. Just one shot, I promise. You're going nowhere and I've got all day. If you don't tell me what I want to know I'll take my time over it.'

Stein looked up at him from where he lay on the ground, his useless left leg stretched out, his trousers soaked with blood, and his screams now moderated to a dull moaning.

In his career with the Company, he himself had killed many times, officially and unofficially, and he'd always believed he was smart enough to die an old man in his own bed. The realization hit him hard that he was in exactly the same position as many of his victims had been, staring into the relentless barrel of a gun. In the instant that he looked up, he experienced the same feeling of hopeless, helpless dread that he'd induced in so many others over the course of his career. He closed his eyes briefly.

'You're Stein?' Murphy demanded, and the man on the ground nodded slightly. 'What have you done with the steel case?'

'Trunk of the car,' Stein gasped. 'In a black bag.'

'Who was the other guy?' Murphy nodded towards the Seat.

'British Intelligence,' Stein said, sweat pouring from his forehead. 'Don't have a name.'

'British?' Murphy murmured to himself, a brief smile appearing. 'That's not so bad. At least not Mossad. Those fucking Israelis never forget. The Brits have a bunch of rules and scruples. They're never going to come after me.' He nodded in satisfaction, lowered the muzzle of the pistol slightly and pulled the trigger. The pistol kicked in his hand, the silencer reducing the sound of the shot to a dull cough. The 9mm bullet hit Stein squarely in the stomach and he clutched at the wound, screaming with the pain. Stepping across to him with unhurried steps, Murphy looked down at him and smiled.

'You said one bullet, you bastard,' Stein gasped.

'I lied,' Murphy grinned, 'and you shouldn't have run.' He lowered the pistol, took careful aim and shot Stein through the head. Only then did the screaming stop.

Murphy gazed down at the dead man with contempt before kicking him once in the ribs, then headed cautiously up the hill towards the Seat Cordoba. Though reasonably certain that he'd find the British agent either dead or seriously wounded, he wasn't taking any chances. It was still just possible that the man was alive and waiting with a gun.

He stepped directly behind the Seat, glanced into the wide-open boot to verify that the black-wrapped bundle was still there. With the Daewoo aimed straight ahead, Murphy stretched out his left hand to ease the boot lid downwards a few inches.

Now able to look over it, as far as he could see there was nobody in the car, either in the front or the back seats. Murphy looked quickly all around him but saw nothing. He eased forward slightly to check the left side of the car first, then the right. That was when he started worrying, because he now registered the blown right-hand front tyre. His bullet hadn't hit the driver, but one of the wheels, which was what had caused the vehicle to swerve off the road. So where the fuck was the driver now?

How could he have got out of the Seat without being seen? Murphy knew he'd watched the car for at least two minutes after it had lurched to a stop, and then he'd put a bullet through the front of the vehicle; he could see both the entry and the exit holes.

Then Murphy remembered something. As the Seat had slid off the road onto the waste ground there had been a short period – just a very few seconds – when the dust swirling around it had almost blocked his view of the car through the Bushnell. It was possible, just barely possible, that the driver, this British agent, could have slipped out of the car through the passenger door.

This realization had come late to Murphy, though his assessment of what had happened was remarkably accurate. Unfortunately for him, it was too late for him to do anything about it.

He whirled round, suddenly conscious that he might have unwittingly made the transition from predator to prey. He swung the Daewoo up to face the threat that he was suddenly sure he was now facing, but he was too late. A lifetime too late.

The bullet from the SIG took Murphy in the right shoulder, spinning him round as the Daewoo clattered to the ground. As he fell back with a shout of pain, stumbling into the rear of the Seat, Murphy looked up at the figure standing ten feet in front of him, and met Richter's ice-blue gaze.

'What's your name?' Richter asked, his voice quiet and controlled.

'Murphy. Mike Murphy.' The response came through clenched teeth as the wounded man clutched at his shattered shoulder.

'Well, Mike, here's the bad news. Some of us in British Intelligence,' Richter said, echoing Murphy's remarks, '*don't* have scruples and *don't* give a flying fuck for anybody's rules. But what I don't do is tell lies, so you're getting the same two you doled out to Stein there.'

Richter altered his aim slightly and shot Murphy in the stomach. The assassin howled with pain and doubled up, falling to the ground. Richter stepped closer and ten seconds later Murphy fell silent permanently as Richter's last bullet blew off the top of his head.

# Chapter 25

The Seat was useless to Richter. The car had three bullet holes in it – one through the boot lid, the others in the driver and passenger doors – and Murphy's shot had not only punctured the right front tyre but also buckled the wheel rim and smashed the brake disc. It was now going to have to be hauled away behind a recovery truck.

But, Richter reasoned, Murphy hadn't just been waiting around there on the road out of Zounáki on the mere off-chance that Stein would turn up there. Obviously he'd been following the Seat, which meant that there was another vehicle parked somewhere in the vicinity. He could hopefully use that to get back to Máleme.

But Richter needed to do a bit of a clean-up first, because he wanted to leave a satisfactorily tidy solution for the Cretan police to find. He first checked Stein's body and found, as he had expected, that the bullet from the sniper rifle had gone straight through the American agent's left thigh – Richter could clearly see the entry and exit points in the fabric of the trousers – and vanished into the scrubland beyond.

The other injuries had all been caused by Murphy's Daewoo pistol, and all the wounds on Murphy's own corpse by the SIG that Stein had originally been carrying. The bullet holes in the Seat were simply that, and they would reveal little information about the weapon that had fired the bullets themselves. Richter's rudimentary knowledge of ballistics reassured him that a round fired from a high-velocity rifle at long range would leave a hole similar to that from a larger but slower bullet shot at close range from a pistol.

Richter eyed critically the two bodies now lying beside the Seat. He then dragged Stein a little further back, and turned him round so that his feet were pointing towards his dead assassin. That looked better.

With a little imagination it was easy to construe this scene as some kind of gunfight between the two men that had ended with both of their deaths.

It would take a lot more imagination to credit that both had managed to shoot each other in the stomach before simultaneously shooting each other in the head, but Richter believed that Fitzpatrick could probably use his influence to make sure it became the accepted account. That way, the open files on the killings of a policeman and two villagers in Kandíra, of the diver near the island of Gávdos, and a man calling himself Curtis in the hospital in Chaniá, could all be closed.

Richter was still wearing the thin rubber gloves he'd donned before approaching Stein in the car park at Máleme, so was reasonably certain that he'd left few traces in the Seat. He placed the Daewoo by Murphy's side, then stepped across to the other corpse. He wrapped Stein's right hand around the butt of the SIG, pointed the pistol into the sky and pulled the trigger. The weapon coughed and recoiled. A paraffin test, if anybody bothered to carry one out, would now show that both men had fired weapons shortly before they died.

He checked Murphy's pockets, found a set of car keys as expected, and the magazine from the Dragunov, which he hadn't anticipated. Richter put both of these in his jacket pocket, lifted the briefcase from the passenger seat and the black-wrapped steel case out of the boot of the Seat, and set off down the hill.

A few minutes later he locked both items safely in the boot of the Peugeot he'd found parked a quarter of a mile away, and began climbing up the hill to the north of the parked vehicle, looking for a sniper rifle. When he discovered it, Richter whistled softly. It was a long time since he'd seen that particular model. For a few moments he wondered what to do with it, then shrugged, tossed the magazine down beside it and headed back down the hill. He'd let some Cretan local find it and add it to his private armoury.

JAMES BARRINGTON

## Central Intelligence Agency Headquarters, Langley, Virginia

Just after nine, Henry Rawlins knocked on the door of John Westwood's office and slumped down, uninvited, in a leather chair in front of his desk.

Westwood watched him quizzically. The CIA Director of Personnel was a most infrequent visitor to his domain: in fact, as far as Westwood could recall, Rawlins had never before even been in his office. When they met at all, it was usually at high-level meetings and conferences elsewhere, or over meals in the supergrades' dining room at Langley.

'Good morning, Henry,' Westwood said. 'Unusual to find you defending democracy on a weekend.'

Rawlins smiled thinly. 'I'm not absolutely sure that's what the CIA is doing, and I personally don't get involved if I can avoid it. I generally leave that to you full-time warriors.'

'So what's special about this Saturday, Henry?'

Rawlins smiled again, but didn't answer the question. 'I hear you've been running checks on some pretty senior guys, John,' he said, and Westwood nodded. 'What's it all about?'

'Right now, Henry,' Westwood replied, 'I'm not really sure. What I do know is that the Company was involved in some kind of deep black operation back in the seventies, somewhere in the Mediterranean region. A short time ago a Greek diver found a crashed Learjet near the coast of Crete. What research I've been able to do has demonstrated a definite link between that same deep black op and the crashed jet. The moment the news of the Lear's discovery hit the press, somebody here in America began eliminating every CIA agent who'd originally been involved in that operation. He killed three former agents, all long retired.'

Rawlins raised his eyebrows. 'Who were the victims?'

'Charles Hawkins, James Richards and Henry Butcher.'

Rawlins shook his head. 'I don't think I ever ran into any of them.'

'You probably wouldn't have, Henry: they were well before your time. In fact, all three of them retired over ten years ago.'

'But if they're long retired, why the hell did somebody need to kill them?'

'That,' Westwood said, 'is what I'd like to know. But whoever the

**400**

killer is, he's absolutely ruthless. He not only killed Hawkins, but he took out his wife as well, and Henry Butcher was already in a deep coma in a hospital when he was murdered. What's worrying me is that the killer probably still works right here in this building. And that's why I've been running about trying to find someone who fits the very basic profile I've so far been able to put together.'

'Which is?' Rawlins asked.

'He had to have been employed by the Company at least as early as nineteen sixty-nine or seventy, probably in Operations or Intelligence, and he's likely to be still working here now in some senior position.'

'And that's it?' Rawlins asked, incredulous.

'That's it,' Westwood confirmed, 'and that's why I've been tying up your staff, Henry. I have to say I didn't expect a personal visit over it,' Westwood added with a smile.

Henry Rawlins smiled back. 'Normally I wouldn't bother, but this morning we received a high-priority signal request from CIA London, and my staff considered it important enough to call me in. The British Secret Intelligence Service has been inquiring about a bunch of people they believe were CIA officers in the early seventies.'

'Really?'

'And guess what,' Rawlins added, 'some of the names they've got are the same as those you've just mentioned.'


## Western Crete

Richter drove Murphy's rented Peugeot up to Tavronítis and then turned right towards Chaniá and Réthymno, putting some distance between himself and the two corpses he'd left behind. He stopped in Máleme, dumped the Peugeot there and reclaimed his own Renault hire car. He then drove out of the town towards Chaniá. On reaching Plataniás, he pulled off the road and reached into his jacket pocket.

For obvious reasons, he had switched off both the mobile phones he was carrying when he'd donned the old man's hat and coat. Now he switched them both on again and, selecting the mobile that Ross had given him, fished out the notebook in which the dead man had written the contact number for SIS Crete. He dialled this and asked for Fitzpatrick. Thirty seconds later the SIS man was on the line.

'I've taken care of that matter we discussed,' Richter said.

'That's "taken care of" as in what, exactly?'

'You could describe it as a terminal solution. The man who encountered Charles Ross is no longer with us, and nor is the cleaner somebody sent out to take care of him.'

'Cleaner?' Fitzpatrick asked. 'What cleaner? It's the first I've heard of that.'

'Me too,' Richter replied. 'I talked to Watson – real name Richard Stein – before he got ventilated—'

'Your doing?'

'Oddly enough, no,' Richter said. 'I had every intention of eliminating him, but somebody else did the job before I got the chance. From what Stein told me, my guess is that this whole operation was a double-blind set in motion by Stein's CIA briefing officer in the States. He sent three agents out here to Crete to totally destroy the wreck of the Learjet and recover all the evidence, and then sent out a cleaner – he was called Murphy – to kill them and take away the evidence. And then, probably, he'd already got somebody else organized in the States to kill the killer.'

'Let me get this straight,' Fitzpatrick said. 'This guy is prepared to kill three or four CIA agents just to eliminate all traces of some thirty-year-old Company operation? Why? What the hell is he trying to protect?'

'I wish I knew. Anyway, I need to explain what happened, so you'll need to take notes. Ready?'

'Ready.'

Richter described the location between Zounáki and Nterés where the abandoned Seat and the bodies could be found. 'Somebody may well have stumbled across them by now,' Richter said, 'in which case the Cretan police will already be involved. I tried to set the scene so that it would look like both men died after a shoot-out, with no third-party involvement. I don't know how good forensic science is here on Crete, so I can't predict how the police will interpret the scene, but there are a few things you should know before you talk to them.

'First, the Cordoba has four bullet holes in it: one through the boot lid, one in the driver's door, another in the passenger door, and one that destroyed the right front wheel. In fact, the hole in the passenger side door is an exit hole, so there were only three hits on the car. All those shots came from a Dragunov sniper rifle that I found around three hundred metres from where the vehicle was stopped.'

'A Dragunov? I've not seen one of those for a while,' Fitzpatrick commented.

'Nor me.'

'What did you do with it – the Dragunov, I mean?'

'I left it where it was. Unless the Cretan police realize the shots that hit the car came from a rifle, not a pistol, they'll have no reason to go looking for another weapon. Obviously, if they find it, the "gunfight at the OK Corral" scenario goes straight out of the window.

'I searched the scene and I couldn't find any of the Dragunov's bullets, or even any fragments. But if the police decide to analyse the traces of copper on the bullet holes in the Seat and compare that with the copper jackets of the nine-millimetre slugs in the Daewoo and SIG pistols, they'll probably find a difference in the composition. That would be a bad idea, so perhaps you can talk them out of conducting too deep an investigation.'

'I'll do my best,' Fitzpatrick confirmed. 'Anything else?'

'Only to request a light touch in checking the rest of the crime scene. I was responsible for the elimination of Murphy – he's the one you'll find holding the Daewoo – and I've no doubt I may have left some traces at the scene. I was wearing gloves, but there'll be hairs, clothing fibres, all that kind of thing.

'The ideal conclusion for the Cretan police to draw would be that Stein killed their officer in Kandíra, and also the diver whose body we recovered from the sea near Gávdos. There's a police officer called Inspector Lavat who's up to speed on those two killings, so I suggest you bring him into the loop.

'In Chaniá, you could argue that Stein killed his colleague, real name Roger Krywald, though he was near death in the hospital, to avoid any possibility of him talking. In fact, according to Stein, Krywald was killed by Murphy.

'Then, back in Réthymno, Stein discovered Charles Ross in his hotel room and killed him. Perhaps you could suggest that Six received a tip-off about this renegade American agent. After that Stein, with four killings already under his belt, tried to escape from Crete – perhaps heading for a boat or helicopter, which he'd arranged to pick him up somewhere on the west coast.

'He'd got himself as far as Máleme when he was intercepted by Murphy – I don't know if that's his real name or an alias, but he's got to be carrying some kind of ID. They drove off the main road and up into the hills, got involved in a confrontation and shot each other to death. End of story, but perhaps you could dress up Murphy's role so that he becomes a US undercover police officer, hot on Stein's trail.'

'OK, that should work,' Fitzpatrick said after a moment. 'What are you going to do now?'

'I don't really know. I've collected what evidence there is to be found, and all the opposition players have been eliminated as far as I know, so I suppose I'll just head back to London and let my section or Six sort it all out.'

'Good luck. Right, I'll get over to Zounáki and fix things out there. Maybe I'll see you again some time.'

'You never know.' Richter disconnected.


### HMS *Invincible*, Sea of Crete

The young communications rating was concerned. The procedures were quite specific, but as far as he could see there was no way he could follow them. So he called the Chief over and explained his problem.

'Leave it to me,' the CPO said, and walked across to the Communications Officer.

'Yes, Chief?'

'Slight problem, sir,' he said. 'We've got a Flash signal classified Secret for Lieutenant Commander Richter, but as far as I know he's ashore somewhere so we can't deliver it within the specified time.'

'Sounds like it's Commander Richter's problem rather than ours, Chief. Give it to me and I'll see if the Ops Department has any kind of contact with him.'

As he left the Communications Centre the officer reflected that he'd never known a junior officer – and in his book a lieutenant commander *was* still a junior officer – to receive so many personal classified signals or, frankly, cause so much trouble to other departments on board any ship. He wished the bloody man would get off the *Invincible* and bugger off back to London or wherever he'd come from.

'Richter?' he said without preamble as he stepped into the Ops Office and saw Ops Three sitting at his desk working out the following day's flying programme. 'Have you got a contact number for him?'

'I have,' Ops Three replied, 'but he's either had his mobile switched off for the last few hours or he's been out of a cell. Why?'

'I've got a signal for him,' the Communications Officer said, thrusting a clipboard at him. 'It's Secret and Flash, and I reckon you've got a much better chance of contacting him about it than I have, so you may as well take it. Sign here.'

'Thanks a bunch,' Ops Three muttered under his breath.

### Western Crete

Richter had ended his call to Fitzpatrick only four minutes earlier, and had just started the engine of the Renault and slipped it into first gear when his other mobile phone – the Enigma issued on the *Invincible* – started to ring.

'Commander Richter? It's Ops Three, sir, on Mother. We've been trying to reach you for some time.'

'Sorry, the phone's been switched off. What did you want?'

'I was instructed to pass some landfall information on to you, sir. An American frigate approached Crete from the west and launched a chopper this afternoon at just after three local time. It flew to somewhere near Plátanos where we think it landed. It got airborne again a few minutes later and flew back to the frigate. Then the frigate itself left the area, and we presume that the helicopter picked someone up.'

Richter smiled slightly before he replied. 'I don't think the man they were expecting actually turned up, because I met him first. Is that it, then?'

'No, sir. I've just been handed a Secret signal for you, precedence Flash. It's in a sealed envelope so that's all I can tell you about it. What do you want me to do with it?'

Richter thought for a moment before replying. 'Open it, please,' he said, 'on my authority.'

'I won't be able to read it to you, sir,' Ops Three said. 'Not even over a secure telephone.'

'I know,' Richter said, 'but you will be able to tell me if I need to get back to the ship in a hurry or do something else.'

'Right, sir.' Richter heard a faint tearing sound and then silence for a few moments as Ops Three scanned the signal.

'Yes?' Richter said encouragingly.

'I don't understand the third sentence here, sir, but the first two are quite clear. You're to report by the fastest possible means to the American naval air station at Soúda Bay.'

That wasn't at all what Richter had been expecting. Having just killed in cold blood someone who was almost certainly a CIA agent or asset, he had rather hoped to be keeping his distance from America and the Americans for some time.

'Who's it from?' Richter asked.

'The originator is listed as "FOE" – that's Foxtrot Oscar Echo,' Ops Three reported, 'and the signal is signed "Simpson".'

'Is there anything else you can tell me without compromising the text?'

'Really there's only one thing, sir. It's the proper name "Westwood". Does that help?'

'I'm not sure,' Richter replied, wondering what the hell John Westwood's name was doing in a signal sent to him from Richard Simpson. At least he could trust Westwood, counted him as a friend. 'OK,' he said. 'I'll get myself to Soúda Bay. Can you get that signal to Soúda Bay Ops or wherever by helicopter so I can pick it up?'

'Yes, sir. That shouldn't be a problem. We've got a Merlin leaving the ship in fifteen minutes to join the ASW screen. I'll re-task it on telebrief to call at Soúda Bay first.'

'Thanks.' A thought suddenly struck Richter. 'Are you still running surveillance out to the west of Crete?' he asked.

'Yes, sir. How did you know about that?'

'Actually, I requested it. You might need a higher authority to confirm it, but there's now no reason for it to continue. I suggest you check with Wings and tell him what I've just said.'

'Right, sir.' Ops Three's voice sounded uncertain. The instructions for the surveillance operation had come straight from Flag Officer Third

Flotilla, *Invincible*'s operating authority. How the hell could a request from a lieutenant commander in the Royal Naval Reserve turn into an order from an Admiral?

'Thanks, Ops Three,' Richter said. 'My guess is I won't get back on board this deployment, but maybe I'll get the chance to fly with the squadron again some other time.'

## Central Intelligence Agency Headquarters, Langley, Virginia

Like Henry Rawlins, Nicholson wasn't normally to be found at Langley over the weekend, but he'd been expecting a signal from the US Navy frigate that had been tasked with collecting Richard Stein or, more likely, Mike Murphy, from the western end of Crete.

Conscious of the time difference between the Mediterranean area and the American eastern seaboard, he'd appeared in his office early, but it wasn't until after ten local time that the signal finally arrived, having been routed through various satellites, the frigate's operating authority and Langley's own communications section. And when he read it, Nicholson knew that his problems were far from over. The signal, shorn of its routing indicators and other dross, was for Nicholson a two-word nightmare. It said simply: 'NO SHOW'.

For two or three minutes he just stared at the words, wondering what the hell could have gone wrong. He knew Krywald and Stein had recovered the case and file because he'd received Krywald's email confirmation of that. He knew Elias was dead because Stein had told him, and he knew Krywald had been eliminated because Murphy had confirmed his death. The only thing Murphy had needed to do after that was locate and eliminate Stein himself, recover the two items, and climb onto a chopper for the ten-minute flight to the waiting frigate.

That wasn't rocket science, for Christ's sake, and it was the kind of thing Murphy did all the time. For a few moments Nicholson wondered if the timescale had been just too tight, but he'd discussed it all with Murphy before he'd even left for the airport, and his operative had seemed quite satisfied with the proposal. Something, Nicholson knew, must have gone tits up.

His priority obviously was to find out what had happened.

Nicholson was methodical, so first he checked his secure email inbox, hoping for a message from Murphy, but found nothing there. Then he took a risk: he used his office telephone to call Murphy's mobile, but just heard a recorded message stating that the phone was switched off. Without much hope, he then tried Stein's mobile, but got the same response – or rather lack of it.

The only option was to email Murphy and find out what had happened. It took Nicholson less than three minutes to compose and send a message to the classified server. He marked it High Priority and incorporated a request for a read receipt: that way he'd know when the email got displayed on Murphy's laptop.

After a moment's thought, he sent an almost identical message to Richard Stein. Then all he could do was sit back and wait.

### South of Zounáki, western Crete

Inspector Lavat stood by the boot of the blue Seat Cordoba and stared at the two bodies lying on the ground. Then he examined the bullet holes in the metal of the Seat, shook his head and glanced towards the higher ground lying to the north of the crime scene. To Lavat, the damage to the car looked as if it had been caused by a rifle, not a pistol – a rifle that he was certain had been fired from somewhere in those hillocks some three or four hundred yards away. But that, he had already decided, was not going to be the official version.

He'd been telephoned an hour earlier by a man he'd never heard of, called Fitzpatrick, and given brief details of the incident occurring near Zounáki. The moment Fitzpatrick mentioned Richter's name, Lavat had been sure that there would be more to these killings than met the eye. And, after a brief initial inspection, he knew that he was right.

The police in Máleme had received an almost hysterical phone call from a female British tourist who had stumbled on the grisly scene whilst out walking, and they had reacted immediately. Half a dozen police officers had been dispatched to the location, and now stood around, making sure that the small but growing crowd of eager sight-seers all kept their distance and didn't contaminate the crime scene.

They were waiting for their forensic people to arrive, and Lavat knew that then his real work would begin.

No experienced forensic scientist could accept the scenario that Fitzpatrick had suggested to Lavat. The chances of two people inflicting virtually identical bullet wounds on each other, and then simultaneously shooting each other in the head, were less than zero. Lavat realized that and so too would the men in white suits when they finally arrived.

But Lavat also knew that that scenario made perfect sense from the point of view of convenience and even justice. Fitzpatrick had informed him exactly who the two dead men were, and Lavat knew that one of them – the one clutching a SIG P226 automatic pistol – was almost certainly the man who had killed his police officer in Kandíra. Fitzpatrick was a little more vague about the identity of the second corpse, but Lavat didn't feel inclined to probe too deeply.

He shook his head again, wondering how best to approach the problem. Perhaps conjuring up an anonymous eyewitness might be the best option: somebody who had actually observed the two men shooting at each other. That might be the best way of persuading a suspicious forensic scientist to doubt the evidence of his own eyes.

Failing that, he guessed he would just have to accept whatever the forensic team decreed, but ignore the conflicting evidence when he came to write the report. After all, the one thing certain was that there would be no court case: this double shooting was a dead end, and was also going to close four open files.

On balance, he was glad Richter had been around, and he was certain he could detect the hand of the Englishman in many of the events following the death of Spiros Aristides. But he was also pleased that Richter was leaving Crete: life there had been both quieter and simpler before he arrived.

## NAS Soúda Bay, Akrotíri, Crete

The armed sentry posted at the counter-weighted barrier guarding the main entrance to the Soúda Bay base took one look at Richter's Royal Navy identity card and raised the barrier.

'You're expected, sir,' he said. 'They're warming up one of the RC-135s for you. Do you know where the flight line is?'

'No,' Richter said, 'I've never been here before.'

The sentry handed him a printed map annotated with directions and supplemented it with a string of verbal instructions. Richter drove on into the base, trying to shift a feeling of unreality engendered by the sentry's casual phrase: 'They're warming up one of the RC-135s for you.'

The RC-135 is a highly specialized and very expensive electronic surveillance aircraft based on the ubiquitous and reliable Boeing 707 platform. It was an RC-135 on a regular patrol out of the States that stood off the Kamchatka Peninsula in 1983 and recorded all the transmissions from Soviet ground stations and fighter aircraft, as Korean Airlines flight KAL007 flew increasingly further off-course into Soviet territory and was finally shot down by a Russian Flagon interceptor. That incident resulted in the loss of two hundred and sixty-nine lives but produced for the West arguably the greatest intelligence coup of the decade, comprising Russian radar signatures, radio frequencies, intercept procedures and all the rest. Appallingly, many Western intelligence analysts considered the sacrifice of so many lives to be entirely justified.

The RC-135 is not only an extremely complex and expensive aircraft, but is also highly classified. The Americans are very reluctant to let anyone anywhere near one unless they have a demonstrable and essential need to know what goes on inside the fuselage. So why, suddenly, was Richter being allowed aboard one as a passenger? And as a passenger to where, exactly?

As he hauled the Renault round a corner and headed towards the complex of hangars, he suddenly noticed the unmistakable shape of a Royal Navy ASW Merlin standing over to his right. He checked the mirrors, braked the car to a halt, then reversed back until he could turn onto the dispersal where the helicopter was parked.

He stopped about fifty yards from the Merlin, switched off the engine and climbed out of the vehicle. The chopper's engines were running and the rotors turning, so he knew that at least some of the crew had to be on board. A ground marshaller was standing in front of the Merlin, wands crossed below his waist in the 'park' position. Richter moved across to him and spoke into his ear.

'Are all the crew still on board the chopper?'

The marshaller glanced at him. 'No, sir. One of the guys from the back got out a few minutes ago. He's over in that building to your right.'

'Thanks.'

The building indicated was about seventy metres away, and as Richter approached the door it opened and a man wearing flying overalls stepped out. Richter recognized him immediately as one of the 814 Squadron aircrewmen.

'Is that for me?' Richter asked, gesturing at the buff envelope the man held in his hand.

'Oh – hullo, sir. Yes, it's for you.' He took a crumpled sheet of paper out of one of the pockets of his overalls and proffered it. 'It's classified Secret, sir, so you'll have to sign for it.'

Richter scribbled something approximating his signature in the space the aircrewman indicated, then took the buff envelope from him. He ripped it open and pulled out the message form. The text was brief and specific:

RICHTER, INVINCIBLE. PROCEED NAS SOUDA BAY IMMEDIATE. JOIN FIRST AVAILABLE FLIGHT NORFOLK VIRGINIA. ON ARRIVAL AWAIT CONTACT COMPANY REP WESTWOOD REFERENCE CAIP. SIMPSON, FOE.

Richter walked back to the Renault and dropped into the driver's seat. He read the message again, then made a decision. He pulled out the Enigma mobile phone and dialled FOE in London. Five minutes later he was talking to Simpson himself.

'I was called up by your old pal John Westwood,' Simpson began, 'and when he found out it was you that was opening cans of worms all over the Mediterranean, he thought the two of you should get together.'

'Get together on what, exactly?' Richter asked.

'Good question. I don't know, and nor does Westwood, but it looks as if someone in the States is going around permanently silencing CIA personnel who were involved in a deep black operation the Company ran in the early seventies.'

'So?'

'So there's a link to what happened on Crete. A direct link. Pretty much all Westwood has been able to dig up is the name of the operation.

Everything else – all the documentary evidence and all records on the CIA's database – seems to have been destroyed. But the name's interesting. It was called "CAIP", spelt Charlie, Alpha, India, Papa,' Simpson added. 'The same as the initials on that steel flask and the file you've recovered from those Yankee comedians.'

# Chapter 26

Richter was feeling the strain. His sleep on Friday night had been interrupted by the news that Stein's hire car had been spotted, and Saturday had been, by any standards, a very full day. He was sitting in a surprisingly comfortable seat in the darkened rear compartment of the RC-135 – none of the electronic surveillance devices had been switched on, and three of the consoles were shielded by tied-on shaped plastic sheeting so he couldn't even see the displays – and he was now trying to make some sense of the CAIP file.

The problem was, it was full of what looked like complex medical information, none of which meant anything to Richter: his medical expertise basically encompassed taking an aspirin whenever he had a headache. He hadn't yet found any explanation of what 'CAIP' meant, or even what the initials stood for, and he guessed that this file wasn't a stand-alone. As far as he could see, it dealt only with the strictly medical aspects of whatever CAIP involved. No doubt there had been other files at Langley – presumably already destroyed if what Simpson had said was accurate – which would have contained more general information about the concept and scope of the operation.

Stein's briefcase lay on the seat beside him, the sealed flask tucked beside Richter's two mobile phones and his Browning Hi-Power, none of which he'd found the time or the inclination to return to the ship. The steel case was still wrapped in its black dustbin bags but was now, as an additional precaution, locked in a sealed heavy-duty plastic box and tucked away under an adjacent seat. Next to it was Richter's overnight bag, noticeably bulkier than when he'd packed it on board the *Invincible* what seemed like weeks ago.

The X-ray machine operator in the military departure lounge had thrown a fit when he'd registered what was in the briefcase, and another one when Richter had put his overnight bag through, but that hadn't stopped him taking the two cases onto the aircraft unopened. Richter could be very persuasive, and the orders that had caused the ground crew to start pre-flighting the RC-135 had come from a level whose authority couldn't be ignored.

Richter closed the file, replaced it in the briefcase and snapped the lid shut. None of it made much sense to him. His best guess was that thirty odd years ago a bunch of American scientists had found, or stolen, or maybe even bought, the lethal bug that was sealed in those remaining steel flasks. They'd been returning to the States when fighter interceptors from some hostile power, maybe Libya, had shot down their aircraft, plunging them and the deadly pathogen they carried to the bottom of the Mediterranean. A subsequent search, if there'd been one, hadn't found the wreckage, and eventually almost everyone had forgotten about the lost Learjet.

Over the intervening years world opinion had shifted, and now it was no longer acceptable for any nation – and certainly not America, the world's supposed peacekeeper – to be seen as involved in any aspect of biological warfare. So when that Greek diver had stumbled across the wrecked Lear, somebody at Langley had decided that the once-buried evidence should be re-buried permanently, and had sent a team of agents over to Crete to recover what they could and destroy the rest.

That more or less made sense, but why all the killings? That was what he didn't get. Killing everyone involved seemed an extreme reaction if Richter's 'lethal bug collected for research' hypothesis bore any relation to the facts. What had started out as an obscure thirty-year-old puzzle had rapidly turned into a massacre, with three CIA agents and the mysterious Murphy – who Richter guessed had been a Company-employed hitman – all now dead. Plus five Cretans: the police officer; Spiros Aristides, his nephew and the two villagers.

In fact, Richter's hypothesis was wrong in every respect bar one: a team had indeed been sent to Crete to recover what they could and destroy the rest. All his other assumptions were inaccurate, however, because he was looking at the problem from the wrong end.

He was still trying to make some sense of it all as he drifted into sleep.

## Norfolk, Virginia

'So who do you reckon is knocking off your ex-CIA wrinklies?' Richter asked, before yawning prodigiously as Westwood threaded his Chrysler Voyager through the light late-morning traffic heading for Interstate 64.

When the RC-135 touched down, Westwood had been waiting for him at the airbase in Norfolk and had whisked Richter away as soon as the aircraft had come to a stop in the dispersal. The plastic box containing the steel case was now in the back of the car, and Stein's briefcase and Richter's overnight bag were both sitting on the rear seats.

Westwood shook his head. 'I wish I knew – and I wish I knew why. I'm hoping you and I can get our heads together and sort this mess out.'

'We'll do our best. Thanks for organizing the ride – pretty impressive stuff, getting the use of an RC-135 as an executive jet. They could improve the in-flight catering, though. Coffee from a Thermos and a couple of packs of sandwiches won't ever get them into the "My Favourite Airline" charts.'

'You're lucky you even got that.' Westwood changed lanes and accelerated. 'I had to call in a bunch of favours first and then clear it with my boss.'

'You heard what happened on Crete, I suppose?'

Westwood nodded. 'Yes, your Mr Simpson briefed me on a secure telephone link, not that it was much help to me. What I still can't figure out is why anybody would decide a thirty-year-old covert op is still so sensitive that any people involved with it have to be killed on the off-chance that they might talk about it.'

'I think *I* can,' Richter said.

'Go on. I'm listening.'

'I think Stein was more or less right. I think the guys involved in CAIP had found some lethal bug somewhere, and were taking it back to the States for use as the basis for a biological weapon. According to the CDC people on Crete, the bug contained in the flasks acts a bit like a combination of Ebola and Lassa Fever, but it's much, much faster than either of them. Lassa kills in weeks, Ebola within a few days, but catch this one and you're dead in a matter of hours.

'That suggests to me that they'd probably found this bug somewhere in the African rain forest, because that's where most of the real nasties like Marburg and Ebola have come from. Perhaps they'd staged out of Egypt or Israel, or somewhere similar, just stopped for a refuel, and their next stop was going to be a Spanish or British airfield for another top-up before the hop across the pond.'

'But it's still ancient history,' Westwood objected. 'That plane went down over thirty years ago. Why the hell should anyone care about it now?'

'Maybe because the US has always vehemently denied any involvement in biological warfare. Your government always maintains that all its research is aimed at defensive, not offensive, measures. Imagine the outcry if somebody found proof that the CIA was involved in discovering naturally occurring viruses, which Fort Detrick or wherever was then developing into biological weapons for offensive purposes.'

Westwood remained silent for a few moments, then shook his head. 'Sorry, Paul, I don't buy it. In that case, all we'd have to do is claim that the bugs in those flasks were intended for delivery to the CDC, to allow us the opportunity to develop antidotes. Who could ever say that that wasn't the truth? You talked about *proof*, and the flasks don't prove anything, not really.'

'OK,' Richter conceded, 'that does make sense. But maybe your phantom killer is a lot more paranoid than either of us, and he's not willing to take a chance on his name being linked with this operation.'

'Maybe. We'll get him, though. With what's in the file, I'm hoping we can nail this bastard real quick.'

'There's one thing I've just remembered that might help,' Richter said. 'I had quite a little chat with Stein back on Crete, and the only really solid piece of information he gave me was the name of his briefing officer, which was "McCready".'

Westwood looked interested, then shook his head. 'I don't recall that name from the research I've done,' he said. 'I can check it out at Langley tomorrow, of course, but my bet is that he was either employed solely as a briefing officer for this operation, and not beyond that, or else he was using an alias. That would have been pretty much standard procedure for an operation of this classification.'

'And there's something else,' Richter said. 'Something that really worries me.'

'What?'

'The steel case,' Richter replied. 'According to Stein there were four flasks inside it. Three were still sealed and one had been opened by the Greek diver, but there were spaces for twelve flasks altogether. So who's now got the other eight? Did Aristides sell them on to someone, or did somebody take them out of the aircraft even before Aristides found it? If opening a single flask can kill everyone who comes close to it, do you have any idea what sort of damage a terrorist group could do with eight containers of this bug?'

'Shit. You got any more bad news I should know about?'

## Lake Ridge, Virginia

About once an hour since he'd got up, Nicholson had been using his home computer to access the classified server, but he was still waiting for a read receipt from either Murphy or Stein to signify that they'd now opened the emails he'd sent them. On repeated attempts to contact their mobiles, each time the system had reported the phones were switched off.

This was the worst possible news. It suggested that both men were either dead or imprisoned, or otherwise unable to get access to their computers or phones, and that almost certainly meant that somebody else had now gained possession of the flasks and the classified file. As far as Nicholson knew, no other intelligence services had any interest in the matter, so the most likely organization to have become involved was the Cretan police force.

That might or might not be a good thing, but he had to find out exactly what had happened, because until he knew he couldn't take any remedial action. For some minutes Nicholson sat and considered his options, but he realized virtually immediately that he really had only one choice. The sole usable asset he now had on Crete was the CIA agent living and working the *persona* of Captain Nathan Levy, United States Air Force, and all he could ask of him was to investigate, since Levy was strictly a support agent. For anything beyond that, Nicholson was going to have to fly yet more people out to the island.

He checked a small notebook in which he'd listed – quite illegally according to CIA regulations – the contact details of all the people he had already tasked in any connection with this operation on Crete. He opened his email client, copied Levy's address into the 'To' field, composed a message, marked it High Priority, added a read request, and then pressed 'Send'.

With the message on its way, Nicholson began to feel better, but he knew it would probably be Monday midday, Crete time, before Levy would reply. However, the time difference meant that his reply should be posted on the classified server by the early hours of Monday morning, Eastern Standard Time, so he wouldn't have that long to wait.

### Haywood, Virginia

'It's no good,' Westwood said, tossing down the red Ultra-Secret classified file and looking across his study at the couch where Richter lay sprawled, half-asleep.

'No?' Richter sat up, yawning, but looking interested. Tired but interested.

'I was going to use this,' Westwood tapped his finger on the file in front of him, 'to cross-reference the names of any agents who fitted the rough profile I prepared. I'd already checked out the senior agents listed on the inside front cover. That got me nowhere, because they're all dead.

'In fact,' he added, 'it was the killing of the two retired Company agents that sparked our interest in what was going on in the first place. The problem is that all the junior agents are referred to in the file either by their initials, sometimes only by single initials, or by their Christian names. Sometimes they used two or three initials at the start of a memo and then only used single letters after that. It's real confusing now, but probably made good sense at the time, when everybody knew exactly who "B" and "R" and "John" and "Mike" were.'

'How many different sets of initials are we looking at?'

Westwood glanced down at the paper on which he'd been making notes. 'I've got eleven sets of three initials, six sets of two letters, and fifteen single initials, and there's really no way I can make any sense of them. I mean, right here in this tasking sheet I've got "CRP", "P", "CP" and "RCP". That could be one person if the "RCP" is a misprint for

"CRP", or two, or three, or even four different people, and I can't see any way of finding out which at this stage.'

'And the Christian names?'

'Half a dozen different ones,' Westwood said, again reading from his list. 'I've got Dave, George, John, Mike, Oliver and Steve. And unless I've missed something, these guys are never referred to by their initials, because none of them match. There's no "J" or "D", for example. And I've checked the initials and the names with the agents that I'm guessing might have been involved way back, but none of them match, apart from "John", three times, but that's not real surprising.'

'Can we look at it from the other side?' Richter interposed. 'Is there anything in the memos to show what CAIP was supposed to achieve?'

'No. Apart from the medical stuff, they're all just routine: requests for motor transport, inquiries about aircraft availability, booking briefing-rooms, that kind of thing. Nothing with any details. I think you're right. Almost everything in this file deals with the very specific medical aspects of CAIP. The other files, the ones that as far as I know were destroyed back in nineteen seventy-two, probably dealt with the overall picture. Unless we can identify Mr X and persuade him to tell us what the aim of the operation was, I think the only way we're going to find out is if the Company vets some of our senior medical specialists and gives them clearance to analyse this file. Maybe they could translate this stuff into something mere mortals could understand.'

'So what now?'

'I don't know,' Westwood said, 'but I guess the first step is to take all this stuff' – he gestured towards the red file and Stein's briefcase – 'and show it to my boss, Walter Hicks. But the problem is we've still only got a bunch of initials and six Christian names. We can't start accusing any-one only with that, and particularly not any of the senior guys now at Langley.'

'I can see that,' Richter said. 'Accusing somebody who out-ranks you of being a multiple murderer is not the way to make friends and influence people, unless, of course, you can prove it, and you certainly can't do that with what we've found so far. If you're wrong, you'd spend a very long time working very hard trying to make people forget. It's your call, John, but my advice would be don't involve Walter Hicks until you've got more than some initials to go on. I think the best option would be a bit of finesse here.'

'Meaning what, exactly?'

Richter got off the couch and moved across to sit opposite Westwood at the desk. He rubbed his tired eyes then leaned forward. 'Let's sketch out a scenario. According to Stein, the man we're looking for has been calling himself McCready. I know that's almost certainly an alias, but let's use it for the moment as a convenient name for our bad guy.' Westwood nodded. 'Now, he's sent three agents to Crete to recover this file and the steel case with the flasks inside it, and also to blow up the Learjet. He's probably been keeping in regular contact with them by email or mobile phone or maybe both.

'They'll have been keeping him informed, so he'll know that they successfully destroyed the jet and found the case and all the bits. He'll probably have been told that the diver had been eliminated, and that Krywald was terminally sick in Chaniá hospital, and he'd certainly arranged a pick-up for Stein from the west end of Crete. I know that because Stein told me so, and the *Invincible*'s radar tracked a helicopter that launched from an American frigate, landed somewhere at that end of the island and then returned to the ship.

'I'm guessing that McCready also briefed Murphy to eliminate Krywald, find and kill Stein and recover the steel case. I assume both Stein and Murphy had been briefed about the pick-up by helicopter, and this McCready didn't much care which of them made it, as long as one of them did. If Stein got there before Murphy found him, fine: McCready could take care of him in the States. If he was already dead, Murphy would have recovered the steel case and he'd be the man the chopper collected. Probably Murphy would walk into a bullet or a sub-way train or something else fast-moving and lethal once he'd handed over the case to our mystery man.'

'I can't argue with any of that,' Westwood said.

'OK, then look at what's happened since. The chopper left the rendezvous empty-handed, with Stein and Murphy being no-shows because both of them were already dead. The frigate no doubt signalled Langley through some covert route informing McCready that nobody had appeared. Once he heard that news, I presume he started trying to reach Stein or Murphy by email or mobile phone, but for obvious reasons he's not going to get a response from either. So for the first time since this operation started, he's completely in the dark. He's got no idea what's happened to either Stein or Murphy, or who's currently got possession of the steel case.

'He'll probably guess that the Cretan police have got involved – maybe they just got lucky and arrested Stein, or picked up Murphy or something like that – so he thinks that the police have his case. Now if I was McCready, I'd want some sort of information, and I'd want it fast. I'd task any asset I had located anywhere near Crete to get on to the island and investigate. Then I'd be thinking about sending a new team over there to pick up the pieces the first team dropped.'

'So?' Westwood asked.

'So how about we bring Mike Murphy back from the dead? We email this McCready character, tell him Murphy had to run for his life after he'd killed Stein, didn't make the rendezvous with the chopper, so had to fly back to the States commercial. That would explain why he hasn't replied to any emails McCready might have sent, and why his phone's been switched off all this time. We tell him Murphy's here in America, complete with the file, steel case and its contents, and ask where he wants to fix the handover.'

'That,' Westwood said after a few moments, 'might just be the best idea you've ever had.'

'Obviously you don't know me as well as you think, John. Back in the UK I'm known as a fund of wonderful ideas. Just ask anyone who knows me.'

'Yeah, right,' Westwood smiled briefly. 'What about the practicalities? Do you happen to know what email addresses McCready and Murphy were using?'

'No, but it doesn't matter. I had to borrow Murphy's car after the shooting stopped, then I decided to liberate his laptop and his mobile, on the grounds that he wasn't going to be needing them any more. I've also got Richard Stein's laptop and mobile, and an unfired SIG P226 automatic with a couple of spare magazines I found in Stein's luggage. The SIG hasn't got a serial number, which makes it a potentially very useful bit of kit. In fact,' Richter added, 'I've now got two laptop computers, four mobile phones, and a Browning Hi-Power pistol as well as the SIG, and not one of them belongs to me.

'Murphy's laptop will have copies of all the emails he's received and probably those he's sent as well, and he'll have been using his mobile phone to dial whatever ISP McCready has been using. All we have to do is hitch the phone to the laptop, switch on and hope for the best.'

'Why "hope for the best"?'

'Because Murphy probably has some kind of password protection built in to his machine. If it's a Windows password it's not a problem – a mentally retarded gibbon could work its way round one of those – but if it's a BIOS password or something more sophisticated it could be a lot more difficult.'

'I didn't think computers were your thing, Paul?'

'They're not,' Richter replied, 'but this guy Baker back at Hammersmith has been giving me a crash course. We've just done basic security. I'm a fast learner and I've got a good memory.'

Six minutes later Richter had everything connected up on the corner of Westwood's desk. He tried the Nokia mobile first, turned it on and watched the screen. There was no request for a SIM or phone password and the phone merely displayed the signal strength and battery level.

'So far so good,' Richter said, and pressed the power button on Murphy's Toshiba Satellite Pro. A light illuminated to show that the hard drive was working, and the opening screen appeared. Then it all stopped and a BIOS password request box popped up in the centre of the screen.

'Shit.'

Westwood didn't seem fazed. 'I'll get one of our IT guys out here to bypass it,' he said, and reached for the phone.

'On a Sunday afternoon?' Richter asked.

'I carry a fair bit of weight around here, Paul,' Westwood replied. 'Of course I can get somebody out on a Sunday.'

The technician arrived just over an hour later. He didn't look like a computer nerd – he was around thirty, clean-shaven, wearing blue jeans and trainers, white button-down shirt and a red sweater – and he was carrying a large aluminium briefcase.

'Is this it?' he asked, before sitting down in front of the open laptop. Westwood nodded. 'Do you know the name of the owner?' the man asked.

'Mike Murphy,' Westwood said.

'OK,' the technician muttered, and began pressing keys. 'What programs do you want to access?'

'It's essential we get into his email client software,' Richter said, 'but we'd prefer to be able to access everything.'

Six minutes later the technician stood up and picked up his case.

'Is that it?' Westwood demanded. 'What was it?'

'Always try the obvious first. His name was Mike Murphy, so I tried "MikeM", "MMurphy", "MikeMurph" and so on. It turned out he was using "TheDoubleM". It was about the twentieth option I tried. I've checked the other programs and none of them are password-protected. The dial-up networking script and the email client – he's using Outlook Express – both have their passwords stored, so you shouldn't have any other problems.'

By the time Westwood had closed the front door behind the technician, Richter had already opened up Outlook Express and was scanning the contents of Mike Murphy's inbox.

'Here we go, John,' he said. 'There are three messages from McCready in the inbox, the last sent on Friday, advising him of the rendezvous near Plátanos at fifteen twenty on Saturday afternoon. I'll just check his sent messages now . . . OK, nothing of great interest, just acknowledgements of what McCready has told him. Ah, this one's different: he's just confirmed that Krywald has been dealt with at Chaniá, which at least bears out what Stein said.'

Richter switched on Murphy's mobile phone again and made sure that the data cable was firmly secured at both ends. He turned to the computer and accessed the dial-up networking script. The default option was a telephone number in the United States, but the name Murphy had given the connection wasn't what would have been expected if it had been one of the major ISPs like AOL. He'd just called it 'Crete', which suggested it was only a temporary connection.

'This is probably it, John,' Richter said, and clicked 'Dial'. The mobile phone dialled the number as the two men watched the screen. About half a minute later, the computer broke the connection once the single message on the server had been downloaded.

'Bingo,' Westwood said. 'Just the one message, but McCready's getting restless,' he added, as he scanned the text.

'OK, let's put him out of his misery,' Richter said, and began composing the message they'd agreed to send. It was fairly long, and they made several changes to try to make it as authentic as possible.

'Are you happy with that, John?' Richter asked, as Westwood read the finished text for the third time.

'I think so. He's possibly going to smell a rat but I'm betting that he's so desperate to retrieve the evidence that he'll still agree to a meet. After all, this' – he gestured at the screen, – 'could have happened.'

Three minutes later, Richter clicked 'Send and Receive' and watched the screen as the message vanished.

'And now?' Westwood asked.

'And now we wait,' Richter said. 'The ball's in McCready's court.'

# Chapter 27

**Monday**
**Lake Ridge, Virginia**

Nicholson hadn't expected a response from Murphy or Stein after such a long silence, being fairly certain that both men had been either killed or captured. But when he checked his email a few minutes before going to bed just before midnight on Sunday he immediately saw the read receipt for the message he'd sent to Murphy, and also a reply from him.

Murphy sounded flustered, and as he read his message Nicholson could understand why. The killing of Stein had gone badly wrong. The police had turned up almost as soon as he'd pulled the trigger, and Murphy had had to run for it, barely getting away with the steel case, and being forced to avoid police pursuit by heading up into the hills, missing the rendezvous with the helicopter. He'd apparently had to sneak onto the ferry up to Kíthira and make his way from there to the Greek mainland before he could catch a flight out of Athens to Amsterdam and from there to New York. But the message confirmed he had in his possession the steel case, the Ultra Secret file and everything else that Krywald and Stein had been able to retrieve.

After reading the email half a dozen times, Nicholson leaned back in his seat to consider his options. He was quite certain that the message had been sent from Murphy's laptop, simply because of the read receipt, but that didn't necessarily mean that Murphy had sent it.

On the other hand, the events described in the message were certainly plausible, and would explain why he'd heard nothing further from Stein – because he was already dead – and why Murphy himself had been out of contact for so long.

For a few minutes he toyed with calling Murphy's mobile phone, just to see if he could confirm the man's identity from hearing his voice, but then rejected that idea, because whether Murphy was alive and waiting to complete the last phase of his contract or dead or languishing in some Cretan jail didn't actually make too much difference.

What Nicholson knew was that whoever had sent the email, whether Murphy or somebody else, knew far too much about CAIP and that meant that he really had no choice. He had to meet him, find out who he was, and then eliminate him. Nicholson spent a few minutes deciding exactly how to respond, and in particular where he should specify as a rendezvous, then clicked 'Reply', and quickly typed his message. He read the text twice, then pressed 'Send and Receive', shut down the computer and went to bed.

### Haywood, Virginia

Richter woke suddenly at four-thirty in the guest bedroom of John Westwood's spacious house, staring at the unfamiliar surroundings and wondering not merely where he was, but also, for a brief moment, who he was. Some people suffer from jet-lag flying east to west, others vice-versa. Richter belonged to the rather smaller group that suffered it whichever way they flew long-haul, and this had ruined another night's sleep.

He knew from past experience that there was no point in even trying to get back to sleep, and he didn't think Sally Westwood would appreciate him blundering around the house in the pre-dawn darkness. He switched on the bedside light, padded across the room to the low book-case beside the door and scanned the titles. They seemed to be mainly Aga sagas and chick-lit, and Richter guessed that the room was usually occupied by Sally's female friends overnighting, but he found a rather battered Clancy novel on the bottom shelf and took that back to bed with him.

Jack Ryan had just been informed by Admiral Greer that he was to give a presentation at the White House about the missing Russian sub-marine 'Red October' and its renegade captain when Richter's alarm went off. He silenced it, put the book down on the bedside table and walked into the bathroom for a shower – the guest bedroom didn't run to a bath, which Richter would have much preferred. He always believed he did a lot of his best thinking while in the bath.

He appeared in the kitchen just after eight. Sally was on her way out of the door shepherding the two Westwood children in front of her, and heading for her Cherokee Jeep and the school run over to Culpeper. She waved a casual hand towards the cooking range.

'Hi, Paul,' she called, 'ham and eggs are in the oven. Just help yourself. I'll be back in about an hour. Make toast if you want it,' she added over her shoulder as she pulled the door to behind her.

Richter headed for the coffee pot instead. He found a mug to fill, added milk, then walked into the study. Westwood was sitting at his desk and staring at the screen of Murphy's laptop. He looked up as Richter entered.

'Morning, Paul. Sleep well?'

'Not particularly,' Richter said. 'I'll sleep a lot better tonight, when this lot's over. What news?'

'I think we've set the hook.' Westwood wore a smile of triumph. 'McCready's replied already. He's given Murphy a good dressing-down for being out of contact for so long, and he wants to collect the stuff at eleven this morning.'

'Where from?' Richter asked.

'One of the Company's regular safe houses. It's about twenty miles from here. I've been there a few times before.'

'Do you know it well?'

'Pretty much. There are sensors covering the drive, external cameras, alarms on all the doors and windows, and also a secure briefing-room installed in the cellar. That's a room within a room, soundproof and airtight. The Company uses this house for sensitive debriefings, that kind of thing.'

'Staff?' Richter asked.

'Just one. He's a retired Company man employed as a permanent caretaker.'

'OK, we shouldn't have any trouble from him. What about walls and fences?'

'It's surrounded by hedges. Most of the properties in that area are fairly open, and the Company decided that building a wall would attract too much attention.'

Richter nodded. 'Right. It's obvious McCready's setting a trap. Once Murphy's handed over the goods, he'll be planning a "wham, bam, thank you, Mike" pay-off. He'll get a bullet in the back of the neck and his body will be dumped in a shallow grave somewhere. We need time to think this through. Send him a reply as Mike Murphy, John, but tell him you're still in New York or somewhere and that the earliest you can get there is four this afternoon. That'll give us time to get our beans in a row.'

## Lake Ridge, Virginia

The first thing Nicholson had done that morning was call in sick to Langley. This was merely a courtesy – as a Head of Department he reported to the Director of Central Intelligence and nobody was going to check his attendance record – but he had three meetings planned during the day, all of which he told his PA to cancel or reschedule.

Then he drove down the road to a gas station – not the one he normally used – and parked beside the pay phone at the side of the lot. He made one short call to a Virginia number, then got back into his car and drove home.

He had left his computer switched on, expecting the confirmation email from Murphy, and as soon as he got back to his house he checked the inbox. The first message he looked at was from Murphy, explaining that he couldn't make the morning rendezvous. That wasn't entirely surprising, as Nicholson had no idea where the other man was in America, but he had no problem with the revised rendezvous at four in the afternoon. It just gave him more time to organize things over at Browntown. Nicholson sent a brief acknowledgement, climbed back into his car, drove to a different pay phone and made another call to the number he had dialled previously, then returned home again.

He left the house a couple of hours later, heading for the meeting he had just arranged, and after making a final check of his inbox, hoping that Levy would have replied. In fact, Levy was typing his response to Nicholson's query as the CIA officer drove away from his property. All he'd been able to discover from his contacts was that two men had been found dead after some kind of a shoot-out at the western end of the island, but the Cretan police weren't looking for any third party. At that stage, Levy had no idea of the identity of either victim, but both were believed to be American.

If Nicholson had received Levy's email, he might have deduced that the dead men were Stein and Murphy, and hence been better prepared for his subsequent encounter at the safe house, but it didn't arrive for a further forty-five minutes.

## Browntown, Virginia

The safe house was located deep in the Virginia countryside, at the northern end of the Shenandoah National Park and on the outskirts of Browntown. Richter guessed that the location had been picked, at least in part, because of easy access from Washington and Langley along Interstate 66.

It looked, from Richter's vantage point some four hundred metres away, in all respects like a typical small country property. The binoculars didn't help much: through them the house looked exactly the same, only a lot closer.

'We could have a hell of a long wait here, Paul,' Westwood said. 'It's not ten yet.' The two men were lying side by side at the edge of a small copse of trees, watching the house through binoculars.

They'd started out immediately Westwood had transmitted the email message to McCready, and hadn't bothered waiting for a reply. Richter was certain that whoever was hiding behind the McCready alias wouldn't go to the safe house until 'Murphy' had agreed a time and place for the rendezvous. But it was essential, both men had agreed, that they themselves were there and ready in position well before anybody else arrived. They needed to assess exactly what the opposition strength was before they even thought about entering the property.

Richter had dialled the secure server using Murphy's laptop just before Westwood pulled his Chrysler to a halt about half a mile beyond the safe house, and had downloaded the confirmation from McCready that he would reach the safe house at four. Westwood had parked the Voyager in a side road, but left it in plain sight. As he explained to Richter, cars half-hidden in woods always looked far more suspicious than vehicles parked right out on the street. Then they'd moved on foot until Westwood had spotted the roof of the safe house beyond the trees, and only then had the two men left the road and headed up towards the copse.

'Early birds, worms, that kind of thing, John,' Richter replied. 'Anyway, it's a fine day. We've got sandwiches and coffee and two pairs of binoculars. If nobody shows, we can at least improve our knowledge of ornithology.'

'Yeah, right.' Westwood didn't sound either enthusiastic or convinced.

For nearly four hours almost exactly nothing happened. They saw a lot of birds, a handful of rabbits and a couple of squirrels, and got bitten by an interesting selection of insects, some of which they saw but most of which they didn't.

To begin with, they both watched the house. Then they took that task in turn, because few activities are more terminally tedious than staring through binoculars at a scene that simply doesn't change. They drank a coffee each at about eleven, and a little after one ate the sandwiches Richter had prepared.

Westwood was unimpressed with his choice of filling. 'Cheese and pickle or cheese and pickle, Paul? What the hell kind of choice is that? I don't even like cheese.'

'In England, we call it Hobson's Choice, John,' Richter replied, not taking his eyes from the view through the binoculars. 'The cheese was in your fridge, the pickle was in your cupboard. All I did was put the two together between a couple of slices of bread. So just eat it and stop bitching about it.'

Westwood sank his teeth into the sandwich, then: 'Why Hobson's Choice, Paul?'

'It's supposed to derive from a man named Hobson who ran a livery stable in Cambridge a couple of hundred years ago. Apparently when you hired a horse from him he offered you a choice of exactly one. You either took it or walked, hence Hobson's Choice. You finished?'

'I guess.'

'OK, your turn to watch. Don't take your eyes off the house.'

At thirteen fifty, Westwood muttered the single word: 'Showtime.'

Richter rolled over onto his stomach and in one fluid movement swept his binoculars to his eyes. Two cars were driving slowly – much more slowly than normal traffic – down the road towards the safe house. The leading vehicle turned into the short drive and stopped right outside the house itself, while the second car carried on.

'The lead car will be McCready's,' Westwood murmured, unconsciously lowering his voice although there was no possibility he could be overheard. 'The second car is probably his muscle. They'll be checking the area, looking for people like us.'

'Right,' Richter said. 'How many, do you think? Can you see?'

'No, but we'll know soon enough, I guess.'

'Yes. Once they're satisfied we don't have a fully equipped SWAT team waiting in the wings they'll go back to the house.'

'Just remind me again,' Westwood said. 'Why, exactly, don't we have a fully equipped SWAT team waiting in the wings?'

'Evidence, John, evidence. All we actually possess is a few emails on a stolen computer, a classified file that nobody without a degree in medicine can understand, a bunch of stiffs out on Crete, and three sealed vacuum flasks. So far we don't have anything that implicates anyone that we can identify.'

'And there's another reason, isn't there?'

'Yes, there is,' Richter said. 'I got dragged into this because my boss was looking for a really shitty little job to give me. Since then I've been pulled off a ship, where I was having a pretty good time, and hauled all over Crete following one lead after another. I've been exposed to a lethal pathogen, I've had a bunch of explosives blown up right under me, I've been shot at, and I've had a fellow professional killed more or less right in front of my eyes. All that, as far as I can see, is down to this McCready character – and I don't like unfinished business.'

'OK, OK. I didn't expect an extract from *War and Peace*. Right, someone's getting out of that car.'

Both men concentrated on the scene unfolding at the safe house. The driver's door opened and a tall, bulky man climbed out and pushed the door closed.

'Got him.' Westwood then paused for a few moments. 'Jesus Christ, that's a surprise. It looks like our man is John Nicholson. He's head of the Intelligence Directorate, and he wasn't even *on* my list. But he does fit, I guess, if only because of his Christian name. And *that* must be the caretaker,' he added, as the main door of the house opened and a grey-haired figure emerged. He walked across to the car and stood talk-ing to Nicholson. Then he pointed towards the double garage adjacent to the house. As Richter and Westwood watched, the door swung open by remote control. Nicholson headed towards the house while the care-taker climbed into his car and drove it into the garage.

'He'll only want one car to be visible in the driveway when Murphy arrives,' Westwood observed, then paused as a second car emerged from the garage and halted in front of the house. 'OK, that's probably the caretaker's motor. He'll want the man out of the way for the rest of the day.' The caretaker climbed out of the vehicle, pointed his remote to close the garage door, and walked back into the house.

Five minutes later the main door opened again and the caretaker re-emerged. He climbed into his car and drove away from the house and down the road.

'He'll have been explaining the security systems and other stuff to Nicholson, I guess,' Westwood commented, not taking his eyes off the scene.

'Here come the bad guys.' Richter watched as the other vehicle, the one that had been behind Nicholson's when they arrived, reappeared down the road, turned into the drive and stopped outside the safe house. Three men got out and looked all around them, then two of them walked over to the house and went inside while the third began walk-ing slowly around the property itself.

'That figures,' Westwood said. 'They'll have two guards inside covering Nicholson, and the third guy outside to intercept anyone who wanders onto the property by accident and to shoo away neighbours or salesmen.'

'OK, John,' Richter lowered the binoculars and rolled on to his side to face Westwood, 'now we know the strength of the opposition, are you happy with the plan we worked out?'

Westwood nodded. 'We figured there would be up to four heavies plus Nicholson and maybe the caretaker as well, so the odds are actually better than we calculated,' he said. 'Are you sure you can handle this, Paul, because it really will be my neck on the line in there?'

'Trust me, John. I can take care of them.'

'You'll have Sally to answer to if you don't,' Westwood added, and Richter smiled briefly at him.

'Just trust me,' he said again. 'It's what I do.'

For another hour the two men lay silently, studying the house through their binoculars, but saw no sign of movement apart from the patrolling guard.

At three twenty Richter turned to Westwood again. 'It's time, John. I know you won't need it, but good luck in there.'

'Right,' Westwood eased up into a sitting position and glanced at his left wrist. 'I've got three twenty-one.'

'Check,' Richter said, looking at his own watch. 'You should be outside the house by three forty-five, but that's not critical. But four zero five is, OK?'

'I've got it, Paul. Four zero five. Just be sure you're ready by then.'

'I will be. They'll be expecting you to be armed, so are you carrying?'

'No,' Westwood replied.

Richter reached into his inside jacket pocket, pulled out the Browning Hi-Power and passed it over. 'It's got a full magazine, but you shouldn't have to use it. The safety catch is on and there's one in the chamber. Just remember it belongs to the Queen and I've had to sign for it, so I would appreciate getting it back sometime.'

Westwood nodded. 'Right now, making sure your paperwork gets completed properly is the least of my worries, but I'll do my best. You've got the SIG?'

'You bet,' Richter said.

Without another word, Westwood moved backwards into the relative darkness of the copse, and began making his way down towards the main thoroughfare and the side road where he'd parked his Chrysler.

For fifteen minutes Richter did nothing, lying motionless to watch both the house and the approach road. The outside guard didn't seem to be following any set pattern in his patrolling of the grounds, but Richter guessed that would change after Westwood had arrived. Once the fly was in the web the spider could relax.

At three thirty-five Richter himself started down towards the safe house across the largely open countryside that lay in front of him. Even when the guard was out of sight he moved as quietly as possible, keeping low just in case one of the other men was watching through a window.

By three forty-five, now only twenty yards from the boundary of the property, Richter crouched down behind some bushes. He could see an easy way into the grounds almost right in front of him – a narrow gap in the hedge that he reckoned he could squeeze through – but he was going to wait for Westwood's arrival before he moved again.

He heard the Chrysler Voyager before he saw it, heard the noise of its tyres on the road. He saw the light-coloured roof of the vehicle moving slowly, decelerating further to make the turn into the driveway. And then he saw Westwood himself in the driving seat as the car pulled up outside the house.

As Westwood had explained, the drive was equipped with sensors to detect any vehicle approaching the property, so Richter wasn't surprised when the main door of the house opened at almost the same moment as the outside guard reached the Chrysler.


John Westwood braked to a halt and switched off the engine. He opened the door just as a man walked over and stopped beside it. His jacket was hanging open so Westwood could see the bulge of a shoulder holster and the butt of an automatic pistol.

Beyond him, the front door of the house swung open and another man peered out. It wasn't Nicholson, and Westwood heaved a sigh of relief. That had been one of their worries, since Richter's plan called for Westwood to get inside the house before any of them realized who he was.

'Your name?' the man standing beside the car demanded.

'Mike Murphy,' Westwood said. 'I'm expected here.'

The guard gestured for Westwood to lift his arms above his head and then frisked him expertly. He found the Browning almost immediately – Westwood had simply tucked it into the rear waistband of his trousers – removed the magazine and worked the slide to eject the round already in the breach, then tossed the pistol and the magazine onto the driver's seat of the Chrysler.

When he was checked again, Westwood realized that the man was looking for a wire. After a moment, the guard stepped back, satisfied. 'Follow me,' he said.

At the front door of the house, the other guard stood waiting and now stepped back to precede Westwood into the building.

As Westwood walked down the hallway, he prayed again that Richter was up to it.

The moment the outside guard turned to escort Westwood to the front door, Richter moved. He slipped through the hedge and ducked down immediately. As soon as the patrolling guard was out of sight, he stood up again and sprinted across to the house, flattening himself against the wall and concealed between two large bushes. Whichever direction the guard now approached from, he would hear the man's footsteps on the gravel path before the guard could see him. That was all the edge Richter needed.

He eased the SIG P226 from the waistband of his trousers. The extra length of the attached silencer made the weapon much more cumbersome than a normal pistol, but Richter was more than willing to trade that inconvenience for the ability to fire nearly silently.

But the guard moved much more quietly than expected, and he was within ten feet of Richter's hiding place before he heard him. Richter eased back against the wall and ducked down slightly, waiting for the man to pass. But as the guard drew level, his peripheral vision must have detected the intruder for he swung around, simultaneously grabbing for his shoulder holster.

Richter dropped the silenced SIG and launched himself off the wall like a torpedo out of a tube. He didn't want to kill the guard: he had no quarrel with him or the other two men inside the house. They were just doing a job, maybe hired for the day or perhaps junior CIA agents. But Richter needed to subdue him quickly, because the clock was already running.

Westwood followed the guard across the entrance hallway and into a spacious inner hall. Before the man proceeded any further he stopped and motioned for Westwood to lift his arms above his head.

'The guy outside just checked me,' Westwood said, raising his hands.

'And now I'm checking you.'

Apparently satisfied, he gestured for Westwood to follow him again, heading towards a door set in wooden panelling, which Westwood knew led down to the underground briefing-room. So far, things were going more or less as Richter had predicted.

Outside the soundproof entrance of the cellar room below, he pressed the bell twice. Then he opened the door, pushed Westwood inside, and pulled it closed behind him.

The lighting in the briefing-room was bright and harsh after the comparative gloom of the house above, and Westwood had absolutely no difficulty in recognizing the other figure in the room, seated at a small table. But Nicholson stared back for a few seconds without apparent recognition before his face darkened.

'Westwood, you meddling bastard,' he spat. 'Where's Murphy?'

'Murphy didn't make it.'

Nicholson nodded as if it was the answer he had been half-expecting. 'I suppose you think you've been clever, trying to trace me through the database.'

'Seems I succeeded.'

'Whatever,' Nicholson waved a hand dismissively. 'I was going to arrange for you to have an accident anyway,' he added, picking up a pistol from the table and levelling it at Westwood's stomach, 'but now I won't bother. You can just disappear.'

'Dead bodies have a habit of turning up inconveniently.' Westwood forced a certain bravado into his voice.

'Not in this case. There's a disused well just about five miles from here. It's not marked on any maps, and it's full of the bones of people who've been foolish enough to cross me. I'll cut your tongue out just to keep you quiet, then I'll drop you down it, and you'd better pray the fall kills you. Otherwise it'll take you days to die.'

Even used to the hardened attitudes of his Company colleagues, Westwood was shocked by the ruthless venom evident in Nicholson's tone, and again prayed silently that Richter knew what he was doing.


As Richter crashed headlong into the guard, he groped for the man's hands as they tumbled backwards onto the neatly trimmed lawn fringing the gravel path. The guard had managed to pull out his pistol – a nine-millimetre Austrian Glock – and was trying to bring it to bear when Richter grabbed his right wrist and twisted it up and back.

'Pull the trigger now, and it'll be the last thing you do,' Richter panted in the man's ear, pushing his hand further back until the pistol barrel was directly under the guard's chin.

As the man suddenly relaxed. Richter seized the barrel of the Glock with his left hand and twisted it away. But at that moment the guard brought his left knee up hard towards Richter's groin. Feeling the sudden movement, Richter twisted sideways, taking the impact on his outer thigh, as he tossed the Glock behind him.

The guard pulled himself away and scrambled to his feet. Richter recognized immediately from his stance that he'd been trained in one of the martial arts.


'I think you're forgetting something.' Westwood took his eyes from the barrel of the pistol and looked up at Nicholson's face. 'If you kill me, you'll never recover the CAIP file and those flasks. I've already made certain they'll get into the hands of someone who can ensure the maximum exposure.'

For a moment, Nicholson just stared at him, then he threw back his head and laughed.

'I expected better from you, Westwood. Do you have any idea how corny that routine sounds? It's just bullshit and you know it.'

'You want to take a chance that I'm bluffing? Walter Hicks knows where I am. He knows that I'm meeting you here.'

Nicholson stood up and moved closer. 'The most Hicks can possibly know is that you're supposed to be meeting a man named McCready. There's absolutely nothing to tie me to McCready, so I'm quite happy to take the risk. Even if you have lodged the evidence with someone else, I can soon persuade you to cancel your arrangements.'

'Dream on,' Westwood murmured.

'It's no dream. You're vulnerable, Westwood, and you know it. I reckon if I strapped your wife and kids into a row of chairs in front of you and started cutting slices off them you'd change your mind real quick.'

Nicholson smiled and, for the first time in his life, Westwood literally felt his blood run cold – a cliché come hideously to life – as he realized Nicholson would do exactly what he threatened. The man's life and his career were on the line, and he would do whatever it took to contain the situation.

The guard stepped forward, left arm extended in front of him, the hand open and ready to grab, his right hand flattened into a killing blade, just waiting for the opportunity to strike.

Karate. Richter recognized the stance, but still he didn't move. The man took another step forward, then lunged for Richter's jacket with his left hand, his right swinging downwards and sideways. If the blow had connected it could have broken Richter's neck, but the moment the guard moved, so did his opponent.

Richter stepped forward, blocked the strike with his left hand and turned to his left, stepping under the guard's right arm and seizing his wrist with both hands. Then he straightened up, pulling the guard's arm down and towards him, while simultaneously bending forwards.

The momentum of his strike had slightly unbalanced the guard and Richter's move did the rest. The man stumbled forward, then somersaulted over Richter's bent back, but the Englishman didn't let go. He held on to the man's arm, hauling it backwards as the guard's body hit the ground hard, instantly dislocating his shoulder.

He screamed briefly but Richter hadn't finished. He released the guard's arm, leaned forward and hit him hard in the stomach, driving the breath from his body. Richter reached into his own pocket, pulled out a roll of brown adhesive tape and a couple of plastic cable ties. He rolled the guard onto his front, pulled his arms roughly behind him and lashed his wrists together with the ties, then pulled a length of tape off the roll and gagged him. Richter half-carried, half-dragged him across to the wall of the house and dumped him beside it. Then he stood up, surveyed his work and nodded in approval.

Richter crossed to the gravel path, picked up the Glock and stuck it into his rear waistband. Then he retrieved the SIG and began walking cautiously around the house towards the main door, keeping close to the wall and, hopefully, out of view of the security cameras. Halfway there he glanced at his watch. Three fifty-three. Just about right.

*

John Westwood just stared at Nicholson silently, then looked down to sneak a surreptitious glance at his watch. Eleven minutes to go.

'Late for something?' Nicholson demanded, his pistol still holding Westwood captive.

'No,' Westwood replied. 'I was just wondering when you'd get around to telling me how clever you've been, and what you're planning to do next with whatever's contained in those sealed vacuum flasks. What have you done – sold them to al-Qaeda or some other bunch of deranged lunatics?'

For the second time since Westwood had been pushed inside the secure briefing-room, Nicholson just stared at him. 'You have,' he said eventually, anger flaring in his eyes, 'absolutely no idea what you're talking about. You think I would sell out the Company? Fuck you, Westwood, I'm a patriot, and I'm doing everything I can to protect the Agency, and our country. Once I get my hands on that stuff it's going straight into an incinerator.'

Westwood affected incomprehension, although he had guessed that Nicholson's intentions had been something like that. 'I don't understand. Why go to all this trouble to recover the flasks if all you're going to do is destroy them?'

'You don't understand, Westwood, because you're stupid and ill-informed.'

'I'm only ill-informed because you destroyed all the files,' Westwood snapped.

Nicholson nodded impatiently. 'Yes, but if you'd done your job you'd have seen that those files were destroyed with the highest possible authority.'

Westwood nodded. 'And why would the President of the United States himself have gotten involved in sealing a bunch of CIA files?'

'That remark just shows the pitiful depth of your ignorance.'

Nine minutes to go.


The main door of the house was unlocked. Richter pressed his ear against the wood, listening for any sound of movement inside. He wasn't entirely sure that he would be able to hear anything through its thickness, but he had only lived as long as he had by taking care to check everything twice.

He double-checked the SIG again – full magazine, a round in the chamber and the decocking lever up – then reached out his left hand to turn the handle and open the door. As he had hoped, certainly half-expected, the hallway was empty. Their fly was already caught in the web: now closeted with Nicholson, Westwood had been the only visitor they were expecting, so the guards had clearly relaxed. The building alarms were switched off because of their frequent comings and goings: the most they would be likely to have left switched on was the driveway sensor, and Richter hadn't approached down the drive.

He headed down to the inner hall, stopped close beside the wall and listened. A faint murmur of voices was audible from a short corridor leading to his right, so he followed the sound, treading slowly and care-fully. At the end was a half-open door, and Richter could see from the corner of a wall cupboard inside that it was the kitchen.

He brought the SIG up into combat stance position, kicked the door fully open and stepped inside the room. Like a snapshot, the action there had been suddenly frozen. Two men sat facing each other across a wooden table, coffee pot on the stove behind them. One man's hand had arrested its movement halfway to his mouth, a piece of buttered toast clutched in his fingers: the other guard had his right forefinger thrust through the handle of a coffee mug. Both their mouths hung open in shock, their eyes now fixed on the SIG P226 with its long silencer.

'Afternoon tea, is it?' Richter observed contemptuously. 'Now' – the silenced muzzle of the SIG moved gently from one man to the other – 'in this kind of situation there's always a hard way to do things, and an easy way. The hard way is you both stop filling your faces and reach for your weapons, then I shoot you. That's easy for me but hard for you, and it also makes a lot of extra work for the caretaker here who'll have to clean your blood and intestines and stuff off the wall behind you.

'That's not a good option for you, OK, so let's work on the second alternative. I'll talk you through it, but to make things easier, let's have some names. You first.' He gestured to the man sitting on the right.

'Blake,' the guard replied shortly.

'OK, Mr Blake, just keep that piece of toast in your hand in case you get hungry later. Now, with your left hand take your pistol out of its holster, finger and thumb only on the butt.'

The guard nodded agreement, his eyes still fixed on the SIG. Moving carefully, he pulled back the left side of his jacket and reached awkwardly for his pistol. He tugged it out of the holster and put it on the table in front of him.

'Very good,' Richter said. 'Now finish your toast, then lace your fingers together and put your hands on your head.'

He watched carefully as the guard complied. 'And you are?' he asked, moving the SIG slightly to point directly at the other man.

'Henderson.'

'Same routine, Mr Henderson. Move slowly and carefully.' He didn't need to add any kind of a threat: the SIG did that for him.

'Now,' Richter said, 'perhaps one of you is carrying a back-up piece – a small revolver in an ankle holster or something. If you are, now's the time to tell me, because if I find out later, it's back to the hard option. I'll only ask you once: is either of you carrying a second weapon?'

He was rewarded with two shaking heads. 'OK, now, on your feet, both of you. There are two things I want you to do, both of them easy. First, where are the television monitors and control panel for the security system located?'

'In the den, just off the inner hall,' Blake replied.

'That's good,' Richter said. 'Now we'll just walk down the hall and open the main door.'

'What then?' Henderson asked, a quaver in his voice. 'You're going to shoot us somewhere once we're outside?'

'No,' Richter said. 'I've got no quarrel with either of you. At present you're just in my way. The second thing I want you to do is climb into the car you arrived in, drive away and forget you ever came here. Oh, and collect the remains of your buddy before you go. He's around the left-hand side of the house, trussed up like a turkey for Thanksgiving.' Richter realized he was getting the hang of the language. 'I'll be watching you on the CCTV system, so just make sure you do what I've told you. OK? If I see either of you here again,' he added, 'I'll kill you immediately.'

The small procession reached the front door. Henderson opened it cautiously and stepped outside, glancing behind him and still unsure of what would happen. Blake took a step forward, then span round in the doorway. He dropped his arms and lunged for Richter's gun hand.

It wasn't the brightest of moves, given that Richter was at least two paces behind him and carrying a pistol. Richter stepped back, easily avoiding the outstretched hand, then stepped forward and rammed the end of the SIG's silencer into Blake's solar plexus. The man fell gasping to the floor and for good measure Richter kicked him none too gently in the groin.

'Henderson, pick him up and just get the hell out of here,' Richter snarled. 'I'm losing patience with you two idiots.'

He watched the two men stumble through the front door, then pushed it closed and slammed the bolts home. Richter hurried back to the inner hall, located the den and stepped inside. The car parked on the drive outside was clearly visible, as Blake, bent almost double, climbed slowly into the rear seat. As Richter watched, Henderson came into view, half-dragging the other guard Richter had subdued earlier around the side of the house. He seemed to be protesting furiously, but Henderson ignored him and shoved him into the back of the car. He glanced over at the house for a moment before getting into the driver's seat, then started the engine and drove away.

Richter looked at his watch. Four zero four. On the button.


'So where are the flasks now?'

'I don't know,' Westwood shrugged.

'What the fucking hell do you mean? Of course you know where they are. If you didn't, you wouldn't even be here, so don't try and play games with me. Remember, I can have your wife and kids brought here within an hour, and I can have you talking within three minutes of my starting work on them.'

Westwood nodded. 'You probably could,' he said, 'but it still wouldn't help. I can't tell you what I don't know, and I don't know where the flasks are because I haven't got them.'

'Bullshit,' Nicholson snorted. 'I don't believe you.'

'You will,' Westwood said. 'Just think it through. I've been here in Virginia every day for the past week. The flasks were discovered in a steel case on Crete. How the hell could I have got hold of them?'

'You sent someone over,' Nicholson suggested.

Westwood shook his head. 'No, I didn't – someone else recovered them from Stein. Your hired killer Murphy blundered onto the scene, yes, but he was far too late. He collected a lead lunch, courtesy of the guy who's now got them.'

Nicholson felt for the first time as if the situation was slipping out of his control. 'So who is this man?' he demanded.

Westwood shook his head. 'All in good time – and there's something else. I didn't come alone.'

'This house is secure. My men are in control here,' Nicholson snapped.

'Are you so sure about that?' Westwood glanced again at his watch. Four zero five. He mentally crossed his fingers. 'So if somebody pressed the buzzer of that door now, that would be one of your men, right?'

'Yes, but nobody's going to press the buzzer, Westwood. My men have orders not to disturb us.'

As his voice trailed away into silence, the shrill sound of the buzzer cut through the briefing-room.


Richter had found his way down to the cellar and stopped outside the closed door to the secure room. He had then checked his watch yet again, taken something from his pocket and placed it in the middle of the floor just in front of the door, then stepped to one side and pressed the buzzer, twice.


For several long seconds John Nicholson did nothing. Then he motioned Westwood across to the side of the room where he could keep an eye on him while opening the door. He checked that his pistol's safety catch was off, walked across to the door and slipped the lock.

He eased it open a couple of inches and called out, but there was no reply. Then he glanced through the gap and saw what Richter had intended him to see. A small flask stood innocently on the floor a couple of feet away, the letters 'CAIP' clearly visible on its side.

And then the heavy door swung violently inwards, catching Nicholson sharply on the side of his head. He dropped the pistol and fell back, crashing to the floor. In his last seconds of consciousness, he heard a brief exchange begin between Westwood and the new arrival.

'Is that the way we planned it, or not?' an unmistakably English voice inquired.

'It's probably taken ten years off my life,' Westwood replied, 'but yes, Paul, that's the way we planned it.'

# Chapter 28

## Monday
## Browntown, Virginia

The third guard's name was Ridout, and to say he was annoyed considerably understated the case. Henderson had ripped the duct tape from his mouth before hauling him to the car, and as it turned out of the drive and onto the road, Ridout expressed his sentiments loudly and volubly.

'That scruffy blond bastard's not going to get away with this,' he grimaced. 'Nobody kicks me around like that.'

'You won't be doing anything about him until we fix your shoulder,' Henderson said, pulling the car off the road less than a quarter of a mile on.

'We're going back?' Blake asked hopefully from the back seat, the pain from his bruised testicles already easing.

'We're going back,' Henderson confirmed, switching off the engine and climbing out. 'Now this is going to hurt,' he warned, motioning Blake to grab Ridout around the chest.

'Just do it,' Ridout snapped, his face white and sweating.

Henderson seized his upper arm and with one swift movement pushed upwards and out. There was an audible click as the end of the humerus snapped back into its socket, the sound immediately eclipsed by Ridout's howl of pain.

'Jesus Christ,' Ridout gasped, his voice weak and strained. Cautiously, he rotated his right arm. 'It still hurts like hell,' he said, 'but I can move it.'

'Right,' Henderson continued to the rear of the vehicle. 'We've got Kevlar jackets and three Uzis here. We can take that guy easily, and Murphy as well.' He opened the boot and passed out the bullet-proof jackets, then used his security key to unlock a steel box bolted to the floor. Inside were four Glock 17 semi-automatic pistols, three Uzi sub-machine-guns and six boxes of ammunition.

With hardly a word spoken, they donned the jackets, picked up a pistol and sub-machine-gun each and swiftly began pushing 9mm shells into the magazines. Six minutes after Henderson had halted the car they were ready to go.

'How do we get back inside?' Blake demanded.

'The back door,' Henderson said. 'It's got an electric lock and an external keypad, and I know the code.'


Nicholson came to slowly, a searing pain on one side of his head where the door had struck it. For several seconds he had no recollection of where he was, but then recognized the briefing-room. He tried to stand up but his arms and legs refused to respond. He looked down and saw that his wrists were lashed firmly to the arms of the chair. He also realized that his jacket had been removed.

When he examined the small table in front of him, he noticed a strange collection of objects – a SIG automatic pistol, a kitchen knife, a container of salt, a tin of lighter fluid and a box of matches. Beside them stood the object that he'd seen earlier outside the briefing-room: a small metal vacuum flask bearing the letters 'CAIP'. Near by, West-wood and another man – fair-haired and slightly untidy – were standing staring at him.

'This is Paul Richter,' Westwood began, 'who sorted out your thug Murphy on Crete—'

'Let's just get some answers to a few simple questions,' Richter interrupted. 'First of all, what was CAIP?'

Nicholson shook his head firmly and then wished he hadn't as a bolt of pain shot across his skull.

'OK,' Richter continued, 'it's facts-of-life time. You've now got two choices. Tell us about CAIP and you might walk out of here alive. Clam up, and we're going to do some unpleasant things to you until you do tell us. It's up to you.'

Nicholson still said nothing. The other men exchanged glances, then Westwood turned away. 'I'll go put the kettle on, Paul.'

Richter walked across and ripped both sleeves off Nicholson's shirt.

'John's gone off to boil a kettle of water. When he brings it down I'm going to pour it over your left forearm. That should get the skin bubbling and blistering nicely.

'Then' – he gestured towards the table – 'I'm going to take this kitchen knife and score the skin several times. You'll bleed, but I'll put a tourniquet on your upper arm so you won't bleed to death. Then I'll rub kitchen salt into the wounds, pour lighter fluid over it and set fire to it. And once the flame's gone out, I'll start all over again.

'When I eventually get down to the bone, I'll do the same on your other arm, then begin on your legs. I've got all day, so if you don't tell me what I want to know you'll never walk or have the use of your arms again. And after all that, I've still got the flasks, so even if you hold out saying nothing to the end, I've still won. You just think about that now while the kettle boils.'

Richter smiled, but there was no humour or compassion in it, and Nicholson realized that whoever this Englishman was, he was perfectly capable of doing precisely what he'd threatened. Nicholson knew that, because he'd seen eyes like those before. He looked at such a pair in the mirror every day while he shaved.

'Of course,' Richter said, 'you can save yourself a lot of pain if you just answer a few simple questions.'

Nicholson silently shook his head. Just then the briefing-room door reopened and Westwood walked in, carrying a steaming kettle. Nicholson couldn't take his eyes off this simple domestic appliance as Westwood stepped across to the table and put it down.

'I don't like this, Paul,' Westwood's voice was low and concerned. 'It's barbaric, and it's not something I'm prepared to participate in.'

'Don't worry about it,' Richter said. 'Just go upstairs and watch the monitors, in case the hired help decide to come back. I'll call you down when Nicholson's decided to talk.'

Westwood nodded, his face still troubled, and headed back to the door. As it swung closed behind him, Nicholson raised his voice at last. 'You wouldn't dare.'

Westwood couldn't hear what Richter replied, and he was halfway up the stairs before he heard Nicholson's first scream.

\*

Henderson had worked out a kind of plan. It had to be quick and dirty, because the three of them guessed that the blond-haired man meant to do Nicholson harm, and they had no time to work out anything complex or sophisticated.

Murphy was an unknown quantity: he could even be the fair-haired man's accomplice. Whatever, Henderson had decided that the safest option was to take him down too. Murphy had encountered Ridout and Henderson when arriving at the house, so it was Blake who was going to provide a diversion while the other two men entered the property at the rear.

Blake now sat behind the wheel, his Kevlar jacket ready on the passenger seat beside him, alongside the Uzi. A Glock was tucked into his shoulder holster. Henderson and Ridout both sat in the back as Blake turned the car round and headed back the way they'd come. About a hundred yards from the safe house, he pulled the Ford into the side of the road, watched as his two passengers climbed out, then looked at the dashboard clock. He waited three minutes, then drove on slowly and turned into the drive. He parked carefully and took a map from the glove box. Getting out of the car, he then walked across to the front door and pressed the bell.


John Westwood was sitting at the kitchen table, his mind a whirl of conflicting emotions. He could still just make out Nicholson's howls of pain as Richter did whatever he thought necessary to make him talk. He hadn't exaggerated when he'd said he thought Richter's technique barbaric, but at the same time he recognized that Nicholson was unlikely to say anything unless some extreme form of persuasion was applied. Richter's method of persuasion was as extreme as anything Westwood could conceive, so he just hoped Nicholson would cooperate quickly.

The audible sound of the driveway sensor took him by surprise, and he immediately guessed that it meant trouble of some sort. He picked up one of the Glocks discarded on the kitchen table when Richter had disarmed the two guards. After checking that it was loaded and with a shell ready in the chamber, he headed into the den to look at the surveillance monitors. There he saw a Ford saloon outside, parked broadside on to the house so both its number plates were invisible. The guards had been driving a Ford, but so did a large proportion of the population of America. It could just be a travelling salesman or something.

Westwood proceeded to the front door as the bell sounded, checked that the bolts were fully home and peered at the small surveillance monitor fed by the porch camera. On the screen he saw a man staring down at a road map. Westwood pressed the button and spoke into the interphone system. 'Yes?' he inquired.

'Oh, hi,' the figure replied. 'Sorry to trouble you, but I think I'm lost. Can you give me directions to Browntown?'

'Easy,' Westwood began. 'Turn left out of the driveway and—' He turned sharply, having detected a faint sound of movement behind him. He saw the approaching figure and raised the Glock far too late. Henderson easily brushed the gun aside and struck out with the butt of his own Uzi. The weapon crashed into the side of Westwood's skull and he fell senseless to the floor.

Thirty seconds later Blake was also inside the house, pulling on his Kevlar jacket, as Henderson immobilized Westwood with a roll of plastic tape found in a kitchen drawer.


Nicholson had proved tougher than Richter had expected – tougher in trying to protect a secret almost half a century old than made any kind of sense. He'd hoped that Nicholson would simply start talking as soon as he saw what Richter apparently intended to do to him. Unfortunately that hadn't happened. But using the boiling water and lighter fluid was the kind of brutality that really wasn't Richter's style – so he had got physical with Nicholson instead.

The human body is an extraordinarily sophisticated creation, and the human brain the single most complex structure so far identified in the universe. The brain controls the body through nerve impulses, primarily by instructing muscles when to move, and receives feedback from nerves providing information about the immediate environment. One of the principal functions of these nerves is to warn the brain of imminent danger to the body, and in order to achieve this many nerve endings are located in the skin.

Several of the more aggressive forms of martial art target these nerves to incapacitate or kill an opponent, but accurately applied pressure can also be used to cause intense physical pain. Pain, however, that is of brief duration, causes no permanent damage, and ceases the moment pressure is released. That was as far as Richter was prepared to go, and perhaps Nicholson had guessed this because, despite his screams and howls, he had still refused to divulge the secret of CAIP.

Richter looked down at him, considering. 'Maybe I should try a different tactic.' He walked over to the table and picked up the small flask. Then he glanced back at Nicholson and registered the change in his expression. The fear in his eyes was unmistakable.

'Maybe,' Richter walked back across the room, 'I should just shoot a hole in this flask and close the door on you for a couple of days, leaving you at the mercy of these bugs you're so determined nobody else should find. I've seen what they do,' he added, 'and it isn't pretty.'

He stared at Nicholson, tossing the flask from one hand to the other. 'Of course,' he said, 'if I do that I still won't know what the hell these bugs are, but I can probably get the CDC or else Porton Down to examine one of the other flasks and find out. But you'd be dead, so I still wouldn't know what you were planning on doing with them. It's getting close to the time when you have to make a choice: either die here in a locked room with only a flask full of lethal germs for company or start telling me all about CAIP.'

As Richter studied Nicholson's expression he saw the first signs of a smile appear on the man's face, and realized in the same instant that his gaze was focused somewhere behind him. He span round to find Henderson standing in the open door of the briefing-room, and himself looking straight down the muzzle of a Uzi sub-machine-gun.

Nicholson's mocking laugh echoed round the room. 'I think the cavalry's just arrived, don't you, Richter?'


John Westwood came back to consciousness slowly, squeezing his eyes closed against the pain lancing through his head. He tried to move his arms, to lever himself off the floor, but discovered immediately that his wrists were bound tightly together, his ankles too. He felt the stickiness of the tape on his lips.

He forced his eyes open to register he was lying on the floor of the hallway. The 'lost traveller' looking for directions to Browntown was standing right in front of him, aiming a Glock pistol straight at his midriff. As Westwood glanced up, Blake smiled down at him, then kicked him hard in the stomach.

Westwood retched, or tried to, against the tape keeping his mouth tightly shut. Then Blake leaned down and ripped the tape off his face. Westwood choked, vomiting on to the carpet in front of him. His lunch didn't taste any better the second time around.

'It's all over, Murphy – or whoever you are.' As Blake said it, Westwood knew immediately that Richter had been taken.

Henderson stood to one side, his Uzi covering Richter, as Ridout used a pocket knife to sever the cable ties around Nicholson's wrists and ankles. As soon as he was freed, Nicholson stood up and glared at Richter.

Since Henderson had entered, the Englishman hadn't said a word but was figuring the angles and working out what to do next. He had no immediate idea how he was going to retrieve the situation – not unless one of the three Americans made a bad mistake.

'You want me to waste him?' Henderson asked Nicholson.

'You can eventually, but not yet. He has some information that I need. With the aid of his tools here' – he gestured at the items assembled on the table – 'I think I can persuade him. Meanwhile, shoot him in the legs and tie him up in this chair.'

Then Richter smiled and shook his head. 'No,' he said simply.

The three men stared across the room at him, aware that something had changed, but without knowing what.

Henderson raised the Uzi higher, but Richter just grinned at him. His plan was simple and as risky as hell, but it was absolutely the only choice he had. Otherwise he'd be joining John Westwood at the bottom of Nicholson's well.

'You daren't shoot me,' Richter said, 'not while I've got this baby.' He glanced down at the CAIP flask clasped in front of his chest. 'You and I both know what's inside it, and what happens to us all if it gets punctured. Do you want me to tell your two boyfriends about it, or would you rather explain it yourself?'

For a long moment Nicholson just stared at him, then gestured to Henderson to lower the Uzi. 'The flask contains a lethal pathogen,' he said finally. 'If it gets opened in here we'll all die. Nothing else is changed, though. I still want that bastard strapped into this chair. His pistol is here on the table, so put your weapons down and grab him. Just take extreme care not to damage that flask.'

Ridout gave Henderson a warning glance. 'Watch him,' he said. 'He knows martial arts and he's fucking fast.'

'So what?' Nicholson snapped. 'There are two of you, and you're both professionally trained. Just grab him and let's finish this.'

And that situation, Richter realized, was about the best he could have hoped for. He watched carefully as Henderson and Ridout placed their Uzis on the floor behind them, and began to approach him slowly from opposite sides. Nicholson stood watching with a slight smile on his face.

Richter relaxed, watching everything and everyone. Preparing his body for combat, he stood with his feet slightly apart, his right arm by his side, his left still holding the CAIP flask in front of him.

Ridout was on his right, and Richter guessed he'd prove more cautious in his approach because he'd already taken a beating when he'd encountered Richter out in the garden. Also, having had his right arm dislocated, he would still be hurting badly.

Richter waited until the two men were each about four paces away from him, then he moved in a blur of speed and focused energy. He tossed the CAIP flask in the air towards Henderson, and immediately lunged at Ridout. Nicholson called out something and, as Richter had expected, Henderson stepped backwards and reached up to grab the descending flask. Ridout backed away in reflex, and Richter knew he had only a couple of seconds to get the situation under control.

Nicholson had been right about the SIG, which was lying on the table beside the kitchen knife, but what he didn't know was that the Glock 17 Richter had taken from Ridout was still tucked into the rear waistband of his trousers.

Richter pulled the Glock free, extended his arm towards Ridout, and immediately pulled the trigger. The crack of the unsilenced 9mm weapon filled the room, but Richter didn't wait to see the result of his shot. He swung round to Henderson, whose arms were extended above his head, clutching the flask, noticed the horrified expression on his face, and fired again.

The impact of the bullet in the centre of Henderson's chest knocked the man backwards and he crashed to the floor. As he fell, he released his grip and the flask tumbled, spinning through the air, but Richter ignored it. Having examined it earlier, he knew that simply dropping it could only dent it. It was far too tough to rupture through falling onto a carpeted floor.

Instead, he swung further to his right, levelling the Glock now at Nicholson. The Agency man was reaching down for one of the Uzis, but Richter took less than half a second to focus on his target. He sighted carefully, then pulled the trigger. The bullet smashed into Nicholson's left thigh, smashing the femur about six inches above the knee. The Uzi forgotten, the big man tumbled sideways, screaming in pain.

From the moment Richter had tossed the flask into the air, less than four seconds had elapsed.

In the hallway above, John Westwood heard three rapid shots and a scream of pain. He summoned a smile as he gazed up at Blake. 'You sure your buddies have everything under control down there?' he asked.

'Smart guy.' Blake kicked Westwood in the stomach again, then picked up his Uzi and headed cautiously down the hall.

Richter moved quickly over towards Nicholson, picked up both Uzis, pulled out the magazines and tossed them and the weapons to one side, well out of the man's reach. Then he span back to Henderson and Ridout. He knew both were wearing Kevlar vests, so he guessed that at worst the breath had been knocked out of their bodies.

Henderson had already dragged himself into a sitting position against the wall, and was pulling his own Glock from its shoulder holster. Without hesitation, Richter swung the pistol up, sighted and squeezed the trigger. Henderson's head snapped back as the 9mm copper-jacketed slug punched half his brains through the back of his skull and splattered them onto the wall behind him.

Richter swung his pistol around further, covering Ridout this time. Then he lowered the weapon on seeing that his first shot had missed the Kevlar jacket and had hit Ridout just below the navel. He was clutching his stomach and moaning, and was obviously no threat.

Just then Blake pushed the briefing-room door open and Richter saw the muzzle of a Uzi swinging towards him. He dived sideways, over the top of Ridout, and somersaulted across the floor, landing in a crouch and with the Glock extended in front of him.

Blake pulled the trigger and a ten-round burst screamed across the room towards Richter. Three of the bullets smashed into Ridout, two hitting the Kevlar jacket but the third ploughed into his head, just above his right ear, and killed him instantly. The other rounds pursued Richter's rapidly moving figure, crashing into the wood-panelled walls. As happens with all sub-machine-guns on automatic fire, the muzzle of the Uzi had lifted, and Blake was lowering it to adjust his aim, when Richter fired twice with the Glock.

His first bullet hit the Uzi's pistol-grip, severing Blake's middle finger, and the second passed over the weapon and hit his neck, half an inch above the protection of his Kevlar jacket, and he fell back, dead.


John Westwood had just managed to struggle to his feet, leaning his back for support against the wall, when he saw the door leading to the cellar swing open. He'd intended hopping down the hall to the kitchen, to find a knife to cut the tape binding his limbs, but as the door opened he realized he needn't bother.

Richter glanced both ways as he emerged from the doorway, pistol in one hand and a cumbersome bunch of Uzis, Glocks and magazines clutched to his chest by the other. He nodded to Westwood, dropped the weapons and mags on the floor, and stepped away towards the kitchen. He returned a few moments later with a steak knife, and sliced through the tape binding Westwood's wrists and ankles.

'You OK, John?' he asked, and Westwood nodded. 'Didn't anybody ever tell you never to open the door to strange men?'

'I didn't open the door to anyone,' Westwood protested. 'This door was bolted on the inside, but somehow they must have got in at the back.'

Richter nodded. 'My fault,' he said. 'The back door, off the kitchen, is secured by an electric lock with an external keypad, and obviously Nicholson's men knew the code. It hasn't got internal bolts, but I should have jammed a chair against it or something.'

'What happened down below?'

'We had an exchange of views, and the CIA will be sending out three letters of condolence next week.'

'So who's that still yelling down there?' Westwood demanded.

'Nicholson,' Richter replied. 'I had to take his mind off grabbing a Uzi and ventilating me, so I popped a round through his leg. He'll be walking with a limp for a while.'


Nicholson was lying where he'd fallen, both hands clutching his wounded leg just above the knee. The floor around him was soaked with blood and Richter knew he would die from blood loss if something wasn't done quickly about the bullet wound. He knelt beside him and tied a rough tourniquet around the man's thigh, then applied a broad bandage, taken from a first-aid kit in the kitchen, around the wound itself.

'Now,' Richter said, after Westwood propped Nicholson up against the wall, 'as I was saying before we were interrupted, we want to know more about CAIP. Tell us, and we'll call for an ambulance so you can be in hospital within the hour. If you refuse, then you can probably guess what we'll do.'

Nicholson looked from Richter to Westwood, but just shook his head, his face a mask of pain.

'I don't believe this, Paul,' Westwood murmured. 'It's a covert operation that's over thirty years old and he still won't tell us what it was about?'

'He will eventually. He just needs to be encouraged a little.' Richter stood up, leaned against the wall of the briefing-room and rested his right foot very gently on Nicholson's left shin. 'I'll ask you again,' he said. 'What was CAIP?'

The injured man shook his head once more, and Richter could see him tensing for the pain he knew would come. Richter pressed down harder, then moved his foot backwards, rolling the wounded leg

**455**

sideways. Nicholson's scream cut through the air as he grabbed frantically at his shin, desperate to immobilize it.

'What was CAIP?' Richter repeated, as the howl died away into a moan. 'I can go on all day, Nicholson. You can't, unfortunately.' And he pushed sideways once more, watching the injured man's expression closely for signs of capitulation.

And then Nicholson spoke, almost imperceptibly. 'Stop,' he said, his voice weak and wavering. 'For God's sake, stop. I'll tell you.'

The other two men crouched down in front of him, listening intently.

'I'll tell you,' Nicholson repeated, sweat glistening on his brow. 'I'll explain what CAIP was – and why we did it.'

'OK,' Richter grunted, 'let's hear it.'

As Nicholson began speaking his voice was so low that they had to lean forward to catch what he was saying. 'First, you need to understand the background. What do you know about *Weltanschauung* and eugenics?'

Richter glanced at Westwood, who shrugged his shoulders in incomprehension. 'Not a lot,' Richter replied, 'though I do know what the words mean. *Weltanschauung* is a High German term meaning a world view or philosophy. The fact you've mentioned eugenics suggests you're thinking about Hitler's perverted vision of the future of Germany and the Third Reich. His *Weltanschauung* was that only the strong should survive, and that the toughest of those would become the rulers of the rest, first of Germany, then of Europe and finally of the world. Every other race and nation would be reduced to second-class citizenship, used as a slave-labour force or, in the case of the Jews, exterminated. Basically, the Nazis used the idea as a justification for the Holocaust.

'Eugenics is pretty much the same, but without the jackboots and concentration camps. Refinement and enhancement of the race through selective breeding. It's a discredited, foul idea.'

Nicholson shook his head. 'Not so,' he said, his voice strengthening. 'The idea of eugenics is no different in concept to what farmers and biologists do with plants and animals. They try to breed the hardiest crops, the fastest horses, the most intelligent dogs or whatever. Eugenics is no different.'

'Except that you're talking about human beings,' Westwood interrupted. 'That makes it different. The concept is unacceptable.'

'The government of Singapore would argue with you,' Nicholson said. 'They started a eugenics programme back in 1986. They offered pay increases to female university graduates who had children and at the same time paid grants for property purchase to women who hadn't been to university, as long as they agreed to be sterilized after they'd had one or two children.'

'That's the first I've heard of it,' Westwood said.

'Your ignorance doesn't alter the reality of the situation. The government of Singapore made no secret of their programme, and it was entirely voluntary. If it's successful, the result should be an overall increase in the intelligence level of that nation, and at the same time a reduction in the rate of population growth. Which is,' Nicholson added, 'the second factor.'

'I've no idea where you're going with this,' Richter said.

'You'll see, I promise you. Let me ask you something else – what's the population of the Earth?'

'We don't have time for twenty questions, Nicholson. Get to the point.'

'This *is* the point. The present population of this planet is around six billion, and it's doubling about once every twenty-five years – that's an exponential increase. That means about twelve billion by twenty twenty-five and twenty-five billion by the middle of this century. Some time in the next century the figure would reach half a trillion.'

'So what?' Richter demanded.

'So a global population of that size would mean standing room only, everywhere, and I do mean everywhere. That's a population density of about the same as Manhattan over the entire surface of the Earth, including areas that are presently uninhabited, like the Arctic, Antarctic, Siberia, Amazon Basin and the deserts. Actually, it couldn't get that big, because the food supply would run out long before – you can't build cities on the same land you grow crops on.'

'What's that got to do with the CIA and CAIP?'

'Everything,' Nicholson said. 'In the late sixties and early seventies a bunch of studies were carried out here in the States, and they all came to more or less the same conclusion. Something had to be done to slow down the rate of population growth, and if possible to reverse the trend. Most of the studies suggested that the ideal size for the world's population was between about two and a half billion and five billion people. Even the higher figure is a lot less than we've got right now.

'The most immediate problem was food. Some analysts were predicting that if the population boom in certain countries continued, within the foreseeable future, in just a few decades, the whole world's food supply wouldn't ultimately be enough to feed everyone. America would end up having to supply wheat and other staples, but even that relief would only delay the inevitable. Even with all our resources, there simply wouldn't be enough for everyone to eat, and whole sections of the world's population would end up starving to death.'

'They do now,' Westwood objected.

Nicholson nodded. 'Yes, but that's usually for different reasons. In politically unstable countries the food that we and the voluntary organizations supply often doesn't get through to the people who need it. It's stolen by government officials who sell it, or it gets dumped in warehouses to rot, that kind of thing.'

'This is fascinating, but irrelevant,' Richter snapped. 'Get to the point.'

'It's not irrelevant,' Nicholson responded sharply. 'It's crucial, because it explains the idea behind CAIP. The areas where the population was growing the fastest were identified. Not surprisingly, the Third World was one of them. Africa had always had a high level of infant mortality, but better food and medicines were beginning to reverse that trend: modern science was actually helping create the problem. In the opinion of many analysts, Africa was on the verge of a population explosion, and somebody was going to have to do something about it, soon. And we *did* do something about it.'

'What?'

Nicholson ignored Richter's question. 'Voluntary birth control had been tried in Africa, but that didn't work. The men refused to use free condoms, and the women didn't bother to take contraceptive pills. So a group of senior Company agents was tasked with finding a covert method of keeping those populations in some sort of check, just to slow down this dangerous growth.

'We tried impregnating the wheat and other crops we supplied with drugs that would reduce fertility levels, but that seemed to have little effect, so we looked around at other things. Then the Department of the Army came up with what seemed at the time like a possible solution. It was radical, so we needed high-level Government approval before we implemented it.'

'How high up?' Westwood asked.

'The Department of State,' Nicholson answered.

'And that was CAIP?' Richter suggested. 'What was it?'

'CAIP was the most important operation the Company got involved in throughout the whole of the nineteen seventies. In fact, it was perhaps the most important covert operation of the whole century, and one day the world will be thankful for what we had the courage to do.' There was almost a ring of pride in Nicholson's voice as he uttered these words.

'What were you bringing out of Africa?' Westwood probed.

Nicholson looked at him, and shook his head, grimacing. 'I said it before, your ignorance is total. We weren't bringing anything out. We were taking something in.'

'But the aircraft,' Richter objected, 'was flying westwards across the Mediterranean, away from Africa.'

Nicholson nodded. 'Yes, but it was at the end of the mission, not at the start. We knew even then that we needed to cover our tracks, and that's why we had to order the escorting fighter to shoot it down. The Learjet was supposed to end up in deep water and be lost for ever, but instead it veered off course. I've been waiting since nineteen seventy-two for somebody to stumble across it.'

'So what was it you were taking into Africa?' Richter demanded. 'And what does CAIP stand for?'

Again, Nicholson's voice rose and strengthened. 'We needed to find a simple name that would be meaningless to anyone not involved. It stood for Central Africa Inoculation Program, and that's exactly what it was.'

There was a moment of silence that seemed to stretch for an eternity as the two men stared at Nicholson. Then Richter glanced at Westwood, noticed his look of incomprehension. 'I think I can see where this is going,' he said, 'but I just pray that I'm wrong. Tell us what you were injecting.'

Nicholson shook his head. 'It was a good, simple idea. All we intended to do was reduce fertility levels, bring the population growth under some kind of control. Our only mistake was that we had no idea what the long-term effects would be. It was merely intended to inhibit reproduction – to act as a damper. We never realized—'

'What were you injecting?' Richter asked again. 'What was in those flasks?'

And again Nicholson shook his head. 'We couldn't have predicted the long-term results. We should have spent more time on trials before we started the program, but there was a real sense of urgency at this end. We—'

Richter stood up and kicked Nicholson's shattered thigh. 'Just tell us,' he shouted. 'What the fuck were you injecting?'

Nicholson howled with renewed pain, grabbed again at his leg. He looked up at Richter. 'You fucking bastard,' he cried. 'OK, OK,' he continued quickly, as Richter stepped forward again. 'It was an entirely new substance. The Army scientists had spliced a bovine virus onto a sheep virus, and then modified it further. It had just the characteristics we were looking for, so we tried it by using a smallpox vaccination program as cover. It was only a trial run. We were only out there a few weeks before the program was shut down.'

'Shut down by whom?' Richter demanded.

'The authority came from the President himself. I think he was secretly informed about the program by one of the doctors involved in the African trial.'

'OK, I'll ask one more time. What were you injecting?'

'A virus,' Nicholson said. 'The strain contained in the flasks was extremely concentrated, a mother strain, and its effectiveness was chemically reduced on site by a factor of over ten billion before we could inject it. That's why we needed doctors and scientists to carry out the trial. But we never thought—'

'Oh, Jesus,' Westwood interrupted, with an appalled expression. 'Is he saying what I think he's saying?'

Richter nodded. 'Yes, but I can hardly believe it. What this bastard means is that in the nineteen seventies some rogue element in the fucking American Army developed AIDS to depopulate the Third World – and a bunch of CIA fanatics filled the syringe for them. It's no wonder those files were sealed by the authority of the President. If this ever became public knowledge, the CIA would be finished – possibly the American Government too.'

'Jesus Christ almighty, what the hell do we do now, Paul?'

'What you do, Westwood,' Nicholson said, his voice stronger as some of his previous fire returned, 'is get me proper medical attention to get this leg fixed. Then you give me those flasks and the file. I'll make sure that the evidence is destroyed permanently. That's the only option that makes sense. We cannot, under any circumstances, allow word of this to leak out. The damage to America would be incalculable.'

Westwood glanced at Richter, who shook his head and motioned him towards the door. Westwood moved across there and stood watching as Richter picked up the silenced SIG and gazed down at the wounded man.

'There are a couple of things you should know, Nicholson. This room is soundproof and airtight. The reason we haven't all suffocated so far is because there's a closed-circuit air-conditioning system that keeps the air fresh. But because it's a closed-circuit system it means that any particles that are present in the air stay in the air: only the carbon dioxide is allowed to escape. That's the first thing.'

Richter put the SIG down on the desk, then dragged the small table across the room and positioned it about three feet from where Nicholson was propped against the wall. Then he moved across to where Henderson's body lay and picked up the CAIP flask. He held it in his left hand and peered at it for a few moments, as if seeing it for the first time, then he placed it on the table.

'The second thing is that I believe in responsibility and blame. If your organization was responsible for deploying the AIDS virus in Africa and starting the present pandemic, then your organization should take the blame, either in private or in public. Whether it does or not won't be my decision, but the evidence should certainly not be simply destroyed. It's just barely possible that some of the information in the CAIP file, maybe even the concentrated virus in the flasks, might help find a cure for AIDS, and no matter how slim that possibility, that alone is sufficient justification for not destroying it.'

'But you don't understand,' Nicholson protested through his pain. 'The damage that you could do is—'

'I'll tell you,' Richter cut across Nicholson's protest, 'about damage. Anything anyone might do with this information is totally insignificant compared to the damage your repellent scheme has already done, and not just in Black Africa. You simply don't understand, do you? AIDS could exterminate the entire human race, and it would be your doing.' His last words came out as a bellow and again he kicked Nicholson hard in the leg.

'Get out of here, John.' Richter's voice was suddenly low and controlled. He waited until Westwood had left the briefing-room and picked up the SIG.

Nicholson was howling with pain, his hands clutching desperately at his bloody leg, but Richter's face was without pity or remorse. 'If you have a god,' Richter spoke in a voice as cold as death, 'I hope He can forgive you, because I can't. You are responsible for creating AIDS, so it's only right that you should die from it.'

'No, no! Please! We can work this out,' Nicholson cried out. 'I'll hand over everything, I'll tell you everything I know.'

Richter ignored his sudden pleading. He walked over to the door, then turned and took careful aim. The pistol coughed once and the steel flask on the table bounced into the air. Its side ruptured where the bullet had struck, scattering a dirty brown cloud down towards the injured man. Richter pulled the door closed immediately.

The last thing he heard before the soundproof door slammed shut was Nicholson's despairing wail as the viral spores began to fill his lungs.

# Chapter 29

**Monday**
**Browntown, Virginia**

John Westwood seemed almost in a state of shock as he drove the Chrysler away from the safe house. He'd said nothing since Richter had ushered him out of the place and slammed the door shut behind them.

Richter had left a note for the caretaker, warning him not to go into the briefing-room but to wait for a decontamination team to arrive. He would have to consult Tyler Hardin again, so that the expert could advise what procedures were needed before the room could be safely opened. But all that could wait for a day, at least.

'It's not my call, John,' Richter commented eventually. 'Ultimately, this is your mess and you're the ones who are going to have to clean it up. But I do feel very strongly that you can't just bury it. Going public wouldn't achieve anything except to pillory the CIA and America itself, and you can certainly do without that. My advice is that you take the remaining flasks back to Langley to brief Walter Hicks and suggest that they're handed over to the boffins at Fort Detrick. They just might help in the search for an eventual cure.'

'What are you yourself going to do?' Westwood spoke for the first time. 'Will you tell Simpson?'

Richter nodded. 'Yes. I don't really see I've got much option. If the circumstances were reversed, you'd do the same.'

'I guess so,' Westwood murmured, then straightened slightly in his seat, as if he'd come to a sudden decision. 'Look,' he said, 'the next few days are going to be mayhem over here. I'm going to be spending all my time at Langley explaining what the hell happened back at the safe house – that's the easy bit really – and trying to find an answer to the harder question: why a bunch of rabid neo-Nazi lunatics in the CIA decided thirty years ago that killing off half of the population of Africa seemed like a good idea.

'You probably want to get back home anyway, so why don't we just pick up your stuff at my house and then I'll run you out to Baltimore International?'


## Haywood, Virginia

Richter replaced the Clancy novel in the bookcase – he'd seen the film, knew exactly where the 'Red October' had finished up. He took another look around John Westwood's guest bedroom to ensure he'd left nothing behind that he didn't intend leaving, picked up his overnight bag and Stein's briefcase, and pulled the door closed behind him.

'John,' he explained, as he walked into the kitchen where Westwood was sitting at the breakfast bar, a blank expression on his face, 'I can't take the pistols with me so I'm going to have to leave them here. You can keep the SIG – call it a gift from the late Richard Stein – but if you could get the Browning Hi-Power sent over to the US Embassy in London in the diplomatic bag so I can pick it up, that would be a great help. You have no idea how many forms I'll have to fill in if I don't hand the fucking thing back. I've left both pistols upstairs in the guest room, unloaded and with the magazines out, on the top shelf of the built-in wardrobe. Your kids won't be able to reach them up there.

'You can have this, too,' he said, putting a bulky heavy-duty carrier bag on the kitchen table. 'It's got Murphy's mobile phone and laptop in it, just in case you need to show Hicks the sequence of emails you exchanged with Nicholson. There might also be some other information there that could help you.

'I'm taking Stein's briefcase back with me. I'll get our guys to see if there's anything useful on his laptop, and then I'm going to keep it; it's time I had a computer of my own. And he had a better mobile phone than the one I use back in the UK. Let's call it the spoils of war.'

## British Airways 747, direct Baltimore–London Heathrow, mid-Atlantic

The in-flight movie was crap, Richter knew, because he'd already seen it in the Wardroom of the *Invincible*, what seemed like half a lifetime ago. The in-flight meal hadn't been a lot better – pretty much the only edible part being the roll and butter – and as soon as the grumpy stewardess, or cabin staff operative or hostess or whatever the hell they were being called this month, had taken away his tray, Richter had tried to get some sleep.

That hadn't worked either, and after fidgeting around for thirty minutes trying to get comfortable – a nearly impossible task in the plane's economy section – he'd given up trying and hauled Stein's briefcase down from the overhead locker and opened it up. He'd been vaguely planning to have a fiddle with the dead man's laptop – Richter wasn't quite as computer illiterate as he usually made out – but when he lifted the lid of the briefcase something else caught his attention.

Sticking out of one of the narrow document pockets was a piece of paper. Richter pulled it out, unfolded it and found it was actually six sheets of thin paper stapled together. At the top of the first sheet was the unmistakable dark blue CIA seal, the bald eagle surmounting the white shield with the sixteen-pointed red compass, and the classification – Ultra Secret – stamped in red at the top and bottom of every page, supplemented by a caveat: 'CAIP EYES ONLY'.

He knew immediately, even before reading to the bottom of the first page, exactly what this document was, and where it had come from. It was the executive summary of the aims, conduct and procedures of Operation CAIP. Krywald or Stein had obviously removed it from the file, and Richter could guess why.

It was dynamite, with enough explosive force to blow the Central Intelligence Agency into oblivion, and the only living soul who now knew it existed was Paul Richter.

## Wednesday
## Hammersmith, London

Richard Simpson turned the pages slowly, rereading the document for the third time. Then he dropped it onto his desk and stared across at Richter.

'Where did you get it?' he asked.

'I didn't get it from anywhere, really,' Richter said. 'I liberated a brief-case from this CIA agent named Richard Stein, because it contained his laptop computer and it was convenient for carrying it. I wasn't watching the bloody awful movie on the long-haul back from Baltimore, so I decided to have a play with the laptop instead. When I opened up the briefcase, I saw this bit of paper sticking out of a document pouch. That's it really.'

Simpson looked down and prodded the sheaf of pages a couple of times in an experimental manner. 'So what do you expect me to do with it?' he demanded.

'What worries me,' Richter said, 'and has done since the moment Nicholson finally told us what CAIP was all about, was what the CIA will do with the evidence. Even John Westwood looked totally stunned at the implications, and I would be prepared to lay money there'll be a powerful faction within the Company that will just want this buried.'

'They could be right,' Simpson said. 'Having something like this made public would do immeasurable damage to the American Government, and I don't really see what good it would do to anybody now. AIDS is with us and that's a fact. Whether or not somebody created it, or if it just crawled out of the African rain forest somewhere, seems to me to have become largely irrelevant.'

'But that's not the point,' Richter's voice rose. 'If the CIA was behind this, then the Company should accept some kind of responsibility. I'm not talking about a public blood-letting – I agree that wouldn't help any-one – but some kind of financial reparation wouldn't go amiss. Maybe they could subsidize the cost of the AIDS drugs being used these days. A lot of victims of the disease can't receive treatment simply because they can't afford to pay for it.'

'You seem to know a lot about the subject,' Simpson commented.

'I've done some research since I got back.'

'OK, but you still haven't answered my question. What do you want *me* to do about it?'

'I want you to let the CIA know, through Six if necessary, that we have this document – and that we're prepared to go public with it if the CIA doesn't admit responsibility for CAIP, at least privately, and doesn't offer some form of compensation to those suffering from the horrific disease it helped create.'

There was a long silence in the office. Simpson stared at Richter, then dropped his eyes to the six stapled pages lying on the desk in front of him. When he looked up again, he slowly shook his head.

'I really don't think I can do that,' he said. 'I hear what you say, but on balance I think it's probably better for everyone if we just forget about this and preserve the status quo. In fact,' he added, 'I think it's better if this document never sees the light of day – ever.'

Before Richter could react, Simpson dropped the pages into the mouth of the large document shredder beside his desk and pressed the button. There was a brief ripping sound, then just the whir of the cutting blades. Simpson reached down again and pressed the switch: silence fell.

'So that's it, is it?' Richter demanded. He hadn't even attempted to move as Simpson destroyed the vital document.

'Yes, I think so.' Simpson stood up, rubbing his hands together. 'Unless there's anything else you want to add.'

Richter got up too, and pushed his chair back, then walked slowly across to the door. He reached out for the handle and then turned back to face Simpson. 'Yes, I did quite a lot of research on AIDS yesterday,' he said, 'but that wasn't the only thing I was investigating.'

'Oh?' Simpson sounded profoundly disinterested. 'What else were you looking at?'

Richter smiled slowly and glanced down at Simpson's document shredder. 'Colour photocopiers,' he said. 'It's simply amazing what results you can get from colour photocopiers these days.'

# Epilogue

'The amount of American philanthropy aimed at AIDS is unparalleled and the US funds nearly 30% of the Global Fund's $4.8 billion budget. President Bush recently pledged $15 billion to fight HIV/AIDS over the next five years.'

*Extract from an article by Eric Bovim and posted at* www.TechCentralStation.com

Though what you've just read is a novel, with all the usual disclaimers about people living and dead, the above quotation is genuine, as is the analysis which follows.

## AIDS: An analysis

I have had to take one slight liberty in writing this novel: I have no idea how the human body would react if exposed to an unadulterated 'mother strain' of the AIDS virus, or even if such a thing exists. The physical effects I've described in this book are violent and dramatic, but are by no means unreal. Victims of infection by either a filovirus (Ebola and Marburg) or an arenavirus (Lassa) would suffer very much the same symptoms as those I've described. The only difference would be the timescale, with Ebola Zaïre killing its victims the quickest, usually in about a week to ten days.

As I've said, this book is a novel, but what follows here is fact, not fiction. It should frighten you – it terrifies me.

Despite what the doctors and scientists tell us, the nature of both AIDS (Acquired Immune Deficiency [or Immunodeficiency] Syndrome) and the disease itself are still very poorly understood. The Internet hosts literally thousands of sites where eminently qualified doctors and researchers promulgate their own theories and views about AIDS. Many of these theories are mutually exclusive and contradictory, and even a brief survey leads to the inescapable conclusion that *nobody* actually knows what's going on.

There is no accepted consensus about where and when AIDS originated, how it came to enter the human population, what relationship – if any – HIV (Human Immunodeficiency Virus) has to AIDS[1] and, if you believe some of the specialists, whether the HIV virus actually exists. There is even a groundswell of apparently well-informed opinion that suggests AIDS is caused by recreational drug use, and is not a viral infection at all.[2]

There are a multitude of claims and counter claims, usually completely contradictory. One frequently quoted report stated that by the end of the 1980s some 16,000 health-care workers had become infected by AIDS. Another report, dealing with broadly the same data set, alleged that no health-care workers had contracted AIDS. Clearly one, or even both, of these reports has to be wrong.

In short, we still don't really know what's killing people or what we can do about it.

However, the generally accepted 'official' view of the beginning of the AIDS pandemic is that in the early 1970s an infected green monkey – the source of its own infection being unknown – came out of the rain forest and bit an African, or possibly an African male had sex with an infected green monkey (which it is worth saying is about the size of a chicken), and that single incident precipitated the spread of the disease.

Quite apart from the total lack of any supporting evidence for this quaint folk tale, there are two very sound biological reasons for dismissing the story as complete fiction.

First of all, the AIDS virus bears no resemblance whatsoever to any naturally occurring virus ever found in a green monkey, or in any other primate. Specifically, the codon choices (that is, the sequence of three purine and pyrimidine bases in the virus's ribonucleic acid [RNA] that codes for the production of a particular amino acid by the infected cell) that are present in the AIDS virus are not present in the genes of primates. That means that the chances of the AIDS virus occurring naturally in any monkey, of any species, are microscopically small.[3,4]

The key words in the above paragraph are 'naturally occurring', because African primates have been found to be carrying Ebola and Marburg (both of which are believed by a significant number of researchers to be manufactured viruses) and AIDS, but only after they have been deliberately injected with them for the purposes of vaccine production, medical studies and biological weapons research.

Second, it is rare but not impossible for viruses to jump species. Possibly the record is held by the Hendra virus, a member of the paramyxovirus family (the measles virus is a member of this group), which emerged in 1994 in Australia in a species of fruit-eating bat, but was subsequently found to be capable of infecting and killing horses and cats, as well as human beings.[5] However, viruses that do this are the exception: most are highly specific and cannot jump species unless they have been engineered to do so.

It's also worth mentioning, and then dismissing, the 'Patient Zero' story. This is more or less folklore, but is still for some reason one theory that has been espoused by the Centers for Disease Control and Prevention in Atlanta, Georgia, as well as by a number of other people who should certainly know better.

Patient Zero was Gaetan Dugas, a promiscuous homosexual Canadian airline steward who was diagnosed as HIV-positive in 1980: the origin of his infection remains unknown. He is supposed to have been the source for both the New York and San Francisco outbreaks of AIDS in America, despite the fact that he lived in Canada and travelled primarily to Canadian cities. For him to have been the source of these infections, one has to suppose that, for no readily discernable reason, he only had sex in American cities, but not in Canada. AIDS broke out in 1978 in Manhattan and in 1980 in San Francisco, but not in Toronto or Quebec or Ontario or any of the other cities Dugas is known to have visited.[6,7]

The dates of these American infections are, however, highly significant, as I will mention shortly.

So what really happened?

Absolute proof is almost never found in situations of this type – there is no 'smoking gun' to be discovered – but an analysis of some of the documentation relating to AIDS that has been located by researchers, and a survey of the timescale of various incidents, does point clearly to one appalling hypothesis.

Most of the following has been derived from a variety of sites on the Internet. Readers who are interested should carry out their own research and form their own conclusions. For me, a lot of what follows has the undeniable ring of truth, but obviously I cannot vouch for the absolute veracity of the whole. Readers should also be aware that the URLs I have listed were available when this note was written, but are not necessarily still extant, the Internet being a fluid and dynamic resource.

The story begins in the late 1960s, and one of the first documented references is held in the US Senate Library. It's a record of an Appropriations Hearing that was held in July 1969, when the United States Department of the Army specifically requested (and subsequently received, in 1970) a ten-million-dollar grant to develop a synthetic biological agent that would impair or destroy the human immune system.[8]

Round about the same time, personnel employed by a number of American medical organizations authored articles that advocated similar kinds of research aiming at the development of a hybrid virus that would have the same function.[9]

Then, in the early 1970s, Henry Kissinger allegedly wrote a Top Secret document – a National Security Memorandum that subsequently became known as NSM 200 – which essentially stated that the highest priority of US foreign policy towards the Third World should be depopulation. This memorandum, which was declassified in 1990, was apparently adopted by the National Security Council as official US foreign policy towards the Third World.[10]

Action followed in 1972 when medical teams were sent into Central Africa – into an area that subsequently became known as the 'AIDS Belt' – and administered what was described as a smallpox vaccination to several thousand Africans.[11] This event was followed some time later by the first outbreak of AIDS on the planet.

Earlier, I mentioned the significance of the dates of the American infections. In 1978 a medical programme administered Hepatitis B Vaccine to thousands of male homosexuals living in New York; nineteen months into the AIDS pandemic, five hundred and one of the dead were from New York. In 1980 a similar programme was run in San Francisco, with almost precisely the same results. In both cases, the only common factor in the spread of the disease was that all the victims had either received the hepatitis vaccine or were closely associated with someone who had.[11]

But everybody knows that AIDS is essentially a venereal disease, transmitted primarily by male homosexuals. Isn't it? No, it isn't. At least, not according to the British Royal Society of Medicine, which has stated that AIDS meets none of the criteria of a venereal disease and has suggested that, despite the misrepresentations of the American medical establishment and the American Government, AIDS is not primarily a sexually transmitted disease.[12]

Semen is just about the least effective transmission medium for AIDS, and the virus is only present in microscopically small numbers in the semen of an infected person. Furthermore, condoms are useless in preventing the spread of AIDS, because the virus is less than half the size of the smallest sub-microscopic holes that are found in every condom.[12,13]

But don't take my word for it. As part of the evidence that was submitted in a memorandum to the British Parliament's House of Commons Social Services Committee in 1987, Dr John Seale of the Royal Society of Medicine stated: 'As far as it goes, the tiny research effort into infectivity of bodily fluids indicates that saliva is far more infectious than genital secretions, but that blood is vastly more infectious than either. Consequently, the idea that [the use of] condoms can have any significant effect on the spread of AIDS in a nation is utterly preposterous'.[12]

And: 'Governments all over the world are spending millions of pounds, advising their citizens to prevent AIDS by using condoms on the basis of manifestly fraudulent misrepresentation of scientific evidence'.[12]

A better description of AIDS is just that it's a transmissible disease, and contracting AIDS does not directly depend on your sexual orientation. That said, most research suggests that male homosexuals are primarily responsible for the spread of the disease in Western society but not, in the main, through exchange of semen or saliva. The principal transmission method appears to be through the bleeding that can accompany certain types of homosexual activity.

The best method of contracting AIDS is through an injection. Or you can become infected by means of a blood transfusion, or through a cut on your hand. Or from somebody who has the disease sneezing near you. Some mosquitoes in America are believed to carry the virus.

So what is AIDS? All the independent evidence suggests that it's a manufactured plague. What the AIDS virus resembles more than anything else is a bonding of Bovine Lymphotrophic or Leukaemia virus (BLV) – a virus that targets lymph cells in cattle and is known to cause cancer – and the sheep Visna virus. The only possible way these two different types of virus, which infect completely different species of animal, could bond together would be by someone engineering it in a laboratory, and then further engineering it, possibly by combining it with the human herpes virus, to allow it to make the jump into a human system.

And all the indications are that that is precisely what was done. What is not clear is whether the release of this virus into the population was an act of deliberate genocide or simply the result of shoddy laboratory technique. The medical profession, after all, has a long and less than illustrious history of contaminated vaccinations. Probably the most notable of these was the administration in 1955 of improperly inactivated Salk polio vaccine prepared by the Cutter Laboratories in Berkeley, California. Almost eighty children contracted polio, and passed the disease on to a further one hundred and twenty relatives and friends. Eleven died and three-quarters of the victims were paralysed.

In a chilling foretaste of the media censorship surrounding the AIDS pandemic – of which more later – Bernice Eddy, the doctor who blew the whistle about the Cutter vaccine, was forced out of her laboratory and out of work for daring to suggest the unthinkable.[14]

The Cutter case was a horrendous example of science gone bad, but it certainly wasn't the last such incident. The CDC recorded almost forty-nine thousand adverse reactions to vaccinations between 1991 and 1996, and it was estimated by American health authorities that in this period around 90 per cent of the most severe cases were never reported. Extrapolating those figures, perhaps as many as one million Americans may be harmed by vaccines, and tens of thousands seriously injured, every year.[15]

There are three really terrifying facts about AIDS.

First, it is a very efficient killer with a mortality rate of exactly 100 per cent. AIDS is, just like Ebola Zaïre, a species-killer: the only difference is that Ebola kills in days, while AIDS takes its time. Virtually all the treatments that are currently available are aimed at prolonging the life of the victim, not curing the disease. As far as is known, *nobody* has ever been cured of AIDS – it's just that some victims take longer to die than others.

Second, the worldwide rate of infection has been doubling about once every twelve to fourteen months – an exponential increase. Simple mathematics predicts that, unless some positive action is taken to halt the spread of AIDS, everybody in the world will eventually contract the disease within the foreseeable future. If that happens, the entire human race could cease to exist within one or two generations. As Dr John Seale said: 'The war against AIDS is a war of survival. If we lose, Britain and all her people will perish.'[12]

Third, there is no cure, and it is quite possible that there never will be a cure. For that depressing news, we can thank mathematics as well as virology.

There are at least six different varieties of the AIDS virus infecting the human population, and each is a recombinant retrovirus. The word 'recombinant' means that the virus has the ability to change and recombine into a new strain at will, and it has been calculated that each variety of the AIDS virus has a recombinant potential of about nine thousand to the power of four. For the six known varieties, therefore, the number of possible new strains is inconceivably huge – it's actually the number 354,294 followed by twenty-one zeros. To put that into perspective, we're talking about unbelievably massive numbers, such as the total number of grains of sand on all the beaches in the world, or the number of stars in the universe. To develop a cure for each strain would be simply impossible – the number is just too enormous. And we're nowhere near finding a cure for even *one* strain yet.

But if the foregoing is true, why haven't the news media seized on this information and trumpeted it to the world? Well, it certainly isn't for the want of people and organizations trying to get the information promulgated, but in virtually every case the articles, letters and reports have been ignored, apparently because the information they contained was considered 'too controversial'.

As was stated by Dr John Seale when discussing the infectivity of AIDS: 'The scale of the deceptions and misinformation perpetrated by virologists, clinicians and editors of scientific and medical journals about the infectivity of genital secretions, compared with that of blood and saliva, has been astonishing. In the presence of a new, lethal virus, spreading amongst people, for which no vaccine or cure is in sight, every person would assume that scientists have been working day and night to verify how it is transmitted.

'On the contrary, having assumed for a variety of motives that AIDS is a sexually transmitted disease like syphilis or gonorrhoea, a negligible research effort has gone into the critical matter of transmission. A few preliminary papers were published and their findings have been repeatedly quoted as showing the opposite of what they actually showed. When this was pointed out in letters to the editors of American medical and scientific journals, publication has been refused. No attempt has been made to check or double-check the findings in other laboratories, or to rectify published errors'.[12]

An American doctor, Robert B. Strecker, a practising gastroenterologist who holds a Ph.D. in pharmacology and is a trained pathologist, spent five years investigating the AIDS phenomenon, and then attempted to interest the world in what he had discovered. Virtually every letter and article he wrote was ignored.

Almost in desperation, he and his brother compiled some of the most damaging documents he had uncovered into a report which he called 'This is a Bio-attack Alert'.[3] Copies of this were sent to the governor of every one of the United States, the President, the Vice-President, the FBI, the CIA, the NSA, and selected members of Congress. He got replies from three of the governors and nothing at all from anybody else. His story is typical, and certainly not unique.

What is perhaps not so typical of Dr Strecker is what then happened around him.

First, the CIA warned all agencies that he was a Communist and instructed them not to take anything he said seriously. That, despite the fact that this allegation was a complete fiction, appeared to work.

Second, his office was burgled but, interestingly, only papers and documents were taken, but nothing of any commercial value.

Third, on 11 August 1988, his brother Ted was found dead of gunshot wounds at his home in Springfield, Missouri. He was an apparent suicide, although he had been in good spirits, said no goodbyes and left no note or message. He had been actively assisting his brother Robert in trying to uncover links between the American Department of Defense and the development of HIV.

Fourth, on 22 September 1988, Illinois State Representative Douglas Huff of Chicago was found dead alone at home, the victim of an overdose of heroin and cocaine. Douglas Huff was almost a lone voice in the wilderness, the only person who thought Robert Strecker's theories were of sufficient importance to give him very vocal and very public support. He gave frequent press interviews and appeared on radio and television programmes urging people to be aware of the huge cover-up surrounding AIDS.[16]

Of course, all these events could be completely unrelated, entirely innocent and totally unconnected with Robert Strecker's work. And, then again, pigs might fly but most people would agree that they make unlikely aviators.

So, to return to the question posed earlier, what really happened?

The *least* likely scenario is that, uniquely in the history of virus infections, a naturally occurring sheep virus combined itself with a naturally occurring bovine virus, and simple chance tailored the resulting recombinant retrovirus into a form ideally suited to destroying the human immune system. Then the new virus made two species jumps: first from the sheep or cow in which it had been conceived into a green monkey, and then from the monkey into the human population where it's been wreaking havoc ever since.

Almost nobody who's actually done any proper research into AIDS, instead of simply relying on what's been published in the media, really believes that, but it's still the 'official' explanation. But no matter what one's personal belief, it is possible to easily disprove this theory using the same entirely unrelated discipline already mentioned – mathematics.

Because, even if what may be termed the 'green monkey scenario' is, by some bizarre mechanism, correct, the numbers don't work. As stated above, the rate of infection of AIDS is doubling about once every year. The first cases of AIDS in Africa occurred in 1972. If we assume that there was a single source of infection, and the number of victims doubled once every fourteen months, by 1987 there should have been about 8,000 cases of the disease in Africa. Even if the alleged green monkey had gone on a biting spree – for which, of course, there is not a shred of evidence – and had attacked hundreds of people at about the same time, there would still have been well under one million cases.

The reality is that one of the more conservative studies of the scale of the pandemic by 1987 put the figure at 75 *million*. Other estimates suggested the figure could be almost double that. To achieve the lower of these two figures suggests a first-year infection of around five thousand people – far too many for several entire troops of virus-carrying green monkeys to infect – but well within the number of people who could become victims if the method of transmission was some kind of inoculation programme.

The only way that such a vast number of people could have become infected in such a short time is if the disease had multiple coincident sources. In other words, a very large number of people in the same area had to contract – or be given – the disease at more or less the same time. No other mechanism can account for the sheer scale of the pandemic.

And AIDS broke out almost simultaneously in Africa, Brazil, Haiti, Japan and slightly later in the United States of America: if one infected green monkey managed to achieve this, it must have been the most well-travelled primate in the history of the world. Or is it more likely that the infection was actually transmitted through the smallpox vacci-nation programmes that were known to have been in operation in, strangely enough, Africa, Brazil, Haiti and Japan in the early 1970s, and the hepatitis vaccinations in the States later in the decade?[17]

Independent research suggests that the *most* likely scenario is that in the early 1970s certain WASP-dominated covert factions behind the American Government and military decided to try to eliminate what they saw as particularly 'undesirable' sections of the human race – principally the populations of Third World nations, homosexuals, prostitutes, drug addicts and blacks – and created a disease that would do the job for them very efficiently without a shot being fired in anger.[13]

After all, there would be a huge public outcry if the American Government simply lined up known homosexuals against a wall and shot them (though all the indications are that many members of Congress and the Senate, if not the current British Government and Opposition, would be privately supportive). But killing them secretly with a disease – especially a disease that the American medical establishment is actively and very publicly trying to eradicate – was a far better solution.

Unfortunately, if that were the case, they did the job rather too well, and as a result AIDS now threatens everyone – straight, gay, black, white, you, me, and more especially our children and our grandchildren. Already, babies are being born HIV-positive, and it's probably only a matter of time before children emerge from the womb with full-blown AIDS contracted from their innocent, white, non-drug-abusing, single-partner, heterosexual, American or European parents.

Our children are the future. When infected parents produce infected children, the entire human race stands in jeopardy.

Is it possible that shadowy powers behind the American Government of the 1970s engineered not only the destruction of what they perceived to be undesirable elements infesting this planet, but also the end of our whole civilization?

## References:

1.  'Conspiracy of silence' by Neville Hodgkinson. *The Sunday Times*, 3 April 1994. URL: http://www.virusmyth.net/aids/data/nhconspiracy.htm.
2.  'The AIDS Dilemma: drug diseases blamed on a passenger virus' by Peter Duesberg and David Rasnick. *Genetica* 104: 85–132. 1998. An abstract is available at the following URL: http://www.duesberg.com/papers/pddrgenetica.html or the full article is available at: http://www.duesberg.com/images/pddrgenetica.pdf (this requires Acrobat Reader).

3.  *This is a Bio-attack Alert* by Theodore A. Strecker M.D., Ph.D., 28 March 1986. URL: http://www.umoja-research.com/bio-attack_doc.htm.
4.  *Emerging viruses* by Leonard G. Horowitz D.M.D., M.A., M.P.H., Tetrahedron Publishing Group, ISBN: 0–923550–12–7, page 87.
5.  Hendra virus. Further details of this virus outbreak can be found at the URL: http://www.vetmed.wisc.edu/pbs/zoonoses/Hendra/hendraindex.html.
6.  *Queer Blood – The Secret AIDS Genocide Plot* by Alan Cantwell Jr., M.D. URL: http://gaytoday.badpuppy.com/garchive/health/062397he.htm.
7.  *Emerging viruses* by Leonard G. Horowitz D.M.D., M.A., M.P.H., Tetrahedron Publishing Group, ISBN: 0–923550–12–7, page 95.
8.  Department of Defense Appropriations 1970, Part 6, starting page 104. A transcript is available at URL: http://groups.msn.com/GOVERNMENTGoneWrong/dodhearing.msnw.
9.  For example, W.H.O.'s annual bulletin 1972, page 259.
10.  'The Case of Africa: A dark age or a renaissance?' by Linda de Hoyos. *Executive Intelligence Review*, 8 October 1999, pp. 25–29. A copy of this is available at the URL: http://www.aboutsudan.com/conferences/schiller_institute/dark_age_or_renaissance.htm.
11.  *Did the US Government Develop the AIDS Virus?* Network 23 broadcast on a Los Angeles Public Access Cable Channel. A full transcript is available at the following URL: http://www.totse.com/en/conspiracy/the_aids_conspiracy/aids-us.html.
12.  *Problems Associated with AIDS*. House of Commons Third Report from the Social Services Committee Session 1986–87. Minutes of Evidence (8 April–13 May 1987). Memorandum by Dr John Seale, Royal Society of Medicine. Full transcript at URL: http://www.believersweb.org/view.cfm?ID=519.
13.  'AIDS: Biowarfare Experiment Out of Control?' by Sean MacKenzie, 1993. URL: http://mindgallery.com/hiddenroom/biowarfare.html.
14.  *Emerging viruses* by Leonard G. Horowitz D.M.D., M.A., M.P.H., Tetrahedron Publishing Group, ISBN: 0–923550–12–7, page 487.
15.  *Emerging viruses* by Leonard G. Horowitz D.M.D., M.A., M.P.H., Tetrahedron Publishing Group, ISBN: 0–923550–12–7, page 528.

16.  *'The Strecker Memorandum'*. URL:
     http://www.konformist.com/1999/aids/strecker.txt.
17.  'W.H.O. murdered Africa' by William Campbell Douglass, M.D.
     URL: http://www.biblebelievers.org.au/who.htm.